For Love of
COUNTRY

For Love of COUNTRY

WILLIAM C. HAMMOND

McBooks
Press

Essex, Connecticut

McBooks
Press

An imprint of Globe Pequot, the trade division of
The Rowman & Littlefield Publishing Group, Inc.
4501 Forbes Blvd., Ste. 200
Lanham, MD 20706
www.rowman.com

Distributed by NATIONAL BOOK NETWORK

Copyright © 2010 by William C. Hammond III
First McBooks edition 2022

British Library Cataloguing in Publication Information available

Library of Congress Cataloging-in-Publication Data

ISBN: 978-1-4930-5809-9 (paper: alk. paper)
ISBN: 978-1-4930-6488-5 (electronic)

∞™ The paper used in this publication meets the minimum requirements of American
National Standard for Information Sciences—Permanence of Paper for Printed Library
Materials, ANSI/NISO Z39.48-1992.

To my three sons:
CHURCHILL, BROOKS, AND HARRISON.
No father ever has a greater source of pride.

*All that is necessary for evil to triumph
is for good men to do nothing.*
EDMUND BURKE

Prologue

Off the Barbary Coast, August 1786

THE LOOKOUT STATIONED ON the maintop was caught daydreaming. He was standing on the small oaken platform with arms folded, his back against the mainmast. His gaze was half taking in the white billow of topsail and cloud above, but his brain was seduced by the soporific combination of a hot Mediterranean sun, the comforting sway of the merchant brig as her cutwater sliced through the blood-warm turquoise sea, and, especially, the images of Neapolitan women dancing provocatively in his mind. *Eagle*, out of Boston, was fast approaching her Italian port of call, having traversed the Atlantic and passed through the Strait of Gibraltar. Gladly would he exchange the chaste austerity of shipboard life, along with every bottle of Cutler rum in the hold, for the wanton pleasures of physical abandonment with an untold number of ready, willing, and able accomplices, each endowed with the most beguiling of female adornments. Or so he fantasized.

Given the sailor's distracted state, it is not surprising that he failed to detect the red triangular sails hovering over the distant horizon to starboard. There were nine of them, three to a vessel, and a sharp eye would have observed that the corsairs were sailing in a straight line on a northward course, perhaps two or three cable lengths apart, and the one in the lead was already hauling her wind on a course of interception. But even from the height of the maintop few could have discerned, at this distance, the seven open gunports on the larboard side of the vessels. Or the pistols and wide-bladed scimitars lashed to the hips of their swarthy crews. It was the profile of the xebecs themselves that the sailor had been warned to watch out for.

The angry shouting of John Dickerson, the ship's master, snapped the sailor out of his reverie. Befuddled and transfixed, he stared down slack-jawed at those staring up at him, then shifted his gaze ahead to where Captain Dickerson was furiously pointing. The corsairs were closing fast. They were now near enough for those on deck to clearly distinguish the foremast at the prow of each vessel and the huge lateen yard attached to it at a 45-degree angle. At any moment the long, low, galley-like hulls would surge into view.

Before Captain Dickerson had time to consider his options, the northernmost vessel veered slightly off the wind and opened fire with her forward battery, sending up two warning plumes directly ahead of the merchant brig. Her companions did not waver in their course, kept right on coming at *Eagle*. They would be alongside in a matter of minutes. Cursing with frustration and anguish, Captain Dickerson ordered his mate to heave to.

Eagle's weather deck was twice as high off the water as the xebec bumping up against her starboard side. Nonetheless, the heavily armed boarding party had no trouble clawing their way up on ropes tossed over the brig's bulwarks to secure the two vessels together. On the corsairs' flush decks, pirates brandishing muskets covered them on the ascent while others stood by the 6-pounder guns.

There were eight in the boarding party. All bore the physical attributes of Arabic pedigree except for one, who appeared Germanic— Dutch perhaps, for he was blond and fair-skinned and totally at ease with the ways of the sea. By all indications he was a Christian sailor who, after his capture, had "turned Turk" to join the pirates and avoid prison. Their leader, distinguishable by the length of his jet-black beard, his menacing tone of authority, and the red sash he wore around the waist of his loose-fitting trousers, introduced himself to John Dickerson as *rais* Ali bin Hassan. In broken English he announced that the Americans were now prisoners of Dey Baba Mohammad bin Osman, and would the captain please direct his crew to make sail for Algiers. *Allahu Akbar min kulli shay!*

Among those reluctantly shuffling off to their stations to comply with their captain's order was a tall, sandy-haired, twenty-one-year-old foretopman from Hingham, Massachusetts, named Caleb Cutler.

One

Antigua, British West Indies, August 1786

IT HAD BEEN A MEMORABLE reunion. Richard Cutler had not seen Robin and Julia Cutler, his English cousins, since April of 1782, when Richard and Katherine and baby Will had left Barbados to sail home to America. He had found the family compound much as he had left it on that occasion, tucked in amongst the rolling green fields northeast of Bridgetown, fully engaged in the production of sugar and its by-products. The only major addition to the compound had been a twenty-vat rum distillery, constructed in 1783 adjacent to the boiling house.

Though he considered himself more a sailor than a planter or merchant, Richard had surprised even himself in the joy he took reviewing the entire process with Robin, from the slashing of the cane by Creole slaves wielding machetes, to the collection of juice under great horizontal rollers driven by the sails of two giant windmills, to the boiling in the coppers, to the glorious transformation of cane juice into molasses and sugar, and, ultimately, pitch black rum. Just last month, the first shipments of Cutler rum, fermented for almost three years in thick casks of New Hampshire white pine, had been dispatched aboard the Cutler brig *Eagle* from Long Wharf in Boston to the port of Naples.

With his usual flair for efficiency, Robin had redesigned and retooled the process until every last ounce of juice was squeezed from the cane. Julia's connections to the local families that produced Mount Gay rum had played their role as well in generating tidy Cutler profits, today at their highest level since before the Revolutionary War. The question was, could the Cutler family—with expenses and contractual obligations in England, America, and the West Indies—sustain such profitability now that Whitehall seemed determined to enforce its despised Navigation Acts. It was such concerns that had brought Richard to Bridgetown for a family conference.

During the week he was on the island, that topic had received much attention with no clear resolution. The declaration that America and American ships were off limits to both importers and exporters on the British-controlled islands of the West Indies brought with it a blessing as well as a curse. New business opportunities were there for the taking, and the Cutler family now had the clear incentive to exploit those opportunities. The family's business concerns already extended to Europe, and Richard had much to relate to his cousin about Boston and Salem sea captains who had ventured around the Cape of Good Hope, past the Isle of France, and into Far Eastern waters in search of teas and exotic fabrics. Sugar and rum production would remain at the heart of Cutler commerce, Richard had maintained, but expediency dictated that other untapped markets must now be considered. Total reliance on the old Atlantic trade routes no longer served. In Europe, demand for sugar products was far outpacing supply, forcing prices sharply upward; farther east, the opulence of Calcutta and Canton beckoned.

As lengthy and portentous as those discussions had been, there remained ample time during that week for Richard to become reacquainted with Robin and Julia, always among his favorite relatives, as well as the island that embraced a wealth of blissful memories for him. It was here, on Barbados, that he and his bride had spent the waning months of the war as guests of John Cutler, Robin's brother. John no longer lived on Barbados, having returned to England with his wife, Cynthia, in 1784 to assist with the family's operations there.

Despite his keen frustration at having to withdraw from a conflict in which he had served as a midshipman and then as an acting lieutenant under the command of Captain John Paul Jones, Richard would forever count those months as among his happiest. On this latest visit he had been up early each morning, before the demands of the day could intrude, and had strolled along the white sandy beach where he and his bride had walked and laughed and loved. On those occasions he had talked to her as though she were there beside him, as if by doing so he could magically transport her from their home in Massachusetts and once again be soothed by her melodious English accent and be enraptured by her touch, as gentle and inviting as the lush tropical breezes caressing his sunburned skin . . .

"Mr. Cutler! Mr. Cutler, sir!" The loud rap on the door of his stern cabin jolted him fully alert.

"Yes, Mr. Bryant," Richard replied, recognizing his mate's voice. Quickly he straightened himself in his chair, using both hands to coax back his shoulder-length blond hair. "Come in. What is it?"

The broad-faced and muscular seaman ducked as he entered the small but snug space that defined a captain's privilege. "Good morning, Captain. Cates reports a vessel three points on our starboard bow. Single mast, flying a royal," he added meaningfully. "It's a king's ship, sir. Cates believes she's a naval cutter."

Richard considered that. Matt Cates, the lookout on duty, was a man whose eyesight was normally as sharp as his observations—which was why, in these sensitive waters, Richard had ordered him sent up to the mainmast crosstrees at the first inkling of dawn. Like nearly everyone aboard, Cates had served either in the Continental Navy or aboard a privateer during the war, and was thus well acquainted with British ship design and sail plans. If he believed this ship was a naval cutter, she most likely was.

"What's our course?"

"North by east, sir. Nevis is off to larboard. Clear water lies ahead."

"We're still flying the Jack?"

"We are, sir."

"Very well. I shall be up presently, Mr. Bryant. Please tell the helmsman to hold her course steady."

"Steady as she goes, aye, Captain."

With Bryant gone, Richard cursed under his breath. Every sailor worth his salt knew that what dawn might reveal should be of primary concern to a ship's master, especially when sailing in coastal waters patrolled by overly inquisitive foreigners and erstwhile enemies. That was why he had awoken so early: to update the ship's log at his writing desk and to be ready, just in case. But he had allowed self-discipline to lapse into daydreaming, and the naval officer he once was would not easily forgive himself.

As he tucked the hem of his loose-fitting cotton shirt into his white breeches and tightened the strings at the waist, Richard considered the possibilities. If this was a British warship, why was she bearing down on them from the north? The British naval base on Antigua lay to the east, and he had purposely steered clear of that island, on a wide arc around Guadeloupe and Montserrat. To the north lay the island of Saint-Barthélemy, recently acquired by the Swedes, and the Dutch island of Sint Maarten. Why was a Britisher patrolling those waters, at night, and why did she seem so intent on intercepting a vessel flying the Union Jack, the nationality of which her lookout should already have confirmed? It was as if she had been lying in wait for *Lavinia,* in full knowledge of her pedigree.

Richard picked up a long glass from its becket by the desk, stepped out of his cabin, and ascended the short oaken ladder to the weather deck. There he was greeted by members of the twenty-two-man crew and steady northeasterly trades that ruffled his hair and tugged at his shirt. He squinted northward. The hull of the approaching vessel was just now coming into view: she was thus about three miles away. He glanced up. *Lavinia* was still rigged for night sailing. Her flying jib and jib were furled at their tacks on the jib boom, and her single mainmast topsail was furled tight on its yard. Nevertheless, she was making fair speed close-hauled under fore topmast staysail and the large trapezoidal fore-'n'-aft sails on her foremast and mainmast.

Richard did his best to appear nonchalant as he walked toward the bow of the schooner, his slight limp the result of taking a musket ball in his thigh at point-blank range at Yorktown five years earlier. At the starboard foremast chains he raised his glass and trained the lens on what was now unmistakably a Royal Navy cutter. She carried three square sails from mainsail up to topgallant on a single mast, plus a large fore-and-aft gaff-rigged spanker set out full on her larboard quarter in a following ten-knot breeze. Lunging out from her prow on a line parallel to the deck was a long, black bowsprit that appeared from this distance to be an arrow pointing directly at *Lavinia;* above it a huge white jib billowed out, arced taut as a bow prepared to fire the arrow. She was a fast ship. Too fast for Richard to consider flight.

Suddenly a gun barked on the cutter, the white patch of smoke shooting out to larboard whipped back in front of her by the brisk trades. In the distance a ball whined, increasing to a screech as it shot past ahead of the schooner and slapped the sea, skipping twice before disappearing in a swirl of white water. A 6-pounder, Richard mused. Oddly, despite the threat implicit in such a warning shot, he found himself wondering how so small a vessel could carry so great a press of sail. She could not be more than sixty or seventy feet in length, a good deal shorter than

Lavinia. Must have a deep draught, Richard surmised, and be heavily laden with ballast.

"Shall I order the crew to heave to, sir?" Geoffrey Bryant asked from his side.

Richard nodded. "Yes, do, Mr. Bryant. Any other response would arouse suspicion. And we certainly wouldn't want to do that, would we?" The smile he gave his mate belied the dread that had begun creeping into his belly with the firing of the gun.

The cutter swept past, shortened sail, and wore around under jib and spanker. As she feathered up in and off the wind to lie close a-starboard to *Lavinia,* Richard walked slowly aft toward the helm. Lowering the tip of his tricorne hat to shield his eyes from the sun, he stood glowering at the cutter, his arms folded across his chest, his square jaw set, everything about him the image of a ship's master outraged at being forced to stop at sea.

For a brief span of time the two vessels drifted side by side within pistol shot, each silently contemplating the other across a short, jewel-spattered stretch of water. Then, through a speaking trumpet, the crisp, confident tones of an English patrician shattered the early morning peace.

"What vessel is that?" he demanded to know.

"The schooner *Lavinia,*" Richard promptly called back through his own speaking trumpet. "Out of Bridgetown."

"Bound for where?"

"Saint Kitts."

"Your cargo?"

None of your damn business! Richard wanted to shout back, realizing at once that such bravado would be both futile and foolhardy. This British naval captain not only had license to challenge any merchant vessel under sail, he clearly had the wherewithall to enforce his will.

"Rum and molasses," he replied.

"Are you the ship's master?"

"I am."

"Your name, sir?"

"Richard Cutler."

There was a pause as this information was digested aboard the cutter. Then, in a voice rock hard with purpose: "Mr. Cutler, you will accompany this vessel forthwith to English Harbour. We are sending over a pilot to assist you. Please make ready to set sail."

Richard's tone in reply was equally insistent. "Sir, this vessel has British registry. On whose authority do you act?"

The answer that came back was a thunderbolt. "On the authority of the senior naval officer of the Northern Division of the West Indies Station: Captain Horatio Nelson."

LOCATED MIDWAY along the southern shore of Antigua's heavily indented coastline, English Harbour was the epitome of a British naval base. At its heart was Freeman's Bay, a large circular basin almost completely enclosed by promontories reaching out from the mainland like the claws of a mammoth crab. Once a vessel had gained entrance to the bay, she was protected from the forces of nature by the natural geography of the island. Protection from man was provided by a ring of multilevel stone fortresses glistening with heavy black cannon perched high up in the steep-scarped hills rising above the harbor. From such a vantage point at the core of the Lesser Antilles, the Royal Navy had long held sway over the major sailing routes to and from the rich sugar colonies of the eastern Caribbean, making adjustments in naval strategy and tactics as appropriate, meting out punishments as necessary.

Getting into English Harbour, however, was a tricky business, and it took the skills of a native sea pilot to guide a vessel through the treacherous shallows and reefs that formed the first line of defense against any would-be assailant. Once past the promontories and inside the often windless bay, the vessel would be warped in toward the quays or an anchorage by light hawsers attached to a complex series of wooden bollards and huge iron rings ashore teamed up with an array of anchored buoys.

As *Lavinia* was being hauled shoreward with her sails furled, Richard stood amidships gripping a mainmast shroud. Despite the gravity of the moment, he could not resist taking in the scenery about him. Although he had read and heard much about Antigua, this was his first visit. And he was as impressed by this British military installation as he was by others he had seen in England and the Caribbean. Above, in the Shirley Heights rising abruptly above the harbor, the austere-looking fortifications, observation posts, and army barracks kept watch over the southern approaches to the island and the goings-on in the harbor. The naval dockyards along the western reaches of the bay were abuzz with the bang of hammers; the rasp of saws; and the shouts, curses, and exhortations of foremen and laborers. In the town itself, across the bay, army and navy personnel, and the administrators and tradesmen of empire marched or scurried through thickets of coconut palms, throngs of carriages, and individuals a-horse wending their way along the main thoroughfare and between the clusters of yellowish-brown limestone buildings typical of many West Indian ports.

His gaze swept back to the activity at the naval dockyards and lingered there. Clearly, the British government was investing serious money and manpower to renovate and enlarge these facilities. Not far from the quay to which *Lavinia* was being secured Richard noted what appeared to be a dry dock under construction, the first, he presumed, outside Kingston, Jamaica, the largest Royal Navy base in the West Indies. When that structure was completed, it would save sheathers, caulkers, riggers, and carpenters the three weeks of backbreaking and often dangerous work required to careen a stripped-down vessel over on her side to clean or make repairs to her bottom.

At precisely 3:00 in the afternoon, a chorus of ships' bells clanged pleasantly from the seven British warships anchored in the bay, six bells per ship. As if on cue, a chunky, officious officer of the Royal Navy in the glory of full dress uniform strode up the plank leading from the pier, boarded *Lavinia,* and arrogantly bade the first seaman he came across to go and fetch the ship's master. His pomposity was only slightly curbed when that tall, young, fair-haired seaman with startling blue eyes indicated that he *was* the ship's master.

"At your service, Lieutenant," Richard said, his sarcasm evident.

With a loud harrumph and a jiggle of his bulldog jowls, the officer indicated to Richard that he was to accompany him forthwith in a long-boat. Their destination was the heavy frigate anchored in mid-harbor, a ship Richard had immediately identified as HMS *Boreas* when *Lavinia* had entered Freeman's Bay. He had admired her pale yellow varnish, her sails furled on their yards in Bristol fashion, her three masts stepped with just a hint of rake, and the unblemished black bands running along her gunport strakes. By all accounts she was a magnificent fighting machine, the pride of the Leeward Islands Station. Nothing but the best for Captain Horatio Nelson, Richard thought bitterly. No sooner had that wave of hostility crashed over him, as it often did at the mere mention of Nelson's name, than Richard chided himself for harboring such sentiments. He realized they were groundless, pointless. It should be the other way around, common sense reminded him.

"Good luck, sir," Geoffrey Bryant said as Richard made ready to disembark.

"Thank you, Mr. Bryant," Richard replied. "You have command. Keep the men occupied. The tide turns within the hour and I intend to be sailing with it."

The row over to the flagship was a short one. Richard sat in the sternsheets next to the lieutenant, watching intently as the frigate loomed ever larger. During the war he had been on one much like her in Plymouth Harbor when he was interrogated by British authorities following Captain Jones' raid on Whitehaven. So he assumed that *Boreas* was another Fourth Rate carrying fifty guns, not counting the swivel guns mounted on Y-brackets on her bulwarks and tops, or the murderous carronades affixed to iron slide carriages along her weather deck and quarterdeck, their stubby barrels now becoming visible through gunports cut through the bulwarks. Richard had learned of these newly issued lightweight weapons from his brother-in-law, Hugh Hardcastle, a flag lieutenant in the Royal Navy. First cast in the town of Carron, Scotland, they looked and loaded much like mortars. When fired at close range, Hugh had assured him, their 32-pound shot could wreak bloody havoc. At the time, he was relating to Richard the glory he had witnessed from Admiral Rodney's flagship during the Battle of the Saintes, and the high-pitched tones of excitement and defiance with which he had described the gore and mayhem inflicted by these "smashers," as he referred to the carronades, had seemed very much out of character for that normally staid British naval officer.

At the entry port of the frigate, Richard was turned over to a heavy-set master-at-arms sporting a prominent red handlebar mustache. As he was escorted aft to a hatchway and ladder leading below, he glanced again at the short-barreled iron guns bowsed up tight against the bulwarks. He longed for an opportunity to walk over and inspect them, to see for himself what all the excitement was about.

The scarlet-jacketed marine corporal standing guard belowdecks banged the butt of his musket on the deck to recognize the master-at-arms approaching the after cabin. Once the official had stated his business, the marine rapped gently on the oaken door.

"What is it?" queried a gentle voice from inside.

The corporal opened the door a crack and nodded at the master-at arms to answer.

"Mr. Turner, Captain. I have with me the ship's master of the American schooner, just arrived."

"Very good, Mr. Turner. You may show him in."

The door opened wide and Richard was ushered into a spacious and well-appointed cabin. Sunlight streaming in from open stern windows reflected off the thick glass of the quarter-gallery windows of the dining alcove on the starboard side aft. In the center of the space was a gilt-edged, freshly polished mahogany desk resting on a lush Persian rug laid over the dark red deck, a color intended to mask the splatter of blood in battle. In front of the desk, their high wingbacks blocking much of Richard's view, were twin chairs of impeccable taste, their yellow-floral-on-blue upholstery matched by the thin pad on the settee running athwartship in front of the stern windows. Oil paintings of ships and seascapes graced the walls between rows of books clutched in tight by what must have been specially designed bookshelves. Completing the décor was a curved-front ebony sideboard with gilt handles on the drawers. On its top, among other items, was a silver-sided tray holding cut-glass decanters of various wines and spirits.

"Would you have me stay, sir?" the master-at-arms inquired.

Horatio Nelson rose from the desk, shook his head. "Thank you, no, Mr. Turner. Please leave us. You may close the door on your way out."

After the door clicked shut, each man stood in silent contemplation of the other. They had not seen one another since 1774, twelve years ago, on the quays at Bridgetown when Richard was seeking the whereabouts of Nelson's close friend and former shipmate, Hugh Hardcastle. At the time, Nelson was serving as a senior midshipman aboard HMS *Seahorse* in the Windward Squadron, his age just fifteen, a year older than Richard's fourteen. His meteoric rise through the ranks had become the stuff of legend, and Richard was well aware that it was not just "interest" in Whitehall that had propelled Nelson from a midshipman at the age of twelve to a post captain at the age of twenty. One did not achieve such prominent rank in the Royal Navy at so tender an age unless his superiors saw in him something unusual.

"Well, Mr. Cutler," Nelson said. "It appears Fate has played her hand in our lives once again."

"It would seem so," Richard replied cautiously. Nelson's cheerful greeting had caught him off guard.

Nelson motioned to the chairs in front of him. "Please, sit down. Make yourself comfortable. The sun is most definitely over the yard-arm, so may I offer you a sherry? A spot of claret, perhaps?"

"Thank you, no, Captain." Richard did, however, accept the invitation to sit in one of the wingback chairs. He set his tricorne hat on the desk in front of him, then leaned back, crossing his right leg over his left, all the while returning Nelson's steady gaze. To Richard's surprise, given all he had read about the man's illustrious career to date, Nelson hardly seemed the paragon of a British naval officer. He was a half-foot shorter than Richard and appeared to be somewhat fragile of frame, though it was difficult to discern what might lie beneath the gilded finery of a naval captain's uniform. And finery it was, from the silk of his neck stock to the rich gold-edged and gold-embroidered indigo fabric of his dress jacket. His hair was a shade darker than Richard's and closer cropped, though still sweeping down over his ears, and the eyes making their own careful analysis of the situation were as gray as the sea before a gathering storm. Despite yellow-tinged, almost sickly looking skin— the result, Richard knew, of several near-fatal bouts with malaria—he was nonetheless a distinguished-looking individual who seemed entirely at ease with his rank and destiny; and also with the span of silence that, for Richard, was fast becoming untenable.

"Where should we begin?" the American asked.

The question prompted Nelson back from wherever it was his thoughts had wandered. When he spoke, his tone was decidedly less cordial. "A good place to begin, I should think, is with an explanation. Tell me, pray, why you continue to smuggle cargo in and out of Barbados when you are perfectly aware that by doing so you are in violation of the Navigation Acts."

"With respect, Captain, I protest your accusation of smuggling."

Nelson's dark eyes flashed. "Come, come, Mr. Cutler. Let us not play games. You know damned well that is what you are doing. How can you claim otherwise?"

"I claim otherwise because *Lavinia* has British registry."

Nelson waved that away. "A tiresome ruse," he sighed, shaking his head. "Really, Mr. Cutler, I had expected better of you. These days, a British registry can be purchased for a song, especially by a family like yours with connections in England. Besides, it no longer has legal standing. You are aware of the recent Order-in-Council?"

"I'm sorry, but I am not," Richard hedged.

Nelson's steady gaze told Richard that he was not at all convinced of the American's claim of ignorance. "The decree states, sir," Nelson said, in what was clearly a well-worn speech, "that American vessels are henceforth banned from trade in the West Indies. Shipments to and from these islands are reserved exclusively for British subjects sailing

British-owned and British-built ships. That includes Canadians and Irishmen, but, alas, as a result of our recent squabbles, it most definitely does *not* include Americans. You are in clear violation of that decree, Mr. Cutler, even if I were to accept your registry claim, which I do not. *Lavinia* is American-built and American-manned. And because you are in violation, I have the legal right to impound your cargo."

"Does having the legal right," Richard countered, "give you the moral right? Your Navigation Acts are opposed by many English citizens on these islands. Including, I am told, your superior officer in Barbados, Admiral Hughes."

To Richard's surprise, Nelson actually smiled at that allegation. He leaned forward and beckoned Richard in toward him, looking every bit the school chum about to divulge a grand secret. "Admiral Hughes may be a decent sort," he said, his voice low, conspiratorial, "but I fear he's more a jack-pudding than a fighting admiral. You have no doubt heard of his latest escapade? Poor fellow actually poked his own eye out with a fork whilst chasing a cockroach across his quarterdeck. Now tell me: does *this* seem like a man whose opinions matter?"

Richard was shocked to hear a Royal Navy officer openly disparage a superior; nonetheless, he could not restrain a smile of his own. He had indeed read about that unfortunate mishap, in a Boston newspaper. Try as the Admiralty might to suppress the story, it had leaked out from the forecastle of HMS *Adamant* to the *Bridgetown Gazette*. From there it was picked up by London's *Morning Post and Daily Advertiser* and thus, inevitably, by most other English-language newspapers and magazines around the world.

It took a moment for Richard to suppress the chuckle bubbling up within him. When he had composed himself, he said: "Nonetheless, it is an undisputed fact that your so-called Navigation Acts are strangling these islands. The governor of Antigua has called for their repeal. Governors and legislatures on other islands have joined him. Merchants everywhere are demanding redress. And they are not happy with the Royal Navy either. It is widely acknowledged, Captain, that you are at serious odds with most of Antiguan society. Of course," he added, to drive home the point, "you must realize that. Which is why, I suspect, one hears that you seldom go ashore."

Nelson winced at that assertion. He clasped his hands together and lowered his head down close to them, as though a pilgrim sitting in supplication within his father's parish in Burnham Thorpe. For several moments the only sound in the cabin was the ticking of a small pendulum clock set upon the sideboard. When Nelson did finally sit upright, he peered intently at Richard and spoke in a voice that was at once both weary and wary.

"Mr. Cutler," he said, "the reason I seldom go ashore is because there is very little here of interest to me. I find Antigua to be a vile and sickly place. I greatly prefer Nevis and Saint Christopher—or Saint Kitts as it is now called—but alas, I am not able to spend much time on either island these days. Even if I were, my strong preference would still be to serve my country elsewhere, on some other station. However, I need not remind you that duty is the great business of a sea officer, and in my experience it has never involved a popularity contest. I was sent here to the Leeward Islands Station because my superiors in Whitehall have faith in my abilities. It is to them, and to them alone, that I owe my allegiance. Be assured that I am prepared to grind whatever grist the mill requires to ensure I do not disappoint them."

With that said, both men realized that further discussion on the topic would serve no purpose.

"Where, then, does that leave us?" Richard asked.

"Where does that leave us," Nelson intoned, repeating the words slowly, carefully articulating each as if pondering the significance of the question. His answer apparently determined, he folded his arms across his chest and said with conviction, "I do not know about *you*, Mr. Cutler, but where that leaves *me* is in a rather awkward position. It has always been my policy never to mix personal sentiments with the requirements of the service. But in this instance, for reasons I needn't explain to you, I am prepared to do just that. You are free to leave Antigua and sail home to . . . Hingham, is it not?"

"Yes, sir."

Nelson studied Richard a moment. Then: "You are free to leave Antigua with your cargo intact. But be forewarned," he added in a voice suddenly laced with malice, "you will never again receive such favorable treatment from me. Henceforth, the Royal Navy will keep a close eye on you and your family. We have spies everywhere, including Barbados, and those spies will be monitoring your every move. The next time a Cutler vessel is found in violation of the Navigation Acts, I shall order its cargo and crew impounded, and the vessel seized as a prize. Do I make myself clear?"

"Perfectly," Richard replied, his lips tight. High on his forehead, the scar from an old wound began to pulse.

"Good. Then we understand each other."

"We do, Captain." Richard made to rise. "Will that be all? If I am free to leave, I should like to sail with the ebb tide."

That observation rattled Nelson. "Yes . . . no," he quickly corrected himself, and the hard set of his features dissolved as rapidly as sea mist at a summer sunrise. "A moment, if you please, Mr. Cutler," he fumbled, glancing this way and that before being drawn, unavoidably, into Richard's rigid stare. "I am compelled to ask . . . if I may . . . How is Katherine?"

"Well, thank you."

"Good. I am pleased to hear it. You have a son, I understand?"

"Two, actually."

"Two sons." He half-whispered the words to himself, as if that fact had come as a profoundly sorrowful revelation to him. For a few moments he seemed far away. Then, as though emerging from a trance: "Well, I should think congratulations are in order. They are indeed fortunate young lads, to have such a mother."

"That, Captain, is one thing we can agree upon this afternoon." Richard arose from the chair, taken aback to see the man who had just threatened his family, who indeed could command the respect of nations, so obviously in distress. "Good day to you, sir," he managed civilly.

"Mr. Cutler . . . Please . . . I have but one last request of you." It was a plea that only a heart of granite could ignore. "I would be ever so much obliged if you would . . . see to . . . if you would send . . . dear Katherine . . . my warmest personal regards."

"I will do that, Captain," Richard promised. "And I am certain Mrs. Cutler would want me to send hers to you."

With that, he bowed slightly, turned around, and walked across the after cabin to the door, closing it gently behind him as he stepped out onto the gun deck.

Two

Hingham, Massachusetts, September 1786

FROM 1756, THE YEAR THOMAS and Elizabeth Cutler arrived in America, to the Coercive Acts of 1774 that effectively shut down the port of Boston for the duration of the war, Cutler & Sons had conducted its business from the modest facilities clustered at the end of Crow Point, near the entrance to Hingham Harbor. Costs there were properly aligned with the family's proceeds from shipping. In addition, Crow Point was an easy walk from their home and had sufficient dock and warehouse space to accommodate the family's small merchant fleet of two brigs, two brigantines, and a single topsail schooner.

With the implementation of peace in 1783 and the rapid expansion of American maritime commerce, many Hingham shipping families, the Cutlers included, shifted their business to Boston. Serving the new markets opening up abroad required more ships, better docking facilities, and increased warehouse efficiency. Such amenities flourished in Boston, an hour's sail away from Hingham assuming fair winds. So the Cutlers decided to make the move, maintaining a small office at Baker Yard in Hingham for their own convenience.

For sailors long at sea, rounding up into the narrows of Boston Harbor was usually the most anticipated leg of the voyage, and for the seamen standing by *Lavinia*'s sheets and topsail brace, today was no exception. Little Brewster and seventy-five-foot-high Boston Light were fading fast astern. Off to larboard the triple mountains of Boston Neck—Pemberton Hill, Mount Vernon, and Beacon Hill—loomed close enough for the men on deck to distinguish individuals scurrying about Long Wharf, a half-mile strip of warehouses, chandlers, ropewalks, counting houses, sail lofts, and shipwrights' offices jutting out into the harbor from the foot of King Street, recently renamed State Street. Above and off to the sides, a forest of church steeples—North Church, South Church, so many in between—pointed their white-glossed steeples skyward to the spiritual domain of God, as if to either seek or bestow His benediction upon the commercial domain of Man below. Ships and boats of various sizes, descriptions, and tonnage clogged the harbor, a few under sail, the majority moored to the wharf or to each other, their yards a-cockbill to avoid entanglement, their crews fully engaged in the serious business of loading or off-loading cargoes. Peering down from the gentle slopes of the tri-mountains, as though taking stock of the situation, a stately array of Federalist and Georgian mansions with steeply canted shingled rooftops and brick siding bore witness to just how rewarding such work could be for the owners of the merchant vessels.

"The helm is yours, Mr. Bryant." Richard yielded the long wooden tiller to his mate. Pemberton Point lay off the larboard quarter; Deer Island bore dead ahead. "Take her in."

"Aye, Mr. Cutler. Thank you, sir."

As Richard stepped below to his after cabin, he took satisfaction in the firm, confident commands of his mate directing the crew to stations that brought *Lavinia* close-hauled into Boston Harbor. Soon he would be rounding her into the wind to reduce sail to jib and spanker a-luff until pilot boats arrived alongside to warp her in to a vacant spot along the wharf. To Richard's mind, the way a helmsman guided a vessel to anchorage or dockside revealed much about his seamanship. Through-out this voyage Geoffrey Bryant had not once given him pause to question his seafaring skills, and for that Richard was profoundly grateful. He resolved to talk to his father about promoting Bryant to the rank of ship's master.

There wasn't much for him to do down below beyond jotting down a last entry in the log—careful to note the exact time and weather conditions—and tidying up the space. Although homecoming meant as much to him as it did to any man aboard, he would not be leaving Boston right away. Duty compelled him to spend the balance of the day on Long Wharf. The process of off-loading the cargo required his full attention, to be followed by settlement of wages for his crew after they had the hogsheads of rum and molasses stacked in a Cutler warehouse. And he would need to meet with his father, if his father were in Boston this day; or, if he were not, with George Hunt, the able Boston-based administrator of Cutler & Sons. Only when these and myriad other details had been checked off would Richard board a packet for Hingham.

As it turned out, Thomas Cutler was not present on Long Wharf. After a quick dinner alone at McMurray's, a favorite alehouse located across from Faneuil Hall, Richard was informed by George Hunt that a boat had just departed for Hingham. Before she sailed, Hunt had requested her master to notify the Cutler family of *Lavinia*'s arrival. He also informed Richard that another packet should be on her way in by now and would make the return trip when Richard was ready to leave. Which he finally was, four hours later.

The passage southeast to Hingham provided a welcome relief from shipboard responsibility. He sat alone, propped up against the mast, enjoying the simple pleasures of a fresh southwesterly breeze on his face and the spectacle of a late summer sun casting a brilliant golden sheen over the long string of Boston Harbor islands that both defined and protected Hingham Bay. Richard let his mind wander as he watched one picturesque gem after another pass by to larboard, the sight of each island evoking a distant though clear memory. In their youth, he and his brother Will had sailed out to these islands in search of Indian artifacts and ruins to explore, or wild berries and shellfish to bring home for supper.

One island in particular, once owned by a prominent Hingham Tory named Elisha Leavitt, had been their favorite. Grape Island was an easy row from the Hingham docks. The boys could swim in its sheltered cove when the tide was up or, when it was low, dig for clams in the gravelly sand or wade into the shallows to wrest mussels from the barnacle-infested rocks. Years ago it had also been the scene of a local scandal, one that made Richard smile even to this day. Late one summer evening, as a warm and muggy mist crept over the colony of Massachusetts, Will Cutler had rowed his small catboat in toward the Hingham docks with pretty Sarah Fearing sitting demurely on the after thwart. They had been becalmed out in the bay, Will had told two sets of worried parents, and he had had to battle for hours against a vicious ebb tide threatening to carry them all the way to Hull Gut, a potentially dangerous gap between Peddocks Island and Pemberton Point that could suck the unwary out of Hingham Bay and into the open Atlantic. They were lucky to be alive, he had testified, and would not have made it home had the tide not gone slack just as they were about to be swept away. His explanation stood, for the moment, for indeed it had been a day of fluky winds and an unusually strong spring tide. But the jig was up the next morning when a local fisherman with perhaps an ax to grind informed Thomas Cutler and, worse, Nathan Fearing that during the previous evening, as he rowed his skiff into the harbor, he had spotted Will's boat hauled high up on the beach on the north side of Grape Island, its passengers nowhere to be found amidst the low-lying brush. Richard had never seen his father so angry. Whether his rage was inspired by what Will had allegedly done—whenever Richard put the eternal question to him, Will had responded with a wink and a grin—or by the embarrassment he had caused the Cutler family, Richard had never known for certain.

Will Cutler. A decade had vanished since he had been impressed by the Royal Navy off Marblehead, then whipped to a bloody pulp and strung up from a yardarm after he struck a king's officer in defense of a shipmate. Ten years; yet those vivid memories persisted and still caused Richard's soul to grieve.

As shapes along Hingham Harbor began to resolve into distinct forms, Richard left his perch amidships and strode forward to the jib stay, squinting ahead toward Crow Point. It took him a moment to spot them, but yes, there they were, a short distance up on Otis Hill, just where he had expected to find them. He could see Katherine crouched low beside little Jamie, pointing to the packet and waving his hand for him in its general direction. Richard's sister Lavinia stood next to them, returning his wave with one hand while trying to restrain Will with the other. Young Will. Going on five years now, more than two years older than Jamie, he looked and acted so much like his namesake that his grandmother in her dotage often confused him with her own dead son. He had the same Anglo-Saxon hair and eyes, the same lean and tapered body, the same restless, devil-may-care approach to life that over the years had triggered any number of cuts, scrapes, and bruises—and, once, a broken fibula. He was a handful. His mother was the first to admit that. But her face glowed with pride at the notice Will received from citizens of all ages and the precociousness and free spirit that others found charming and astonishing in one so young.

As the packet was secured fore and aft at the dock, Will shook off his aunt's grasp and bolted forward. Richard stepped onto the dock and walked toward him. Free of the docks and upon dry land, he dropped to a knee and wrapped one arm around Will while encouraging Jamie with the other. Released from his mother's grip if not her attentive eye, Jamie toddled up to his father. At length Richard stood and smiled at his wife. They came together lovingly yet discreetly, as was their custom when in public.

"Richard," Lavinia gushed, when it came her turn to embrace him, "welcome home! Mother and Father have invited you for supper. I know it's getting late and you want to go home, but could you? Please? Annie and I can see to the boys," referring to Richard's other sister. "I promise we won't keep you late."

Despite his deep fatigue and longing to be alone with his wife and sons, to decline an invitation from his parents was unthinkable. Besides, Richard reasoned, it would already have passed muster with Katherine.

"I don't see why not, Liv," Richard replied. He raised his hat to several people passing by and welcoming him home. "Is Stephen here?"

"No. He couldn't leave the business. But he asked me to send you his regards. I must leave tomorrow. Which is why I'm hoping to have some time with you tonight."

"Then let's make it so."

It turned out, in fact, to be a late night. These days, a Cutler family gathering of such proportions was rare. Lavinia, at age seventeen, was married to Stephen Starbuck, a shopkeeper in Duxbury, and Anne, now in her early twenties, was engaged to Frederick Seymour, a gifted Harvard graduate who had insisted on postponing matrimony until he was further along in his medical career and able to support a wife and family in proper style. And with Caleb now following in Richard's footsteps, he too was often at sea, in the Caribbean or the Atlantic or, recently, in the Mediterranean. So Thomas and Elizabeth Cutler were delighted to have this opportunity to regale their family with a healthy round of roast beef, garden-picked vegetables, Yorkshire pudding, bottles of Burgundy, and a day-old berry pie: a meal designed to keep the conversation lively.

The mahogany-veneered Longcase clock in the parlor had chimed twelve times before Richard and Katherine finally took their leave and walked outside into the sticky, cricket-orchestrated night. The whale oil street lamps lining Main Street had been extinguished two hours earlier, but the dim glow of a three-quarter lambent moon was sufficient to guide them past Old Ship's Church to South Street, then left toward their modest two-story cedar-shingled house located a cable length down the road. At the front door, Katherine scooped Jamie up from the baby buggy and carried him inside. Richard followed close behind carrying Will.

"I'll see to them," Katherine insisted once Richard had Will stretched out on the bed next to his brother's. "You're exhausted, Richard. Anyone can see that. Go to bed. I'll be in shortly."

Richard did not protest. When Katherine crept silently into their bedroom a few minutes later, she saw what she had expected to see: her husband stretched out supine on the edge of the red-and-yellow-checkered bed cover. His breathing was already heavy, and his right leg dangled off the side, his foot on the floor, as if he had intended to snatch but a brief respite.

Settling her candle on a bedside table, she lifted his leg up onto the coverlet next to the other and removed his silver-buckled shoes. She managed to get him to move sideways a bit before repositioning the pillow under his head. She then sat quietly on the edge of the bed, gazing down at him, occasionally smoothing back his thick yellow hair and running her fingertips ever so delicately over the scar high on his forehead, the result of a riding accident years ago near her home in Fareham, England, where they met and fell in love. Thinking to make him more comfortable, she unbuttoned his waistcoat and began loosening the strings at the neck of his cotton shirt and the waist of his trousers. Her ministrations caused him to stir and to reach out for her from the deep well of sleep.

She took his hand in hers, kissed it, and laid it back down on his stomach. "No, my love," she said, her lips close to his ear. "Sleep now. We have tomorrow, and the next day. We have so many days."

"I want you so, Katherine," he murmured, his tone throaty and distant, as if he were pleading not to her but to an image faraway in a dream.

"I know, Richard. I know, my love. I want you just as much. But sleep is what you need now." She unrolled a blanket, tucked one end under the foot of the bed and drew the other up over his chest. She gave him a final look as he drifted back into the deep abyss and then blew out the candle.

"Sleep well, my darling. You're home. With me. Safe."

SLEEP HE DID, until almost 10:00 the next morning. He awoke with a start, feeling remarkably refreshed. His first coherent thought was not how absurdly late the hour must be but how quiet the house was. How had Katherine managed that? As a ship's master he was, as much by definition as by nature, a light sleeper, ever susceptible to a sudden heel in a gust of wind, a whine of warning in the rigging, a sudden patter of bare feet on the deck above. If such fleeting phenomena could awaken him, how could two little boys playing downstairs not?

As much as Richard would have preferred to linger at home that morning, he knew his father was expecting him at the Cutler & Sons office at Baker Yard to itemize the accounts of cargo off-loaded in Bridgetown and Boston. Richard planned to tell him some of what he and Robin had discussed, but he would save the finer details for an upcoming family conference that would include Thomas' brother, William Cutler. Richard had learned to his great joy the previous evening that his uncle would soon be sailing from England to Boston on his first trip to America. He had also learned, to his greater joy, that Williams's daughter Elizabeth would accompany him.

"Hard to imagine Lizzy being here," he said to Katherine that evening. They were sitting alone in the dining room off the kitchen, the leaf of the table removed to provide greater intimacy. It was nine o'clock and their sons were a-bed, Jamie flat out from the rigors of play, Will, as usual, miffed by what he deemed too early a bedtime and not averse to voicing his opinion. On the oval teakwood table, a wedding gift from John and Cynthia Cutler, candles flickered in a silver candelabra, accentuating the delicate Wedgwood china and illuminating a bottle of claret and a platter heaped with creamed cod, whipped potatoes, and peas, a favorite meal of Richard's ever since his wife had gathered the courage to try it out on him. Raised in the shelter of privilege and aristocracy, she had become, to her own amazement, a very good cook. Years ago, when they first settled in Hingham, Richard had resolved to hire a local woman who could cook, help with Will, and attend to other domestic chores. It was what she was accustomed to, he had explained to his bride, and he had assured her that they could afford this one luxury if they scrimped in other areas. Katherine would have none of it. She had married an American patriot, she had said, not an English peer. She would learn to be an American wife.

"It *is* hard to imagine," she enthused. "It's been, what, six years since we last saw her in England. I often wonder about her. Her letters don't reveal much."

"No, especially when it comes to men." Richard considered a portion of cod on his fork. "Is there a local lad we might introduce her to?"

Katherine hesitated, and for good reason. Elizabeth Cutler, her best friend since childhood, had been engaged to Jamie Hardcastle, Katherine's youngest brother. Through a horrible twist of Fate, Richard and

Jamie had met on opposite sides in the sea battle between HMS *Serapis* and *Bonhomme Richard* in the North Sea. Wounded by a pistol shot while trying to save Richard's life, Jamie had died in Richard's arms and had been buried at sea. For seven years now, Lizzy had not mentioned another suitor. Her grief seemed inconsolable.

"Henry Ware comes to mind," Katherine said, referring to a modest young man of Unitarian upbringing who was everyone's definition of an eligible bachelor. "But let's not put our eggs in the pudding quite yet. I'm not sure she's ready."

Richard thought to comment that after seven years, it was high time for Lizzy to start getting ready. But he decided from long experience not to press the point. A change of subject seemed politic. "What happened in Hingham while I was gone?"

The conversation turned to local events. Sarah Hersey, a cousin to John Hancock and formerly a prominent resident of Hingham, was returning to town. Sarah had married Richard Derby after the premature death of her physician husband in 1770. Derby, a merchant from Salem reputed to be among the wealthiest and most influential citizens of Massachusetts, died without issue, leaving the entirety of his estate to his widow, who would be returning to the hundred-acre Hersey farm in Hingham to finish out her days.

"Madame Derby," Katherine concluded, "intended to bequeath her fortune to the Harvard Medical School. But she was somehow convinced of Hingham's greater need for a private academy. So she intends to open a school for boys and girls in the center of town. Isn't that a marvel? A school for boys *and* girls! She's asking the leading citizens of Hingham to subscribe to it, and I should think we would . . . What is it, Richard? Why are you staring at me like that?"

"What? Oh. Sorry." He raised his hands in mock surrender. "I admit I was distracted for a moment. I apologize." He leaned in toward her. "But if truth be known, my lady, I was not staring. I was lusting."

Katherine smiled. "You haven't heard a word I've said, have you?"

"I certainly have," he replied indignantly. "Every word."

"Well, then, what was I saying?"

"You were describing, in detail that would make a sodomite blush, how much you have missed me these past few weeks and just what you intend to do to me tonight to prove it."

Katherine pushed her near-empty plate forward, crossed her arms on the edge of the table, and, leaning in toward him, said softly, "Methinks my lord has been away at sea too long and is entertaining impure thoughts. Parson Gay would not approve," referring to Ebenezer Gay,

a local fire-and-brimstone preacher so obsessed with the hideous consequences of original and present-day sin that Hingham citizens of both
sexes scurried across to the other side of North Street when approaching the reverend's home to lessen the odds of a Doomsday scenario
erupting from the pulpit of his front porch.

"Perhaps not," Richard agreed. "But from where I'm sitting, Parson Gay would have to be a blind man not to be entertaining impure
thoughts of his own."

There was ample cause to suggest Gay's vulnerability. Katherine
Cutler was by anyone's standards a beautiful woman, and for this first
evening at home with her husband she had, with Anne Cutler's help,
coaxed her natural beauty to its limit. The scent of rosewater with a
hint of lilac drifted in the air about her, and her pale yellow dress was
one she had carried with her from England to Barbados as a newlywed.
It still fit her perfectly, despite the birth of two sons. Her chestnut hair
had been teased, tossed, and curled with brush and comb until it rolled
and flowed across her shoulders and down toward the gentle curve of
her breasts. On her left wrist she wore a thin gold bracelet, the same
one she had worn that evening twelve years ago when they had first
met in England. The soft hazel eyes that opened wide at Richard's last
remark served as focal points in the graceful blend of her finely sculpted
features.

"Well, my lord," she said in her lilting English accent, "now that Will
seems to have snuggled down, I suggest we do something about those
wicked fantasies of yours. But first, isn't there something you want to
tell me?"

"Tell you? About what?"

"About your voyage to the Indies."

"Oh? I thought I had already told you what there is to tell. What
specifically are you referring to?"

"I am referring specifically to your stopover in Antigua and your
audience there with Horatio."

Richard frowned. "Who told you about that?"

"Geoffrey Bryant. I met him this afternoon on my way to town. He
didn't tell me much, especially when he realized that you hadn't told me
anything. I doubt he'd have much to say in any event, since apparently
he never left *Lavinia*. Only you did, I believe. So might I ask my husband to fill in the gaps? It's a matter of some importance to me."

Her tone was sweet, but it conveyed the firm message that a matter
of such significance would not, could not, be swept under the carpet.
Better to lay it out in the open, say what needed to be said, and clear

the air. He understood; it was an unwritten rule of theirs. But the simple truth was that he could not explain to Katherine why he hadn't told her about his meeting with Horatio Nelson. Which is what he told her.

"Then, can you tell me, is he well?"

"Yes, I'd say he is. He didn't look all that blithe and bonny, as you like to say, but then you know about his bouts with malaria. He looks well enough. And he certainly had no trouble threatening our family and our livelihood. He sends his warmest regards to you, by the way."

"Good. I trust you gave him mine?"

"I did."

"Thank you, Richard."

There was a marked pause in the conversation as Richard ran his forefinger up and down the narrow stem of his wine glass. He knew from experience that Katherine would say nothing further on the subject. It was his move in that intriguing game married couples play with each other, the rules of one match decided by the outcome of previous ones, just as, on a grander scale, legal precedent is established by past rulings in a court of law.

"Have you ever wondered," he asked at length, his gaze flickering back and forth between her and the half-filled glass he now held at arm's length, "how your life might have been different had you married Captain Nelson? Surely you must have. I may not always see eye to eye with the man, but I cannot deny he's a decent sort with a bright future. You said so yourself that day you gave me Gibbon's book. Do you remember that day in Fareham?" He was referring to the second volume of *The History of the Rise and Fall of the Roman Empire* that Katherine had given him as a Christmas present in '78 at his uncle's home in England. It rested today on a bookshelf in the parlor, the letter he had written his parents from France, delivered to Hingham by John Adams, still folded within its pages.

"Of course I remember."

He twirled the stem of the glass between thumb and forefinger. "Well, *have* you ever wondered? I wouldn't blame you if you have. Think on it: the status, the admiration and glory, the jewels and fine clothes and mansions, perhaps a title someday." He held out his arms expansively. "Does this compare with that? Do I?"

She studied his face from across the table. When too many moments of awkward silence had ticked by, she asked, in tones edging on incredulity, "Are those *serious* questions?"

His eyes remained locked on hers. "Yes, I suppose they are."

"Well, my lord, if *that* is the case . . ."

Katherine dabbed at her lips with a napkin and scraped back her chair. Rising, she walked around the table and offered him her hand. "Richard, will you come with me?"

"Of course." He stood up, took her hand in his. "Where are we going?"

"Upstairs. To our bedroom. In the morning, you may ask me if I have answered your questions to your satisfaction."

RICHARD AWOKE the next morning to splatters of sunlight dancing across his face and the rhythmic call of a mourning dove on station near the open window of their bedroom. Dreamily he turned on his side and reached out to draw her in close, for despite their repeated and ever more creative efforts to quench the fires of night, he was, incredibly, primed for her again, the embers of dawn not yet extinguished. She was not there, though the rumpled space next to him preserved the scent of her body. He breathed in that scent and opened his eyes. The angle of the sun told him that it was still fairly early, between 8:00 and 8:30. From downstairs he could hear muffled sounds. The boys were up; therefore Katherine would be up. Sighing audibly, Richard tossed the coverlet aside. "You'd make one pathetic mother," he chided himself just as another, more pleasurable thought crossed his mind. As difficult as it was for him to be away at sea for extended periods, the lifestyle he had chosen did have its benefits. Last night had been one of them.

At the table by the dresser he poured a half-pitcher of water into a pewter basin and splashed it onto his face. He rubbed his chin and jaw, testing for growth. The previous evening he had shaved in anticipation of the night ahead, and he decided this morning he could delay shaving again. He dried his face with a towel, then slipped on an informal ensemble and padded barefoot down the narrow back stairs leading into the kitchen.

The familiar scene before him brought him squarely back into the center of his family. Jamie sat perched in his customary place, buckled in atop a thick slab of wood that brought his tiny waist level with the heavy oaken kitchen table. His breakfast was everywhere in evidence: porridge was smeared on his mouth and chipmunk-like cheeks, on his shirt, on the table, and a very small amount in its bowl. Will had already finished his portion and was playing on the floor amidst two armies of tin soldiers, those painted in red, as usual, having the worst of it from those painted in blue.

"Good morning," Katherine greeted him. "Would you like some tea? The water's hot."

"Thanks, I would." He sat down across from Jamie and made a funny face that ignited a fit of high-pitched squeals. Bits of porridge flew into the air and added to the mess on the chair, table, and floor.

Katherine placed a steaming cup on the table next to a bowl of sugar brought from Barbados in *Lavinia.* Richard gave her hand a quick squeeze, exchanging with her that brief but meaningful glance that lovers give each other after a particularly satisfying encounter.

"You slept well?"

"Never better," he smiled.

Katherine kissed the top of his head before directing her attention to the unholy mess that was Jamie. Richard looked down at his older son.

"Who's the unlucky general today, Will?"

"Cornwallis." Will flicked his fingernail, and the hapless Peer of the Realm flipped over on his side. The battle was over, though Will ignored his father's acclamation, on purpose it seemed to Richard.

"Why the long face?" he asked.

Will glanced up at him, resentment written on his boyish features. "When will you be leaving us again, Father?"

Richard's grin vanished. "What do you mean, Will? Why do you ask? Do you want me to leave?"

"No!" his son cried out. "I don't ever want you to leave, Father. But you always do! Why? Don't you like being home with us?"

Richard felt a lump form in his throat. Will's questions may have been unexpected, but they were not out of character. Challenging the status quo was his standard approach to life, a trait that apparently he had inherited from his namesake. Whether this inbred tendency boded well or ill for the future, his mother and father could only speculate.

"Come over here, Will."

Will shuffled over and sat on the floor before his father. He wrapped his arms around his knees and gazed up inquisitively.

Richard clasped his son on the shoulder and looked him in the eye. When he spoke, it was in that ageless tone of a parent imparting a life's lesson to a child. "Will, you ask me why I leave, why I have to go away so often. When I do, it makes you sad. Sometimes it makes you mad. Yes?"

Will nodded.

Richard nodded back. "Even when my leaving makes you mad, you miss me while I'm gone, don't you?"

Will said nothing.

"I miss you, too," Richard went on, "and your brother and your mother. But there's more to it than that, isn't there?"

Again Will did not answer.

Richard searched about the room, feeling the eyes of his family upon him until he settled on an example. "Will, do you see your toy soldiers on the floor over there?"

"Yes."

"And you liked the sugar you had with your breakfast? And the kite and hoop you play with outside, and your new fishing pole?"

"Yes."

"And unless I'm mistaken, you still hope to have a boat someday to row out in the bay to catch flounder and pollock?"

His son nodded

"Will, think on it: if I stayed home and didn't do my work, I wouldn't make the money I need to buy these things for you. You wouldn't have any of them. Do you understand what I'm trying to tell you?"

Will hugged his knees and rested his chin between them. He rocked back and forth on his tailbone as tiny furrows of concentration sprouted on his forehead. Then he nodded, his mind having drawn a conclusion. "It's alright, Father," he said. "You can go do your work now."

He had not meant it as a joke and was surprised and annoyed when both of his parents broke into laughter. But then he started to point and giggle at Jamie, who was kicking his legs and waving his arms in the air, in response either to his parents' laughter or to the sudden loud knock on the front door.

Katherine wiped her hands on her apron. "I'll go and see who it is," she said. She was shaking her head and smiling as she walked out of the kitchen. When she came back in, her expression had changed dramatically. "Richard, it's your father." She said nothing else. She didn't need to.

Richard was up at once and making for the parlor at the front of the house. Katherine unbuckled Jamie from his chair and set him down next to Will. With a strict warning to them both to stay put and play quietly, she hurried after Richard.

They found the family patriarch staring into the empty stone hearth. When he turned to face them, the shock to Richard was immediate. His father was not a man who gave way to his emotions lightly. As a boy, Richard had admired his father's physical and emotional courage, and his seemingly unfathomable well of knowledge. Others in Hingham felt the same way, and his voice of reason and calm had carried far beyond the borders of the village when the drums of revolution began threatening the colony. Thomas Cutler was at heart a Tory, loyal to king and Parliament, and he had urged the town elders to stand firm and not dispatch the local militia to join General Washington's army encamped on Dorchester Heights. Not everybody in town was convinced of the purity of his motives, however. Some claimed that he was simply trying to salvage his family's shipping business, pointing as proof to the business relationship he enjoyed with his brother William in England. Richard knew the truth. As Captain Jones had once told him, his father belonged to that rare breed of men who act on principle, not self-interest, and Richard had observed for himself on too many occasions how society tends to revile such individuals. He was convinced the truth would come out, and it did—the day contrite British authorities in Boston brought the body of his eldest son home to him. The moment Thomas Cutler gazed down upon that brutalized pulp of flesh he switched allegiance without looking back, going so far as to offer General Washington two of his best merchant brigs for conversion to privateers. At the same time, he had commended his second son, Richard, to the military ambitions of John Paul Jones.

To Richard, as he approached his father in the parlor, Thomas Cutler appeared very much the way he had that horrible day of memory twelve years ago when he had knelt down beside Will's defiled corpse. He was not an old man. He was only forty-nine. But today he looked as though the last vestiges of his youth had abandoned him.

"What is it, Father?" he asked warily.

Thomas Cutler bowed his head. "Good morning, Richard. I must apologize for disturbing you and your family at so early an hour. I'm afraid I am the bearer of very bad news."

"Mother . . . ?" was Richard's first reaction, for Elizabeth Cutler had been suffering ill health in recent months.

"No, it's not your mother. It's . . . this." He offered his son the letter he held in his hand. "A post rider delivered it a short while ago."

Richard unfolded the letter. His eyes swept first to the name at the bottom, signed in the bold script of the U.S. minister to Great Britain. He scanned the text, then read the letter again, this time more slowly.

Katherine asked, "What is it, Richard? Please God, tell me." The pain scrawled in jagged lines upon his face frightened her.

"It's from Mr. Adams," he answered, though he spoke more to himself than to his wife, his eyes continuing to glare down at the letter. "Mr. John Adams."

"Yes, I am well acquainted with Mr. Adams. And?"

He looked at her. "*Eagle* has been seized by Barbary pirates. She's been taken to Algiers. Everyone aboard is a prisoner."

Her hand went to her mouth. "Oh dear Lord no! Caleb!"

"Yes. Caleb. And Captain Dickerson and every member of the crew, all of them men in our employ."

For long, agonizing moments the three Cutlers stood mute, as though frozen in time and place by this horrific turn of events. It was Katherine who came to herself first.

"Please, Pappy, sit down. May I bring you some tea?"

"Yes, thank you, my dear."

As his daughter-in-law left for the kitchen, Thomas Cutler sank onto the soft cushion of an armchair and gazed up at his son with vacant eyes. "What are we to do, Richard? What are we to do?"

Richard could not recall his father ever appealing for his counsel on a matter of such import without first advancing an opinion of his own.

"I don't know, Father," he replied, his mind at a loss for words that might encourage or console. He refolded the letter and placed it carefully under a paperweight on top of the desk. "I don't know."

Three

Hingham, Massachusetts,
September 1786–May 1787

W ILLIAM CUTLER AND HIS daughter did not sail to Boston in September. A month prior to their scheduled departure, Cynthia Cutler, his son John's wife, collapsed under an onslaught of severe abdominal pain. Physicians summoned to the Cutler mansion in Fareham arrived too late to save the baby, so they concentrated their efforts on saving the life of a woman savaged by pain, anguish, and massive loss of blood. She had survived, barely, William informed his brother Thomas in a letter sent to Hingham, but clearly he and Lizzy could not leave England at this time; nor would they hazard a winter crossing. Expect them sometime in early spring, he wrote, concluding with his most devout prayer that God in His infinite mercy would watch over the Cutler family in its time of suffering.

"Amen," Elizabeth Cutler said after her husband finished reading the letter aloud in their parlor on Main Street. She pulled a woolen shawl tightly around her shoulders. Richard wondered why. Her health had improved over the summer. Was her pain more emotional than physical? Local physicians had no definitive answers.

Anne Cutler's face darkened. "That settles it," she said. "Frederick and I are postponing our wedding. I want Uncle William and Lizzy to be here for it, and they'll be here in the spring. We can be married then. Frederick will understand. With so much going wrong for our family, how can I go through with a wedding now?"

"You mustn't postpone it, Anne," her father insisted. "For your sake and for Frederick's, and . . ." his eyes shifted meaningfully from Anne to her mother and then back to Anne, "everyone else's. Please reconsider. You and Frederick have waited long enough. Be married and be happy. Your joy is our joy."

She studied her father's face for a moment, then bobbed her head.

"Thank you," he said softly.

Richard spoke into the ensuing silence. "It's not all bad news, Anne. We've heard from Mr. Hamilton," referring to Alexander Hamilton, a man wielding considerable influence in the halls of power in Congress. During the Battle of Yorktown, Colonel Hamilton had led an assault on a key British redoubt and had credited Lieutenant Richard Cutler with saving his life just as the tide turned—for good—in favor of the Continentals. They had remained in contact ever since. "It seems that Congress is finally ready to do something. A Mr. Barkley has been dispatched to Morocco and a Mr. Lamb to Algiers. From what Mr. Hamilton tells us, their orders are to establish peace treaties with the Barbary States and negotiate the release of American prisoners held there."

It had come as a severe shock to the U.S. government when, a year earlier, the dey of Algiers had abruptly declared war on the United States. Up to that point, America's commercial and diplomatic dealings with the Arab world had been negligible. Many representatives in Congress could not find the Barbary Coast on a map. Like most Americans, what little they knew about North Africa they had gleaned from reading *Robinson Crusoe* or the writings of Miguel de Cervantes. There were aware, of course, that back in '85 the American merchantmen *Dauphin* and *Maria* had been seized by Algerine corsairs and their crews taken to the port of Algiers, where they still remained. These and other incidents involving unlawful seizures of American vessels in the Mediterranean and Atlantic had received considerable press and had done much to stir up a small but growing segment of the population who were outraged over the impotency of their government to act effectively at home or abroad.

Getting American sailors released from Arab prisons, however, was never a complicated matter. It was simply a question of money. Upon seizure of any foreign merchant vessel, whatever the flag of Christendom under which it sailed, ransom payments became due to the sultan of Morocco, or the dey of Algiers, or the bey of Tunis, or the bashaw of Tripoli, depending on which state had perpetrated the atrocity. Toss into the bargain some form of annual tribute, as most European maritime nations had been doing for years, and American merchantmen would be free to sail anywhere they wished in the Maghrib.

To add to America's woes, when the Spanish signed what appeared to be a permanent peace with Barbary in 1783, after fighting with the Moors off and on since 1492 for control of the Mediterranean Sea, America could no longer rely on Spain to protect its merchant fleet. Nor could they rely on Portugal or Britain; those two allied powers had their own commercial interests to consider. Americans did assume, however, that they could rely on the French. Article 8 of the Treaty of Amity and Commerce signed in 1778 compelled France to use its good offices with North African rulers to protect American shipping. With France as a de facto ally in the Mediterranean, and Britain not actively meddling in U.S. affairs in that part of the world, the relatively few Americans who followed current events had cause to be optimistic.

"So you see, Anne," Richard summed up, "there is room for hope."

Anne bit her lip. "Do you think Mr. Lamb will be successful?"

"God willing, yes," Thomas Cutler replied. "We know nothing about the man, but the point is, as Richard said, at least our government is doing *something*. Which, considering its makeup, is an achievement all by itself." He leaned forward in his chair and asked, rhetorically, since he already knew the answer: "Have we heard from anyone besides Mr. Hamilton?"

Silence indicated they had not.

"It's too soon, Pappy," Katherine encouraged, though it was discouraging to the extreme to have received thus far only one response to the many letters sent out. "We need to give them more time."

"I pray you're right, my dear. I pray you're right."

ONCE THE SHOCK of *Eagle's* capture had passed, the Cutler family had called in every chit and favor it had to its credit until the likes of John Jay, John Adams, Benjamin Franklin, and George Washington were made aware of the family's plight. Whether such individuals could do anything beyond what was already being done was doubtful even under the best of circumstances. And these, the Cutlers realized, were hardly the best of circumstances. Congress was focused on itself these days, absorbed in heated debate on whether or not to dissolve the Articles of Confederation and replace them with a more viable form of government. In October, in Annapolis, a convention of nine states had ended with a call to convene a second and more inclusive meeting of all the states the following May in Philadelphia. It would be a truly national convention whose primary purpose would be to resolve the decisive and divisive issue of sovereignty. The delegates would address one central question: Did the Great Declaration grant the states independence from each other as well as from England, or was its purpose to gain independence from England but establish a central government that would have both the authority and the power to act on behalf of all the states? With that question answered, a new national government might then be installed, and the United States could take a more decisive role on the world stage.

"It could take months to decide," Katherine pointed out gloomily late one afternoon in January. She and Richard were huddled before a flaming hearth as she worked on a red woolen sweater she was knitting for Will. The two needles clicked purposefully together, gleaming in the reflected firelight. Outside, homes across South Street appeared as magical structures in a world turned white by whirling cascades of tiny flecks falling silently from an ashen sky. Will and Jamie sat at the window, impervious to the chill, mesmerized by the silent beauty of snow mounding and curving along hedgerows, tree limbs, and on the flat-bottomed, square-ended punt that their father had begun crafting in November for his sons to take out fishing the following spring. "Perhaps years," she added. "What will become of Caleb in the meantime?"

"I wish I knew," Richard replied, hating each word of that oft-used refrain, sick to death of his inability to do something tangible that might lead to the freedom of *Eagle*'s crew.

Christmas had come and gone, and what should have been a happy holiday and a respite from emotional stress had proved to be neither. Try as everyone might to make it so for the children, the forced good cheer had ebbed, inevitably, into undercurrents of foreboding once the boys were a-bed. Even the wisdom and joviality of Benjamin Lincoln, an old family friend who had served as Washington's second-in-command at Yorktown, could not help. Lincoln, who had just returned home to Hingham after quelling a rebellion of disgruntled farmers led by a former army officer named Shay in Springfield, did his best to dispel the gloom. But Caleb's empty bedroom in the house on Main Street proved too somber a reminder of where Caleb was—and where he was not.

"I do know this," Richard complained bitterly. "Unless Mr. Hamilton prevails in Philadelphia, this country will have neither the will nor the means to do much of anything to anyone anywhere. As he once said, our country is despicable in its weakness, and if that doesn't wake

Congress up, we fought the revolution for nothing. It's one reason why Lamb's mission failed, though I still hold the man himself primarily responsible for that."

Although Thomas Barkley had succeeded in part in his mission to Morocco, John Lamb had failed completely in Algiers. As reported in Boston newspapers and confirmed by the *London Chronicle*, Dey Baba Mohammed bin Osman had dismissed Lamb from the royal palace and refused to have any dealings with him. Among the reasons given: the only language Lamb could speak was English; his crude mannerisms and lack of diplomacy offended the dey; and—the reason that dwarfed all others—he brought no money with him, simply a promise to draw funds from a bank in Paris on a note co-signed by America's recently installed plenipotentiary minister to France, Thomas Jefferson. The *Chronicle* had also verified, in a report that seemed to Richard downright condescending, that the French foreign minister, Comte de Vergennes, had refused to honor France's commitments to the United States as called for in the 1778 treaty. America stood alone with but seven hundred ill-equipped soldiers to defend it, and no navy whatsoever.

"What I can't understand," Richard groused, "is why Mr. Jay recommended Mr. Lamb in the first place," referring to John Jay, the secretary of foreign affairs of the Congress. "What in God's name was he thinking? How does trading mules and horses in Tangiers qualify a man to represent our government? How could an intelligent person like Jay have made such a dreadful decision? Had Congress sent Barkley to Algiers instead, Caleb might be home today."

Katherine dropped her knitting into her lap. "It's the same in England, my love. Take William Pitt. When war broke out in America, he stood alone in Parliament in opposition to British policy. And today he is one of the few to contest trade restrictions with America. He believes what we believe, in free trade and open markets. But such men are rarely given their due even if what they have been saying for years turns out to be correct. Self-interest and expediency are the coins of every realm. And that, I'm sorry to say, includes the United States."

"I can't disagree with you, Katherine, though I still hope for better here. Let's pray that what is decided in Philadelphia bears me out."

Katherine waited while Richard got up to drop another log into the flames. When he was beside her again, she said, "I'm mostly through a letter I'm writing to Jeremy. You can read it if you like. Perhaps he can help us."

"How so?"

"Well, for one thing, he's a ranking post captain in the Royal Navy. Hugh tells me he's one of the most respected officers in the Mediterranean Squadron. For another, he often goes out on patrol along the Barbary Coast. Perhaps he has seen something there or has contacts that might prove useful."

Richard did not respond right away. An idea had struck him as Katherine spoke about her brother, and he needed time to think it through. He sat concentrating on the fire, weighing both her words and the possibilities they engendered. When he responded, he kept his tone conversational: "It's worth a try. Please send Jeremy my regards. Tell him I look forward to meeting him someday. Now, tell me about Hugh. What word from him? Is he still in England?"

"He is. 'Sitting on the beach,' as he puts it, though a beach is hardly where he wants to be. Until he's assigned a ship, he's living on half pay at home with our parents in Fareham. His last letter mentioned the possibility of service on the North American Station. Wouldn't that be a treat for us all? Halifax is just up the coast and . . ." She narrowed her eyes. "Richard, what are you thinking?"

He gave her a startled look. "Nothing."

"Yes you are, and I want to know what."

"I wasn't thinking anything," he insisted.

"Not true, my love. I'm married to you, remember? You're onto something."

"It's nothing. A passing fancy." He inclined his head toward their sons standing watch by the window. "Shouldn't you be getting supper ready?" he asked innocently. At the back of his mind he was already framing the contents of yet another letter he would write tomorrow to Alexander Hamilton in Philadelphia.

WITH THE MELTING of the snow, the mood of the Cutler family took a turn for the better. Reports from Philadelphia confirmed that every state had sent its full contingent of delegates to the National Convention. This was important, Thomas Cutler explained to those who would listen, for that gave the convention the legitimacy it required to rule on the critical issues that would decide America's future. Further, it was reported by the press that the northern-dominated Federalist Party led by Hamilton, Jay, and Adams was gaining political ground against the Jeffersonian Republicans, southerners, mostly, who clung with an almost religious tenacity to the principle of states' rights. Such individuals viewed any form of shared sovereignty as anathema.

Under no circumstances, they insisted, should the integrity of the individual states be compromised by a national government, whatever its form; that was the core principle for which the war with England had been fought. Hamilton countered with his oft-quoted conviction that independence backed by a weak military is nothing more than an empty promise.

As Americans awaited the outcome of the debates, William and Lizzy Cutler arrived unexpectedly early in Boston after a swift passage of just eighteen days, the result of steady southerly breezes more typical of Caribbean trades than the perverse westerly winds that normally blew upon the Atlantic in springtime. Soon after the Cutler brig docked at Long Wharf, a flustered George Hunt walked out from the offices of Cutler & Sons and bowed low before William Cutler, apologizing profusely for being caught unawares.

William Cutler put a hand under Hunt's elbow and bade him look up. "There is no need for that, Mr. Hunt," he said with a chuckle. "This is America. No one bows to anyone here." He placed his hand at the small of Lizzy's back. "Unless, perhaps, to a lovely young woman. Mr. Hunt, may I introduce you to my daughter, Elizabeth."

"Ma'am," Hunt said humbly, bowing again and avoiding her eyes as though dazzled by the image of golden hair and delicate feminine splendor standing before him in an ankle-length dress of rich brocade with a richly decorated silk shawl draped across her narrow shoulders. He did manage to collect himself when Lizzy swept him a brief curtsey. "I am honored to meet you, Mr. Hunt," she said. "We have often heard your praises sung in England."

"Thank you, ma'am," Hunt said, adding in a stab at gallantry, "and I have often heard tell of your lady's grace and beauty. Now I understand why." He turned to her father. "Sir, I shall have a boat ready to take you to Hingham within the hour. Please make yourself comfortable in our offices. I shall have tea or coffee brought in, some food, perhaps, whatever you and Miss Cutler might fancy."

"That is kind of you, Mr. Hunt. But I think my daughter and I would prefer to explore your city while we wait." He pointed his cane up State Street to where a gold-domed cupola rose above a substantial red brick building with a prominent balcony built halfway up its east side. "Is that what is now called the State House? Yes? Then it's what we English used to refer to as the seat of royal authority in Boston. Pity it still isn't." He gave Hunt a jovial wink. "Back in an hour," he called over his shoulder. He offered his arm to his daughter, and the two set off at a brisk pace.

Hunt immediately set about to find a small, swift vessel to carry word of the Cutlers' arrival to Hingham, and a larger, more accommodating one to convey them there.

"Lizzy! You're here! You're really *here*!"

Thunder rumbled in the distance and seagulls mewed and circled overhead as Katherine and Lizzy Cutler flew together in a tight embrace on the Hingham quays, their inbred propriety and correct upbringing cast joyously aside in the exhilaration of seeing each other after so many years. It was the same for them all. William Cutler had not seen his brother since Thomas and his wife sailed for America many years earlier. Nor had he met any member of his brother's family here today except Richard, who had visited William Cutler's family in Fareham in 1774 and had lived with him in 1778 after William had pulled every string in his grasp to get his nephew released from Old Mill Prison and into his custody. He was particularly intrigued by his grand-nephews and took great joy in gripping little Jamie firmly at the waist and lifting him high in the air as the boy screeched with delight. "A fine specimen," he announced, setting Jamie down on the ground and gravely offering a serious-looking Will his hand to shake. It was an unguardedly joyful reunion. People passing by on Broad Cove Lane smiled at the Cutlers and at each other, caught up in the family's happiness.

"You look a fright, Tom," William announced with a twinkle in his eye. "A good deal less hair, more girth around the middle, a peg-leg limp, skin that looks more dead than alive—my God, you poor bloke, you look just like me!" They laughed together before William asked, his brow creasing with concern, "How is Elizabeth? You wrote that she isn't in the best of health."

"Much better now. Anne's wedding gave her a lift. And the warmer weather helps. But what really made the difference was the anticipation of you and Lizzy coming to Hingham. It's just what the doctor ordered."

"Glad to be of service," his brother replied. "I must say, I look forward to getting to know her. You two were newlyweds when you sailed for America."

They watched as Lizzy and Katherine wiped away tears, each giggling at the other caught up in the overflow of powerful emotions. Richard laughed along with them, delighted to be once again in the company of people he held so dear.

Only young Will appeared standoffish. Like many boys his age, he regarded shows of personal affection as girlish spectacles to be avoided at all costs. He leaned against a tree with his hands in his pockets, attempting to appear aloof. "Pappy, shouldn't we be getting home?" he said at length. "Father says we should. It's about to rain." As if on cue, there came a louder, closer clap of thunder.

"We shall hop to it, Your Grace," his grandfather said, saluting in a Royal Army fashion that always made Will giggle. He turned toward his brother. "Sir William, pray have yon squire draw up the prince's chariots and we shall be on our way."

A CUTLER FAMILY gathering had to await the arrival of Richard's sisters and was set for the following week. The few days' respite suited everyone, the weight of family issues to be discussed notwithstanding, for the older Cutlers had half a lifetime to catch up on, and Lizzy was eager to lavish affection on her best friend's children. In due course, Stephen and Lavinia Starbuck arrived from Duxbury, though Anne Seymour traveled alone by carriage from Cambridge. Frederick sent his regrets, she announced, but was too busy to take leave of his budding medical practice.

The next day, the family's mood turned somber as they gathered in the parlor of the Cutler home on Main Street. The weather had turned surprisingly cool for late May, and a thick mist hid the sun, adding to the solemnity. Everyone took a seat, the matriarch Elizabeth beside the hearth where a fire popped and crackled, the others flanked out in a wide semicircle around William and Thomas Cutler holding court in the center. Upstairs, in what used to be Richard and Caleb's room and was now occupied by William Cutler, Will and Jamie played war games on the floor under the attentive eye of Edna Stowe, the family housekeeper.

Thomas Cutler led off. "I suggest we postpone discussion of Caleb's release for the moment, though of course that is the most important reason we are here today. Richard has something to say on the subject that I think you will find compelling. Let us first review the state of our business. This is not a separate issue, as you will soon come to realize. It is closely linked to our efforts to free Caleb and the rest of *Eagle*'s crew." He turned to his son. "Richard, you were the last to be on Barbados. Might I ask you to recount for us your observations there?"

Richard was prepared for that question. The previous afternoon he had reviewed today's agenda with his father and uncle. He didn't have to relate much about his voyage to the Indies; everyone present realized what was at stake there and the ramifications of the threat posed by Captain Horatio Nelson. The question was, how should the Cutler family respond to that threat? Richard deferred the answer to his uncle.

"Our original assumption," William picked up the thread, "was that there was no substance to any of this. As Richard pointed out, there is considerable opposition to the Navigation Acts in every British colony and at every level of society. So we chose to do nothing and wait for the storm clouds to blow over, so to speak. Alas, we were wrong. It seems clear, in retrospect, that the Royal Navy intends to follow the letter of the law on this matter, whatever the consequences. Captain Nelson is even now carrying out his threat. There are more British agents on Barbados than ever before, and we are being closely watched in England as well."

"Our own country is spying on us," Lizzy said to Katherine, "waiting for us to make a wrong step. And this despite the frightful taxes we are forced to pay each year."

"Excuse me, Mr. Cutler," Stephen Starbuck broke in. He stood out among the others by the simplicity of the clothes he wore: a plain-cut white shirt, no waistcoat or neck stock, and a drab pair of black trousers and thick cloth shoes that nonetheless were his Sunday best. He was not a Quaker, although he looked like one. He often reminded Richard of Benjamin Franklin in Paris during the war. Not only was Starbuck as comfortably indifferent to current fashions as Franklin was, he possessed the same acuity of mind that allowed him to fly like an arrow to the heart of a matter. "Exactly what do the British expect to gain from the Acts? Liv has told me some of what Richard just explained, but I don't understand their purpose."

"You are not alone in asking that question, Stephen," William said. "It's the old way of doing things: colonies sending raw materials only to the mother country, and the mother country sending manufactured goods only to her colonies. Everyone else is excluded from this internal financial scheme, even, at times"—he pointed to himself—"a country's own citizens. Of course, for such a system to work properly, a country must have a considerable number of overseas possessions capable of producing raw materials. Which England does, of course. As an English citizen I strongly disagree with this policy. I favor free trade because free trade serves everyone, from the Exchequer on down. But the concept of free trade is anathema to the Old Guard, who see it as a threat to the natural order of things and therefore to the country's financial stability. Does this explanation help?"

Stephen nodded.

"Good. Now then," William continued, "since American merchants are denied access to British-held islands, we—meaning the Cutler family in England—are forced to purchase or hire British-built ships and man them with British sailors—or at least sailors who we can demonstrate are not American. As long as the Navigation Acts remain in force, we will ship our goods directly from Bridgetown to Britain and her possessions, and on to Europe, while Cutler and Sons in Boston will continue to service our North American customers. To accomplish the latter, we must arrange to transfer cargoes at sea after they leave Barbados. I suggest the islands of the Bahamas as the site for such transfers. There are too many of them for the Royal Navy to patrol effectively, and the navy is known to turn a blind eye to what goes on there."

"So we are reduced to smuggling," Anne muttered.

"You can look at it that way," her uncle answered her. "Captain Nelson certainly does. Your father and I, however, prefer to think of it as being forced to find more expedient methods of doing business. The bad news—and it *is* bad news—is that the added expense of obtaining non-American ships and crews is putting a considerable strain on our earnings, as you no doubt noted when you received your recent distributions. Call it what you will, we have no choice. We must serve the customers we have to the best of our ability, while at the same time seeking out new customers in new markets that have no trade constraints."

"What new markets?" Lavinia wanted to know.

"The Orient is certainly one. It's quite lucrative, as merchants from Salem have discovered. In Canton we can exchange sugar and molasses for teas, calicoes, nankeens, and silks, then sell those goods here and in England at steep prices. Sweden and Russia are two other possibilities. Those countries—"

Elizabeth Cutler threw up her hands. "Sugar and silk, teas and nankeens," she wailed, her voice a testament to agony and despair. "That's all well and good, William, but in God's name will you *please* tell me what all this has to do with Caleb!"

Her husband reached out to soothe her. "We were just coming to that, my dear." He nodded again at Richard, who rose to his feet. That simple act drew the eyes of the room to him, since up to this point everyone who had spoken had remained seated.

"What I am about to tell you," he said, "I have already reviewed with Father and Uncle William. And with Katherine. It was her letter to her brother Jeremy last winter that inspired what we are now proposing to do. However, we agreed not to settle on any course until we spoke with you today. This must be a family decision, for reasons that will become clear in a moment."

He paused a moment, drew in a breath. "Whatever we might do to free *Eagle*'s crew, we can expect no further assistance from the American government. It couldn't do much even if it had a mind to, since it will take months, perhaps years, to establish whatever form of government is decided upon in Philadelphia and to allow that government to frame our foreign policy. That's the reality of it. There's no point in wasting time debating it. Now that the French have abandoned us, we have no one to turn to but ourselves. So it is to ourselves that we will turn."

He withdrew a small piece of paper from his waistcoat pocket. "The dey of Algiers," he said, consulting the paper, "is demanding $59,496 in ransom for Captain Dickerson and the twenty members of his crew. That number, of course, includes Caleb. It calculates to $2,833 a man, on average. Mr. Lamb assumed that he could secure their release for half that amount. He was mistaken. The dey would not have accepted that sum even if Lamb had brought the money with him. It was a mistake we do not intend to make. We will have the entire amount the dey demands, and we will deliver it to him in gold and silver and Spanish pieces of eight. The dey has made it clear that he will not accept paper currency."

Family members exchanged glances.

Lavinia said: "You say 'we,' Richard. Who actually is going to do this?"

"I am. Congress is prepared to grant me temporary status as an agent acting on its behalf in Algiers. My orders are to sail there, pay the ransom to free *Eagle*'s crew, gather information about Algiers, and then sail to Toulon, to the naval hospital there. While *Eagle*'s crew is being seen to, I am to travel to Paris and report to Captain Jones, passing on to him what information I have managed to obtain. Our minister in Paris, Mr. Jefferson, has already informed Captain Jones that Congress desires him to lead a delegation to Barbary, at a date still to be determined. His mission will be to negotiate the freedom of all Americans held in the Barbary States and to do whatever is necessary to ensure a lasting peace in the area. Captain

Jones is a naval officer respected as much in Tripoli as he is in Paris. He is perhaps the only American who has a chance of succeeding in such a mission."

Silence prevailed.

"Can we assume," Anne asked into the quiet, "that you talked your way into this appointment, Richard? That it was on your initiative, and not our government's?"

"That would be a safe assumption," Katherine answered for him, adding in a voice blending humor with pique, "I had to put him on the rack to get that information out of him."

"I didn't want to alarm you, Katherine," Richard explained, his tone contrite even though the two of them had already settled the issue.

"Will you be in any danger, Richard?" Elizabeth Cutler wanted to know. "I could not bear the thought of having two sons in captivity."

"No, Mother," Richard assured her. "You needn't worry. I will have official status, and I plan to sail under the protection of the Royal Navy. Not in a formal capacity that would violate British policy, but Jeremy believes he can assist me by having his ship serve as an informal escort. I could sail alongside him in *Falcon*," referring to a newly built Cutler topsail schooner, "as he patrols the coast of North Africa. Pirate corsairs respect Royal Navy guns as much as their counterparts ashore. What I have to say to the dey of Algiers may be better received if a British warship is anchored in the harbor alongside my schooner."

"Thank God for that," Elizabeth Cutler sighed. "You're certain of this assistance, Richard?"

"Yes, Mother, I am. I have a letter from Jeremy that confirms it. Look at it this way," he concluded when silence again prevailed. "I can do no worse than Mr. Lamb. Nor suffer greater consequences. The worst that can happen to me is that I, too, will be given the boot from Algiers."

Anne said: "You mentioned a sum of almost sixty thousand dollars, Richard. I assume from what you said earlier that Congress is not providing that sum."

"That's correct. Congress has no money to send, so the ransom money must come from us, as a family. That is why we are gathered here today and why we are seeking your approval to do this. Sixty thousand dollars constitutes almost our entire reserves. As Uncle William explained, we can hardly afford such a loss at a time when Cutler and Sons must invest in new ships and crews, and new markets, in order to survive. The stakes couldn't be higher."

Anne did not demur. "When it comes to a vote, I will vote yes. Everyone in this room will. But I must ask why Congress has no money. It provided funds for Mr. Barkley in Morocco, did it not?"

"It did, but Congress has no more funds available. It has exhausted its resources and has no immediate means to replenish them. Congress has promised us that it will eventually repay the sixty thousand dollars whatever the outcome may be in Algiers and whatever the outcome in Philadelphia. We are at risk only if Congress reneges on that promise. Mr. Hamilton has assured me that it will not, and I believe we can rely on his word."

Stephen Starbuck offered a final perspective. "Richard, please do not misunderstand me. We all want Caleb released, and we all support you. It's a good plan and I admire your creativity and courage. But my concern is this: if the United States continues to pay ransoms for Americans who are illegally held in Barbary, should we not expect to pay ever higher ransoms for ever more Americans illegally held?"

Richard nodded his understanding. "You're right, Stephen," he said. "Of course you're right. That same thought worries me. But it's not up to you or to me or to any of us in this room to decide matters of foreign policy. We are but one family trying to save one of our own and those in our employ. I don't mean to sound callous, but I suggest we set aside your concern until after we have Caleb here at home to worry about it with us."

Stephen nodded his agreement. "Until we have Caleb home," he said somberly.

Four

Portland, Maine, Autumn 1787

T HE DEVIL IS IN THE DETAILS, his father often said, and it seemed to Richard during those waning weeks of summer that the legions of hell had ascended from the depths to conspire against the Cutler family. Having agreed on their course of action, the Cutlers now sought to motivate others to work on their behalf. In his mission to Algiers, John Lamb had been careless with the details, and had failed as a result. Richard vowed that he would not make the same mistakes. Nevertheless, with much of the process outside his control, and with the details bedeviling him at every turn like a biblical swarm of locusts, by the end of August Richard's mood was dark. Even Jamie's silly antics did not have their usual effect, and Will gave him a wide berth when he saw his father in the parlor prowling back and forth like a lion in its cage.

"At least we know that Caleb is all right," Katherine tried to comfort him early one Tuesday morning. They were sitting with Lizzy in the kitchen, its four windows open to allow in the warm, humid breeze. Katherine was watching her husband carefully. She felt his pain and ached for him to *do* something, anything that would give him purpose. *Falcon*'s upcoming shakedown cruise would fit the bill. On Friday, Richard planned to take the new schooner down east to Falmouth. Being back under sail again was the ultimate remedy for whatever ailed him.

"There is that," Richard had to admit.

A year after *Eagle*'s capture, the Cutler family had finally received direct word from Algiers. The letter had been written by Captain Dickerson and had been forwarded by Charles Logie, the British consul in Algiers, to William Carmichael, the American chargé in Madrid. From there it had taken two months to reach Hingham. What Dickerson had to say was encouraging. *Eagle*'s crew was being treated well, under the circumstances. And no one, at the time of the writing, had been sold off to slavery in Tripoli or Tunis, the fate of many other Christian prisoners. The crew, Dickerson reported, was kept together in barracks located near the harbor and had been put to work rebuilding the breakwater, a backbreaking task. Because he was the ship's captain, he was excused from most work details and given leeway to walk about the city during daylight hours. Certain of his crew had been singled out for other duties, he wrote, including Caleb, who had been selected to serve as a domestic servant in the royal palace. Caleb had declined what had been meant as an honor, but he had not been punished for his refusal. And so far, not one American had converted to Islam to secure his freedom, an act encouraged by Arabs who coveted Western seafaring skills for their pirate fleets. The letter ended with Dickerson sending his respects to the Cutler family along with his prayer that *Eagle*'s crew would not be forgotten.

"It was good of the dey to let Captain Dickerson write you," Lizzy encouraged. "He didn't have to do that."

Richard gave his cousin a wry smile. His foul mood was in no way relieved by the knowledge that soon after he returned home from Falmouth, she and her father would be returning to England.

"Perhaps, Liz," he said. "Though I doubt the dey was making any sort of humanitarian gesture. He wants his ransom money, and he expects this letter to expedite the payments."

"How could he possibly know that the Cutler family is going to pay the ransoms, and not your government?"

"I don't think he does. Perhaps he misunderstands the situation. Algiers is small—it's a fortified city much like ancient Sparta. Perhaps the dey thinks that America, too, is a small place where people of influence have the ear of other people of influence, and that's how things get done. That might be the way it is in Africa, and perhaps in Europe, but God is my witness, it is not the way things are in America. *Nothing* gets done here without a colossal effort. I have not yet received the document promised me by Mr. Jay, to give one example, and I have written him *four times*. I'd do better sailing to Philadelphia to get it myself rather than waiting to have it sent here to Hingham."

He was referring to what should have been one of the more easily checked-off details: receipt of the diplomatic passport that would identify Richard Cutler as a representative of the U.S. government in Algiers. John Jay, foreign secretary for Congress since 1783, had assured Richard that he would have this document in hand no later than the first of August. It was now almost the first of September.

"You understand why," Katherine said. "Now that the issue of government has finally been settled, he can turn his attentions to other concerns, including ours."

The issue of how the United States of America would be governed did indeed seem to have been settled. What had been agreed to at the National Convention in Philadelphia by the majority of states had unleashed a flood of celebration throughout the North, some of the joyous backwash spilling over into pockets of federalism in the South and even swirling around Republican high ground there.

The Articles of Confederation, the feeble glue that since 1783 had struggled to hold the states together, had been dissolved. In their place would rise, like a phoenix, a truly national government presided over by an elected president whose political agenda would be held in check by a Congress representing the people; the decision-making and lawmaking power of those two branches would be balanced by a Supreme Court representing law and order. What the press had labeled the Connecticut Plan, because it had been proposed by Connecticut lawyer Roger Sherman, drew from both a New Jersey Plan calling for a legislature with one vote per state and a Virginia Plan proposing a legislature with voting powers based on population per state. Under Sherman's plan, trumpeted by some officials as the Great Compromise, Congress would be divided into two forums: a House of Representatives, its size determined by the population of the individual states, and a Senate to which each state would elect two spokesmen, regardless of its population.

"Yes, well, we'll see," Richard said, his dour mood lifting. "My hunch is you may be right. Never in a million years did I think the convention would accomplish so much so quickly."

"Any chance you might see Agee while you're in Falmouth?" Katherine asked, seeking to reinforce her husband's cheerier disposition.

She was referring to Agreen Crabtree, a man brought close to Richard by their shared experiences during the war with England, first as midshipmen aboard *Ranger,* then as acting lieutenants aboard *Bonhomme Richard,* both ships under the command of Captain John Paul

Jones. During an early morning raid on the English seaport of White-haven, Richard had saved Agreen's life; Agreen had returned the favor, twice, during the battle with HMS *Serapis* in the North Sea. Richard had invested considerable effort in tracking down his former shipmate after the war, finally locating him in what was now Agreen's home on Casco Bay in the Eastern Province of Massachusetts—or Maine, as Agreen preferred to call his native land.

"I'm still hoping," Richard answered her. "I've tried to reach him, apparently to no avail. But he may be there. And if he is, I'll do every-thing I can to convince him to join Cutler and Sons. We always have need of so fine a seaman."

"And so fine a friend. Think he'll take the bait?"

"He will if the bait is a position as ship's master. I think it's what Agee wants, and it's certainly what he deserves. His current employer either has his head buried in the sand or he hasn't a ship to give him."

"I would be forever in his debt," she sighed, "if you could convince him to sail with you to Africa."

"I would be, too," he said, adding with a grin, "though I suspect you'd be the more persuasive in that regard. He was quite taken by you during his visit here. But the chances are slim, regardless. I'm planning to be in Falmouth only a day or two, and for all I know, he's away in some Far Eastern port beguiling some love-struck Malay girl with those outrageous good looks of his."

Katherine walked over to the kitchen windows and flung them wide to let in every gasp of the sultry air. When she came back, she stood behind Richard and began gently massaging his shoulders.

"Well," she said, "whether you see Agee or not, I hope you enjoy your cruise to Falmouth. And you needn't worry about Lizzy and me whilst you're gone. We have our own plans."

He settled back gratefully into her soothing touch. "What sort of plans?"

Behind his back, she smiled impishly at her friend seated across the table. "Oh . . . nothing that a big, brawny sailor like you would find the least bit interesting."

He reached across his chest and took her hand in his, all the while staring across the table at his cousin.

"What, Lizzy?"

Lizzy shrugged.

"*What*, Lizzy?" he repeated.

"I don't know what she's talking about, Richard," Lizzy said, grinning. "Honestly, I don't," she giggled when his eyes narrowed in disbelief.

IT WAS AS BRILLIANT A September day as she could recall, a welcome reprieve from a vicious late summer storm that had lashed the area two days before. The cerulean sky was a perfect match for the unruffled waters of Hingham Bay lapping the shore all around them and a rich complement to the late-summer greens of the trees lining the peninsula's stony shoreline. Ahead, brown stubbles of freshly cut hay lay atop fields rolling like swells on an open sea. World's End, as the peninsula was called, was a part of Hingham set aside by the town's Puritan forefathers as common property for freemen to use for planting or cutting timber, or as pasture for their livestock, much like the Common in Boston. Citizens of Hingham had once clustered their homes together for mutual safety and had been assigned planting lots a considerable distance away from their house lots in town. By the mid-1700s such common land was no longer necessary. Indian attacks had ceased to be a threat, and there was ample farmland south of town on private property. Nonetheless, the electorate of Hingham enacted legislation to maintain the integrity of World's End for the pleasure of future generations.

Katherine nudged her bay hunter over to the right as she returned the wave of a broad-shouldered, fair-haired man tedding hay with a three-pronged pitchfork. "There's your friend John Cushing," she teased when she was close in beside the roan under Lizzy's command. She realized the word "friend" was a stretch, since Lizzy had first met the young man only a week before and had said nary a word to him since except in greeting. "A handsome one, isn't he?"

Lizzy, too, returned John's wave, blushing when she realized it was meant for her, not Katherine. His eyes were hard upon her.

"Joy o' the morning to ye, Miss Cutler," he called out. "A fine day to be out riding."

"It is indeed, Mr. Cushing," she called to him. "What a shame to find you working so hard on such a day."

"I'd gladly work a week's worth," he shouted back, "any morning I'd have the pleasure of watching you and Mrs. Cutler ride by."

As they continued northward at a slow walk, Lizzy could not resist turning in her saddle to look back. He was still watching her. "Must be married, a man like that," she sighed, facing forward again.

"Well, he's not," Katherine said. "He was engaged to a local girl named Mary Thaxter. Mary came down with a terrible sickness not two weeks before their wedding date. John was at her bedside when she died."

"How ghastly. When did that happen?"

"Almost three years ago."

"Three years? And he's not had an interest . . . since?"

"Not to my knowledge."

They rode down the slight incline of Pine Hill toward the sharper incline of Planter's Hill, the highest point on World's End. As they crossed a small field, Katherine asked: "What about you, Lizzy? Have you had an interest . . . since?"

Lizzy fixed her with a defiant stare. "I've been waiting for you to ask me that," she said, adding with what Katherine interpreted as a rebuke, "I'm just surprised it took you so long."

"I don't mean to meddle, Lizzy," Katherine said in apology. "But I can no longer sit by and say nothing. I care too much about you, and I want to help." They were approaching the crest of Planter's Hill. "Here, let's slide off, shall we? We can walk to the top. Rest the horses a bit."

Lizzy did not comment that the horses hardly needed a rest since they had walked most of the two miles from their starting point at the stables near Indian Hollow. She slid down from her saddle and straightened the knee-length cotton culottes she had borrowed from Katherine. Holding the reins in her right hand, she fell into step beside Katherine, her mount trailing behind.

"I'm sorry," Lizzy said when she realized that Katherine was waiting for her to speak first. "I didn't mean to take on like that." She contemplated the ground as they walked along. When at last she spoke, her voice conveyed more gratitude than bitterness. "You *have* helped, Katherine. More than you realize. You and Richard and your family have been so very kind to me this entire summer. I have not felt such . . . peace . . . since . . . well, since the day I learned that Jamie had died."

"That was almost eight years ago, Liz. And look at you. You're still a beautiful young woman. You would make any man proud and happy; any child a wonderful mother. It's what Jamie would want for you. I should know. He was my brother."

"I know he would, Katherine. It's not Jamie. It's me. I feel . . . I feel that no man could ever measure up to him."

Katherine touched Lizzy's arm. "Your love for my brother has always been an inspiration to me," she said. "But understand, Lizzy: no man *needs* to measure up to him. Jamie was who he was, and you loved him for that. You will always love him for that, regardless of who else may enter your life."

Lizzy rounded on her. "That's all well and good for you to say, Katherine. But ask yourself this: Were something to happen to Richard, would you remarry?"

Katherine had not expected the question, though she had considered the answer often enough. "No. I don't think I could. Richard would always be in my heart, living there. But you can't compare my situation with yours, Liz. I've been married to Richard for a long time. We've shared happiness I never thought existed. And he has given me two fine sons and a wonderful family. I would be content to live with the memories. But you don't have those memories yet. God willing, you will have them some day."

Lizzy shook her head in frustration. "What you don't seem to understand," she said, "is how unique your marriage is. I've never seen the like! I've watched Richard watching you, many times this summer, especially when you're not aware that he is. I've seen the longing in his eyes. The *longing*, Katherine! Even after all those years, he's mad for you. He's a glutton for you. What I would give for that! The servants, the finery, the titles, the fancy parties: I'd give them all up, gladly, if only a worthy man would look at me that way!"

"A worthy man just did," Katherine pointed southward, whence they had come. "And there are many others like John Cushing out there, if only you would give them a chance and not push them away."

Lizzy's startled expression collapsed into a long, forlorn sigh. "What good does it do me?" she said, tears welling up in her blue eyes. "Next week I must leave Hingham, a place I have come to love, and sail home to dreary old Fareham."

At the crest of Planter's Hill now, they looked down on the white clapboard houses of the village nestled off to their left at the southern reaches of the harbor; ahead, the peninsula of Nantasket stretched out its long, bony arm along the limits of Hingham Bay. Farther northward, beyond Nantasket Beach, the white-crested waters of the Atlantic glistened in the morning sunlight as Katherine turned to Lizzy with a smile as warm and inviting as the day itself.

"That, my dearest friend, is what we have come here today to discuss."

RICHARD HAD LONG FAVORED Falmouth as a sailing destination. The easternmost town of any consequence in the state of Massachusetts, it was situated on a stubby peninsula jutting out into the island-studded waters of Casco Bay. Its natural harbor afforded good anchorage, and the thick forests growing close to its rocky coastline emitted a heady scent of pine that blended appealingly with the pungent aromas of sea air, even at low tide. It was, Richard had often mused, a rugged land of simple tastes and pleasures where a man could go to bed at night looking forward to waking up the next morning and getting on with his life. The area had a special significance to him because it was the last place on earth his brother Will had walked. In October of 1775, a week before he was flogged to death aboard a king's ship off Marblehead, Will had trudged angrily amid the ruins of a town recently reduced to matchwood by the Royal Navy as punishment for holding a British sea officer hostage earlier in the year.

Richard had worked his crew as hard as he dared during the three-day voyage. Every jack aboard was hand-picked from a pool of volunteers for this precursor to the cruise to North Africa, and Richard had tested them and the schooner at their limits. From Hingham, *Falcon* had sailed deliberately into the teeth of a howling nor'easter; throughout the night her crew had battled shrieking winds, ripping thunder, and wild flashes of lightning as they struggled up ratlines a-weather to set, douse, or double-reef the two topsails. Forward, sailors grabbed on to bowsprit and forestays to set one storm jib, douse it, then set another of different dimensions as the schooner bucked, plunged, and shivered. Amidships, her captain, rain streaming off his oilskins, made mental notes of which jib worked best with the shortened canvas aloft to maximize stability in the frothing seas.

Throughout that first night and well into the second day, Richard was everywhere about the schooner. This was his vessel, his command, and he would come to know every nook and cranny of her just as a man, over time, comes to know a lover. Whether spread-legged for balance at the helm, entwined in the standing rigging shouting encouragement or direction to topmen battling canvas on the yardarms, or deep in the hold searching for excessive seepage between the difficult-to-caulk garboard strakes, he remained visible, always, to his men, sharing their hardships with an almost reckless abandon. Nor was it all for show. These men might obey Richard as their employer, but they would not respect him as their captain unless and until he convinced them that he was a ship's master in whom they could entrust their lives and fortunes. "First among equals" was how he had described the position of a Yankee sea captain to John Paul Jones, and he was determined to be perceived as exactly that aboard *Falcon*. That meant doing nothing rash or foolish. Throughout the second night, when the storm was at its peak, both gaff sails—normally set beneath the topmast yards—remained tightly furled. Even a reefed spread of canvas challenging so fierce a gale might send *Falcon* over onto her beam ends did the helmsman lose control of the tiller.

At daybreak on the third day, with the shriek of the wind easing to a mournful moan, off came the gaskets on the great fore-and-aft sails, and up the masts they went on their large wooden rings. Up, too, sprouted the schooner's three regular foresails at the bow. Now on a broad reach with the wind on her quarter, *Falcon* had seven sails billowing, from her flying jib bent on near the end of the forty-foot jib boom, to the two topsails aloft, to the leech of the massive trapezoid sail on the mainmast, its boom extending a good ten feet beyond the stern. By the time *Falcon* was resting peacefully at anchor off Falmouth, Richard had determined that this was her fastest point of sail, faster even than a beam reach. Her crew logged her speed at more than fifteen knots at one point, a highly satisfactory result, especially when one factored in the weight of the reinforced planking on her deck and along her bulwarks and gunwales. Richard was more than satisfied. Benjamin Hallowell's shipyard in Boston had done its job once again. It had produced a vessel not only of beauty, but of fluid grace and function that any sailor would be proud to call home.

With the sun now low on the horizon, Richard allowed his crew some much-needed time for recuperation. They would sail with the ebb tide the next afternoon. The cruise home, he had already decided, would be less demanding, whatever the conditions at sea. He had pushed the men hard on their outward voyage, and the storm had provided him with what he needed to know. The old adage—if your vessel has a flaw, a storm at sea will find it—had proven its reliability. *Falcon* needed a few modifications— he wanted to more evenly distribute her ballast, and he'd see her helm tightened and another coat of tar on the shrouds—but these were minor adjustments compared with the flaws a shakedown cruise often brought to light. By year's end, he speculated, she'd be ready to put to sea.

A knock on the door of the after cabin brought him back to the present. "Enter," Richard called out.

The door opened to admit a stocky, black-haired sailor. Like the other twenty-four members of *Falcon*'s crew, he had served his young country in the Revolutionary War. After his father died and left the family farm to his oldest brother, Abel Whiton had returned to the sea to make a living. Aboard *Falcon* he served triple duty as foremast topman, ship's cook, and coxswain of the captain's gig.

"Will ye be having supper aboard, Captain?" he asked.

"Yes, Whiton," Richard replied, stifling a yawn. The previous day and night had strained his resources to the limit. "I'll go ashore in the morning. Please wake me at six bells and have the gig called out."

"Aye, Captain. And as ye'll be eating aboard, I'll be serving up a flounder Tom Gardner brought in not an hour ago. She's a plump fish, sir. As plump a flounder as ever I've seen. He and the men want ye to have it."

"Please thank Gardner for me," Richard said, with feeling. It was no big matter, a fish. The sea was full of fish. Yet Richard was keenly aware of how unusual it was for common sailors to offer any sort of gift to their captain, especially a captain who had just put them through hell.

"I'll do that, Captain. And sir? It'll take me an hour to prepare your supper, so in the meantime, might ye snatch some shut-eye? If I may, sir, you've hardly slept a wink since we left Boston. The men are concerned."

"Thank you, Whiton," Richard said, smiling despite himself. A part of his mind wondered how John Paul Jones would have reacted to such a suggestion by a member of his crew. British sea captains held a somewhat different perspective on shipboard protocol than their American counterparts. "I think I'll do that."

"Very good, sir."

As Whiton made his way forward to the galley he was surprised to see a stranger approaching, someone who had apparently made his own way below.

"May I help ye?" Whiton said, his senses alert. He did not recognize the tall, sinewy man, although he recognized a fellow sailor by the deep, leathery tan. The stranger's shock of reddish-blond hair was streaked white in places and was tied back at his nape with a simple piece of cod-line. He was dressed in baggy white trousers and a blue cotton shirt that was rolled up to his elbows and open at the neck. When he brought a finger up to his clean-shaven chin, the muscles in his forearm rippled.

"It's all right," he assured Whiton in a deep voice. "I'm an old friend of your captain's. I received permission t' go below from that gray-haired fellow up there on anchor watch."

"Mr. Tremaine? Well, if Mr. Tremaine gave you his permission . . . Mr. Cutler is aft, in his cabin. I should warn ye, sir, he's done in. He may already be asleep."

"I'll take care not t' scare him," the visitor promised.

He walked softly aft and listened at the door of the cabin a few moments before cracking it open and peering inside. Richard was seated at his desk, but he had turned his chair around and was facing aft with his feet up on the narrow, crimson-cushioned settee running athwartship afore the stern window. That window was open, and Richard appeared to be looking out to southwestward, toward the town of Cape Elizabeth, where a massive structure clearly defined as the base of a lighthouse stood on a far-off promontory known locally as "the Neck."

The visitor cleared his throat. No response. He cleared it again, this time with more authority. Still no response.

He walked over to the settee and sat down opposite Richard, who, as Whiton had foretold, was fast asleep. For several moments the man sat quietly, gazing across at his friend as the manuscript pages of their history together unfolded before him in oft-read passages. They had last seen each other when Agreen Crabtree had unexpectedly dropped anchor off Hingham two years ago. Two years; yet here, today, that span of time seemed little more than the blink of an eye. So profound were his feelings that he was for a moment unable to speak. He managed to summon enough of himself to shout out, with all the outrage of a captain on his quarterdeck, "Good *God*! And t' think I once thought t' join up with this sorry outfit, where the captain sleeps all day while his crew fishes!" The result was gratifying.

Richard's eyes flew open. He blinked once, twice, as if in the confusion of collecting his wits he was unable to comprehend either the rude manner in which he had been awakened or the apparition sitting before him with a silly grin on his face. Then his eyes focused and both men were on their feet, each first gripping the arms of the other, then throwing that aside and embracing with hard slaps on the back.

"Dam*n*ation, Agee, are you ever a sight for sore eyes!" Richard held his friend at arm's length and inspected him. "How long have you been in Falmouth?"

"We call it Portland now, Richard," Agreen replied with an enormous grin. "A couple o' days, t' answer your question. I was aboard my brigantine, workin' away, bein' the good servant that I am, when I noticed this fancy topmast schooner prancin' about the harbor. As

I'm watching her I'm thinkin' her crew hasn't a clue how t' handle her proper; she's bound to smash up there on the lee shore. So who else could be her captain if not my long-lost friend, Richard Cutler? And who else in his right mind would have the gall t' paint such a beautiful hull *yellow*? So I rowed over."

"What you mean is, you got my letter."

"Well, that too," Agreen chuckled. "So what brings you up here, my friend? To offer me a king's ransom t' quit my employ and join yours, so I can fish up there on deck with your crew?"

"Nothing quite so glamorous, Agee." Richard motioned to the settee. "Have a seat. We have some catching up to do."

The time invested in catching up was brief. After a few minutes, Richard said, "We can talk more about this over supper. You can stay aboard?" Agreen nodded. "Excellent. Now, Agee, here's the situation. *Falcon* was launched a month ago. This is her shakedown cruise, as you know from my letter. For a destination I chose Falmouth—excuse me, Portland—for reasons you understand and also because there was the outside chance I might find you here."

"So this here's a social call?"

"Far from it."

"What, then?"

"I have a business proposition for you. I can't pay you a king's ransom, but I can pay you a fair wage if you'll agree to join me on *Falcon*'s maiden voyage."

"Where to?"

"Algiers. With a stopover on the way at Gibraltar."

Agreen whistled softly. "Algiers. Jesus, Richard. You're takin' her right into the lion's den."

"I am. That's why she's painted yellow. Ben Hallowell recommended it. Dark paint absorbs heat and cracks a ship's planking."

Agreen nodded, his face grave. "I assume this has to do with *Eagle*? Everywhere I go, people still talk about it. And they're still mad as hell."

"As well they should be. It's why the states acted as boldly as they did in Philadelphia. America is tired of being pushed around, Agee. I'm going to Algiers to get Caleb and his shipmates out of there. This *will* cost my family a king's ransom, but it's worth every piece of eight we have to pay."

"An' you're asking me t' join you on this cruise?" Agreen asked rhetorically.

"Yes. As *Falcon*'s sailing master. With the understanding that should you choose to remain in the employ of Cutler and Sons after we return home, you'll be awarded a vessel of your own, most likely this very schooner. We'll have with us a crew of twenty-five men, the same men you saw up on deck. Each is skilled at more than catching fish, I assure you. And we'll be going armed into the lion's den, Agee. Do you remember meeting General Lincoln when you were in Hingham? He's requisitioning six 6-pounders for us through our mutual friend Richard Dale," referring to a fellow prisoner-of-war in England and *Bonhomme Richard*'s first lieutenant. Dale was one of the few former Continental Navy officers who retained meaningful connections with what remained of America's military.

"Carriage guns, Richard? On a merchant vessel?"

"Yes. And swivel guns. And not just on *Falcon*. Mr. Jay is calling on all American merchant captains to arm their vessels because we have no navy to protect them. There aren't enough guns to go around, so we had to act quickly to get them."

Agreen reflected on that. "That's the reason for the reinforced planking I noticed on deck."

"Yes. She couldn't take the recoil without it. I'm certainly not going into the Mediterranean looking for a fight, but I'll be goddamned if I'm going in there unarmed. We won't have much, but at least we'll have something. *Falcon* will be outfitted as close to a naval vessel as our country has today. And I intend to command her like a naval vessel. With your help, I pray. So what do you say, Lieutenant Crabtree?" Richard forced his voice to sound casual and bright. "Are we shipmates again?"

Agreen scratched the nape of his neck, his brow furrowed in concentration. He stared beyond Richard, out the window to the few lights visible ashore. When his eyes flicked back, Richard saw sadness and disappointment in them.

"God is my witness, Richard, I want to do this. I'd sell my soul t' help you and your kin, you know that. But I'm not my own man the way you are. I work for Mr. Sloane, and he has me bound t' him like a prisoner to a stake. He won't take kindly t' my leavin' his employ. And he'd make things right nasty for me around here if I jumped ship."

"Is Mr. Sloane here in Portland?

"He is."

"I'll pay him a visit in the morning."

"For what purpose?"

"To buy out your contract."

Agreen shook his head. "He's a nice enough man, Richard, all else bein' equal. But when it comes t' money, all else ain't equal. Not with him; not by a long shot. Things tend t' get a mite sticky if he finds himself at the wrong end of a bargain. He pays good wages, I'll give 'im that. So it'd cost you plenty even if he were inclined t' release me."

"It's worth plenty to me and my family, Agee, to have you in our employ. Do we have a deal?"

Agreen snorted. "Not so fast, my friend," he cautioned. "Not so fast. We're makin' progress, but we're not there yet. We've got some serious negotiatin' still t' do. Since you're askin' me t' quit my position, I have t' consider my own interests, t' do what's right by me. For starters, there are three conditions that must be met before I could even consider signin' up with your outfit."

"Name them."

Agreen held up a finger. "First, I want t' stay a spell with you and your family before we sail for Algiers." He held up another finger. "Second, I want t' get t' know your sons better." He held up a third. "Here's the clincher, matey, the deal-breaker: I want time alone in your kitchen, without you stickin' your nose in where it ain't wanted, t' sit an' ogle your wife."

Richard maintained a poker face as he pretended to weigh the pros and cons. Then, with a heavy sigh: "Damn your sorry eyes, Agee, you have me in a corner. It goes beyond my better judgment, but I see I have no choice. I accept your terms." He stood up and offered his hand.

Agreen stood up and shook it solemnly. Then they both burst out laughing.

RICHARD HAD MUCH to relate to his family on his first evening home. That Agreen Crabtree would be joining *Falcon* on her cruise to Algiers was the most heartening news. The fact that he would be stopping off in Hingham on his return voyage from North Carolina sometime in October added to the family's pleasure. To Richard's surprise, given what Agreen had told him about his employer, Peter Sloane had readily agreed to release Agreen from his contract on the condition that he completed two final runs to Baltimore and Wilmington. There was no need to buy out the contract, Sloane had informed Richard once he understood the facts. *Eagle*'s fate, he declared, could be the fate of any American merchant vessel—his own included.

The timing seemed ideal, for it would take another two to three months to prepare *Falcon* for sea and tie up the remaining loose ends. Several of those loose ends had been tied up during his absence, Richard discovered. His father informed him that they had received the letters of credence confirming Richard as an American emissary that John Jay had promised, and William Cutler announced that his family's share of the ransom money would soon be on its way to Gibraltar, where it would remain in the custody of Captain Jeremy Hardcastle pending *Falcon*'s arrival there.

The family discussion then shifted to another topic, one equally pleasing to those present, especially Richard, who had learned to his joy that very afternoon that while William Cutler would be departing on schedule for England, his daughter would remain behind. Elizabeth Cutler would continue to occupy the spare room in Richard and Katherine's home on South Street where she had stayed all summer.

"Isn't it wonderful, Lizzy staying with us?" Katherine purred several hours later to her husband. He was lying on his back in bed with two goose-down pillows propping him up. The house was quiet; on either side of the bed the amber glow of candles flickered. When Katherine dropped her nightgown and slipped between the thin sheets, the heady tropical scent of frangipani filled Richard's senses.

"Yes," he agreed, welcoming her into his arms. "And it's wonderful to see my uncle so pleased."

"He's pleased because Lizzy is so happy." Katherine laid her head on Richard's chest. "He told me he can't remember when he last saw her this way. He completely supports her decision."

"*Her* decision? When did she decide this? While I was away?"

"Yes. We were out riding one day and, well, the subject sort of came up."

"Sort of came up?" He kissed the top of her head. "Do you really expect me to believe that? I'd wager serious money that General Cutler here has been mapping out her campaign for some time, waiting for the right moment to pounce."

"I shan't take that wager," Katherine said. "And you'll be interested to learn that I saw Lizzy walking with John Cushing today down by the harbor."

"John Cushing? I hadn't thought of John for Lizzy. Now that I do, I think well of it. They have much in common."

"They do, but let's not get ahead of ourselves. There are a lot of eligible bachelors about town. The point is, Lizzy is finally ready to find out for herself just how many there are. She's in no hurry to get serious about anyone. The fun is in the hunt, as she's about to find out." She snuggled up closer. "It will be nice to have her company whilst you're away. She'll be such a help with the baby."

Richard stroked the firm flesh of her back down to the smooth silk of her buttocks. "Yes, I suppose," he said, turning slightly, preparing to take her fully in his arms. "Though I doubt Jamie would appreciate you calling him a baby. He's three years old, after all."

Katherine brought her lips to his ear and a whisper to her voice. "I wasn't referring to Jamie."

It took a moment to register. "Katherine! You're with child? Are you sure?"

"Have I been wrong before?"

He embraced her with a passion born of elation abruptly tempered by a surge of guilt. He slumped back onto the pillows. "A baby, Katherine. Sweet Jesus, a baby. And here I am, leaving you when you need me the most. Just as I did before Will was born."

She lifted her head and looked him in the eye. "You mustn't think that way, Richard," she scolded, surprised by his reaction and wishing to relieve him of an unfair burden. "You must never, never think that way. I'll be surrounded by family and friends here, just as I was in Barbados. You needn't worry. You mustn't. What you are doing for Caleb and *Eagle*'s crew is so very important." Her voice relaxed when she added: "So you see, my love, our daughter and I will be in good hands."

"Our daughter? What makes you so sure it's a girl?"

"It's only fair. You have your two boys. Now it's my turn."

He took her hand and kissed her fingers. "Since you're making all the decisions here," he said, "what do you propose to name the lass?"

"Diana."

"Diana, is it? Why Diana?"

"No reason. Other than I happen to like the name."

"I see. And I am to have no say in the matter?"

"None whatsoever." She kissed him. "Any other questions you'd like to ask about the baby?"

"Yes." He locked his eyes on hers and held them there. When she cocked her head in question he asked: "Is it mine?"

She ran the tip of her tongue along her lower lip. "Richard Cutler, you are a filthy beast with what I can only describe as very odd preferences in lovemaking. I'm onto you. You know that, don't you?"

"Of course I know that," he grinned. "It's why you married me."

She held his gaze for a moment before laying the side of her head gently back down on his chest. "To answer your question, I can't be absolutely certain the baby is yours. I do recall there being quite a bit of activity back then. You can imagine how difficult it is, keeping account of all the whos and whens. So let's just say I *hope* the baby's yours."

He slapped her bottom. "You're nothing but a wanton hussy," he declared, his voice becoming thick with rekindled desire.

"I know, my lord," she whispered, her voice, too, becoming throaty, any lingering banter fading away as she caressed the rigid strength of his loins, felt him probe the liquid folds of hers. "Isn't that why you married me?"

She opened her mouth, her tongue dueled with his. He grasped her, turned her on her side, tossed aside the light coverlet, and brought her beneath him. He entered her easily, smoothly, blissfully, her fierce desire preparing her to receive him in a single powerful thrust. Later, after he had poured himself into her and her tremors had subsided, he lay on his back with her arm wrapped tightly around him.

Her last words before he drifted away were both soft and compelling: "I love you, Richard. I shall always love you, and I am so very, very proud of you."

Five

At Sea, Spring 1788

IT WAS FITTING THAT THE ARRIVAL of *Falcon*'s ordnance in Boston, under sail from Baltimore, took an agonizingly long time. Such had been the case with most details since the Cutlers had settled on their course; why should the resolution of the most crucial detail be any different? Delays had heaped upon delays, some due to human error, the majority simply the result of trying to get things done in a fledgling republic where bureaucrats lacked any practical experience. Someone in higher authority had to approve each step along the way. But who? What was the protocol? Most important, who should one turn to—or away from—to ensure that blame, if levied, could be deflected elsewhere?

Richard Dale finally managed to wade through the bureaucratic quagmire to secure the weaponry he had requested for *Falcon*. His source was *Alliance,* the last American frigate to see action in the war with England. After the Treaty of Paris was signed in 1783, she had been decommissioned and put up in ordinary in Baltimore to await her fate. Ben Franklin had advocated giving her as a gift to the dey of Algiers in lieu of ransom money, a proposal supported by, among others, the powerful Biddle family in Philadelphia. In the end, however, most of the frigate's guns were removed and she was sold off to private interests to serve in the China trade.

Even after six of *Alliance*'s thirty-six guns had been officially consigned to Boston, along with eight of her swivel guns, the vessel selected to transport them would not sail from Baltimore until its master had determined who was footing the bill. John Jay had promised American shipping entrepreneurs that Congress would help pay the cost of arming their vessels. But what, exactly, did that mean? Just how much was Congress prepared to pay? Who would approve such payments? Of greatest mystery, where would the money come from? Under the Articles of Confederation, government efficiency had been a rarity. With the Articles now cast adrift and a new ship of state under way without, as yet, a working compass to guide it, the term "government efficiency" had become an alehouse joke.

Their frustrations mounting, the Cutlers had finally decided to pay for the guns themselves and to send one of their own vessels to Baltimore to get them. Alexander Hamilton was again quick to promise that the U.S. Treasury would repay all expenditures incurred in the rescue of American sailors abroad—once the government was able to exercise its newly granted authority to raise funds by taxing its citizenry. An increasingly skeptical Thomas Cutler had put that letter in a drawer with all the others.

By the time the last loose ends had been tied off, the thick blanket of winter snow had melted sufficiently to reveal tiny buds of the new season beneath and Diana Cutler had been welcomed into the world by a family praising God that both mother and daughter had made it through what had proved to be a difficult pregnancy.

"She will be our last child," Richard vowed to Katherine one evening in mid-April. They were sitting side by side in their bedroom beside a wicker cradle in which Diana slept soundly at last, her tiny stomach taut with her mother's milk. "I shall not see you suffer like that again. I thank God I was not able to sail before Diana was born. I could not have without knowing that you both were safe."

Katherine was in no mood to protest. The pregnancy had been an ordeal, with more weight gain, bloating, and sickness than she could have expected following Jamie's relatively easy birth. Unwillingly but inevitably during those difficult weeks she had revisited in her mind the fate of Cynthia's baby in England. That fearful image of a tiny, bloody corpse had consumed her waking hours and intruded upon her dreams. As much by her own desire as her doctor's urging, she had remained a-bed for much of the last two months of her pregnancy.

"I am eternally grateful for Lizzy," she said, rocking the cradle gently with her hand. "She was a godsend, truly a godsend, especially with the boys. Your mother was a love, of course. She did what she could. And Anne and Lavinia helped out whenever they were here. But Lizzy was

always here. We would not have come through as we did, without her."
Wearily, sadly, she put her arm around her husband's waist and laid her
head against his shoulder. "She's taking Will to see you off tomorrow in
Boston, you know."

"She'll be at Long Wharf, yes, but she'll not be there to see *me*
off."

She looked at Richard and smiled. "It's amazing, isn't it? Who would
have dreamt it? They make such a handsome couple. And yet their back-
grounds are so different."

"So are ours," he reminded her. "I was a lowly sailor from the colonies. You were English gentry, destined to become a matriarch of titled
blood. Rumor has it that King George himself carried a torch for you."

"Oh, posh," she laughed. "Today, even his stable boy would not so
much as glance at this bedraggled mass of flesh."

He put his arm around her. "This bedraggled mass of flesh," he said,
"could arouse a dead man."

She squeezed his hand at her waist. "Thank you for saying that,
Richard, even if we both know it isn't true." Her tone turned suddenly
grave. "You *will* be careful, won't you, darling?" She was imploring him
as much with her eyes as her voice. "Please, my love, be careful. I can
bear the thought of you being away at sea. I'm used to that. But I cannot
bear the thought of you in danger." She forced a smile, as though reading his mind. "Don't fret. I shan't break down on the jetty tomorrow or
cause a scene. I am a daughter of the Royal Navy, remember? But you
must promise me that you will take no unnecessary risks and that you
will do only what you must to bring everybody home safely."

"That I can promise," he assured her.

THE NEXT DAY WAS STORMY, though not fiercely so, the cold, sleet-
flecked rain persisting in a blustery wind gusting to twenty knots
judging by the whitecaps rolling into Boston's inner harbor. The foul
weather had at least the benefit of providing a diversion from the stress
of leave-taking. Will took it like a man, lingering only briefly in his
father's embrace at Long Wharf as *Falcon*'s crew labored with stay-
tackle to transfer three heavy wooden chests from the Hingham packet
into the schooner's hold, storing the $20,000 worth of specie near the
munitions brought aboard earlier in the week. Thomas Cutler was
thinking as much of Caleb returning as he was of Richard leaving, and
his handshake in farewell was firm, encouraging.

"Go with God, Richard," he said simply. "Bring your brother home."

Not surprising to Richard was the fact that Agreen and Lizzy were having the hardest time saying good-bye. Agreen had spent the previous night aboard *Falcon* with the rest of the crew, making final preparations for departure. During the early weeks of the past winter, when *Falcon* had been tethered against the quays in Hingham, he had spent most nights aboard her, preferring the Spartan accommodations of his cubicle-sized cabin to the goose-down bedding available to him in the spare room on Main Street. In more recent weeks he had been lured ashore not so much by the hospitality of Richard's family as by the warmth and welcome he discovered in the company of Lizzy Cutler.

"Is she spoken for, Richard?" Agreen had asked him in February— and several times since—and Richard was certain he would ask it again now as they sat together at the table in his cabin. The oilskins hanging on hooks on the back of the door dripped rainwater mixed with salt spray onto the deck. The coastline of Massachusetts was disappearing astern as *Falcon* knifed her way eastward through the frigid waters of the Atlantic under shortened sail and the attentive eye of her mate, Micah Lamont.

But Agreen did not ask that or any other question. He sat brooding, his eyes transfixed upon the steam curling up from the tin mug of coffee brought aft from the galley by Abel Whiton.

"You did a fine job getting her ready," Richard said, to break the silence. "She's shipshape to satisfy an admiral. And I'm pleased to note that you haven't forgotten how to properly bowse the guns."

Agreen gave him a grin at that, and a mock salute. "Just lookin' t' make sure you get your money's worth, Captain."

Although Agreen was one of the highest paid employees of Cutler & Sons, Thomas Cutler had had no trouble justifying the amount. Trouble was, by Agreen's own account, he had no notion of how to spend or invest such wages. So he had asked the Cutlers simply to hold his money for him, withdrawing enough to put some coin in his pocket and to purchase, for Lizzy, a bright red woolen scarf that he gave her the evening before he sailed *Falcon* to Boston to load supplies and munitions.

"Somethin' t' remember me by," he had told her as he handed her the gift. She had smiled at that, closing her eyes and holding the delicate fabric warm against her cheek. Then, to his surprise and that of Richard and Katherine, who were watching them, she had taken hold of the scarf by its ends and flicked the middle over Agreen's head, around his neck. She drew him to her and kissed him, her mouth open, her lips lingering on his.

"Something to remember *me* by," she replied when at last she stepped back, her hand on his cheek.

Richard sipped his coffee, savoring the heat and taste of the bitter liquid as it coursed its way down his throat. When he looked up, Agreen's momentary flash of humor had vanished, and his eyes had returned to the mug he held firmly in his hand on the table.

"Will Dr. Brooke be joining us?" Richard asked.

Agreen glanced up. "What?"

"Dr. Brooke," Richard said, referring to Dr. Lawrence Brooke, the ship's surgeon. Brooke had served in that capacity aboard *Bonhomme Richard,* and Richard had sought him out in Boston specifically for this cruise. Brooke, being on the brink of retirement with most of his patients referred elsewhere, had accepted. Although a reclusive and somewhat officious little man, Lawrence Brooke was an unusually gifted physician, one whose services would be sorely needed on this voyage. "Will he be joining us for coffee?"

"I doubt it. I invited him as you asked me to, but he told me he wanted t' work some in his cabin." Agreen revealed a hint of a smile. "The man ain't much for small talk, is he, Richard? Then again, neither am I, today. I don't know what the hell's gotten into me."

"I know what's gotten into you," Richard said, "and it's something good. I suggest you accept it for what it is."

"That's easy for you t' say, matey." He sounded almost in pain.

"Anything I can do?"

"No," Agreen replied, then reversed himself. "Yes, Richard, there *is* somethin' you can do. For starters, you can tell me t' slack off and change tack. You can tell me t' stop livin' in this goddamn fantasy world and get a grip on myself. You can tell me t' remember who I am and where I come from and what a frickin' fool I am t' think a woman like that would have anything t' do with a man like me."

Richard shook his head. "I won't tell you any of those things, Agee, because none of them is true."

Agreen gave him a bewildered, exasperated look. "Hellfire," he exclaimed. "Lizzy was born an' raised in England. By your kin, Richard, in luxury. I've *seen* the place she hails from. It's a frickin' palace a hundred times over compared t' the hovel I grew up in. An' that was in *Maine,* for Chrissakes!"

Richard shrugged. "What's wrong with Maine?"

Before Agee could answer, a shout from the weather deck forestalled him. Both men instinctively glanced up to the deckhead, their senses alert for the stamp of feet on the ladder leading below that would signal a message from a lookout.

When they heard nothing further, Richard continued: "You ask why a woman like Lizzy would want anything to do with a man like you? Maybe it's because she's a good judge of character. So is my father. He's a wise man, Agee, as I'm sure you agree. He was the one who proposed doubling your wages." That forced a weak grin out of Agreen. "My father once told Will and me something I will never forget. What he said was, 'Boys, as you grow older and make your way in the world, you will meet what will seem like many different kinds of men. In reality, there are only two kinds: those who are decent and God-fearing—the majority—and those who are not. The way to tell the difference, and the way to take the true measure of a man, is to observe how he treats people he cannot possibly use to his advantage. The better he treats them, the better the man he is.' A worthy observation, wouldn't you say?"

Agreen sat in silence.

"Look at it another way," Richard pressed. "Have you considered that what Lizzy sees in you is what I see in you? What my entire family sees in you? What every man-jack aboard this schooner sees? That night you gave Lizzy the scarf. She kissed you and you blushed as red as a lobster in a boiling pot. *You*, Agee, a man who's had every inch of his body kissed by God knows how many women the world over. You blushed. And the point is, so did she. That, my friend, is when I knew. About you *both*. There's feeling there. You know it and I know it. I can't predict the future any better than you, but it seems to me that you have every reason to be hopeful about Lizzy. Katherine agrees. And she's rarely wrong in these matters."

"You reckon so?" Agreen asked, at length, a flicker of optimism brightening his face.

"I reckon so."

Apparently willing himself to leave the subject of Lizzy behind, Agreen leaned forward with a serious glint in his eyes. "Seeing as how you have all the answers, Captain Cutler, I have one more question to ask you: Where on God's sweet earth did Dale find those fire-arrows we have in our hold? I've heard of 'em, but I've sure as hell never seen one before yesterday."

He was referring to an odd piece of ordnance that Richard Dale had managed to secure for *Falcon* in addition to the more traditional round-shot, grape, and langrage. It was a four-foot-long, thick metal shaft with an iron arrowhead at its tip and a wasp nest–like mass attached to the shaft just behind the arrowhead. Dangling down from the shaft on each side of the wasp nest were two long silver chains capped with menacing double prongs in the shape of fishhooks. The mass itself was made of hemp fiber, its hollow center stuffed full with sulfur, gunpowder, paint, pitch, saltpeter, anything and everything combustible.

"My guess is North Carolina," Richard replied, "somewhere along the Outer Banks. Ocracoke was home base for Blackbeard for a while. Dale only said in his message that these arrows were Blackbeard's weapons of choice. One look at them and you can see why. I'm glad we have them, though since we only have three, we can't test-fire one at sea. If it comes to that, we'll just have to hope that Blackbeard knew what he was about. Which I suspect he did."

He drained his mug and placed it back on the table. "We do have enough shot to exercise the guns, however. And we'll start doing that on a daily basis. It's been awhile since any of us has held a linstock."

"When do you propose we start?"

"No time like the present, Lieutenant."

Falcon WAS BUILT to accommodate a ship's complement of thirty sailors in addition to her officers and surgeon housed in the four after cabins. Which is why she had fifteen bunks built in against her hull in the crew's quarters forward, the assumption being that one watch would come on deck to sail the vessel while the other watch went below. That she had a crew of only twenty-five on this cruise was based on a second assumption: that on the homeward voyage she would have *Eagle*'s crew aboard, and several of them would be too ill or weak to stand watch or perform other shipboard duties.

A crew of twenty-five was sufficient to sail the schooner. It was barely enough, however, to sail her *and* service her guns. If they were forced to fight a battle in foul weather, things could, in Agreen's words, get a mite fiddly. *Falcon* had six carriage guns mounted on her flush deck, three to a side, each calibrated to fire a 6-pound ball a distance of up to one mile. In addition, she had eight swivel guns mounted on Y-brackets on her bulwarks, four to a side; each of the tiny cannon was designed to fire a canvas bag crammed with grapeshot. When fired at close range, these cast-iron balls, each weighing a half-pound, could cause havoc on an enemy's deck.

A 6-pound carriage gun normally required a crew of four. Richard had *Falcon*'s guns operating with crews of three, with a fourth man moving between guns to help out whenever possible. Three guns to a side, nine men total, plus one man at each of the four swivel guns per side left twelve men plus her mate and sailing master—and her captain when he was not at the guns—to sail the schooner during a battle, a bare minimum possible only in fair weather, on a relatively flat sea, and with fore-and-aft sails furled. The three gun crews thus served guns on both sides of the schooner, which meant that *Falcon* could fire her starboard battery or her larboard battery, but not both at once. The consequences of being trapped between two enemy ships at close range would be dire, especially since, without anyone available to haul munitions up from the area in the hold that served as a magazine, they would need to position much of their powder on deck, each flannel bag a potential bomb if struck by enemy shot.

"Captain Jones once said," Richard had told the assembled crew before the first gun drill that first day out of Boston, "that you judge a man-o'-war not by the number of her guns but by the skill of her gunners. You know the story of *Ranger*. She was a small sloop-of-war, but she never lost a fight against a Royal Navy brig or frigate. Not with Captain Jones in command. *Falcon,* too, is small. But she's as fine and fast a vessel as sails this ocean. And I say to you that she will never be outsailed, outmaneuvered, or outgunned by Barbary pirates—or anyone else, by damn!"

As the days blended one into another, daily life aboard *Falcon* settled into a predictable, time-consuming routine that would delay the ship's arrival in the Mediterranean by as much as a week, but was nonetheless a routine that Richard believed was critical to master.

After breakfast at 8:30, both watches set about practicing man overboard drills and sail drills. The more experienced seamen who would be called upon to navigate the vessel in the event her small complement of officers was incapacitated had lessons in spherical trigonometry as well. Drills were performed under the watchful eye of Agreen Crabtree, whose blue-water experience exceeded that of everyone else on board, including the captain. Assisting him was Micah Lamont, the schooner's mate, who worked side by side with the crew as he directed their efforts either on deck or aloft in the rigging.

After dinner at noon and a half-ration of rum, gun drills began under Richard's direction. For the first week it was pantomime, conservation of round-shot and powder being deemed paramount until the guns could be run in and out rapidly and flawlessly. By the start of the third week Richard noted significant improvement in the time it took to free the guns from their breeching ropes, tamp down the flannel bags of powder into the barrel, insert the ball, tamp that down, then haul on the side-tackle until the muzzles of the guns had run outboard through the square ports cut through the bulwarks. The improvement came as no surprise to Richard. He had fully expected it. These Yankee sailors were bred to battle and needed only to get back into the natural rhythms of gun evolutions.

From 3:00 until supper at 5:30 the crew had free time, save for those on watch duty or the extra hands required in bad weather. Candles were extinguished at the start of the first watch at 8:00, which was also the start of the six-hour, off-on rotation for alternate watches during the night. The system was an innovation introduced to the Continental Navy by Captain Jones aboard *Ranger,* in defiance of the time-honored rotation of four hours on, four hours off. Captain Jones had found the new procedure more to his liking—as did his crew, who performed better with two extra hours of sleep.

AT THE CAPTAIN'S signal, Micah Lamont cast out two empty cooper's barrels from the stern and watched them splash into the sea in *Falcon's* wake.

"Barrels away, Captain," he called back.

"You have the helm, Tremaine," Richard said to the leathery-skinned, gray-haired sailor who was twice the age of anyone else aboard. Tremaine had signed on with the frigate *Raleigh* during the war, first as surgeon's mate as a way to be mustered into the ship's books, then switching to quartermaster's mate when the opportunity arose. Unlike many sailors, Nate Tremaine did his job because he loved doing it. He had little expectation of promotion or bonuses, and lacked much desire for either.

"Aye, sir," he said, taking hold of the long, horizontal tiller.

Agreen brought a speaking trumpet to his lips. He was standing beside the mainsail, which was tightly furled on its boom, its canvas dripping wet from a thorough soaking given it by Seaman Isaac Howland lest a stray spark from a recoiling gun waft over and set it ablaze. "All hands! Stations t' wear ship! Stand by the lee braces! Step lively there, you men!"

Sailors sprang to action to bring *Falcon's* topsails and a full set of foresails around and lay her on a reciprocal course. Richard divided his attention between the three gun crews to starboard and the watch he held in his hand. Today would be their third drill with live shot, and he was challenging his gunners not only to hit the target, but to knock several more seconds off the time it took to fire, worm and sponge out, reload, and fire again. His goal: the deck cleared for action in three minutes, a gun firing every forty-five seconds, and two discharges per sixty seconds for the smaller swivel guns.

Almost as one, each of the three gun captains raised his right hand, indicating his gun was ready. Richard checked his watch. "Fire as they bear!"

At the forward-most gun, Tom Gardner dropped to a knee and sighted his target bobbing up and down thirty yards off to starboard. Not satisfied, he pushed the quoin a notch further under the breech to raise the barrel a notch. He rose to his feet, stepped to the side, and blew on the slow-match glowing at the end of his linstock. He dropped the tip to the vent, and a flame flashed out, followed a split second later by the roar of the gun. In a blaze of orange flame, the carriage crashed back until checked by its breeching ropes. All eyes on board searched the sea for the splash. There it was—a plume of water shooting up three feet to the right of the barrel and slightly short of it.

"The devil!" Gardner cursed aloud. He ordered his crew to reload.

Seconds later, Phineas Pratt fired his gun, overshooting the mark.

The third gun fired, dead-on. With a resounding *crack!* thick shards of oaken staves splintered into smithereens.

"Well done, Blakely," Richard called out to the gun captain. "A direct hit, and record time running out your gun. You and your crew have earned an extra tot of rum this evening." In a louder voice, directed at the entire ship's company: "We shall splice the main brace for every man aboard do we repeat that performance on the next volley!"

A cheer went up, followed by laughter when a sailor standing by the jib sheets shouted out: "Is that Cutler rum you'll be issuing us, Captain? Or are we finally getting the good stuff?"

"Very amusing, Hobart," Richard shouted back. He cast a fond eye upon Increase Hobart, a red-bearded, broad-shouldered bull of a man who had sailed with Cutler & Sons from its earliest days. "That comment earns you an overnight in the brig, with naught to eat but the weevils shaken out from Whiton's biscuits!"

Another round of good-natured cheers and back-slapping of Hobart got Richard to thinking, again, that the daily gun drills were essential not only for the safety of the schooner and her cargo, but for the morale of her crew as well. It gave them something to do, a healthy competition that broke up the daily routine and monotony. He was reflecting further on this when suddenly there came a cry from aloft.

"Deck, there! Sail ho!"

"Where away?" Richard shouted up. He sensed from the tone of voice that what the lookout had sighted was not a merchant vessel.

"Two points abaft the larboard beam," the answer was shouted down. "She's barely hull-up, sir. I can only make out her tops'ls and t'gallants."

Everyone aboard instinctively glanced in the general direction, and saw nothing but open water. Given his height advantage of eighty feet and his excellent eyesight, Matt Cates could spot a billowing topgallant almost twenty miles away on the earth's curvature. Those on deck could see only half that far.

"Very well, Cates. I'm coming up."

Richard doffed his heavy woolen sea coat and handed it to Lamont.

"Steady as she goes?" Agreen asked.

"Yes, for now, Agee. I doubt she's a pirate in these waters. Spanish or Portuguese, more likely."

With an agility and speed that in his early days of sailing would have been unimaginable to him, given his inbred fear of heights, Richard clambered up the ratlines on the foremast shrouds to the topmast yard. Ignoring Cates' offered hand, he swung a leg over the pine spar and secured himself against the mast. He took the glass and held it to his eye, extending and retracting it until a pyramid of stacked sails came into sharp focus. He held the glass steady until he had determined the vessel's course relative to his own.

"What is she, sir? Can you make her out?"

"Not yet, Cates," Richard replied, squinting into the lens. "She's ship-rigged and flying plain sails to t'gallants. A large brig or a frigate, I'd wager." He strained to identify the ship's flag, but the distance was too great and the white billowing square sails on her mainmast blocked his view. Added puffs of canvas suddenly billowed out.

"She's setting her stuns'ls," he remarked, more to himself than to Cates, "aloft and a-low. And she's doing it smartly." He collapsed the glass. "She's showing us her speed, Mr. Cates. So I suggest we show her our heels. Keep me informed."

Grabbing hold of a foremast backstay, he crossed his legs over it and let himself down hand under hand to the larboard bulwarks. "Whoever she is," he shouted out to the crew after jumping down onto the deck, "she finds us interesting." He turned toward the helm. "Bring her up two points, Tremaine."

"Two points, aye, sir," Tremaine replied. He checked the compass. "New course: east by north, a half north."

Since leaving Boston *Falcon* had followed an easterly course between 38 and 42 degrees north latitude, Gibraltar lying a little south of east of Boston. In the prevailing westerly breezes and generally fair weather, navigation had not posed much of a challenge. As they approached the Azores to starboard, Richard had ordered a course altered slightly southward to take advantage of an unusual northeast-bound current that Agreen had discovered on an earlier voyage, an offshoot of the powerful Canary Current leading south to the Cape Verde Islands and the more powerful North Equatorial Current streaming across the Atlantic to the Caribbean Sea.

"Any change in her course, Cates?" Richard shouted up.

"Aye, sir," Cates shouted down. "She's dropped her leeward stuns'ls and is heading east."

"Can you make out her flag?"

"Not yet, sir."

"Very well. Keep me informed."

Due east, on the frigate's course, lay the Strait of Gibraltar, the eight-mile stretch of water separating the southern tip of Spain from the northern tip of Morocco. As much a pathway connecting Europe and Africa as a seaway linking the Atlantic to the Mediterranean, the narrow passage had served as a stepping-stone into the heart of Europe for the Muslim armies that swept across North Africa and northward in the eighth century. For seven hundred years the North African Muslims—or Moors as people of mixed Arab and Berber descent were called—held sway on the Iberian Peninsula, dispelling the barbarism of the Dark Ages by introducing literature, science, and medicine that the Arabs of Babylon and Damascus had inherited from the ancient Greeks and Persians. Not until 1492 were Spanish and Portuguese forces finally able to break the stranglehold of Muslim occupation by capturing the city of Granada, the last outpost of Islam in Europe. Since then, Spain and Barbary had continued the fight—at sea—for control of the Mediterranean, with no meaningful peace treaty signed until 1785, just three years ago.

"Appears that we're both headin' for the Strait," Agreen commented, peering through a spyglass at the topsails of the mystery ship, which had come into view for those on deck.

"So it would seem," Richard agreed. Though the odds were long that this frigate was a pirate vessel, he would take no chances, not with the treasure *Falcon* carried in her hold. His eyes went aloft, searching for a flutter or a luff anywhere among the schooner's press of canvas to indicate a slight loss of wind power. He found none.

Throughout the rest of that day the two vessels held their relative positions. By nightfall *Falcon* seemed to be gaining ground. At dawn the next day, the sharp eyesight of Matt Cates confirmed that indeed they had gained ground, though the frigate—or whatever she was—remained visible through the spyglass and did not alter course when land was sighted and coastal traders were suddenly everywhere, sailing in and out of the busy Spanish port of Cádiz. *Falcon* sailed swiftly through a gathering storm past Cape Trafalgar, through the Strait, and toward their destination, barely visible through the drizzle and fog: a 2.53-square-mile spit of land dominated by a monolith that since 1713 had been a British territory and was reputed to be the most heavily fortified piece of real estate in the history of the world.

Falcon's entry into Algeciras Bay was duly noted by the Royal Navy. As the schooner approached Gibraltar from the west, a British gunboat sailed out to reconnoiter. She was an odd-shaped, beamy vessel rigged with two masts, each with a four-sided lugsail. Her rounded bow and sturdy construction reminded Richard of a Dutch herring-buss he had once seen in the English Channel. Except that this vessel carried a 24-pounder gun mounted on her bow and what looked to be long nines mounted amidships, one on each side.

When the gunboat was close alongside, an individual dressed in a heavy blue sea coat cupped a hand to his mouth. "What vessel is that?" he called up, his crisp patrician accent announcing him as an officer.

Richard identified himself and his command.

"Yes, Mr. Cutler, we've been expecting you," the man replied cordially. "Welcome to Gibraltar. I am Lieutenant Hollingsworth, at your service." He pointed toward a massive limestone structure looming eerily through the fog above a small indentation along the western edge of the spit. "You may take station over there, sir. Rosia Bay is that cove you see beneath the fortress. You needn't concern yourself with the tide—it's of minor consequence in these parts—but do mind the depth. It's twelve fathoms. Rather a sharp drop-off, you see. But it affords good holding for your anchor, and you'll find no currents there. Am I understood, sir?"

"You are, Lieutenant," Richard called over to him.

"Very well, Captain. If there is anything I might do for you, you need only ask anyone you see to have me summoned. My name, again, is Lieutenant Charles Hollingsworth, attached to His Majesty's ship *Guardian.* Captain Hardcastle insists you be shown every courtesy during your visit here. I am off to inform him of your arrival. He will be sending further word to you shortly. Good day to you, sir. Again, my warmest welcome."

"Thank you, Lieutenant," Richard said, touching his tricorne hat in deference to the officer's rank. "You have been most kind. We shall proceed to the cove directly."

Agreen had watched this exchange with ever-widening eyes. "Well slather me with butter and fry me up brown," he muttered as the gunboat sailed away toward the Mediterranean Squadron anchored to the north. "There you go again, Richard. I've never seen anyone dive so deep and come up so dry. Next thing you know, they'll be floatin' out a red carpet t' parade you in. Sure must be nice, knowin' people in high places."

Richard gave Lamont the order to steer for Rosia Bay, then turned to look at Agreen. "This has nothing to do with me, Agee," he said. His relief at finally having his vessel under the protection of Royal Navy guns was immeasurable. "Credit goes to the Hardcastle family." He smiled wistfully. "Except for the father. He'd as soon fire a broadside into me."

An hour after *Falcon* dropped anchor in the horseshoe-shaped cove the British officer had indicated, the mystery ship that had pursued her rounded up unchallenged into the bay, the red cross of Saint George on her ensign fluttering listlessly in the damp, heavy air.

Six

Gibraltar, August 1788

"**B**OAT COMING ALONGSIDE, SIR." That's the navy for you, Richard thought to himself: an underling advising a superior officer of the blatantly obvious. He and Lamont were standing amidships watching a gig approach *Falcon*. Eight oars worked together in nearly perfect synchrony. Each oarsman was dressed in a blue-and-white-striped jersey, white duck trousers, and a straw hat bound with a wide strip of blue cloth around the middle, its sparrow-tailed ends hanging over the rim. A midshipman served as coxswain at the tiller. Beside him sat what any farmer from Concord could readily identify as a British sea officer.

Richard maintained a deadpan facial expression. It was he, after all, who had insisted on following naval regulations aboard *Falcon*. "Thank you, Mr. Lamont," he said. "I shall welcome the boat myself."

"Toss oars!" they heard the coxswain shout. At his command, eight oars, their blades striped in blue, rose as one into the air seconds before the gig gently bumped against the hull of the schooner. Moments later, an elegantly dressed officer stepped through the larboard entry port.

Richard bowed slightly. "Welcome aboard, sir," he greeted the officer. "My name is Richard Cutler. I am master of this vessel. This is my mate, Micah Lamont."

The officer bowed to each man in turn. "I, sir, am Edward Cobb, second lieutenant of His Majesty's Ship *Invincible*, at your service. I trust you had a pleasant voyage from Boston?"

Richard had recognized the name of the ship as his brother-in-law's command. "It was uneventful," Richard replied, "therefore pleasant."

"Just so." Cobb cast an eye about the schooner, his gaze settling first on the six guns bowsed up against the bulwarks. He then took in the sails furled tight on their booms and yards; the halyards, sheets, and braces coiled neatly on their pins; finally, the clusters of crew scattered about the deck, regarding him curiously.

"A fine vessel you command, sir," Cobb said, with genuine admiration. "I have long praised American shipwrights. They make graceful ships. Fast ones, too. This one even outran her escort."

"Her escort, Lieutenant?"

"Quite." Cobb's pewter gray eyes twinkled with mirth. "*Redoubtable,* the frigate you surely noticed attempting to overhaul you. She's the fastest vessel in the squadron, so her officers claim, though apparently not the fastest vessel currently in Algeciras Bay. I must say, you put quite the twist in Captain Swanson's knickers."

"I apologize, Lieutenant. I don't take your meaning."

Cobb stepped closer, his tone turning serious and confidential. "It was by Captain Hardcastle's order, Mr. Cutler. He advised all ships patrolling the Atlantic to keep an eye out for you, and if sighted, to escort you in. Can't be too careful these days, can we, what with Spain's peace treaty with the Barbary States and with Portugal in the pirates' pocket. Algerine corsairs are now free to sail out into the Atlantic, boldly as you please, to do their dirty work."

"I see. I must thank Captain Hardcastle for his thoughtfulness."

"Which, sir, he hopes very much you will do this evening," Cobb said, stepping back, his tone again light and airy. He reached into an inside pocket of his uniform coat and drew out a square piece of paper, folded to form an envelope. Impressed with a signet ring where the four flaps met in the center was a seal of red wax with the Hardcastle family crest of twin stag antlers and a shield. "It's an invitation to supper," he said, handing over the envelope, "in his cabin at three bells in the second dogwatch. May I respond favorably on your behalf?"

Richard broke the seal, unfolded the paper, and scanned the invitation. "You may indeed," he said.

Cobb's gaze shifted beyond him, and Richard turned to see Agreen and Lawrence Brooke approaching. "Ah, there you are, Agee. I was wondering where you'd gone off to. And I'm glad to see you up on deck, Doctor." He indicated the British officer. "This is Lieutenant Edward

Cobb, of His Majesty's ship *Invincible*. Lieutenant, I introduce you to my sailing master, Mr. Agreen Crabtree, and our ship's surgeon, Dr. Lawrence Brooke."

Cobb clicked his heels together and bowed. "Delighted, I'm sure."

"Lieutenant," Agreen acknowledged. He thrust out his hand in greeting. Cobb hesitated a moment, then shook it firmly, as he did the hand of Lawrence Brooke, who said in formal fashion: "Welcome aboard, Lieutenant. We are honored by your presence."

"The honor is mine, Doctor." Another bow, then: "I must be getting back to my ship. We will send a boat for you this evening, Mr. Cutler. Good day to you, gentlemen." He touched his hat, then turned toward the entry port.

Richard stopped him. "A word, if you please, Lieutenant."

Cobb turned back. "Yes, Captain?"

"I have a favor to ask. A procedural point, actually. We've had a long voyage and my crew could do with some shore leave. How does one go about obtaining permission for shore leave?"

Cobb smiled. "Permission is not required, Mr. Cutler. Gibraltar is at your disposal. And as a former navy man, you may be interested to note that this is one of the few bases where the Royal Navy does not allow 'wives and sweethearts' aboard a ship out of discipline. There's no need for such allowances," he explained when Richard seemed not to comprehend. "Sailors here are free to take shore leave whenever they're off duty. There's no place for them to run to, you see, do they have a mind to desert," he explained further. "As to your procedural point, I can verify from personal experience that you will find both the alehouses and the ladies of Gibraltar most accommodating."

With that, he was off.

The prospect of spirits and loose women had not eluded Micah Lamont. "Might I inform the men of their shore leave, Captain?" Lamont asked, trying hard to mask his own anticipation.

"Yes, do. But make certain it's only half the crew at a time. And make certain everyone is back on board by the start of the second watch. I'm holding you responsible for that, Mr. Lamont. The men must understand that we are guests here. I will not tolerate disorderly conduct ashore. Anyone brought up for disciplinary action will have his privileges suspended."

"I'll tell them, sir," Lamont acknowledged. He saluted, more in appreciation of Richard's words than as a requirement. Richard had not pushed naval discipline that far aboard *Falcon*.

"What are your plans for the evening, Agee?" he asked more casually after Lamont had disappeared down a forward hatchway and Dr. Brooke had strolled forward to stretch his legs. "Are you going ashore?"

Agreen gave him a bewildered look. "Are you kiddin', Richard? *Me*, pass up an opportunity like this? You old married fart, don't you realize what's sittin' in some alehouse over yonder, just waitin' for a bloke like me? Damn right I'm going ashore."

Richard grinned at that response.

"Yep," Agreen went on in a quieter, absent sort of way, "I know *exactly* what's waitin' for me. Some good shore cookin', that's what. It took some doin', but I finally lured the good doctor out of his grotto. Reckon we'll go find us a place in town and while away the hours discussin' whatever it is that men like us discuss when forced t' make conversation with each other. It won't be doxies, though. Brooke doesn't seem t' have much interest in women. Even if he did, I doubt he could do much about it, if you catch my drift."

Richard studied his friend. "You're not abstaining because of me, are you, Agee? I don't give a hoot in hell what you do."

Agreen chuckled. "Because of *you*, Richard? I don't think so, matey. An' seein' as how you've got no qualms with any o' this, I suggest that after you've filled your belly with the fine food and wine your Royal Navy chums are serving up, and I've finally managed t' ditch Lawrence, you and I meet at some cathouse ashore. Don't matter which one. They're all pretty much the same. We'll find us a pretty little knob an' do the jig with her together, the way *real* shipmates do. I'll even pay the chippy if you think you're up to it, so t' speak."

When Richard remained expressionless, Agreen laughed out loud and slapped him on the shoulder. "Ease your sheets a little, wouldja, Richard? I'm just kiddin' around! Enjoy yourself, and don't you worry about your sailing master. He's fixin' t' have a grand old time cavortin' ashore with the doctor!"

AT PRECISELY SEVEN that evening, the captain's gig from HMS *Invincible* slid alongside the yellow hull of the American schooner. A sailor standing in the bow caught a deadeye on the larboard main-chains with his boat hook and held the small boat steady. Up on deck, Richard stepped through the open entry port, then swung around and lowered himself into the sternsheets by way of a makeshift ladder secured to the schooner's side. Once aboard, he settled in next to the midshipman at the tiller and waved to Pratt, Hobart, and Howland peering down at him from the bulwarks.

After exchanging the usual pleasantries with the coxswain, Richard sat in silence as the oarsmen rowed the boat over to the naval squadron's anchorage. Only the steady creak of oars rising and dipping, rising and dipping broke the silence. Richard took advantage of the lull to survey the western face of Gibraltar, now revealed to him by an evening sun streaking through broken clouds. Through the dissipating fog and mist he saw what appeared to be a gargantuan battle cruiser of mythical proportions pointing north, the magnificent height of the Rock looking like an old-fashioned poop deck rising high above the Mediterranean. There was even what seemed to be a ship's hull, a substantial wall running close to the water's edge from as far north as he could see all the way south past the fortress to Europa Point at the southern tip of the rocky promontory. Interspersed along the wall every fifty feet or so were clusters of star-shaped batteries housing cannon of various firepower standing in defense of official and private buildings of Spanish, British, and Italian construction. And, to his surprise, he saw Moorish construction too: holding a commanding position where a gentle slope gave way to a steep escarpment a third of the way up to the top of the Rock loomed a massive stone castle in a triangular shape resembling an Egyptian pyramid. Attached to the castle was a square-turreted redoubt replete with merlon battlements and a huge stone archway flanked on both sides by thick stone walls that zigzagged down along the embankment to the wall at the water's edge.

The coxswain followed Richard's gaze. "The Tower of Homage, sir," he explained, his seasoned tone suggesting prior experience acting as tour guide to visiting dignitaries. "That's what we English call it. The Moors call it Al Qasabah. It was built in the fifteenth century after the Moors recaptured Gibraltar from the Spanish. Quite a sight, isn't it? The British governor lives on the top floor of the redoubt."

"I'll be damned," Richard marveled, awed by the sight and wondering what it must have cost the Spanish to finally wrest this fortress away from the Moors.

A glance to the right or left of the castle confirmed how heavily fortified Gibraltar was, and why the Spanish had failed during the Great Siege of 1779–83 to take back from the British what was, geographically if not by the Treaty of Utrecht, Spanish soil. All along the escarpment were natural caves of various sizes, giving the impression of an enormous, two-mile-long honeycomb of gun ports. The iron black of cannon muzzles protruded everywhere like the dark tongues of unseen beasts lurking in their dark depths. In areas devoid of caves the British had erected additional gun batteries, armed to the teeth with 64-pounders—some larger, it seemed to Richard, if guns of such enormous size existed. And from his current vantage point out on the waters of Algeciras Bay, away from the dominance of the fortress and the sheer rock cliffs, he could see high up on the very peak of the Rock what he would have deemed to be impossible: silhouettes of mammoth cannon arrayed in back-to-back formation. One rank faced north toward Catholic Spain, the other south across the eight-mile Strait toward the empire of the Prophet: the North African realm of Islam.

When the coxswain ordered his crew to ease on their oars, Richard turned his attention to the ships attached to the Mediterranean Squadron lying at anchor dead ahead. All the ships he made out were frigates save for two: a 74 with a long white pennant fluttering from her foremast truck identifying her as the flagship; and another, a 64, Jeremy's ship. Richard was familiar enough with British ship construction to know that 64s had become the orphans of the Royal Navy: too large and cumbersome for frigate duty but not large enough in this modern age to take position in a line of battle during a major fleet engagement. Still, these ships held their own in special assignments, and the mere threat of her broadside—thirty-two guns firing mostly 24-pound shot, or roughly 750 pounds of iron per broadside—was enough to keep all but the mightiest of predators at bay. Compare that weight, Richard brooded, with *Falcon*'s broadside: a puny 18 pounds.

The reception awaiting him aboard HMS *Invincible* was entirely in keeping with a Royal Navy ship. Once he had climbed the steep steps built into the frigate's tumble-home and was standing at the larboard entry port, a side party of ship's boys, dressed in finery from their polished buckled shoes to the clean white tips of their cotton gloves, piped him aboard, the high-pitched squeals of their bosun's whistles continuing until a petty officer gave a quick chopping motion with his hand and they ceased abruptly.

Lieutenant Cobb, there to greet him, snapped a crisp salute. "Welcome aboard, Mr. Cutler," he said hospitably.

Richard returned the salute. "Thank you, Lieutenant."

"Allow me to escort you aft, sir. Captain Hardcastle is eagerly awaiting you."

Richard was eagerly awaiting his first meeting with Jeremy, too, but he could not resist giving the ship a quick once-over as he followed

Lieutenant Cobb aft toward the captain's cabin lodged beneath the quarterdeck. Not surprisingly, he found nothing even remotely in violation of the strict code of seamanship demanded by the Royal Navy. What did command his attention, and caused him to slow his pace, were the stubby 32-pound carronades mounted on traversable slides that he could see up through the open serpentine railing on the quarterdeck. They were the same sort of guns he had admired aboard HMS *Boreas* in Antigua. These and the long guns on the weather deck featured the new and more efficient flintlock firing mechanism set off by yanking a lanyard. This recent innovation in the British navy had reduced the linstock and powder quill to backup status in case a flintlock misfired.

Just then, a small, tail-less, brown creature with a furry white chest scampered out from beneath the quarterdeck overhang. It stopped abruptly at Richard's feet and stared up at him with an arrogant "what the hell are you doing aboard this ship" look. The creature then launched into a tirade of furious scolding chatter before wheeling about and scampering back whence it had come.

"There's a monkey on deck!" Richard shouted out incredulously to Lieutenant Cobb, who turned around to grin back at him. He realized how absurd his words must have sounded, but taken aback as he was, he didn't know what else to say.

"It's a rock ape, actually," Cobb informed him. "They're from Morocco. Every ship in the squadron has one. They make interesting pets, or so I'm told."

Richard joined Cobb under the overhang. "You could have fooled me," he said, glancing warily to starboard as if expecting another assault. "I don't think that fellow likes me."

"That fellow doesn't like anyone," Cobb said.

If the sentry standing at ramrod attention before the captain's cabin found anything amusing in that exchange, his face did not show it. It remained as blank as the spotless white of his trousers and pipe-clayed belts, and the faultless blood red of his dress uniform coat. Two black chevrons on the lower sleeve identified him as a Royal Marine corporal. He snapped his sea-service musket to his side and banged its bronze-tipped butt on the deck as the lieutenant approached.

"Captain Cutler of the American schooner *Falcon* to see the captain," Cobb declared.

"Sir!" the sentry replied. He pivoted on his heels and knocked on the cabin door.

"Yes?" a voice called from inside.

"Captain Cutler to see you, sir," the sentry announced. "Of the American schooner *Falcon,* just arrived."

"Very good. Please show him in."

"I shall leave you now, Mr. Cutler," Cobb said, as the sentry opened the door and stepped aside. "I hope you enjoy your evening." He gave Richard a final salute, which Richard returned.

"Mind your head, sir," the marine corporal cautioned as Richard ducked into the grandeur of a post captain's day cabin. He heard the door close gently behind him as he entered the room.

"Richard! By God! How delightful to meet you after all these years!" Jeremy Hardcastle, decked out in the blue, gold, and white of a senior officer's dress uniform, rose from his chair at a small desk by the larboard galley windows and strode over with hand outstretched.

"Wonderful to meet you too, Jeremy." Richard shook his brother-in-law's hand firmly. "Katherine has told me much about you. Be warned: she has you sitting high on a pedestal."

"Does she now!" Jeremy smiled. "Well, at least I'm in good company up there. It's where you've been perched ever since the day she met you."

Jeremy's effusive greeting dispelled any tension or unease Richard might have felt before meeting his in-law as quickly as the fog had earlier dissipated in Algeciras Bay. Gripping Richard's upper arm gently with his right hand, Jeremy guided him toward two blue-on-yellow wingback chairs set this side of the small desk where he had been sitting, near the edge of a deck covered with a decorative black-and-white-checkered canvas carpet.

"May I offer you a glass of sherry?" he inquired. "It comes from Jerez and is really quite excellent. I do credit the Dagos for producing such a fine spirit."

"I'd welcome a glass, thank you."

As Jeremy fetched two cut-crystal glasses and a decanter of sherry from the selection of spirits available in fitted racks directly above an ornately carved mahogany sideboard, Richard glanced around him. During his years at sea he had been privileged to witness the splendor and dignity of a British captain's after cabin, as far removed from the stench and squalor of the crew's quarters forward in the forecastle or the rough-and-tumble of the midshipmen's berth four decks below on the orlop as Kensington Palace was from the slums of East London or the carnival air and whores of Southwark Fields. This cabin was as opulent and commodious as any he had seen, simply because this was the largest British warship he had ever been aboard. A large, rectangular ebony chart table dominated the center of the room; beyond it, on the starboard side, was another sitting area with a brocade couch and chairs set beneath another set of gallery windows just aft of a 12-pound gun bowsed up against a closed gunport, the blood red of its carriage and truck a bold complement to the gleaming black of its muzzle. A formal dining alcove beyond was balanced on the larboard side by the captain's sleeping alcove, its door closed. In between, in the stern windows, thick glass panes afforded a blurred view of the Tower of Homage at sunset. Arrayed upon the walls of the day cabin were a number of nautical paintings as well as an impressive number of books arranged on shelves specially designed to prevent them from falling out during rough weather.

Jeremy walked over with a glass of sherry in each hand to where Richard was standing. "So tell me," he said as he handed a glass to Richard, "how is my darling sister? It's been too long since I last saw her."

"She's well, Jeremy. She sends her love to you."

"And my two nephews, whom I am sad to say I have never met?" He clinked his glass against Richard's. "Cheers, my good man."

Richard sipped his sherry and took a moment to savor the delectable taste. "They're just what you'd expect of two strapping lads," he replied. "Full of mischief and a constant worry for their poor mother. And I'm pleased to report that you now have a niece. Her name is Diana, born just before I sailed. She'd make you proud. A lovely little lass."

"No surprise there, if she takes after her mother."

"Which, praise God, she does."

"Then I believe congratulations are in order." He raised his glass. "To Diana Cutler: may she forever serve as the apple of God's eye and the pride of her mother's fleet."

"To Diana Cutler," Richard said, raising his own glass. "But if you don't mind, Captain, I'd prefer the word 'squadron' to 'fleet.'"

Jeremy laughed. "Done, Commodore, by your leave."

Each man took the measure of the other as they sipped their sherry. As Richard had expected, Jeremy was as physically striking as his siblings: as tall as Hugh and as graceful as Katherine, with Hugh's wavy brown hair and finely chiseled features, and an easy air of authority about him that seemed more a birthright than anything gleaned along the pathway to the quarterdeck. Only his eyes, ice blue and piercing, seemed uniquely his own, inevitably drawing one in toward him. Like his brother Hugh—and, Richard had to admit, like their father—everything about Jeremy Hardcastle exemplified how the British Admiralty desired its officers to appear and act in public.

Before Jeremy sat down on one of the wingback chairs, as if sensitive to their stark difference in dress, he removed his uniform coat and hung it on a hook by the door leading into his sleeping cabin. Richard took a small canvas satchel from a side pocket before removing his own coat. With both men now similarly clad in white trousers, shirt, waistcoat, and navy blue neck stock—notwithstanding the more elegant cut of clothes fitted by a London tailor—they at least appeared to be equals.

Richard placed the satchel on the small round table between them. "I have several letters with me," he said. "One is to you, from Katherine. Another is to her parents. A third is from Lizzy Cutler to her parents. I am hoping you can have the two letters to Fareham sent by naval courier. I also have letters from me and my crew to our families back home in Boston. Might I ask you to see to them as well?"

"I will attend to them personally, Richard. And I have a package for you, which you must remind me to give you later this evening." Without further explanation, Jeremy steered the conversation back toward family news. "I heard that Lizzy is in America. I must say, I have felt sorry for that poor girl during all these years. So much to live for, so lovely, yet never truly happy. She is a living tribute to Jamie, but I fear it's a sacrifice offered for no real purpose. It's not what my brother would have wished for her. It's certainly not what *I* might wish for her."

"No," Richard agreed. He thought he detected in Jeremy's tone a sentiment for Lizzy that went beyond brotherly love or concern, and offered nothing further.

"So," Jeremy interrupted his own thoughts, "to the business at hand. You are sailing to Algiers. As you are aware, we have chests of gold and silver waiting for you in the hold, sent here by your uncle. In value, it is roughly £7,500. That sum does not include another £2,500 worth contributed by my father. If my math is correct, that totals $45,000 in American currency."

"Your *father*?" Richard exclaimed, stunned to his core.

"Yes, my father," Jeremy confirmed.

"But . . ." Richard hardly knew what to say. "Was this Katherine's doing?"

"No. Not directly. Your uncle informed my father about your plan to rescue Caleb, and my father offered to help. It's that simple."

Richard shook his head. "Forgive me, Jeremy, I mean no disrespect, but it *can't* be that simple. Your father has had it in for me since the day I first laid eyes on his daughter."

"That is true," Jeremy admitted. "But I suspect there are things you don't fully understand about my father, Richard. He's a proud man, and he's Royal Navy to his core. Perhaps saltwater does run through his veins, as some people say. But be assured that he loves his daughter. He loves her very much. And he was quite clear in his own mind what he wanted for her in life and in marriage when the two of you fell in love."

"Whatever it was, it did not include me."

"No, it did not. You were, after all, a colonial. Admittedly, a colonial from a good family with good English connections, but a Jonathan nonetheless who would deny his daughter her rightful place in English society."

Richard grimaced. "Did love never enter his equation? Did he not care who Katherine might actually *desire* for a husband?"

Jeremy chuckled. "Never, Richard. In my father's view, if love comes about, it does so as the result of doing one's duty. It is not something to be sought out or coveted, such as a title bestowed by the king. Yes, I can see you don't agree with that perspective, but think on it: is his view so outlandish? Whatever his social class, every father wants his daughter to rise a notch or two as a result of marrying well. I should think your father would want the very same thing for your sisters, Anne and Lavinia. You will want the same for Diana someday."

"Well, if it's fancy titles your father admires," Richard blurted out, "you should remind him that I am master of an American schooner." Instantly he regretted uttering something so inane.

Jeremy chose to ignore it. "What my father may have believed back then, Richard, is not necessarily what he believes today. Old age tends to mellow a man. He is retired, as you well know, and could hardly be considered wealthy. His gift to you and your family is his way of saying that perhaps he was wrong about you, that he recognizes the joy and comfort you have given his daughter. So really, in a way, it *is* Katherine's doing. Her letters home speak volumes."

Richard struggled to accept the incomprehensible. "Your father is *apologizing* to me?"

Again Jeremy chuckled. "Don't press your luck, Commodore. In his prime, my father would have told the Almighty to sod off did He try to force an apology out of him. I daresay, though, that what we have here is as close to an apology as you or anyone else is ever going to get.

"Now then," he continued, his tone turning serious, "tomorrow, or whenever it suits you, we will need to transfer the chests we hold here on *Invincible* over to *Falcon*. I have detailed some men to help. I also have a lighter standing by to supply you with water and victuals."

The first warm glow Richard had ever felt for his father-in-law was suddenly doused by a cold, sinking sensation. Jeremy's words hit him like a thunderbolt.

"Excuse me, Jeremy. Perhaps I was misinformed, but I thought it would be the other way around. I thought that we would be transferring chests from *Falcon* onto *Invincible*. You're escorting me to Algiers, are you not? I had understood that we would sail there together."

Jeremy shifted uneasily in his chair. For several long moments he contemplated the glass he held at his lap. When his eyes came to Richard's, they were filled with regret. "You were not misinformed," he said softly. "That was both my plan and my most devout wish."

"But plans have changed."

"I daresay they have."

"Orders from Whitehall?"

"Quite so. His Majesty's government now deems it inadvisable for a British warship to be seen escorting an American vessel anywhere along the Barbary shore."

"I see." Richard drained his glass and set it carefully on the table, drawing out the process to consider the ramifications and consequences of *Falcon* going it alone. Nothing that came to mind was in any way encouraging. In fact, he *did* see. It was, after all, the way of the world when it came to America. But still he was unprepared for it.

"I had not looked forward to telling you this, Richard," Jeremy said after another lengthy pause. "Please try to understand my position. I'm at an absolute stand here. My hands are tied."

"Apologies are not necessary, Jeremy," Richard said. "I do understand."

Just then the door to the cabin opened and the captain's steward stepped inside, pushing a wooden cart on wheels before him. He was the one person aboard *Invincible* free to enter the after cabin at will, and he did so this evening with a considerable flourish.

"Good evening, Captain," he said cheerfully as he strode aft from the pantry toward the dining alcove. "Supper will be ready in twenty minutes, at 8:30 as you requested. May I bring you anything at the moment?"

"Yes, thank you, Bowen. Please bring over a bottle of Bordeaux and two fresh glasses. Leave another bottle open on the dining table." He glanced at Richard. "I believe we shall have need of both bottles this evening."

"Very good, Captain."

Twenty minutes later Bowen ushered Richard and Jeremy into the dining alcove. The stylish Chippendale table there could comfortably seat ten people, which Richard assumed it often did when the captain was entertaining other officers or officials from ashore. Tonight the captain's steward had set places for two, one at the far end of the table, the other at the corner beside it nearest the hull. Toward the middle, the flames of three candles in a silver candelabra flickered in the gentle sea air wafting through a stern window hooked slightly ajar.

Once seated, and with a generous portion of what appeared to be some sort of fowl placed before him, Richard allowed the steward to ladle fresh peas, roasted potatoes, and cooked carrots onto his plate, leaving room for an assortment of olives and nuts and slices of freshly baked bread laid out on separate plates nearby.

"Will there be anything else, Captain?" Bowen inquired after half-filling two glasses of red wine and expertly wrapping the base of the bottle in a white napkin.

"Thank you, no, Bowen."

"Very well, sir. I shall return in half an hour."

"This is delicious," Richard remarked after he had consumed a forkful of the meat. "What is it?"

"A local partridge," Jeremy replied. "It's a favorite dish of mine, and one I thought you might enjoy. Gibraltar is full of birds. Most of them are migratory, but these birds prefer to stay."

"And be eaten."

"Yes. Rather accommodating chaps, aren't they?"

They engaged in small talk, with Richard continuing to make a show of enjoying his supper though in truth he no longer had much taste for food. His appetite had been struck down by his brother-in-law's thunderbolt. Ultimately he asked: "Have you met the dey of Algiers, Jeremy?"

"Bin Osman? Yes, on several occasions."

"What can you tell me about him?"

Jeremy took a sip of wine and dabbed at his lips with his napkin. "He's no fool, I can tell you that. And despite his diminutive size, he's as proud a man as any I've met. He might humble himself before Allah, but there the list ends."

"An interesting way to put it. What else?"

"He has taught himself several languages. He speaks English better than most of my countrymen. And he's quite elderly, near eighty.

That's significant because he has ruled longer than anyone else in North Africa. Regimes in that part of the world tend to be rather temporary, you understand. The dey does not rule as a hereditary right, as does the British king, for example, but entirely at the pleasure of the *ozak,* his council of janissaries—Turkish soldiers who owe their allegiance not to the dey, but to the grand sultan of the Ottoman Empire in Constantinople. Should the dey displease the *ozak,* an assassin is likely to put a quick end to his reign. Stop me if I'm telling you what you already know."

Richard shook his head. "I don't know any of this. How has bin Osman managed to survive for so long?"

"As I said, he's no fool. He's a tough old bird who does not abuse his office, as others have before him. In his youth, so the story goes, he was apprenticed to a shoemaker and earned a reputation for hard work and decency. Since he's of Turkish ancestry, he was able to work his way up through the ranks until he achieved the title of *khaznaji,* or treasurer, a position regarded as equivalent to an heir apparent—a prince of Wales if you will. His reputation is that of a simple, frugal man who does not shrink from using piracy and terror as instruments of government policy, and who does not tolerate loose morals or spirits or tobacco. He is widely respected for those beliefs, since they sit at the heart of Islam, in theory if not always in practice. When the former ruler copped it forty years ago, bin Osman was voted in."

"You make him sound almost admirable."

"That's exactly the point, Richard. He *is* admirable to those he serves. If you're going to judge a man, do so using his standards, not your own. It's a mistake we English often make."

Richard pressed on, his voice laced with derision. "So Mohammed bin Osman dispatches pirate corsairs to prey on unarmed merchant vessels and enslave and torture their crews. Yes, I can understand why people find him so admirable."

Jeremy's face tightened. "I certainly do not wish to imply that *I* admire the dey," he huffed, "or that I approve of his ways. However reprehensible I find him and his ilk, though, I advise you to first size up your enemy before you endeavor to bring him down."

Richard's shoulders slumped. "I'm sorry, Jeremy. I meant no offense."

"No offense taken. The dey of Algiers has thrown your brother into the brig. You have every reason to hate him."

"Please, carry on."

"I will, but first, may I offer you more partridge? Anything else? No? Right, then, at least allow me to pour you some more wine. Your glass is dreadfully empty."

Richard did not protest, though the rich meal reinforced with several glasses of wine was beginning to slow his thinking. He forced himself to sip more slowly, to keep a grip on himself.

"There are essentially three points you need to understand," Jeremy said, settling into an explanation that Richard suspected had by now become quite familiar to him. "I'll try to keep them brief and simple—though admittedly there is precious little about our Muslim friends that fits comfortably under either of those terms.

"First, you must recognize that Muslims do not believe that what they are doing violates civil or Islamic law. To the contrary, their religion encourages holy war, or jihad, against nonbelievers. That most definitely includes you and me, and everyone else who does not pay homage to the Prophet Muhammad or follow the Koran, the Islamic sacred book that Muslims accept as the word of God dictated to the Prophet. So you see, all this has a religious undertone to it.

"However—and this is my second point—while religion is important to the Muslim as an individual, its role is secondary in affairs of state. Put another way, what to you and me is piracy on the open seas is, to the dey and his council, simply good business. The tribute he receives from European powers to protect their shipping in these waters and the ransoms he receives for the release of captured sailors are critical to the economy of Algiers and the other Barbary States."

"So the dey not only supports acts of piracy, he directs them."

"Just so. And I might add that he earns a pretty penny in the process: one-fifth of every tribute paid, one-fifth of every ransom paid, one-fifth of the value of every foreign cargo seized. The captain and owners of the corsair receive half, and her crew and soldiers divide up the balance. A rather tidy arrangement, isn't it? Does it happen to remind you of anything?"

"Privateering?"

"Well done. Bravo. As I recall, during the recent war your privateers were quite successful in the Atlantic and Caribbean doing precisely what Barbary corsairs are doing today in the Mediterranean."

"That's hardly a fair comparison, Jeremy," Richard protested. "America was at war with England at the time. Every nation accepts privateering as a legitimate activity in times of war."

"Ah, you've put your legal finger right on it. Brilliant." Jeremy raised his glass in a silent toast. At Richard's confused expression he explained: "To you and me, Richard, and to everyone else of a Western mind, peace exists until a state of war is declared between two nations. Muslims, however, tend to look at things a bit differently. They believe that a state of war exists ipso facto with an infidel country until a temporary peace has been declared with that country. That notion has its roots in Islam, since Islam is forever fighting what Muslims believe is a holy war against nonbelievers. That's just my opinion, of course. You'll not find that in the Koran. And incidentally, the purpose of jihad is not strictly to convert nonbelievers by force. It is, rather, to remove obstacles to their conversion to Islam. To achieve that goal, force often becomes necessary."

Richard contemplated that. "And a temporary peace can be declared only if and when another nation pays a financial gift, or tribute, to the ruler?"

"Exactly so."

"We call that blackmail in America, Jeremy."

"We call it blackmail in England, too, Richard. But to repeat myself, the Muslims don't see things our way. Mind you, the dey does not desire peace with every nation, only the most powerful ones, such as England. The others he'd prefer to prey upon and take his profit from their cargoes and sailors. Cheers." Jeremy drained his glass, gripped the bottle, and after glancing over at Richard's half-full glass, refilled his own. "And by the by, you may be interested to know that in Arabic, the word 'corsair' does not mean 'pirate' as many people believe. It means 'privateer.'"

Richard settled back in his chair. "What's your third point?"

"Sorry?"

"Your third point. You said there were three points I need to understand."

"So I did. Let me see . . . I should let up a bit on the wine . . . Ah, yes. My third point is that taking innocent people for slaves has been going on for centuries, by Christians and Muslims alike. Barbary corsairs have raided the coasts of Ireland and England and as far north as Iceland to cart off and sell off whomever and whatever they can. Britain has returned the favor by raiding villages in northern and sub-Saharan Africa and making slaves of Berbers, Moors, and Negroes. France, Spain, Holland, and many others have all followed our example. As have you chaps in the colonies—quite enthusiastically, I might add. So you see, Richard, we are *all* guilty in the eyes of God—or Allah, if you prefer."

The door opened and the steward reappeared carrying a silver tray. The conversation ceased momentarily as Jeremy and Richard watched him set the tray on the dining table. After removing the used dishes and glasses, he served heaping spoonfuls of a steaming pudding into two blue-flowered china bowls. He placed each bowl just so on a plate in front of each diner along with a clean wineglass.

"Figgy-dowdy," he announced imperiously to Richard, "prepared to the captain's specifications. May I suggest a bottle of port to complement the pudding?"

Richard put a hand over his glass. "I'd best not, else I—"

"A capital suggestion, Bowen," Jeremy interjected. "Please make it so. And Richard, I suggest you take my first lieutenant's cabin tonight. He's ashore at the citadel. Pedestal or no, my dear sister will see me keelhauled if you should fall overboard on your way back to your schooner."

"Thank you, Jeremy," Richard said, his speech slurring slightly despite his best efforts to control his tongue. "And thank you for the many courtesies you've shown me and my crew. You have been most kind."

"Nonsense, my dear fellow. We're family. It's the least I can do. Now, then, before we both set three sheets to the wind, there is something I need give you. I mentioned it earlier when we were both sober as church mice." He motioned to his steward, who had uncorked the port and was engaged in pouring out the contents. "Bowen, kindly bring me the packet on the smaller desk by the inkwell."

When the steward had brought over the thick canvas package and departed the alcove, Jeremy opened it and removed a folded British flag, on top of which was a sheet of paper with a scalloped edge on one side and odd-looking bold black script cut off at the jagged edge.

"The flag, you may recall," he said impishly, "is the Union Jack. I'd advise you to fly it when you leave Gibraltar. Barbary pirates are less likely to interfere with a vessel flying the Jack. In the event they do, show this to their *rais,* their captain." He handed over the sheet of paper.

"What is it?"

"It's a passport of sorts. Every corsair captain in the Mediterranean has a half-sheet to match this paper. If the two sides fit together, you are free to sail on your way."

"Is that what comes from paying tribute?" Despite himself, Richard could not suppress a note of sarcasm.

"England does not pay tribute, as such, to any Barbary state. Arabs have too much respect for our guns to demand it. As a matter of diplomacy, however, we do from time to time present the various deys and beys with gifts—for example after a new ruler has been installed. Which tends to happen quite frequently, as I told you.

"A further point, whilst we're on the subject. I have notified Charles Logie, our consul in Algiers, of your pending visit. No doubt he has informed the dey. I have never met Mr. Logie, and I have little information to give you about him. I do advise you to be wary of the French consul, a certain Monsieur de Kercy. Your own envoy—a chap named Lamb—relied too much on his good offices, and came to regret it. Which leads me to my main point, a warning, actually: trust no one in Algiers, Richard. And I mean *no one*. It's the proverbial den of thieves. And do not believe for an instant that because you represent the United States in Algiers you have diplomatic immunity there. More than one foreign consul has found himself in an Algerian prison for the crime of upsetting the dey."

Richard nodded. He had heard similar words of caution from others.

"By the by," Jeremy said with just a trace of slurred speech, "I had another distinguished guest for supper not two weeks ago. He sat in the very chair you're sitting in now."

"Oh? Who?"

"Captain Horatio Nelson. He's a dear friend of mine. I believe you have made his acquaintance?"

Richard allowed the beginnings of a grin.

"Yes, well, ahem, I informed Captain Nelson of your pending arrival here and he insisted on sending you his warmest personal regards."

"That was very decent of him," Richard commented.

"Yes, well, Horatio is a very decent sort of man. But perhaps there's another reason for his bestowing such benevolence upon you. He's getting married, did you know?"

"I did not. To an Englishwoman?"

"Rather. Her name is Frances Nisbet. Her uncle is the governor of Nevis. She's a young widow with a young son, Josiah. Her former husband was quite a bit older than she. He was, in fact, the family doctor who tried to save her sick father, whom Fanny adored. He wasn't able to, alas. In any event, Captain Nelson was on his way home and did me the honor of nipping in."

"I'm glad you told me. I wish him the best in his marriage."

"Yes, I'm sure you do."

Despite the late hour, Jeremy showed a seemingly limitless capacity for conversation and alcohol. As his inquiries and observations and opinions rained in, the thought came warmly to Richard's mind that Jeremy Hardcastle was, after all, Katherine's brother and a very fine man.

Jeremy was keen to learn about the goings-on in Philadelphia, where a new Constitution had been completed the previous September and now awaited ratification by two additional states before it could be signed into law. Richard was surprised to learn how much of American politics and policy Jeremy already knew, as he picked Richard's brain for further details. What was his take on the convention? Who among the delegates did he know personally and what was his opinion of them? How would the proposed two houses of Congress actually function if both were popularly elected? What city would serve as capital? How serious, in fact, was the rift between the Federalist North and the Republican South? Would the infant republic be split asunder as a result of that rift? Most pressing: who among the nation's elite would be called upon to serve as its first president? General George Washington, one supposed.

"Only a fool would not think so," Richard declared, his patriotism roused by Jeremy's enthusiasm despite a surfeit of wine. "It's his fate, Jeremy. He didn't prevail against overwhelming odds during the war in order to step aside now, when his country needs him the most."

"Handsomely said, sir. Handsomely indeed, in light of all we've managed to knock down." He drained his glass a final time and placed it emphatically on the table, signaling the end of the evening. "I need not remind you that Europe is watching with keen interest what is happening in America. I do not envy General Washington his fate."

"Nor do I, Jeremy. It's no easy matter making the impossible become the inevitable. But if there's one man up to the task, it's General Washington. Stand by the signal halyard to see what happens next."

Seven

Algiers, August 1788

"ENTER," RICHARD GREETED A loud rap on the door. A lanky young sailor opened the door of the after cabin and cautiously poked his head inside.

"Ah. Chatfield. Report, please."

"We have clear seas, Captain, save for three fishermen to northward. And, sir? We have thrown over the log-line and Mr. Crabtree desires me to report a speed of nine knots. Current course: northeast by north, a half north. The wind has veered a point, and remains steady."

"Thank you, Chatfield," Richard said. He was leaning over a chart laid out on the cabin table and held in place by small stone blocks at the corners. "Your watch is relieved at four bells, correct?"

"Yes, sir."

"Very well. Report to me again at that time."

"Aye, Captain."

Richard returned to his chart of the western Mediterranean. Bracing his legs to counteract the sharp heel of the schooner, he gripped a parallel rule firmly in hand and walked it from the compass rose to their last position of dead reckoning an hour ago. Agreen was sailing *Falcon* as close to the wind as she could lie, so the wind veering a point had brought them a point southward. He picked up his dividers and measured nine sea miles on the latitude scale at the side of the chart. Using the dividers to measure that distance along the edge of the rule, he penciled a light line on the chart from their last position and indicated their new position with a tiny bold circle, carefully noting beside it the time and reported compass heading. By his reckoning they were now roughly twenty miles from the Spanish port of Cartagena, on an approximate line of latitude of 38 degrees north, with the Balearic Islands dead ahead over the horizon. By sunset, he calculated, they could make their southerly jog through the wind and proceed close-hauled direct to Algiers, assuming the wind remained as is.

The chart indicated that Algiers lay four hundred miles almost due east of Gibraltar, a fifth of the way along the two-thousand-mile Barbary coastline stretching from Salé, Morocco, eastward to the city of Derna in Tripoli. *Falcon* could not sail due east—strong headwinds from the Levant prevented it—but due east was not Richard's preferred course. When he learned that he would be sailing without a Royal Navy escort, he had plotted an indirect route along the Iberian Peninsula, keeping just beyond sight of land and sailing with topsails furled to render *Falcon* less conspicuous to another vessel. His chosen course increased the distance on this leg of the voyage by one-half, but that did not trouble him. It was a safer route. The British flag fluttering on his ensign halyard, coupled with the *laissez-passer* Jeremy had given him, afforded some comfort. But he was in no position to tempt Fate.

Since leaving Gibraltar two days earlier, he had ordered the men to sleep by the guns on their regular starboard and larboard watch rotation. Keeping the men on deck and maintaining a high level of readiness was essential for the safety of the schooner as well as the mindset of the crew. It was a tiring regimen, but they would soon drop anchor off the coast of Algiers. As for himself, the knowledge that a large part of his family's fortune resided directly below him in the hold—and that he alone was responsible for its safekeeping and delivery—was enough to keep him on his toes. And so it would continue, he realized, until he and *Eagle*'s crew were well clear of North Africa.

Wearily he sat down at his desk and reviewed, once again, the numbers as he understood them. He had with him seven chests of hard specie worth $68,000 in U.S. currency, $9,000 more than bin Osman had demanded two years earlier from American envoy John Lamb for the release of *Eagle*'s crew. Nine thousand dollars seemed a good and necessary hedge, and Richard again gave silent thanks to Henry Hardcastle for his unexpected generosity—something he had done more conspicuously in a letter he had written his father-in-law from Gibraltar.

Still, certain questions remained unanswered. There was no way for Richard to know who else might be imprisoned in Algiers. His primary mission was clear—to secure the release of *Eagle*'s crew—but could he negotiate the release of other American sailors in the event he found any? Certainly, as an envoy of his government he had to try. He did know that the crews of *Dauphin* and *Maria* had originally been taken to Algiers in 1785. But the French Foreign Ministry had reported that most if not all of them had been sold into slavery elsewhere along the Barbary Coast. If that be true, though, why had the dey allowed the crew of *Eagle* to remain intact in Algiers? Precise figures were hard to come by because nations rarely publicized the price they paid to ransom their citizens. But it was rumored that both Russia and Sweden had recently paid $1,500 per able-bodied seaman, and $2,500 for an officer. If *that* be true, why were the ransoms being demanded for American sailors so high—almost twice as much?

His thoughts were interrupted, briefly, by a report from Phineas Pratt. Conditions were unchanged, Pratt announced, though Dr. Brooke had come topside, clearly feeling the effects of a rolling sea.

Richard nodded, with sympathy. The good doctor was no sailor and had suffered bouts with seasickness throughout the voyage. Yet overall he seemed quite content. On occasion he had joined the three ship's officers at supper and had regaled them with stories about his experiences in the Continental Navy, stories that became ever more fanciful as more rations of rum found their way into his glass. That was before Gibraltar. Once *Falcon* had departed the British fortress, Richard had suspended rum rations for everyone, himself included.

Thirty minutes later there came another knock on the door.

"Reporting as ordered," Peter Chatfield said as he respectfully entered the small cabin. "Sea conditions and course remain the same, Captain. We have sighted what looks to be a Spanish felucca, but that is all."

"Thank you, Chatfield. Please be at your ease."

Richard gazed up fondly at the ruddy-faced, tow-haired youth. The two were well acquainted. Chatfield lived three houses down from him on South Street, and his parents were close friends of Richard's own parents. At nineteen, he was *Falcon*'s youngest crew member. Nonetheless, he could hand, reef, and steer as ably as any man aboard, and he performed every task asked of him without complaint. He could also play a tune on the fiddle to lift the soul of even the most salt-encrusted tar. Plus he had another God-given talent—the reason Richard had summoned him today.

"Chatfield," Richard said, "you are a fine sailor, and you have helped keep morale high aboard ship since our first day out of Boston with your music. I am glad that you are with us. If you continue in our service, a brilliant future awaits you."

Chatfield blinked, caught off guard by the unexpected praise from his captain and employer. "Thank you, sir," he said somewhat sheepishly.

"However," Richard went on, "in Algiers I shall have need of another of your skills. You are a gifted artist, Chatfield. I have seen many of your drawings and sketches. Your attention to detail is quite extraordinary, especially when it comes to landscapes."

"Why, thank you very much, sir," Chatfield replied, more boldly this time, the pride of the artist showing through.

"As you know, from Algiers we are sailing north to the naval base at Toulon. The French government has granted us entry for a limited time to allow *Eagle*'s crew to receive medical attention as necessary and to recuperate before we head for home. From Toulon, Mr. Crabtree and I will be traveling to Paris to meet with Captain Jones. I am commissioned by our government to pass along such intelligence about Algiers as I am able to gather. He and his delegation will use that information in their mission to the Barbary States, which we can assume will take place soon after our new government is installed. Captain Jones will be negotiating peace treaties there, as well as the release of all remaining Americans held prisoner in North Africa."

"I understand, sir," Chatfield said. That information was common knowledge aboard *Falcon*. Richard had explained it to the crew soon after they had departed Boston.

"Here's where you come in, Chatfield. As soon as we reach Algiers, I want to put your artistic skills to work. Specifically, I want you to draw whatever you see—the city, the harbor, the islands, the fortifications, everything—in as intricate detail as possible. I don't know how much of this sort of thing Captain Jones may require, but I do know he can't have too much information. Since we won't be in Algiers a long time, you will have to work quickly and diligently. When I go ashore, you will accompany me as my aide-de-camp. Take mental notes of what you see, write down what you can, and sketch everything when you get back aboard. This will be your sole responsibility from the moment we arrive in Algiers to the moment we leave. I have made Mr. Lamont aware of this. Do you have any questions?"

"No, Captain," Chatfield said.

"Good lad. And Chatfield," Richard added offhandedly, "there's a reason you'll want your artwork to be at its best. Captain Jones himself will be reviewing your drawings—as, I suspect, will General Washington."

"General Washington, sir?" Chatfield gulped.

"Quite possibly," Richard assured him. "And others of his cabinet as well."

THE CITY OF ALGIERS faced eastward on the western slope of a wide, horseshoe-shaped bay sculpted into the dry hills of North Africa, so later that afternoon Richard ordered *Falcon* through the wind, on a new course south by east. If the wind held, they should sight El Marsa at the bay's northeastern tip by the evening watch of the next day, their fourth day out of Gibraltar.

Falcon's American-style schooner rig did not go unnoticed as the ship crossed the Mediterranean. On three occasions the lookout reported glints of sail to the south or east that appeared to be on a course of interception. As before, Richard took no chances, assuming every vessel of consequence they encountered was a pirate. He ordered evasive action, relying on the schooner's speed to outrun any would-be predator.

The third vessel, spotted rising to windward during mid-afternoon, proved more difficult to shake off than the first two. She was a three-masted barque, the largest vessel they had encountered since leaving Gibraltar. The schooner's inherent advantage over a square-rigger—her ability to lie two points closer to the wind—was no advantage now. *Falcon* was already close-hauled, sailing by the wind; the barque was upwind with the wind at her back, presumably her fastest point of sail. Richard had two choices: he could either try to outrun her as the schooner currently bore, with North Africa somewhere over the horizon and with the barque closing on an oblique angle of interception; or he could do what he did: wear his ship around, order the two topsails shaken out, and flee back toward Spain with the wind on the starboard quarter, *Falcon*'s fastest point of sail. When *Falcon* showed her heels, the barque at once adjusted her sails in pursuit, keeping pace and even seeming to narrow the gap between them until the black cloak of a moonless night settled over the Mediterranean, ending the chase. When Agreen ordered the crew to bring her back around and shorten canvas for night sailing, Richard resolved to keep the two fore-and-aft sails reefed throughout the next day and to approach Algiers under cover of darkness.

RICHARD SET HIS course toward the mammoth Bay of Algiers and the lighthouse that the chart indicated was on Penon Island, the largest of numerous islands scattered about the approaches to the city of Algiers. Their vast number and varying sizes reminded Richard of the islands of Casco Bay at the approaches to Portland, Maine. Jeremy had informed him that there was also a fort on Penon, an island connected to the mainland by a man-made mole, and he had described other seaward batteries apart from the city to the north and south. Fort Barbarossa to the south, named after the red-bearded Turkish grand admiral whose galley fleets finally drove the infidels from Algiers in 1529 and ended more than two centuries of Spanish occupation, was the crown jewel of Algeria's defenses.

Richard decided to delay his final approach into Algiers until dawn, lest an unknown vessel without proper identification signals attempting to breach the harbor defenses by night set off an alarm. He was expected here, and he would sail in under American colors. His understanding of diplomacy was that so long as he remained within the bay, in sight of Algiers, his diplomatic credentials protected him and his crew from harm or capture—unless, of course, he somehow offended the dey.

Its connection to the mainland gave Penon Island the shape of a sideways L running west to east out into the Bay of Algiers. The lighthouse was on the island's northern tip. On its southern end, the fort guarded the entrance to the inner harbor, accessed through a sizable gap in a breakwater running a half-mile southwestward on a straight line toward Fort Barbarossa. As Richard took in that smooth-faced, well-maintained breakwater, the thought sprang to mind that here, no doubt, was where American slave laborers, his brother among them, had endured many tortured hours.

As *Falcon* approached Penon in the relative cool of early morning, Richard stood by Agreen at the tiller. He held his breath, forcing himself to concentrate on the schooner's course and to act as if the fort's massive cannons, about to come to bear at point-blank range, were of minor consequence. *Falcon*'s crew took their cue from the officers, though no one, including Richard, could resist a glance at the two-tiered alabaster fortress looming off to starboard. Above it, at the pinnacle of a towering, slender, unadorned turret, an enormous green flag bearing a long white crescent stirred lazily to life in the awakening breeze. Below, on the parapets, turbaned soldiers in white with a red sash slanted across their chests kept vigil among rows of massive black cannon, the bore of each barrel as wide and menacing as the largest guns on a Royal Navy First Rate.

"We're through," Agreen said casually once they had sailed beyond the threat of instant annihilation. "Where to, Captain?"

Richard slowly let out his breath as he surveyed the inner harbor with a spyglass. It was a fine anchorage, the many islands at its approach and its two breakwaters providing shelter against foul weather coming from any direction. What vessels he could see lay quietly at their moorings, and they made for an eclectic collection. Anchored within the shadow of the fort was a flotilla of narrow-beamed xebecs, most with three lateen-rigged masts, the two largest carrying a square sail on the foremast. Nearby were three other vessels of distinctive pedigree: an old-fashioned Portuguese caravel with a high poop deck; three high-prowed galleys equipped with oars and a single mast that appeared to be built along the lines of an ancient Viking raider; and an odd-looking three-masted polacca, a local merchant vessel, with lateen rigs on her foremast and mizzen framing a square rig on her mainmast. He searched about, to no avail, for the barque that had pursued them two days before. Nor did he find *Eagle,* although that came as no surprise. She had either been sold off, he speculated, or presented as a gift to bin Osman's overlord in Constantinople.

Richard pointed toward a stone jetty jutting out into the harbor from shore. "Might as well go all the way in," he said. "There's deep water in there, and I see no advantage in anchoring out here. There's no easy escape from this place, should it come to that."

"Can't argue with you there," Agreen replied. In a louder, more authoritative voice: "Stations to drop anchor! Trim the sheets there! Stand by to douse the jib!"

As the schooner glided in toward the jetty, Richard walked forward with his spyglass. He focused the lens as he swept the glass up and down, right and left, taking in a city set slightly back from the harbor and encased within a ten-foot-high wall that followed the contours of the outermost structures in remarkably straight lines. The two outer walls, to the north and south, ran up a gentle slope of hills and slanted inward toward each other without actually meeting at an apex to form a triangle. Instead, the top of the triangle appeared to be lopped off, with the two sides connected north to south by a much shorter wall. Algiers thus appeared as a giant trapezoid facing eastward. Within those walls, Jeremy had informed him, lived more than fifty thousand people.

At first glance the city seemed remarkably clean, almost blindingly white, the stark stone of its multistoried, flat-roofed buildings reflecting the rays of the early morning sunlight so fiercely that he had to shield his eyes from the glare. Since the walled city lay upon the slope of the hill, it was easy to pick out individual buildings. Certainly he had no trouble identifying the most imposing structure of all, situated a quarter of the way up the trapezoid. Built centuries ago as a fortress for the ages, it rose a majestic one hundred feet into the air amid a complex of stately buildings and a grand mosque surmounted by an enormous white cupola. Towering over the mosque, and attached to the side of its Moorish-arched entryway, was a single, thin minaret with what looked like a whaling ship's crow's nest attached to it three-quarters of the way up. Richard collapsed the spyglass, thinking that Jeremy had not exaggerated when he described the magnificence of the royal palace known locally as the Qasbah.

"You have your work cut out for you," he said crisply to Chatfield, who was standing by the fife rail at the foremast, absent-mindedly flaking out a topmast sheet as he took in the sights. "I suggest you get to it."

Chatfield looped the coiled rope over a belaying pin. "Aye, Captain," he said.

Richard walked aft. "Mr. Lamont," he directed the mate, "you may call the men to breakfast. Please ask Whiton to send up a pot of coffee for Mr. Crabtree and me."

"Right away, sir," Lamont said.

Richard joined Agreen at the taffrail, as caught up as his crew by the strange and exotic landscape that stretched out before them. Together they watched the palm-rimmed city stirring to life within its walls, and even more so outside them, amid a sea of white tents so numerous that they seemed to be laying siege to Algiers. Caravans, Richard speculated, preparing to set off into the great sandy wilderness of the Sahara Desert. Here and there they saw camels loping lazily among thickets of date palms and fruit orchards, and they were close enough to hear the distant Arabic of men engaged in morning routines. Richard's eyes swung back to the base of the city, to the wall directly ahead at the end of the man-made mole where a huge rectangular entryway with a triangular roof gave access into the city. Camel drivers were leading in a troop of the single-humped beasts; on either side of the gate, attached to the outer rampart high up near an esplanade on top of the seaward-facing city wall, were five structures that looked like giant black meat hooks.

Richard dared not speculate on what those evil-looking monstrosities might be used for.

"Coffee, sir," a voice announced from behind. "Whiton asked me to bring it up. He's serving breakfast to the men."

Richard turned to see Isaac Howland holding a pot of coffee in one hand and the ears of two cups in the other. "Thank you, Howland," he said absently. "Leave the coffee on deck."

"Aye, Captain," Howland said. He dropped to one knee and put down the two cups. "Allow me to pour a cup for you and Mr. Crabtree."

He was in the midst of doing that when suddenly, from all about the city, there came a piercing shriek of trumpets—a cacophony followed moments later by the high-pitched, doleful-sounding wails of men. So unexpected and piercing was the auricular onslaught that Howland jerked upward, upsetting the cups and spilling coffee on the deck.

"Jesus Christ in heaven!" Agreen cried out as the din abated. "What in hellfire was that ruckus all about at this early hour?"

Richard had his spyglass trained ashore. "It's the Muslim call to prayer," he said, squinting through the lens. "Get used to it. You'll be hearing it several times a day."

"Can't wait," Agreen groused as Algiers went quiet. Both inside and outside the walls, men had dropped to their knees and were bending far forward toward the rising sun like so many Druids at ancient Stonehenge. "Hell of a thing, makin' people pray," he added. "An' makin' 'em bang their heads on the ground t' do it!"

"Maybe." Richard continued to squint through the lens. "Just be careful who you say that to, Agee. Men have lost their heads here for lesser blasphemy." He handed over the spyglass and pointed ashore to where the mole connected to the mainland. "Have a look at that long building over there. The one whose roof you can see the other side of the wall, down by the gate. What do you make of it?"

Agreen adjusted the focus. "Army barracks?"

"That's what I thought at first. But you'd more likely find army barracks inside the forts. My hunch? It's a prison. Caleb could be sitting in there as we speak."

Agreen nodded grimly. "Think Caleb knows we're here?" he asked, more to make conversation than to learn the answer. He had asked that question before.

Richard replied as he had before. "That depends on what the dey wants Caleb to know, Agee."

"Think *anyone* knows we're here?" Agreen asked, searching about the shore and the other vessels at anchor for some sign acknowledging their presence.

Richard took a sip of lukewarm coffee. "They know, Agee. They know. All we can do now is wait."

WAIT THEY DID, until well past noon, when the searing heat became so oppressive that even a brisk easterly breeze skimming off the Mediterranean could do little to mitigate the effects of the brutal desert sun. The crew was on deck, most of them lounging beneath spare canvas sunshades strung horizontally from the foremast to the mainmast shrouds, eight feet up from the deck to permit the free circulation of air beneath them. At least topside there was a breeze. Belowdecks, conditions were as insufferable as the wait. The sun was on its downward arc and the hard black tar on the standing rigging was beginning to lose its texture when finally they spotted a slender little boat with a high, curved prow coming toward them from the jetty. Six men worked the oars, one seated in back of the other. In the sternsheets, beside the coxswain, sat a man of European descent—a Frenchman judging by the gold-on-white Bourbon flag fluttering from the boat's stern.

At *Falcon*'s entry port, Richard, dressed in loose-fitting shirt and trousers, greeted a short, stubby man clad in finely cut clothes that nonetheless failed to conceal the natural consequences of gluttony. He emerged on deck panting from the exertion of climbing up the short rope ladder. His brow glistened with sweat.

Once aboard, the man managed to collect himself. "*Bonjour,*" he said with some flourish, bowing from the waist. "*Vous êtes capitaine Cutler, n'est-ce pas? Je m'appelle Jean-Baptiste de Kercy. Je suis le consul de France ici à Algiers.*" He paused when Richard seemed not to comprehend, then asked, "*Vous parlez français, capitaine?*"

"No," Richard lied. He thought it best not to reveal too quickly his fluency in French. Somehow, he sensed, this deception might work to his advantage later. "I apologize, sir. I do not speak French. Nor do any of my crew."

Kercy cast a skeptical eye at the Americans gathered about him, as if to take their measure along with their captain's. He pulled a handkerchief from an inside pocket of his formal coat and wiped his brow.

"*Vraiment? C'est dommage. Mais, pas de quoi.*" He shifted to English, which he spoke hesitatingly and with a strong accent. "It is good that I speak English, *non?* Monsieur Logie, *le consul d'Angleterre,* is not here. He is called to Tangiers, *alors.* So, *capitaine,* I alone have the honor to welcome you and your *compagnie* to Algiers. But that is good, *oui?* We are friends, Americans and French?"

We used to be friends, Richard thought to himself. "We are indeed, monsieur," he said diplomatically.

"*Bon. Alors, monsieur,* the dey is informed of your arrival. He extends his *salutation, aussi* . . . also, *une invitation* for . . . uhm . . . *un rendezvous* . . . at the palace, at the Qasbah, *demain à onze heures*—ah, that would be at 11:00 tomorrow morning. The time is *acceptabl*e to you?"

Do I have a choice? Richard wondered. Aloud he said, "Quite acceptable, Monsieur de Kercy. Thank you. But I am curious: Is there not a call to prayer at noon? In which the dey must participate?"

"*Oui.* That is so."

"Then why a rendezvous at 11:00? That gives us only an hour."

"*Exactement, capitaine.* The dey believes this first meeting will not take long." Kercy either did not notice Richard's raised eyebrow or chose to ignore it. "*Maintenant, capitaine,* I have the *plaisir* of extending to you another *invitation. S'il vous plaît,* do me the *honneur* of staying with me as my guest, in my home in Algiers."

Richard had expected such an invitation from either the French or the British consul. Despite the unique opportunity such an invitation would provide to gather intelligence, he had already decided to decline. He would not ignore Jeremy's warning: *Trust no one.* Nor could he ignore his personal responsibility for the family fortune stored in *Falcon*'s hold, to say nothing of the schooner and her crew.

"Thank you, Monsieur de Kercy. Your offer is gracious and very much appreciated. Personal reasons, however, require me to remain aboard my vessel."

"*Mais pourquoi, monsieur?*" Kercy's voice carried a tone of incredulity mixed with hurt feelings. He raised his hands, palms up, as beads of sweat trickled from his forehead down the side of his face into his short-cropped, sorrel-colored beard. "Your ship and men are safe here. I offer you a good room, good food, and wine, up there, near the Qasbah, where you will find the heat, um, not so hot." As if to underscore his point, he again mopped his brow. "*Aussi,* we have much to discuss, you and I. I am your friend, monsieur. I have influence here. I can help you."

Richard bowed in diplomatic fashion. "I do not doubt that, Monsieur de Kercy. I mean no disrespect, but I must remain aboard my vessel."

"Is it *peut-être* the company of Monsieur Logie you would prefer?" Kercy asked, with what seemed like forced humor. "Because he is English? Like your wife?"

Richard bristled with resentment at the mention of his wife. She had no place in this exchange, and he had to fight back an urge to respond from the heart.

"No, sir," he said. "I assure you, I would give Monsieur Logie the same reply."

Whatever de Kercy saw in Richard's eyes convinced him. "*Eh bien.* As you wish, *capitaine.* I must accept your *décision.* And I will do what I can for you. Tomorrow, if you wish, I will accompany you to the palace. Protocol is very important here. I can help you with that, at least."

"I would be honored, Monsieur de Kercy."

"*Eh bien.*" He turned back toward the entry port and the small boat awaiting him. "*Adieu, Capitaine* Cutler. *À demain.* Until tomorrow."

Richard stepped in front of him. "Before you go, Monsieur de Kercy, may I ask you to show me where the Americans are being held?"

"*Certainement, monsieur. Le prison est là,*" he pointed, "near the gate you see. It is called Admiralty Gate. It is also called the Gate de Jihad. On the other side of the wall is the prison—*vraiment,* there are *trois* . . . three, *prisons,* one in back of the other, in the area we French call *la marine.*" He indicated the same low-lying roof that Richard had noticed that morning.

"Thank you," Richard said. He stared at the building, oblivious to Kercy's grunts and mild oaths as he battled his way down the short rope ladder leading into the tender.

As NIGHTFALL CREPT across the unruffled waters of the bay toward the bare-soiled Sahel Hills rising off to westward, cooler, more refreshing breezes wafted through the open windows of *Falcon*'s stern cabin where Richard, Agreen, Lamont, and Dr. Brooke had gathered for supper. Their mood was somber. No one said much simply because there wasn't much to say. Lawrence Brooke did try to inject a note of optimism when he said, "Tomorrow, Captain, you will see Caleb. And we will know the condition of *Eagle*'s crew."

"I pray that is so," Richard replied, and said no more on the subject. After so many months of planning and posturing and preparation, of conniving and cajoling, of soldiering through the depths of anxiety, here they were at last in Algiers, in all likelihood within hailing distance of those they had come to rescue. Today was Wednesday. By Friday, God willing, they would be bound for France and the medical facilities at Toulon.

Even the normally chatty Abel Whiton went about his business in silence as he served and cleared away the dishes of a routinely simple meal of salt beef, hardtack, and the few carrots, cabbages, and apples that remained from the stores loaded aboard at Gibraltar. As soon as propriety allowed, Dr. Brooke excused himself from the table, to be followed shortly by Lamont. Agreen remained seated.

"Anything I can do for you, Richard?" he asked when they were alone.

Richard forced a smile. "I appreciate your asking, Agee, but really, no, there isn't. Get some rest. We have a long day tomorrow."

Agreen hesitated a moment. When Richard met his gaze with silence, he said, "Well, since it appears you won't be requirin' my wit and charm this evenin', I reckon I'll mosey along. Good night, Richard." He scraped back his chair, rose to his feet.

"Agee?"

"Yes?" Agreen looked down. In the feeble light of four flickering candles he thought he glimpsed dampness in Richard's eyes.

"Before you leave, Agee," Richard said, his voice quavering a little as he looked up from where he was sitting, "I need to tell you what it has meant to me to have you on board this cruise. I don't mean to embarrass you, but I need to say this. I would have been hard-pressed to do any of this without you. Just knowing that you were here whenever I needed you has meant more to me than I can express. I also want you to know what I hope has long been obvious to you—that you will always be more than just a friend to me. You're my brother, Agee, as much a brother to me as Will or Caleb. And whoever finally succeeds in sweet-talking you into dropping anchor—and I hope and pray that someone will be Lizzy, because I know how well you'd treat her—is going to be one hell of a lucky woman."

Agreen stood stock still. His Adam's apple bobbed up and down once, twice. His mouth opened, but no words came out. At length he half-whispered, "Thank you, Richard. Thank you for sayin' that. It means everything t' me. You know the feeling's mutual." He forced a smile and in a louder voice more like his own said, "As to what I've done on this cruise, in case you've forgotten, Captain, that's my job. Why you're payin' me so damn much money t' *do* my job, I haven't a clue."

Richard burst out laughing. "Get the hell out of here, Lieutenant," he said, waving him away.

"Aye, aye, Captain." Agreen saluted, performed a military about-face, and left the cabin.

Eight

Algiers, September 1788

RICHARD WAS UP BEFORE the change of watch at 6:00, shaving in front of the small, round mirror nailed on the wall of his sleeping cuddy and washing himself as best he could in a pint of water brought up from the hold the previous evening. By the time Whiton knocked on his door with a round of coffee, Richard was dressed in his Continental Navy uniform of white knee-breeches, white cotton stockings, dress blue uniform coat with silk neck stock to match, and black leather shoes with polished silver buckles—an ensemble that fit him just as well as it had when he had last worn it after the Battle of Yorktown years ago. Left off, purposely, was the traditional cotton waistcoat. Algiers was too hot for that. Otherwise he looked every thread the American naval attaché acting on behalf of his government—except that, Richard reflected glumly, his country had neither a navy nor a consulate nor a viable government for which to act.

At 10:30 he met Agreen and Chatfield by the larboard entry port. The rest of the crew was present as well—Pratt, Tremaine, Howland, Gardner, Blakely, all of them save for those on station by the oars in the bluff-bowed captain's gig, swung out from its place of storage between the fore and main masts and waiting to ferry Richard to shore. They had all come to see their captain off.

"It's time, Richard," Agreen said. He pointed ashore at the great double doors of the entry gate swinging open. A troop of men emerged onto the narrow strip of stone between the water's edge and the east-facing wall of the city. Kercy and his small entourage walked among what looked to be four janissaries dressed in collarless buttoned-up vests, cassocks with short sleeves, white turbans, and red leather slippers. Each of the Turkish soldiers carried a wide-bladed scimitar lashed to his waist by a wide red sash, and each gripped a six-foot, iron-tipped lance.

"*Enfin, mes enfants, allons-y,*" Richard responded with forced good humor. His jibe targeting Kercy, ashore and out of earshot, drew gentle laughter from the crew and cut the tension. He gestured to Chatfield to go down into the gig. "*Falcon* is yours, Agee. Remember: no one comes aboard in my absence."

"Understood," Agreen confirmed, realizing, as did Richard, that if it came to that, there was nothing he or anyone else could do to prevent a swarm of Arabs from coming aboard and doing whatever they wanted. "Good luck, Richard."

Each man saluted the other and turned away.

THE WALK FROM the jetty up to the royal palace took twenty minutes. It was not far, but the climb was steep, and Kercy was panting so loudly with the effort that eventually even small talk became impossible. The party had to pause now and then to allow him to catch his breath. That suited Richard, for he needed time to consider his surroundings, to think. Once through the Gate of Jihad, he had scanned the prison area to his right, straining to make out who and what he could within a jumbled array of one-story, flat-roofed buildings that largely blocked his view. Every man he saw was wearing the traditional Arab headdress and *haik* or *burnoose* tied with a silk belt.

As they walked on, his gaze took in a spider's web of winding streets so narrow that a normal-sized man with arms outstretched could touch the buildings on either side. Snaking off in eccentric directions, these streets formed an exotic white-stoned labyrinth whose exit would have been impossible for the uninitiated to discover were it not for the royal palace looming high above them, as much a guidepost for travelers within the city as was the lighthouse for mariners out in the bay. Occasionally Richard made some comment to Kercy or silently indicated a building to Chatfield, something for him to take note of and sketch later on the tablet he had brought with him. But mostly each man kept his own counsel as they waded single-file upstream against a flow of exotic humanity that readily gave way to foreigners in company with armed palace guards.

What Richard observed along the route was beyond anything his imagination had predicted. On many streets in these depths of Algiers were individual bazaars, or *souks,* where merchants hawked their inventories of black olives and beeswax, leather hides and wooden sculptures, coffee and salt and beans, jewelry and silks of various colors and designs, each commodity and its traders grouped together in a designated area, apparently to ensure a competitive market. From within cozy nooks of bakeries and coffeehouses flowed the animated chatter of patrons debating the affairs of the day along with alluring scents that helped to mitigate, just a little, the constant and sometimes overpowering stench of fresh animal dung, coffee beans roasting in frying pans over open fires, and the gut-wrenching stink of freshly tanned animal hides.

The men, on foot or riding on mules, were richly attired. As for the women, it was impossible to tell; their long black *burkhas* and veils covered all but their eyes—eyes careful to avoid any sign of interest in the foreign men approaching them. Here and there, within makeshift stalls containing rich displays of medicinal powders and liquids, were what had to be physicians dressed in flowing white *djellabas* dispensing advice and medicines to those in need, their services apparently free of charge since coins never seemed to change hands. Smooth-domed mosques were everywhere, some of immense size with magnificent marble archways in Moorish tradition, each mosque designed in the round to ensure that every worshipper inside held equal status in the eyes of Allah. Near each mosque was a one-story alabaster *madrasa* where dark-haired schoolboys strolled outdoors in discussion with teachers or played with a ball near circular marble fountains splashing cool water.

As they approached the Dar al-Imara, the grounds of the royal palace, the din and reek so prevalent in the lower part of the city gradually abated. Here abided a different world, one centered on a broad rectangular area about the size of the Common in Boston, size being about the only basis of comparison. The residences along its periphery were more stately and ornate than any the party had seen so far, most of them two-story affairs constructed in spotless white brick and marble with decorative wrought-iron balconies set under front-facing windows. Gracing the quadrangle were numerous courtyards with fruit orchards and scented plots as well cultivated as any English garden. The few men they saw were walking with purpose from what Richard presumed was one administrative building to another, or into the palace itself, positioned in the geometric center of the quadrangle, its huge towering stone façade standing as testament to Man's rule on earth.

Piracy does have its benefits, Richard mused as he absorbed such majesty and opulence in a desert land that otherwise had little to enrich it.

Shy of the main doors of the palace, within a courtyard rife with blossoming flowers and the heady scent of honeysuckle, Kercy called a halt to collect both his thoughts and his breath. "*Vous êtes prêt, capitaine?*" he asked. Then, remembering himself, "You are ready, Captain?"

"I am," Richard replied, with more conviction than he felt at that moment.

"*Bon. Alors,* when we go inside, I will review with you the protocol of the court. We have"—he consulted his waistcoat watch—"*vingt minutes*—twenty minutes—before the audience with the dey. As I have told you, protocol of the court is not difficult. But it is very important. If you do not follow exactly the rules, you will insult the dey, and that, *mon ami,* you do not want to do. As for the rest," he added with a smile and a slight shrug, "that is up to you."

"I understand," Richard said.

At 11:00 the door to the audience chamber opened and a golden-robed court official summoned them deeper into the palace. Kercy led the way. At the doorway to the innermost region he paused between two towering, scimitar-wielding Turkish guards. Bowing more from the neck than the waist, he announced to the court, in French, the arrival of Richard Cutler from the United States of America in the company of his aide-de-camp, Peter Chatfield. With an imperious movement, Kercy turned to his right and held out his arm toward Richard, as a circus barker might do when introducing the next act.

It was Richard's cue to enter, and he did so stiffly, replicating the consul's bow as best he could while his eyes flicked about the chamber. He saw five men in what was, surprisingly, a sparsely furnished sanctuary. Four of them stood, ranged on either side of a fifth man who was seated in a substantial though largely unadorned wooden chair with a high back that seemed, to Richard, hardly the seat of royalty. The proportions of the man in relation to his throne created an incongruous image. Although dressed in ornate turban and rich silk robes, Mohammed bin Osman was scrawny and of insignificant height, while his heavy wooden throne was tall and gracefully curved. He might have been mistaken for a child were it not for his thick black eyebrows and chest-length black beard, which was tied off in a number of tight, separate strands embellished with tiny beads of various colors. To allow his feet to touch an ornately decorated stool set on the marble floor, he had to sit slightly forward with his elbows on the armrests, giving the impression that if he were ever to lose his temper he would spring forward from his seat of power to personally smite the offender. From somewhere within the vast chamber—Richard could not determine where—came the soft, wistful melodies of an oud.

"Welcome to my palace, Monsieur de Kercy," the dey said in English to the French consul. "It is a pleasure, as always. Please make the introductions."

Kercy walked halfway from the doorway to the throne and stopped. He bowed to the dey, just as he had before, then turned and gestured to Richard to join him.

After Richard had performed his requisite bow, careful to keep his arms straight down at his sides, Kercy first introduced the dey of Algiers, whose dark, deep-set eyes fastened on the tall, blond-haired, blue-eyed Anglo-Saxon standing before him. To his right was a man identified by Kercy as the *khaznaji,* the royal treasurer. Beside him stood the *vekil kharj,* the quartermaster of the Gate of Jihad, who served his master as foreign minister. On the other side of the throne, to Richard's surprise, stood a broad-shouldered man dressed not in the silk cloak and cassock of the two ministers but rather in white-pleated canvas breeches, a half-buttoned-up garment that was more a vest than a shirt, and red Turkish shoes. On his head was a pleated, off-white turban, and at his waist he carried a Damascene knife and scimitar held in place by an elaborately woven silk *cuzaca.* He was introduced as a *rais,* a sea captain.

It was the fifth man present, however, whom Richard found the most intriguing in this fortress of Islam. He was bearded and dressed in a white shirt covered by a black cassock that descended to his knees. On his feet he wore slippers with heels, as Kercy had explained all Jews living in Algiers were required to do, and a black headdress that fell like a half-sleeve to the nape of his neck. He held papers in his hand and was stationed next to a plain wooden desk replete with other papers and writing implements.

With the introductions and formalities over, Dey Baba Mohammed bin Osman wasted no time getting down to business. His hooded ebony eyes flashed at Richard, but he spoke softly. "Welcome to Algiers, Captain Cutler. Do I understand correctly that you come as an emissary of your government?"

"You do, Your Excellency."

The dey's thin smile revealed his pleasure with that salutation. "And you have come to Algiers to negotiate the release of American prisoners of war?"

Jeremy was right, Richard mused. This man is slippery as an eel and speaks near perfect English. And he speaks in lies. Aloud he said: "I have come to Algiers to secure the release of twenty American seamen and their captain, yes. But I have not come to negotiate their release. That has already been done, Your Excellency. You yourself set the price of ransom two years ago, and you announced that price publicly."

"So you say. What is your understanding of the price?"

Richard withdrew a piece of paper from his coat pocket and read a figure he could have recited in his sleep. "Fifty-nine thousand four hundred and ninety-six American dollars." He looked up. "To be delivered to your *khaznaji* in gold and silver ingots and pieces of eight."

"You have brought this amount with you?"

"I have, Your Excellency."

"As described?"

"As described, Your Excellency."

"And is that the entire sum you bring?"

"I have brought a little more, Your Excellency, in the event you are holding other American sailors whom I might ransom at the same price."

"I see." Bin Osman motioned his *khaznaji* and *vekil kharj* to his side. As they huddled together speaking in a tongue he did not understand, Richard glanced askance at Kercy. The Frenchman stared rigidly ahead.

When the whispered conference broke up, the dey's voice hewed a sharper edge. "Mr. Cutler, you are a representative of your government? Yes or no."

Richard did not immediately respond because he did not understand why the question had been repeated. "I carry American papers, yes, Your Excellency," he hedged. "But I do not have an official rank. I am here in Algiers as a private citizen. I intend to pay the ransom you have specified from my family's accounts."

"Am I to understand, then, that you have the same lack of authority as did Mr. Lamb, your government's previous emissary?"

Richard was uncertain where this line of questioning was leading. A sudden surge of dread overwashed the anxiety that had already bound his stomach into a knot. "I have come to Algiers," he repeated, "to pay the ransoms required to free American seamen you have detained here."

This time bin Osman summoned Kercy to his side. Richard watched the consul walk formally toward the throne. He bowed low before the dey, his hands at his sides, and remained in that position as he and bin

Osman conversed quietly in French. Richard strained to hear. He could not hear much, but what he could make out suggested that the dey was not entirely pleased with what he had heard so far, and that at least one source of his displeasure was the French consul. Their discussion concluded, Kercy walked slowly backward to his place beside Richard without ever removing his eyes from bin Osman.

The dey stoked his beard, looked at Richard. "Captain Cutler," he said, "I must insist that you stop speaking to me in riddles. You either are or you are not a formal emissary of your government. I was informed that you are, which is why I agreed to receive you today, to discuss the terms of release of American prisoners of war. However, as surely you are well aware, we can accomplish nothing before we negotiate a treaty of peace between our two nations. No release of prisoners can take place before such a treaty is signed and an appropriate tribute paid. The question I again put before you is therefore very simple: Are you or are you not prepared to negotiate such a treaty?"

No one had advised Richard of the need for such a treaty. Nor had he spoken in riddles. He had spoken the truth, a truth of which bin Osman had been made formally aware months ago. He felt himself being drawn into a trap. If he replied to the dey in the affirmative, the money he had brought with him might have to be used, in its entirety, for a purpose he was unprepared, unqualified, and unauthorized to perform. Even if peace treaty negotiations did prove successful, it seemed all but certain that Caleb and his shipmates would not be released until additional funds were paid. If he answered in the negative, however, the dey might consider his presence in Algiers of no value to him, and all would be lost.

He fought to keep his nerves under control. He needed time to think, to weigh the ramifications more carefully. But time was a luxury he did not have. Not so much as a minute. He looked straight at the dey. "Be assured, Your Excellency," he said in a level voice, "that I do serve as an emissary of my government. Should you desire confirmation of my status, my aide-de-camp carries my papers with him."

"That will not be necessary, Captain Cutler."

"Then, may I ask Your Excellency to state your terms?"

Bin Osman deferred that question to the *vekil kharj*, who read from an official-looking document handed him by the Jew: "As to terms of peace between Algiers and the United States of America," the minister formally announced, "His Majesty Mohammed bin Osman requires a sum of four million Algerian *muzunas*—in value, one hundred thousand American dollars—that will—"

"I don't have that amount," Richard blurted out, his face darkening. Kercy shot him a warning glance. Protocol forbade interruptions.

The foreign minister pursed his lips, continued in a ceremonial tone: ". . . that will guarantee peace between our nations for a period of five years. During that time your ships are free to trade anywhere in the Mediterranean Sea and the Atlantic Ocean without interference from Algiers. There remains the matter of annual tributes. His Majesty in his infinite mercy agrees to settle that matter at a later date. His Majesty declares that with this treaty in place, American prisoners of war in Algiers may be released upon payment of the ransom specified. It is Allah's wish, praise His holy name."

As the Muslims in the chamber repeated those last four words, Richard set his gaze on Kercy. He willed the French consul to look at him, talk to him, counsel him. When Kercy remained stoic, eyes forward, Richard swung his gaze back to bin Osman.

"Your Excellency," he said evenly, forcing himself to bow low in consular fashion, "there is an apparent misunderstanding that I am confident we, as men of goodwill, can resolve. As I have stated to this court, I am an emissary authorized by the government of the United States to pay the ransom to free its citizens. I am not authorized, however, to negotiate a peace treaty with Algiers. I did not bring the requisite tribute. I have only enough funds with me to ransom the Americans you are holding."

Bin Osman gave another of his thin smiles. "Ah, but you can secure whatever funds you need, can you not, Mr. Cutler? You travel from here to Paris, no? To meet with Captain John Paul Jones? We are informed he is coming soon to Barbary to negotiate treaties with the four states. That being so, may we assume that he has—or will have—the requisite tribute? To ensure that such treaties are signed? Surely a nation as rich as yours should find this a trifling matter."

That last remark would have made Richard laugh were any of this a laughing matter. But it was something else the dey had just said that shocked Richard to his core. *Who had informed bin Osman of his pending audience with Captain Jones?* That mission was a state secret, or so he had presumed. Richard had told no one about it outside of his family. Nor had Alexander Hamilton informed anyone, so Richard had been assured, other than the French foreign minister, who had to be informed when Hamilton requested access to the French medical facilities in Toulon. Vergennes was a longtime friend of the United States, the one reliable ally America had in the French court in addition to the marquis de Lafayette. Who might Vergennes, in turn, have informed of this mission?

Richard's eyes again flew to Kercy and then back to the dey. "Your Excellency," he said, straining to reverse the setback, "you speak the truth. I am to see Captain Jones in Paris. He, not I, is the emissary authorized to negotiate treaties of peace on behalf of the United States. I would be honored to convey to him the terms for peace you have proposed between our two nations. As for today, may I request that Your Eminence demonstrate your generosity and goodwill by releasing into my custody the Americans you hold here, at the price you have specified. I assure you that Captain Jones will consider these factors most favorably when he negotiates the terms of peace. By granting this request, you will be serving both your cause and the glory of Allah."

Again the thin smile. "You speak like a diplomat, Mr. Cutler," the dey said, in a tone that did not necessarily convey a compliment. "I believe your government makes a grievous error in sending Captain Jones to me instead of you. Yesterday, I might have considered your request. Today, alas, I cannot. One of your highest-placed diplomats has recently informed this court that America no longer wishes to negotiate the release of any of its citizens at any price, or to pay tributes of any kind. So if I release the prisoners I hold, I have lost . . . how do you Americans say . . . my bargaining chips. Nor would that be the end of the matter. Other nations might follow suit. There would be no further payments. You are a man of business, are you not, Mr. Cutler? Surely you can appreciate why my agreement to your request would be very bad business. My superiors would not be pleased. Allah would not be pleased."

Richard was stunned by the dey's words. "Who is the American diplomat you refer to?" he dared ask.

"Your consul in Paris," bin Osman informed him, "Mr. Thomas Jefferson. You know of him, I must presume, since I am advised that you will be visiting him when you are in France."

Advised by whom? Everything was happening too quickly. Yes, Richard did know of Thomas Jefferson, and yes, he had been ordered to report to him when in Paris. Jefferson was widely rumored to be George Washington's choice for secretary of state once the new republic was established and Washington had been elected president. Richard was aware that Jefferson opposed paying tribute to any country sponsoring piracy or terror—for the very reasons advanced by Stephen Starbuck during the family conference in Hingham—but would Jefferson so deliberately and publicly knife Richard in the back while at the same time sabotaging the mission of Captain Jones to North Africa? It was unthinkable. It made no earthly sense. But would the dey make such a claim were it a total fabrication?

"I find that hard to accept," was all Richard could say, and he said it without much conviction.

The dey nodded at Kercy.

"It is true, monsieur," the consul confirmed. His voice was low, melancholy, as though Jefferson's statements on tribute had sucked the wind out of his sails as well. "I will show you his letter. It came to His Majesty the dey from my ministry in Paris a week ago."

Richard felt despair overriding his anger and frustration. He forced himself to concentrate on the few cards he held—cards that, despite all, might yet provide a wedge inside the prison door.

"Captain Cutler?" the dey prompted him.

"Excellency?" The word came out softly, with no strength to it. Richard was beginning to accept the unacceptable: that his mission to Algiers had failed as assuredly and miserably as that of his predecessor.

Bin Osman sat back in his throne, a motion that lifted his feet off the stool and made him look, for an instant, like a bearded gnome sitting in a highchair. Yet not a flicker of amusement danced in Richard's eyes as he returned the dey's dark stare.

"Captain Cutler," bin Osman said in the conciliatory tones a father might use when offering parental advice to a child after first chastising him, "I can see you are an honorable man. I admire that. We hold your brother and you are doing what you can to have him released. I admire that as well. I too have a brother. If our roles were reversed, I would do as you are doing.

"I am therefore prepared, out of respect for you and to show the mercy and love of Allah, to make a certain . . . how shall we say . . . accommodation. We understand, you and I, why I am unable to release all of the American prisoners at this time. However, for the value of two hundred thousand *muzunas*—five thousand of your American dollars—I will release your brother to you. He is a fine young man. I see pride and accomplishment in him. Perhaps you are aware that I once offered him a position as a servant in my residence. I meant it as a high honor, though he was delighted to refuse." Bin Osman chuckled at his turn of phrase. "So you see, Captain Cutler, for his sake and for yours, I am willing to bend the rules, as you Americans like to say. You may take your brother to Paris with you, if you wish."

Five thousand dollars, Richard realized, was twice the amount a sea captain fetched in the ransom market, and three to four times the price for a common sailor. This was extortion on a grand scale. However tempting the lure thrown out to him, Richard forced himself to ignore the bait. He at once understood what message his acceptance of the dey's offer would convey to the rest of the world about Americans' values and the sanctity of the freedom for which they had shed so much blood. The fledgling United States would be seen as something Richard fervently believed it was not: another platform for duplicity and treachery on the world stage, its citizens as subject as the citizens of other nations to the deceit and betrayal of those in positions of power and influence. Of more immediate concern, what message would his ransoming Caleb send to the rest of *Eagle*'s crew, all of whom were relying on Cutler & Sons for their well-being and the well-being of their families back home? Richard could well imagine their reaction to watching Caleb sail off to freedom while they remained abandoned to their fate in Algiers.

Richard could hardly keep his fury in check. "Your Excellency," he managed in a tight voice, "may I propose another solution?"

Bin Osman arched his thick eyebrows. "By all means do so," he replied.

"I propose," Richard said, "that for the same sum of two hundred thousand *muzamas* I be granted two requests. First, that I be allowed to meet privately for one hour with my brother and Captain Dickerson at a location of your choosing. And, second, that my surgeon be allowed to examine every American prisoner held in Algiers."

Bin Osman's jaw fell. "That is *all*, Mr. Cutler? You are willing to pay so much for so little?"

"It is no small matter to me, Your Excellency, to see my brother and his shipmates alive and well."

Bin Osman glanced questioningly to his left, at his *khaznaji* and *vekil kharj,* and then to his right, at the sea captain who stood with arms folded across his chest, the bulge of arm muscles visible under his thin shirt. He, too, returned the dey's glance without comment.

"Done," the dey announced. "Your requests are granted, Captain Cutler. At 4:00 this afternoon I will send guards to the jetty to escort you and your surgeon to the prison."

"Thank you, Your Excellency," Richard said with glacial formality. He bowed once, quickly, then turned sharply on his heel and began walking out of the royal chamber, motioning to Chatfield to follow him. The two guards at the door made no move to stop him. Kercy, aghast at the breach of diplomatic protocol, hastily took his leave with a series of bows and backward steps. Once out of the royal chamber, he hurried after Richard.

"*Capitaine*! *Capitaine* Cutler!" he panted as he caught up with him. "You have insulted His Majesty by leaving so. You must go back and apologize. *Maintenant! S'il vous plaît, monsieur!* You must!"

"Fuck His Majesty," Richard threw over his shoulder. He rounded on the consul, his lips curled in contempt. "*Je crois que tu comprends très bien ce mot 'fuck,' Monsieur de Kercy, non?*"

The consul stood speechless as Richard and Chatfield made their way down the narrow, dirty streets of Algiers toward the Gate of Jihad and the harbor where *Falcon* rode peacefully at anchor.

Nine

Algiers, September 1788

THE AGE-OLD TRADITIONS OF Christmas had always been faithfully observed by the Cutler family. Early on Christmas Eve, friends and neighbors gathered at the Cutler home on Main Street to sing the songs of the season and to enjoy mulled cider or a drink of hot rum, water, and sugar. Later, after supper, the family dragged the Yule log through the front door and into the sitting room hearth, sprinkling it with spiced cider just as their Saxon ancestors had done and later setting aside a burnt fragment to tie to next year's log, thus carrying the tradition forward in perpetuity. Later still, with his brood huddled before the fire and his wife seated beside him, Thomas Cutler read by candlelight the familiar passage about the decree from Caesar Augustus as Caleb and Lavinia, the youngest of the five children, stifled yawns, determined to carry the magic of this evening as far into the night as their parents would allow.

The next day, Christmas, was the only morning of the year that the children eagerly attended the First Parish service, for they had placed bets among themselves on how long Parson Gay's sermon would last. Halfway through the diatribe, inevitably, Will would set his younger siblings to quiet giggling when he covertly stretched out his mouth with his middle fingers to mimic the austere facial features of the good reverend. And they knew that a present or two awaited them after the service, as well as a Christmas feast of roasted venison, sweet potatoes, fried onions, candied apple rings, and pies so choice with buttery crusts that even the adults rubbed their stomachs and groaned contentedly when the meal reached its reluctant conclusion.

There was nothing merry, however, about the Christmas of 1775. Will was with his family in spirit only, as he forever would be, and the revolution that had claimed his young life was spreading like a wildfire throughout the colonies. Elizabeth Cutler did what she could to inject a sense of purpose into the family's traditions. Richard, approaching sixteen and now the oldest child, understood the role he must play for the sake of his siblings, especially sweet Anne, whose grief over Will's death seemed inconsolable. But it was a role he could not play. He missed Will terribly. There was no reconciling his sorrow and rage. Caleb tried to cheer him; time and again during those days leading up to Christmas he begged Richard to play checkers with him or go outside in the bracing air for a game of sticks and hoops. Richard always put him off, promising to play some other time.

So it was that Christmas morning in 1775 that Caleb approached Richard as he sat alone at the kitchen table where the family would soon gather for supper. He held a package in his hand, wrapped simply in paper, and this he gave to his older brother. Richard separated the folds. Inside was a wooden model of a ship. He balanced it in his hand, immediately aware of the significance of the gift. Will had been a master whittler, and for each of the past three years he had given Richard a model ship as a Christmas present. Richard kept the collection upstairs on his dresser as a shrine to his brother's memory, the intricate detail of the masts and yards, and the standing rigging fashioned from their mother's sewing thread testifying to the loving care Will had invested in each model, a gift to a brother whom he, in turn, loved.

What Richard now held before him, however, was no masterpiece. It was the crudest of ship models, essentially a block of wood with its center cut out to form a quarterdeck in the stern and a forecastle in the bow. Two twigs were stuck in holes knocked in the wood with a nail: one a bowsprit, the other a single mast rising from the center of the hacked-out section.

Richard looked at his brother, at eye level with him because Richard was seated. "Thank you, Caleb," he said. "I like it. But . . . why?"

Caleb's lips began to quiver. Tears sprouted from the corners of his eyes and coursed down his smooth cheeks. He choked on his reply; when finally he was able to speak, his words came out as a high mournful wail that was at once both accusation and supplication.

"I'm your brother too, Richard. I'm your brother too!"

A GENTLE RAP on the cabin door broke the reverie. "Yes? Enter."

Micah Lamont stuck his head inside. "Seven bells," he announced, adding, when Richard appeared nonplussed, "You asked me to come to you at seven bells, Captain."

"Yes, of course. Thank you, Mr. Lamont." Richard glanced down at his watch to confirm the time of 3:30, a motion that allowed him pause to collect himself. "We will weigh anchor as soon as Dr. Brooke and I are back aboard. Please prepare *Falcon* for departure."

"Aye, Captain."

Richard's mood had eased somewhat since his return from the dey's palace. Once aboard, he had gone below to his cabin and shut the door, remaining there, alone, for nearly two hours. When he emerged, he summoned his two officers and the ship's surgeon to his cabin, reviewed with them what had transpired at the royal court, and advised them that they would be departing for France that very evening. They would not, however, be sailing to Toulon. The medical facilities there were no longer needed. They would sail instead to Lorient, a French seaport on the Bay of Biscay. Lorient was considerably closer to Paris, he explained, and it was a seaport with which both Richard and Agreen were well acquainted. From there they would travel to Paris to meet with Captain Jones.

"We will be gone less than a week," Richard concluded, glancing at his mate, who would be in command of the vessel during their absence.

"Understood, Captain," Lamont replied.

"Are you ready, Dr. Brooke?"

"Ready, Mr. Cutler," the frail, gray-whiskered surgeon replied. He patted his brown leather medical bag for emphasis.

"Good. Agee?"

"Five thousand dollars in gold coin accounted for," Agreen assured him, "and secured in the gig."

"Thank you. Gentlemen, it's time."

On deck, Richard motioned to the surgeon to step down into the gig. Ashore, by the jetty, ten Muslim soldiers, dark as mahogany and heavily armed, waited by a mule-drawn wagon.

"Good luck, brother," Agreen said. He squeezed Richard's shoulder.

Ashore, the mayhem so palpable in the morning was by now far less in evidence. Perhaps that was the natural way of Algiers, Richard mused as he sat in the gig's sternsheets and observed the relative tranquility outside the walls. Earlier in the day, before his audience in the royal palace, this area had been crammed with herdsmen and traders and government officials and exotic beasts. At this hour, only a few individuals were walking about, each dressed in the flowing white robe and turban of an ordinary Arab citizen, none of them paying much attention to the gig or its passengers. Perhaps, he speculated, the relative quiet and lack of visible humanity were due to the soldiers standing at attention by the jetty. The soldiers were clearly on His Majesty's business, and judging from their iron demeanor, God help any man stupid or unlucky enough to get in their way.

When the two Americans stepped ashore into the blazing late-summer heat, they were searched for weapons and then escorted through the intricately decorated Gate of Jihad. Once inside the city walls, the party split in two. Four soldiers headed straight up toward the Qasbah with the treasure wagon. The six remaining soldiers guided the two Americans along a dirt pathway set between the city's east-facing wall and a long row of what Richard assumed were administrative buildings, set so close together that there was hardly enough space to walk between any two of them. The sights and smells and sounds that had assaulted Richard's senses earlier in the day were here less noticeable, as if this area had been declared off-limits to ordinary citizens and the ruckus and stink that they and their animals generated.

When they arrived at the last building, a dreary one-story, white-washed affair featuring narrow, glassless slits for windows, the officer in charge of the detail ordered a halt and signaled to the Americans to stay put. Richard watched the officer enter the building and then examined, to the extent possible, the area directly behind it. He could see the first prison barrack clearly enough—it rose two stories higher than the administrative building set in front of it—but he noticed no movement either inside or outside its walls.

The turbaned officer reemerged and summoned the Americans inside. The building's interior was refreshingly cool, though it took awhile for Richard's eyes to adjust to the relative darkness. Two Muslim soldiers took up positions by a wooden doorway to his right, one on each side, as the officer indicated to Lawrence Brooke that he should follow three other guards through another door on the other side of the building leading outside to the prison compound. He spoke emphatically in Arabic to the two remaining guards before holding up one finger to Richard: one hour, the time he had purchased. He then followed Brooke and his escort outside.

Richard stepped between the guards, opened the door. Caleb was up in an instant and walking toward him with a noticeable limp. A second man rose to his feet but remained standing beside a thick wooden table where he and Caleb had been seated.

Caleb was thinner than Richard had ever seen him, his skeletal frame only partially concealed by the large shirt with open sleeves that he wore along with baggy cotton trousers and sandals. He was bearded, unkemptly so, and his eyes and cheeks were hollowed. But his embrace was firm and unflinching, and his deep-set blue eyes glistened as he embraced his brother. "Richard! By God, I feared I would never see this day!"

Richard was so overcome that words utterly failed him. He held Caleb at arm's length and stared at him, then clasped him to his chest. So frail was Caleb that Richard could feel his ribs through his shirt. Still he could not bear to release him. It took several minutes, several precious minutes, for the severity of the moment to ease its bite.

"You look well, Caleb," Richard managed at last. "Better than I expected."

Caleb forced a smile. "I manage. We all manage. We have Captain Dickerson to thank for that." He indicated the man standing by the table. "He's done so much for us," Caleb explained. "Each day we're fed a pound of bread and some bits of camel meat. That's standard prison fare. But Captain Dickerson is able to procure some decent food for us every now and then, and he makes certain our clothes are boiled once a week. The Arabs respect him. He's the reason we're still alive—or at least not sold off to some worse form of slavery."

Richard released his brother, walked over to the table. "Thank you, Mr. Dickerson," he said, gripping the man's hand. "Thank you for your care of my brother and the crew." He was grateful Dickerson was in the room. Had he not been, Richard knew, it would have been impossible to keep his frayed emotions in check.

"My duty, Mr. Cutler," Dickerson said in reply.

There was a brief, awkward silence, broken finally by Caleb. "How are Mother and Father, Richard? And Anne and Lavinia?"

Richard turned around. "Everyone is well, Caleb. They send their love to you, of course."

"And Katherine?"

"Beset daily by Will and Jamie's mischief. And Caleb? You have a niece. Her name is Diana. She was born just before I sailed from Boston."

"A niece. Diana Cutler." Caleb shook his head in wonder. "A beautiful name for a beautiful lass."

"She is that." A wave of powerful emotion surged between them when Richard added, his voice cracking, "Had we had a son, we would have named him Caleb."

Caleb smiled. He quelled the wave of emotion with, "Well, that means that you and Katherine will just have to keep on trying until you have another son."

Richard held up his hands defensively, relieved for the distraction. "No promises, Caleb. It was not an easy birth."

Fifteen minutes had elapsed. Forty-five minutes remained. Richard's eyes flicked from Caleb to Dickerson and back again. "When were you informed that I was coming here?"

Caleb deferred the answer to his captain.

"I learned about it from the guards," Dickerson said. "I've managed to pick up a little Arabic, since as an officer I'm excused from heavy labor. I am even allowed some freedom to walk about the city, on my parole. See here." He drew up his trouser leg to reveal a thick iron ankle bracelet, a badge of special status. "Two days ago, we were informed by the French consul—ah, I see you have met Monsieur de Kercy—that you had an audience this morning with the dey."

"And have you been told . . . about what happened during that audience?"

"The result," Caleb confirmed. "Not the details."

Richard quickly summarized the proceedings, purposely omitting the possible role of Thomas Jefferson. He still could not fully accept the dey's claims about the American consul, and he would not relay deeply troubling information that might cause the prisoners to lose hope. He did dwell, in detail, on the final offer the dey had made to him. "I pray you understand, Caleb," he concluded, "why I had to refuse it."

Caleb's blue eyes met Richard's with an expression of deep concern, not for himself. "Of course I understand," he said. "We have a country to build, don't we, and a revolution to justify. Besides, Richard, even if you had accepted the dey's offer, I would not have left Algiers with you. Under no conditions would I leave here without my shipmates."

Richard's desire to walk over and embrace Caleb again proved almost irresistible. But he felt the seconds ticking by, and in any event, that would only have embarrassed his brother. "Are other Americans being held here? In addition to *Eagle*'s crew?"

"Yes," Dickerson replied. "Five from *Dauphin* and three from a brigantine out of Charleston. At one time there were fifty-one captives here besides ourselves. But most of them have been sold off elsewhere. One of them converted to Islam," he added bitterly. "And Mr. Cutler, I have the sad duty to report that three of *Eagle*'s crew have departed this life."

"Who?" Richard heard himself ask.

"Nathan Reeves, Ashley Bowen, and Joshua Winter."

"How?"

"Reeves and Winter from the plague, three months ago. Bowen was executed, not two fortnights after we got here. He went off his head and tried to escape. Trouble is, as you've seen for yourself, there's nowhere to escape to. We warned him about that, to no avail. They brought him back from the desert half-starved and raving mad, cursing Allah and the dey and every Arab that's ever lived. They tortured him for his heresy. He was still alive when they spiked him on a hook on the outside wall. It took him two days to die. It was a warning to the rest of us. We could see his body every day while we worked on the breakwater. They left him hanging there until nothing was left but bones picked clean by the birds."

Richard was too appalled to speak right away. Three good men lost, Christian men, fine, able-bodied seamen. Reeves and Winter hailed from Weymouth; both were married with young children. Bowen, hardly in his twenties, hailed from Cohasset. He had wed a comely Hingham girl just a month before *Eagle*'s final voyage. Richard had stood up for him at their wedding.

"I'll write to their families," he said, as if to himself alone. "And I'll ask Katherine to look in on Mary. She's so young. She'll take this very hard."

"Aye, that she will," Dickerson agreed.

"And I'll write Father," Richard pledged in that same faraway tone that nonetheless contained a timbre of iron resolve. "Cutler and Sons will not forget these men or their families. We take care of our own. Please tell them that, Mr. Dickerson. Make sure they understand."

Richard's fury over the injustice and savagery of these deaths was bubbling up like hot lava from its core and in danger of spilling over. He paced back and forth until he was able to calm his nerves somewhat. More minutes ticked by.

"There is something else I must ask," he said, his hardened gaze taking in both men. "You say that other ships' crews were brought here, but then were sold off elsewhere. Why has *Eagle*'s crew been kept intact here in Algiers? Why haven't you *all* been sold as slaves?"

Caleb nodded. "It's a question we've asked ourselves, Richard, more than once. I've already given you one reason: Captain Dickerson. But we're convinced there are other reasons. As near as we can tell, it was back in February that bin Osman was informed of your sailing here with ransom money. That was when they stopped transferring prisoners from Algiers."

Richard did the calculations. Four months was the correct time frame. In early February Alexander Hamilton had informed the Cutler family that Congress had officially notified the court of Dey Mohammed bin Osman of *Falcon*'s pending visit. But the proceedings that morning seemed to indicate that bin Osman was expecting the Americans to be bringing almost twice the amount of money they had actually brought with them. Who had given the dey that impression? And why?

He put those questions to Caleb. Dickerson replied. "Kercy, is my bet," he said, an assertion that did not surprise Richard. What *Eagle*'s captain said next did surprise him: "Though it could just as well have been the British consul. I don't trust Logie any more than I trust Kercy, I don't care how many gifts of food and coin he gives us. It's blood money, to my mind."

"What are you saying, Mr. Dickerson?' Richard asked. "That the British are also involved in this . . . ?" He wasn't quite sure what he meant by "this."

"I'm sorry to say they are, Mr. Cutler," Dickerson said. He gave Richard a look of pure disgust. "So are the Spanish. So are the Dutch and Swedes and Danes. So are the Portuguese. But our primary suspects are the British and French, for a good reason."

"Which is?"

Dickerson shrugged. "As the two strongest maritime powers in Europe, they have the most to lose."

"From what? American competition?"

"Precisely. The way I see it, Mr. Cutler, all Europe is conspiring against us. To protect their trade routes, you understand. America is a threat to them. Not a military threat; God knows, the Kingdom of Naples could overrun us in a month. No, the threat they see is the size and range of our commerce. And our claim to free trade. That claim has their merchants up in arms. The truth is, Mr. Cutler, America stands alone. Europeans mean to cripple us economically, and they are getting all the help they need from the four Barbary States. This much I've learned from my privileges here: the treachery of these people knows no bounds. Europeans are using Arabs and Arabs are using Europeans in a combined effort to prey on our country. We're the world's whipping-boy, and without a navy to protect our trade, there's not much we can do about it."

"That's a serious accusation, Mr. Dickerson," Richard said. "If I understand you correctly, you are accusing the Barbary rulers of acting in concert with the British and French against America's commercial interests."

"You understand me correctly, Mr. Cutler. Mind you, there are no formal alliances involved. That would be too obvious. But the alliances are real enough, mark my words. Of course, I can't prove any of this. It's just what my bones are telling me."

Over the years the Cutlers had learned to rely on what Dickerson's bones told him. There was good reason why Thomas Cutler had given him command of *Eagle*.

"Is there any evidence you can offer? Anything I can pass on?"

"No, I'm afraid not. And what good would it do if I could? America is powerless to do anything to stop these abominations. In any event, my evidence is what I see with my eyes and hear with my ears. I have heard that Queen Maria of Portugal has persuaded Whitehall to deny Royal Navy escorts to American merchant vessels in the Mediterranean. And I know for certain that Kercy and Logie have urged bin Osman to seize American ships. I have heard this said in what little Arabic I understand and in what questions I've had answered.

"There's more," he continued. "We believe the two consuls have supplied the dey with specific information on the whereabouts of American ships in the Mediterranean—information gained from their own country's warships out on patrol. I am convinced that is how *Eagle* came to be seized."

Richard's thoughts, as Dickerson spoke, went to Jeremy Hardcastle. He could not believe that Katherine's brother had anything to do with such duplicity and treachery. Whitehall, yes; Parliament, maybe; but not Jeremy. That was unthinkable.

"And," Dickerson went on, "the consuls have advised bin Osman that America is a fruit ripe for the picking—a rich country easily able to afford whatever tributes the dey might decree. Bin Osman knows

nothing about America, Mr. Cutler. He relies on his ministers and foreign consuls to supply him with information, and he tends to accept
whatever he's told. Of course, it doesn't hurt that what he's told is what
he wants to hear."

The door to the spartan chamber opened. A Muslim guard entered.
He pounded the haft of his spear on the floor and held up five fingers,
then another five. Ten minutes. After the door banged shut, Caleb gave
his brother a somber look.

"Richard, there's something else—something that may be worse
than anything we've discussed so far. I pray to God I'm wrong, but I
think it possible that bin Osman set terms today that he knew you could
not accept."

"Why would he do that, Caleb?" Richard asked warily, as though
he was about to be offered the final piece of a puzzle and feared what
fitting it in would show. "What would he gain?"

Dickerson said, when Caleb hesitated, "The ransom money you
have in your hold, Mr. Cutler. He can take it without having to release
a single prisoner."

A shadow passed over Richard's face. The same thought had
occurred to him that afternoon in his cabin. "I have diplomatic immunity," he said, sounding unconvincing even to himself.

"In theory you do. But only in theory. And only as long as you remain
in Algiers. I hardly dare say it, Mr. Cutler, but at this very moment you
and your crew may be in greater danger than any of us here in this
prison."

Richard nodded slowly. He could not argue.

"You're sailing tonight, Richard?" Caleb asked.

"Yes," Richard replied.

"For home?"

"For France. I'm to report to Captain Jones in Paris. He has been
appointed to lead a delegation to Barbary to negotiate the release of
American prisoners and to establish terms of peace with the Barbary
States."

"Are you a part of that delegation?

"Not to my knowledge."

"What will you tell Captain Jones when you see him?"

"I will tell him everything I've learned about Algiers during the past
two days, including what you just told me. There must be something in
all this that will help him in negotiations."

"When is his delegation due to arrive in Algiers?"

"I don't know," Richard had to admit. "It hasn't been decided. Our new Constitution is being approved by the individual states. Massachusetts ratified it in February. Maryland ratified it in April. That leaves only two more states to make it official. Next February we will elect a president, and you know as well as I that it will be General Washington. He has publicly stated that if he is elected, the release of American sailors held in North Africa will be a top priority of his administration."

"In another year or two, then," Caleb said, unable to prevent frustration and misery from creeping into his voice.

"As soon as humanly possible," Richard vowed.

Dickerson intervened. "We understand, Mr. Cutler. We realize that you are doing all you can. Your coming here has given us hope, no matter how the negotiations may have turned out. We'll make it. You have my word on it, sir. We'll make it."

Caleb had a more personal perspective. "Richard," he said, "be careful. Not just in France. Be careful leaving Algiers."

That Caleb, a prisoner in this sweltering, stinking, godforsaken hole of a city for nearly two years, could worry about *him* at a time like this would have entirely broken Richard were it not for Captain Dickerson walking over to offer his hand.

"Godspeed, Mr. Cutler," he said.

Richard gripped the firm, leathery hand. "Godspeed to you as well, Mr. Dickerson," he said, his voice a study in anguish, "and to the men. Tell them not to lose faith. Tell them their families are being well taken care of. Tell them their country is doing everything possible to get them released."

"I'll tell them," Dickerson promised.

As Richard turned to his brother one last time, the door reopened and this time both Muslim guards trooped in. Somehow, from somewhere, Richard had to find the heart to say good-bye and the spine to walk away.

Caleb made it easier for him. He formed a fist with his right hand and brought it up over his left breast, the way he had done in younger days when mimicking the Roman general Fabius Maximus. "Strength and honor, Richard," he said, not melodramatically as he had done when play-acting as a child, but with a wry smile at the corners of his mouth and a twinkle in his eyes.

Richard brought a fist over his own heart. "Strength and honor, Caleb," he said in reply, relieved beyond measure that Caleb had grown into a man capable of smiling at his situation no matter how deep the abyss of despair.

Richard turned and departed the chamber, to await Dr. Brooke outside and then to make all haste to leave Algiers.

Ten

At Sea, 100 Miles North of Algiers, September 1788

THE DWINDLING LIGHT OF dusk revealed nothing untoward maneuvering upon the waters of the Maghrib, at least nothing that two lookouts perched high above in the crosstrees could detect. Richard decided to call them back down to the deck for the night. The moon in its first phase was but an arched yellow sliver—how fitting, he thought, that on this of all nights the moon should mirror the crescent on the Algerian flag—and the light it cast was too feeble for Peter Chatfield and Matt Cates to put to much use.

"Tremaine, take the tiller," he said, indicating to Micah Lamont that he would be relieved from duty once Richard had confirmed the schooner's course, speed, and standing orders. "To review, I want four men on watch throughout the night," he told Lamont. Mr. Crabtree has the first watch. I'll take the second. You have the third watch, with Tremaine at the helm. Before sunrise I want all hands on deck and Chatfield and Cates back up in the crosstrees."

"Understood, Captain," Lamont said. He yielded the tiller to Nate Tremaine. "I have already informed the crew."

"Good. Now please pass word for Tom Gardner to come aft."

"Aye, Captain. Will there be anything else, sir?"

"Nothing else, Mr. Lamont. Go below and get some rest. I'll send word if I need you."

A moment later the ruddy-jowled, powerfully limbed seaman who served as senior gun captain lumbered toward the after deck. "You sent for me, Captain?"

"Yes, Gardner. Are the guns primed and loaded?"

It was a rhetorical question. While *Falcon* was still within the Bay of Algiers, Richard had ordered the six guns released from their breeching ropes and loaded—with grapeshot in two, chain-shot in the third, both sides. At the same time he had ordered extra shot and flannel bags of powder brought up from the hold and stored in specially designed racks built in along the mid-deck section between the guns. There too, wrapped loosely in spare canvas like some dreadful sea creature dragged up from the depths, lay the three four-foot-long projectiles that Richard Dale had secured for the ship's arsenal before it left Boston.

"Loaded and run out as ordered, sir."

"Good. Now, as I have informed Mr. Lamont, tonight we shall post three two-hour watches. Pratt has the first watch, Blakely the second. I want you on deck for the third. Before dawn, at the start of the fourth watch, I want every member of the crew on deck. At that time, if need be, I shall take personal command of the guns. Understood?"

"Understood, Captain." Gardner snapped a salute, a hard-to-break old habit that reflected his service as senior gunnery officer aboard the 32-gun Continental Navy frigate *Raleigh*. "You may depend on me."

Richard returned the salute. "I always have, Gardner."

With Gardner gone, Richard strode a few steps aft to larboard, toward Agreen, who was leaning against the taffrail peering southward across the dark sea. Increase Hobart and Isaac Howland had taken lookout positions, one on each side of the schooner abaft the mainmast; two other seamen stood watch afore the forward chain-wales.

Richard and Agreen stood side by side in silence, alert for any unusual sound out there in the gloom: words shouted in Arabic or, above them in the rigging, a sudden flutter of sail that could indicate either a shift in wind or—less likely, considering who had the helm—the schooner veering too far into the wind. *Falcon* was sailing due north on a beam reach, a moderate easterly breeze square on her starboard beam. Richard had specified in the night's sailing instructions that she would remain on this tack for another six hours. They would then come off the wind on a course that would take them through the Strait of Gibraltar, along the southern coast of the Iberian Peninsula, and northward past Lisbon toward the Bay of Biscay and the French port of Lorient.

"I have the deck, Richard," Agreen said at length. "I suggest you follow the advice you gave Lamont and go below."

"I'm enjoying the night air, Agee. If it's all the same to you, I'll remain topside for a while."

"Always glad for your company." Agreen stretched out his arms to loosen tense muscles. "Think I'll take a gander 'round the deck, maybe check the guns while I'm at it. I'll be back quicker than a rooster chasin' a hen in heat," he added cheerfully.

As Agreen walked slowly forward, pausing to have a word with Increase Hobart, Richard glanced southward for the hundredth time since sunset. He could see little beyond the few feet of white wake bubbling out from the rudder, but that didn't matter. He had a premonition that they were not sailing alone this night, a premonition that nagged at him in whispers of warning from Caleb and Captain Dickerson. *Perhaps they were wrong,* he defied the whispers. Perhaps they had misread the situation. Perhaps Agreen and Lamont shared his premonition simply because they were taking their cue from their captain. Was not the dey aware that Richard was to meet with Captain Jones, a man on a mission that would expedite payments of ransom and tribute to bin Osman and other Barbary rulers? Why would he attempt to thwart that mission? What would be the incentive? Down whatever path such reasoning led, however, it always ended at the same pitiless blockade. It was not only what the dey had to gain by taking *Falcon,* which was a king's ransom. It was also what he had to lose, which was nothing.

His thoughts went inevitably to Caleb, to Dickerson and *Eagle*'s crew, to the treasure undelivered in his hold, to his sons Will and Jamie and his daughter Diana, to so many people: Katherine, her brothers, and especially her father, who finally was beginning to think well of him—every member of his own family and others, lifelong friends and neighbors among them, those families of his employ who had relied on him to prevail in Algiers, to bring their men home. Rage bubbled through his veins; he felt his hands coil into fists. He had always been taught to play by the rules: the rules of law—English law—that his country had adopted. Those rules had been inculcated in him since he was barely old enough to understand the difference between right and wrong, when Will was alive and able to explain such things to him. The righteous will always win out in the end, Parson Gay had thundered from his pulpit in Hingham; good will prevail over evil, his father had assured him; never hate your enemies, his Uncle William had counseled, for hate clouds your mind and your ability to respond effectively. Well, Richard thought, I am here to tell you, Uncle, that I *do* hate my enemies. God is my witness, I hate them for what they have done to my friends, my country, my blood. Jeremy was right: Algiers is nothing more than a den of thieves with no laws or rules other than those ordained by a petty dictator surrounded by sycophants and cutthroats. *But think on it,* his inner regions taunted him, *think on it.* Is Algiers really so different from other states? Had not his brother been executed under English law, specifically the Twenty-second Article of War decreed by Whitehall? How was justice served in that travesty? Where was the "winning out" there? What "good" existed in any of this? The temptation to pound his fist on the taffrail and scream out to the Almighty was proving irresistible. It was tempered only by a sympathetic hand placed on his shoulder and a voice, equally sympathetic, inquiring, "Captain, are you all right?"

The question jolted him. He glanced to his left where Lawrence Brooke was staring at him with an expression fraught with worry.

"I apologize, Doctor," Richard managed. "What did you say?"

"I asked if you are all right, Captain. It doesn't take a physician to see that you are deeply troubled. May I ask, is it your brother?"

Richard pushed back his long hair with both hands, gently massaged a throb in the old wound high on his forehead. "Yes," he allowed. "Caleb and his mates and a host of other people you don't know. It appears their faith in me has been misplaced."

Brooke's response was a look of disbelief. "Captain," he chastised, "that is one of the most unfair statements I have ever heard. What are you thinking? That you failed in Algiers?"

Richard let silence be his answer.

"Then you are wrong," Brooke went on. "Dead wrong. Impossible demands were placed on you in Algiers; still you did everything you could for those men. Your brother realizes that. So do his shipmates. It's what they told me when I examined them in prison. No one blames you for what happened, so why blame yourself? It defies logic, Mr. Cutler. Our visit to Algiers has inspired hope. Not just among *Eagle*'s crew but in every American held captive in North Africa. These men need such hope to survive."

For what must have seemed to Brooke a prolonged span of time, Richard continued to stare out into the night. Finally he lowered his eyes to the deck and said softly, "Thank you for those words, Doctor. They mean a lot." He shook his head to exorcise the demons abiding there and said in a more natural tone, "Did you come on deck to take the air, Doctor? Or is there something I can do for you?"

Brooke shook his head. "There is nothing you need do for me, Captain. I came on deck to tell you that I have finished my report on the prisoners. I gave it to Abel Whiton to put on your desk."

Richard smiled. There was no need, aboard *Falcon,* for Brooke to walk all the way forward to locate the captain's steward, in order for the captain's steward to walk all the way aft to the captain's cabin carrying what Brooke had gone forward to give him. Brooke was indeed a product of naval regulations, Richard mused, regulations that specified that only the captain's steward was permitted inside the captain's cabin without a formal invitation.

"Thank you, Doctor. I shall look forward to reading your report. Briefly, how did you find the men?"

"I found them in remarkably good health, Captain, considering what they've been through. In remarkably good spirits, too. As I said, your coming to Algiers was just the tonic they needed. They could hardly believe you were actually there."

Richard nodded his understanding. He motioned to Agreen, who had made the rounds of the deck and was now standing discreetly by the bulwarks a short way away, a black shadow in the dim glow thrown off by a flickering candle enclosed in a lantern attached to the binnacle. He was confirming the compass heading reported by Tremaine. "Anything to report, Agee?"

Agreen came closer, shook his head. "Nary a lick, Richard. The wind's picked up, so we're makin' a good six knots to northward. It's as quiet out there as a nunnery at midnight, and everything aboard is shipshape. The guns are ready, should we require 'em."

"God willing we won't," Brooke said somberly. "But I'd best go below to prepare for that eventuality. A pleasant night to you both, gentlemen."

"And to you, Doctor," Richard replied. He checked his watch and turned to Agreen. "You'll be needing sleep for tomorrow, Agee. Go below. I have the deck."

Agreen glanced up at the main topsail, the breeze ruffling his reddish-blond hair. "I've a mind t' remain topside," he replied, continuing to stare upward at the topsail and the star-studded sky beyond. "If it's all the same t' you."

"Always glad for your company," Richard said.

LAMONT ROUSED THE FIRST and second watches from their bunks at 4:00 the following morning. Men groggy from lack of sleep clambered up the forward hatchways and took position at preassigned stations either by the guns or by the standing rigging. When the ship's complement was assembled on deck and the first slivers of dawn were giving form to the eastern horizon, Lamont sent Chatfield and Cates scurrying up the ratlines. In a consuming, eerie silence broken only by the creaks and groans of block and tackle, the slap of water against the bow, and the snap of the American ensign coming to life in an awakening breeze, they waited, captain and captain's steward alike, until the horizon became clear enough to distinguish sea from sky, friend from foe.

The cry came from high up on the mainmast crosstree. "Deck, there! Sails ho!"

"Where away?" Richard demanded, though he already had his glass trained to the southeast.

"Broad off the starboard quarter, Captain. Eleven, maybe twelve miles off. I see . . . two sets of sail, sir. Each has a square sail forward, a lateen on the main and mizzen. They're hull up."

Yes, there, the tips of white, Richard said to himself. Looping the strap of the glass over his shoulder, he jumped up onto the bulwark by the mainmast chain-wale and climbed the starboard shrouds to get a better look. He laced his arm in and around the rigging and held the glass steady to his eye. With a sudden burst of clarity there they were, two xebecs, the largest and presumably the fastest vessels in the pirate fleet they had seen anchored off Penon Island. They were making good speed on a close haul: white water flew out from their cutwaters beneath taut bellies of white canvas. Richard did a quick calculation. His schooner was fast, certainly, but fast compared with a standard-built vessel such as a frigate or brig. In a race she'd be hard-pressed to stay ahead of these low-lying, narrow-beamed, sharp-prowed vessels built specifically for speed.

He collapsed the glass, slithered down a backstay to the deck. "Right on schedule," he muttered to Agreen, just as Micah Lamont said, "Shall we change course to westward, Captain, and set the tops'ls?"

"No, Mr. Lamont," Richard responded. "That's what they're expecting us to do. Bring her to the wind on a new course, north by east."

"North by east, sir?" Lamont said in disbelief.

"You heard me, Mr. Lamont! North by east!"

"Aye, Captain. North by east it is, sir."

He had pictured it all in his mind only a few hours ago, exactly as it was happening now: xebecs appearing like apparitions of the night, coming at them from the southeast, giving chase as *Falcon* fled toward . . . where? The charts showed no safe harbor within reach. The chase might take awhile, but its outcome was inevitable. There was nowhere to run, nowhere to hide, no one to turn to save the British squadron at Gibraltar, assuming that *Falcon* could get there before being over-taken, and assuming, if she did, that the Royal Navy was disposed to help them. Both assumptions, he realized, were long shots, especially the first. No, he had concluded, his stomach twisting at the mere thought of it, there was only one salvation for *Falcon* and her crew: fight or sur-render. For him, the choice was clear. He had told Agreen his plan and Agreen had agreed.

He strode forward to the mainmast, the eyes of his crew upon him. "Men," he shouted in as loud and steady a voice as he could manage, "out there"—he pointed to starboard—"are two pirate corsairs. You saw them in Algiers. They are coming for us. They are coming for our treasure. They are coming for our ship. They are coming to take us as slaves. They are coming for our Christian souls. I swear to you on all that is holy that they shall have none of these things!"

To a man, the crew roared out their agreement.

"We may be outmanned and outgunned," Richard cried out the obvi-ous, "but we are not undone. We can outmaneuver them. We can out-shoot them. And we have surprise on our side: they are expecting us to flee, not fight. *And* we have with us a secret weapon courtesy of Black-beard and *Queen Anne's Revenge*. I say we introduce these bastards to Mr. Edward Teach! I say we show them that Americans will no longer take their abominations lying down! I say we avenge *Eagle's* crew and pay them back with some of their own! Are you with me, lads?"

To a man, the crew cheered again.

Richard raised high his tricorne hat. "Then let us clear for action! Arm yourselves with pistol and musket, and take your battle stations. God be with you all!"

Men cheered anew as Richard turned on his heel. "Mr. Crabtree," he called out. "Bring her up full and by and join me below. Mr. Lamont, please relieve Mr. Crabtree at the helm."

As *Falcon* swung a point further into the wind, Richard hurried below to the after cabin. From his sea chest he removed a treasure: a finely wrought, well-honed sword with a gilded lion's head on the haft.

It had been a gift from a young Swiss woman of noble blood whose acquaintance he had made in Paris during the Revolutionary War. He secured the sheath to his belt and walked over to a side table where he flipped open a rectangular mahogany box. He withdrew two Kelvar flintlock pistols issued to him as a lieutenant in the Continental Navy and hooked one of them onto his waistband with a prong attached to the left side. The other pistol he handed to his second in command when, moments later, Agreen stepped into the cabin.

"I doubt we'll need these, Agee," he said, willing his voice calm. "If we're close enough for small arms, we're done for. But at least we can take one or two of them with us."

Agreen checked the frizzen for powder. "I'm with you, Richard," he said grimly. He tucked the muzzle of the pistol behind the waistband of his trousers. "We all are. If we're goin' down, let's go down fightin'. America needs t' make a stand somewhere. We'll make it here and now." He grinned as a thought came to him. "I'd give a lot t' have seen the look on those pretty Arab faces when they saw us turnin' *toward* 'em. I'd wager they haven't seen *that* for a spell."

Richard smiled back, the smile of a wolf. "One thing is certain: they won't try to sink us. Not with the treasure we have on board. They'll aim for our rigging to disable us, and then take us by boarding. Should it come to that, Agee, should they succeed in grappling us, we cease fire and lay down our arms. If I'm unable to give the order, you give it. I know what I said up there. But I won't see these good men die for nothing."

"It wouldn't be for nothing," Agreen said softly. He put a hand on Richard's shoulder. "But don't worry, Captain. If need be, I'll carry out your order."

Up on the weather deck, Americans were preparing for a fight that, judging from the rapidly decreasing span of blue water separating *Falcon* from the two xebecs, was less than thirty minutes away. Gun crews had removed tompions from the muzzles of the guns and stood by with sponges, rammers, and worms. Butt ends of linstocks were secured in tubs of water; their upper ends glowed with hot slow-match twisting like snakes around the three-foot-long forked sticks. Gun captains had removed quoins from their beds under the breeches to elevate the muzzles as much as possible. Wet sand was strewn about the deck to provide better footing in the slurry of spilt blood, and the canvas wrap covering the three fire-arrows had been removed to expose their sharply honed, polished arrowheads glistening in the early morning sun.

Richard had every confidence that Gardner and Pratt and Blakely would tend to the guns. Save for actually launching the fire-arrows, these men had experienced, many times, the evolutions of naval gunnery. Richard's primary concern at the moment was *Falcon*'s position relative to the two xebecs.

He and Agreen walked to the starboard railing amidships and scanned the sea to windward. So far, at least, his expectations were on target. The first xebec, the one closest to the schooner, had responded to his jog to the northeast by setting a new course to the west-northwest. The one following behind maintained a northerly course with a little easterly to it. So they were splitting apart from each other, Richard observed. In ten minutes *Falcon* would pass the first xebec. Good, but not good enough. He needed more power.

"Set the fores'ls?" Agreen asked, as if reading Richard's mind.

"Yes, do, Agee."

Agreen waved to Tremaine at the tiller, who at the signal nudged *Falcon* into the wind. As the schooner's sails luffed and she momentarily lost way, Agreen signaled to the three foredeckmen stationed by the jib sheets and halyards. Up shot the jib, followed by the flying jib—two sets of triangular white canvas that reinforced the best efforts of the fore topmast staysail to such an extent that when Tremaine brought her back on her course full and by, *Falcon* sprang forward like a frisky colt given free rein at last.

They were making ten, eleven, perhaps twelve knots. Richard put the glass to his eye and noted with satisfaction that the xebec to windward had lost some of the driving power in her massive square foresail. It still drew, braced hard over, but with less authority than when the wind was on her quarter.

"We might outrun 'em on this tack," Agreen speculated, referring specifically to the xebec to windward. Her consort was now positioned to the south and west of them.

"Perhaps," Richard said, having considered that possibility, "though I doubt it. Those lateens are of no small consequence, Agee. And even if we could outrun them, what then? Where would we go? We have no more friends to the east than we do to the west."

Just then, the xebec doused her great square sail and trimmed in her lateens, settling closer to the wind on a course that seemed to parallel *Falcon*'s, but on closer inspection had more east to it. It was a course of interception.

"There's your answer, Agee," Richard said, pointing. He lunged to grab hold of the starboard railing as *Falcon* heeled sharply to larboard in a gust of wind. The early morning breezes had hardened to a steady fifteen knots, strong enough to raise whitecaps on the waves and splatter spume across the schooner's foredeck. "See that xebec there? Even without her squares'l she's able to keep pace with us. She has two sails to our five, and our relative positions haven't changed much." He spoke with genuine admiration.

"So their plan is t' circle around us an' trap us between them in a vise."

"That's how I see it. And I'm happy to oblige. It's imperative we keep the xebecs apart. Any hope we have depends on it. But with this wind kicking up, we need our larboard side up, not down. I aim to take that xebec first," pointing to the one ahead, to windward. "We'll need to change tack before we engage."

Agreen nodded. "That thought had occurred to me."

"We're two peas in a pod, Agee." Richard faced forward with a hand cupped at his mouth. "Gardner!"

Tom Gardner stepped aft, gripping the larboard railing for balance. "Captain?" he called when he was within hailing distance.

"Man the larboard guns and remove the aprons," referring to the metal covering placed over a gun's touchhole to protect powder inside from rain or sea spray. "Await my order. After the first round, reload the two forward guns with grape at full charge, the after gun with a fire-arrow at half charge. Got it?"

"Aye, aye, sir!"

As Gardner ordered the gun crews from the starboard side over to larboard, Agreen said to Lamont by the tiller, "At my command, bring her on a new course due south."

"Due south, aye, sir," Lamont acknowledged.

The xebec to leeward remained south and west of them, and was now making her turn to north-northeastward. To windward, the other xebec was closing in rapidly, intending, apparently, to sweep in ahead of *Falcon* and rake her bow with the starboard guns. She was close enough for the Americans to see her every detail with the naked eye: her white bowsprit; the ship's boat lashed upside-down between the foremast and mainmast; the ornately carved, extreme overhangs on her stem and stern; individual seamen and marines on deck, others secured high in the rigging like so many bugs caught in a giant spiderweb, the polished steel of their muskets and scimitars glittering in the bright sunshine. *Falcon*'s crew could also see the black muzzles of guns, ten of them—6-pounders, Richard surmised, much like his own—protruding through the bulwarks on both sides.

No one aboard *Falcon* had difficulty with the calculations. The Americans were outgunned forty to six, and perilously outmanned. The mathematics of defeat, Richard thought bitterly. But at least *Falcon* had a fighting chance. *Eagle* had sailed into these waters unarmed.

Agreen looked hard at Richard. The xebec to windward was closing fast. The xebec to leeward was farther away but closing nonetheless. The vise was beginning to close.

Richard nodded once in reply to the unspoken question.

"Ready about! Stations for stays!" Agreen shouted through a speaking trumpet. "Ready! Ready! Hard a-lee!" he barked a moment later. *Falcon* turned into the wind and through it as sailors in her bow eased off the larboard jib sheets while others amidships gradually hauled in the booms on the great fore-and-aft sails, keeping the sails drawing as long as possible to maintain her speed.

Richard kept his glass on the xebec to windward. His view swept across her deck to the helm, where, more to his disgust than his surprise, he brought into focus the *rais* who had stood beside the dey's throne in the royal palace. He was shouting something forward through a cupped hand, but stopped short and shifted his gaze toward the schooner as if sensing the eyes of his enemy upon him.

"Helm's a-lee!" Agreen shouted. It was the signal to release the headsheets to larboard and haul them hard in to starboard. As *Falcon* veered through the wind, her crew adjusted jib and mainsheets until all sails were drawing full on a beam reach, on a course due south.

Falcon and the windward xebec were now almost upon each other, sailing on opposite tacks, the heel to starboard in the strengthening breeze elevating the schooner's larboard guns. As the xebec approached, her larboard guns were pointing down toward the water.

The *rais,* caught off guard by the schooner's sudden surge southward, let fly the sheets on both lateen sails, causing them to shiver and thunder in protest and their great booms to jounce and swing wildly back and forth across the deck. But that single action brought the heel abruptly off her; she was gliding forward on an even keel now, her bow nosing slowly, instinctively, into the wind as her gun crews struggled to make ready the larboard guns.

"*Fire! In sequence!*"

A tongue of orange flame lashed out from *Falcon*'s foremost starboard gun, vomiting a shower of white sparks in its wake. The foredeck was enveloped in a gray cloud of acrid smoke that quickly carried off to westward as fifty balls of half-pound grapeshot streaked eastward. Screams rent the air: Arab sailors and marines caught in the path of the deadly outpouring reeled backward on deck or plunged from the rigging. Moments later a second blast delivered a second payload of grape, the effect of a giant blunderbuss fired at point-blank range. Again the screams, again the sickening plunge of men from aloft, some, lifeless, falling like stones, others with arms and legs flailing wildly until they splashed into the sea or crashed onto the deck below. A third gun roared in perfect synchrony, sending a wheeling mass of chain-shot end over end, humming and whirling into the enemy's mizzen shrouds, digging iron teeth deep into hempen rope, slicing through the lee shrouds, causing the mizzen to teeter perilously back and forth.

As *Falcon* swept past, the xebec fought to reverse her position, to bring the wind behind her and shape a course to westward. Richard held his glass on her stern. He could see scores of confused and excited men, one—the captain—waving frantically toward the larboard guns, then up to the rigging, then to the foredeck where sailors were struggling to lower the huge square sail from its yard. The crew was having a hard time of it, Richard noted, his lips pursed tight in satisfaction.

"There goes the element of surprise," Agreen commented, as awed as Richard by the effect of a murderous broadside without one gun answering. "Now they know we're serious."

"Rely on it." Richard scanned the waters with a naval officer's eye.

Forward aboard *Falcon*, the gun captains had ordered their crews through the evolutions that would have the three larboard guns reloaded in less than a minute.

To westward, perhaps a quarter-mile away, the other xebec rushed to enter the fray. She had doused her square sail and was sailing under her two close-hauled lateens.

"Bring her about, Agee," Richard ordered. He was envisioning a course in his mind that would take them on a reverse S, up between the two xebecs, first dispatching the one to windward before looping to westward to challenge her approaching sister. He estimated he had five minutes, no more. "Lay her fifty yards to leeward of our friend the *rais*."

Agreen ordered *Falcon* around on the opposite tack, on a course one point west of north.

Ahead, the wounded xebec was making headway to northwestward, toward her consort. If she maintained that course, however, she would be exposed to a rake on her bow or stern, at *Falcon*'s pleasure, since the schooner had every sail drawing and could maneuver at will. The *rais* had to make a choice: either allow his ship to continue westward in the hope and prayer of joining her partner to pass the baton of battle, or turn, now, to present her larboard broadside to the oncoming schooner. Richard was banking that he would do the latter and stay in the fight, motivated less, perhaps, by duty and honor than by fear of the dey's wrath if he should fail him.

Falcon was but a cable length away when the xebec swerved to southward, unleashing her broadside as she did so. It was an onslaught as ill timed as it was ill managed. A single 6-pound round shot hit the schooner, punching harmlessly through the foresail and then the mainsail a few feet behind it before plunging into the sea astern.

The xebec was helpless now, at least for the time it took to reload her guns. With her square sail raised and a damaged mizzenmast, she could not wear ship and present her starboard battery.

The second xebec had closed to within two hundred yards.

Richard saw his chance. With *Falcon* on her northerly course, she came broadside to broadside with the wounded xebec and unleashed her starboard guns. Flames shot out from her forward gun, then her middle gun. But the results were negligible. On this round, the xebec's top-hamper was empty of sailors, and those on her deck had taken cover behind the bulwarks, just as Richard had suspected they would.

He walked quickly to the after gun, where the iron bolt of the fire-arrow had been thrust into the muzzle from outside the gunport. Its wasp nest of muslin and the combustibles it contained lay snug against the railing, its long chains with their barbed hooks at the end dangling down toward the sea. At Richard's command, Blakely leaned out from the starboard bulwark and touched the hempen mass with a sizzling linstock. Instantly it burst to life, a bright yellow ball of fire. Richard took the linstock from Blakley, blew hard on the end to stimulate the flame, then stepped aside and settled the glowing tip on the touchhole.

"This is for you, Caleb," he breathed. "And for you, Ashley."

A puff of smoke burst at the hole just as a flame of powder raced down the priming quill into the heart of the gun where a powder canister had been rammed down to the breech. The powder exploded, propelling the gun carriage backward in a screech of wheels and the fire-arrow forward in a straight shot at the enemy, its flight purposely slowed by a half-charge of powder. Its entire four-foot length seemingly awash in flame, the arrow streaked toward its target like some ancient fireball hurled by a Crusader's catapult at a Saracen fortress.

The arrow struck the main lateen sail abaft the spar, halfway up, its iron tip piercing through, its barbed hooks grabbing hold of canvas and wood with the tenacity of an eagle's talons clutching a frightened prey. The arrow's flight jerked to a halt and the fire in its soul reached out to consume everything around it, setting off a conflagration that threatened the very life of the xebec.

Richard had a hard time tearing his eyes away from the rapidly spreading flames. "Bring her off the wind!" he shouted to Lamont at the tiller. He pointed at the approaching xebec. "Sail directly at her!" To the gun captains: "Reload the starboard guns! Handsomely now, you men!"

The second xebec was almost upon them. They had less than a minute before a second engagement that everyone aboard *Falcon* realized would not be as one-sided as the first.

The first volley came sooner than Richard expected. Swinging suddenly onto a more southerly course, the xebec unleashed her larboard battery just as *Falcon*'s gun crews were scrambling across the deck.

"Down! Everyone down!" Richard screamed, as ten guns roared almost as one. A perfectly timed broadside—half the guns aimed high, at the rigging, the other half aimed level, at the schooner's deck—pummeled *Falcon* with round-shot. His warning came too late. To his horror, Richard saw four men fall amidships, Phineas Pratt among them. Then a shot struck the mizzen with such force that it took out a chunk of pine near the base, launching splinters of wood into the air with the fury of precisely aimed lances. One long, jagged splinter harpooned Nate Tremaine in his left side, beneath his ribs. The old sailor dropped to his knees, remained there a moment as if in prayer, then collapsed face-down onto the deck, blood running in a red rivulet from his mangled torso toward the larboard scuppers.

When Richard seemed momentarily stunned by what had just happened, Agreen stepped forward and bellowed, "Starboard guns! *Fire!*"

Falcon's starboard guns returned fire just as a thunderous explosion astern stunned the sensibilities of survivors on both sides. The fire on the first xebec had burned down to the magazine. Where moments before a vessel had struggled for life, only open water remained.

"Reload!" Agreen cried out.

"Both arrows in the larboard guns!" Richard shouted, back in command. He looked hard at Agreen. "We have one chance, Agee. One chance only. We have to make it count."

Agreen nodded. He understood perfectly what Richard intended.

Both vessels were back on course, sailing right at each other. The outcome would be decided in a half-minute. *Falcon* was sailing to the northwest, the xebec to the southeast. They were bow to bow, each making good speed despite the cut on the schooner's mizzen. Richard stood hard beside Agreen near the tiller. He stared darkly ahead at the death or redemption, or both, fast approaching his command.

The span of water separating the two ships narrowed to seventy feet. Sixty feet. Richard unsheathed his sword . . . fifty feet . . . and raised it high in the air. Still the two vessels came at each other, the bowsprit of each aimed directly at the other like two medieval knights jousting full-tilt from opposite ends of the lists, lances out, winner take all. At twenty-five feet Tom Gardner set the two remaining wasp nests ablaze, seconds before Richard sliced his sword downward.

"Up helm! Bring her off! Starboard guns . . . *Fire!*"

An unholy discharge of flames, smoke, and shot erupted from both vessels at once, as the xebec veered into the wind the instant *Falcon* fell off it. Grape and langrage screamed into *Falcon*'s rigging as round-shot pulverized her bulwarks, smashing through them, launching shards and splinters in all directions, deep into wood and canvas and the flesh of men staggering backward from the brutal impact. A block crashed to the deck near Richard, followed immediately by a broken topsail yard and, moments later, a silent serpent of rope. Agreen was down, though in the stinging smoke Richard could not determine where he was hit or how badly he was hurt. Others, too, succumbed to the maelstrom of iron balls and wooden spears that lasted but a few seconds yet seemed, to those alive aboard *Falcon,* a purgatory without end.

Then, abruptly, the two ships were disengaged, sailing haphazardly away from each other. It took only a short time, in this wind, for the smoke to clear. Dazed, his ears ringing, his left arm barely able to clutch the mizzen for support, Richard forced his eyes astern. As gruesome as the scene was aboard *Falcon,* that on the xebec was much worse. Both fire-arrows had found their mark. She was in irons, her bow facing into the wind, the fire in her sails and rigging spreading rapidly down toward her deck, rendering her inoperable. Men who had witnessed the fate of their sister ship tried desperately, vainly, to douse the blaze with buckets of water and a pump hose. Others abandoned ship, apparently preferring death by drowning to incineration alive.

Richard fell to his knees beside Agreen, pain searing through his shoulder. He had barely enough strength left to turn the body face up, visions of Jamie Hardcastle dying on the deck of *Serapis* flashing through his befuddled mind. He saw a shard of wood embedded at the base of Agreen's neck and a blotch of red spreading down his shirt. He saw, too, a mass of blood on the side of Agreen's face, an inch above his left ear—a glancing blow from falling tackle, perhaps, for he could see no hole in the skull, nor feel one. Not knowing what to do next, he began unbuttoning Agreen's shirt, one-handed, to at least get to the wound and somehow stem the flow of blood. He felt a hand on his arm, pushing it aside.

"I'll see to him, Captain," Lawrence Brooke said.

Richard gave the surgeon a look edging on hysteria. "Doctor," he croaked, "he must not die. *Agee must not die.*"

Brooke had already gently pulled the splinter from Agreen's throat and was packing the wound with gauze. "Captain," he said hurriedly yet firmly, "you have done your work for today. Allow me to do mine. Once I have seen to Mr. Crabtree I'll be examining that shoulder of yours. You are losing too much blood."

It was only then that Richard looked down at his left shoulder and arm, and saw that they too were soaked in red.

"See to the men first, Doctor."

"I'll see to them." Brooke summoned Gardner and Howland, both staring mutely in turn at the havoc aboard their own vessel and the fiery spectacle astern. "Take Mr. Crabtree below to his cabin," he said to them. "Gently now, lads. Easy does it." When Agreen was gone, Brooke examined Richard's upper arm. Using a surgeon's scalpel to cut away the shredded cotton, he ran his eyes over the crimson pulp of flesh and the fractured sliver of white bone visible inside it. "You have a serious wound, Captain. You're in shock, so you may not feel the pain just yet. But you will." He withdrew a thick white piece of cloth from his medical bag and placed it squarely over the mangled tissue. "Hold this bandage with your right hand. And don't move. I'll be back with some laudanum. I need to set that bone."

Despite the doctor's order, Richard struggled to his knees as soon as Brooke had stepped forward to take a quick inventory of the horrors that lay ahead for him on the surgeon's table. As he did so, a fierce stab of pain assailed his shoulder and a wave of dizziness overcame him. He leaned against the starboard railing for support, peered over it.

"Shall we search for survivors, sir?" Lamont called out cautiously from the tiller.

Richard stared astern at the xebec, now drifting aimlessly, the fire in her belly burning low to the waterline. *Falcon* was too far away for him to determine how many of her crew, if any, were floundering in the water beside her. He glanced forward. Increase Hobart lay on his back not ten feet away. Part of his skull had been blown off and his brains oozed out onto the deck. Richard tried to count the number of his own crew standing by the mutilated rigging, but even that minor effort proved too taxing. All he could draw from his wretched state was the assurance that *Falcon* had somehow prevailed and the knowledge that in victory he would have a terrible butcher's bill to pay.

"No, Mr. Lamont," he managed to rasp. "Lay her on a course for Cape Sicié, as best you can. Apparently we have need of the medical facilities at Toulon after all."

With that, he slumped down to a sitting position, his back against the bulwark. He muttered a brief prayer for the dead and dying, then closed his eyes to the horror as blessed unconsciousness finally settled over him.

Eleven

Toulon, France, Fall 1788–Spring 1789

RICHARD CUTLER, PROPPED up on three pillows, his forehead creased with furrows, tossed his head this way and that as if to escape the sight of something unbearable. The naval hospital was chilly. Early that morning an orderly had latched the large double windows of the cavernous chamber to make certain they remained shut against breezes that were abnormally cool for late October in the South of France. Nonetheless, rivulets of sweat snaked from Richard's brow into the coarse stubble on his chin, mingling there with the salt of tears born from the anguish of his dream.

The abyss separating them was vast and deep. Increase Hobart and Nate Tremaine stood apart from him on the other side, in front of a third figure Richard could not make out. Others had gathered in the distance behind them, faceless forms that seemed to stop and hover for an instant before retreating farther back from the edge, as if, having accepted their fate, they were simply waiting for the other three to join them.

"I'm sorry, Captain," Hobart shouted over. "We can't come across. It's too wide. We must remain here."

"No, Hobart," Richard shouted back. "There must be a way across. We just need to find it." His eyes shot right and left, searching frantically for a pathway to deliverance. "Don't give up on me, men. Please God, don't give up on me. You don't have to go!"

"Aye, we do, Captain," Hobart shouted again, less forcefully. "It's our time. I'm sorry we failed you."

"You did not fail me, Hobart," Richard replied, his own voice softer, restrained in resignation. "You have never failed me. Nor you, Tremaine. None of you has. You are the finest men I know."

Just then Peter Chatfield stepped forward from behind his two shipmates and approached the rim of the abyss. He raised his right hand as if in benediction and said, without a trace of tremor in his voice, "It has been an honor to serve you and your family, Captain. I regret nothing. Please, do not mourn for us. We are at peace. It is very beautiful here." As one, he and Hobart and Tremaine began walking slowly backward toward the faceless forms, fading deeper into obscurity with every step, until it became impossible to distinguish one from the other.

"The honor is mine," Richard called after them, choking on his words. His arm raised in farewell, he was prepared at last to accept God's will. "The honor is mine."

"*Capitaine* CUTLER? HE FELT someone gently but persistently shaking his right shoulder. "*Réveillez-vous, monsieur. Réveillez-vous.*"

For an instant Richard was not certain who was speaking, why he was being awakened, or even where he was.

The man who had spoken was dabbing at Richard's forehead with a cool, damp cloth. "*Capitaine,*" he said kindly, "*vous avez le cauchemar. Réveillez-vous maintenant. S'il vous plaît, monsieur.*"

Richard blinked up at an orderly wearing a spotless white coat, a neatly cropped goatee, and an encouraging smile. His eyes searched the room, looking for something familiar, until he got his bearings. Yes, he remembered now. He had been carried here on a stretcher he knew not how many days ago. The sizable room was divided with white curtains into small cubicles to afford a semblance of privacy to each patient. His space contained a nightstand next to the bed, two chairs near its foot, and a chest of drawers directly across from the foot of the bed against the curtain.

When he tried to raise himself up on his elbows, he felt a jab of pain shoot down his left arm. He winced, swearing under his breath.

"*Prenez garde, capitaine,*" the orderly scolded him. "*Tenez, je peux vous aider.*" He inserted another pillow under Richard's head and carefully brought him up to a sitting position.

"*Merci,*" Richard said when the pain had subsided. He looked questioningly at the orderly. "*Le docteur Brooke, est-il ici?*"

"*Je crois que oui,*" was the reply. "*Je le chercherai. Un moment, s'il vous plaît.*"

As the orderly disappeared in search of Lawrence Brooke, Richard breathed in the heavenly aroma of fried eggs and bacon. He had not eaten a square meal in days; he had not tasted eggs or bacon since their first day out of Gibraltar. His stomach growled in anticipation.

"*Pardon,*" he said to the orderly upon his return. "*J'ai une faim de loup. Est-ce que je peux avoir quelque chose à manger?*"

"*Certainement, capitaine.*" The orderly gestured in the general direction of the hospital kitchen. "*Votre docteur est entièrement maître de votre petit déjeuner.*"

True to the man's word, a few minutes later Lawrence Brooke pushed aside the curtains of the cubicle. He was followed by a second orderly bearing a tray laden with fried eggs, bacon strips, toasted cheese on bread, two rolls, and hot coffee. With a look that seemed to express mild disapproval, the orderly settled the tray on the table next to Richard's bed and departed.

Brooke pointed at the tray. "Nothing 'petit' about that 'déjeuner,' eh, Captain? I had to ruffle some feathers out there in the kitchen, but I was finally able to convince the director of the hospital that you require more than bread and chocolate to get better. This'll put some meat back on your bones." He picked up the tray and placed it on Richard's lap, pausing after he did so to inspect the bandage and sniff it closely for any hint of gangrene. Detecting none, he said with a satisfied air, "Please, Captain, have at it. I've already eaten."

Richard dug into a breakfast more delicious than any he could remember.

"I tried for roasted potatoes," Brooke said, taking a chair and enjoying the spectacle of his captain eating so ravenously, "knowing how much you enjoy them. But these French think that potatoes are fit only for animals to eat. Imagine believing such a thing with people out there starving."

"You did fine, Doctor," Richard said. "Just fine, thank you. Are the others in the hospital eating as well?"

"Those able to, yes."

Richard understood that Brooke meant no criticism, but guilt stroked through him nonetheless—guilt for enjoying such fare while others under his command could not, either because they were too injured or because they were dead. He set his fork down.

"Have you made the rounds this morning, Doctor?"

"I have."

"And?"

Inexplicably, Brooke bowed his head. "Mr. Crabtree is progressing," he said, avoiding Richard's questioning gaze, "though it will be a while before he's back on his feet. That shot that glanced off his leg fractured his kneecap. As painful as it is for him, it will heal, over time."

"How much time?"

"It's difficult to say with that kind of injury. I'd give it four months, at a minimum. But his prognosis, overall, is good. The wounds to his neck and head are coming along. He lost a lot of blood, as you did, Captain, but you both will pull through. Thankfully, there's no need to hurry things along. From what I'm hearing, it may take longer to repair *Falcon* than to repair her two senior officers. Since you and Mr. Crabtree aren't going anywhere anytime soon, you may just as well settle in and enjoy the local flavor."

"Doctor, my family . . ."

"I took the liberty of writing your father, Captain. I reported to him that we have been delayed in Toulon for the winter and that you and Mr. Crabtree have been wounded, though you both are recovering nicely. I did not give any other details. You can supply those later."

Richard let his head sink back down onto the pillows, yielding to a surge of relief and to the fatigue that had plagued him since the battle. Moments passed in silence save for the distant sound of a three-way conversation in French. Then a premonition compelled him to open his eyes and look at Dr. Brooke. "What is it, Doctor? What haven't you told me?"

Brooke had been staring down at his hands. He slowly raised his eyes. "I regret to report, Captain, that we have lost another shipmate. He went during the night."

"Peter Chatfield."

"Yes, but how . . . ?"

"Go on."

"He fought hard to the end," Brooke said, blinking. "It's a blessing he went, for he could never have recovered from his injuries. I didn't want to tell you this, Captain, not in your condition. I know how fond you were of Chatfield."

Richard slumped back onto the pillows. "And the others?" he murmured.

"The others will pull through, Captain. You may depend on it."

THOSE FIRST FEW WEEKS in Toulon passed calmly, quietly. Richard remained in the naval hospital, drifting in and out of consciousness, largely oblivious to the passage of time or to specific dates. It was not until the crisp air of autumn was yielding to the frost of winter that his condition improved sufficiently for him to go outside and take the air, although he was still unable to stand for more than a few minutes at a time. His strength returned slowly but surely.

One day in late November the port captain of Toulon came to visit him at the hospital. He had come on official business, document case in hand, to determine the sequence of events prior to *Falcon*'s arrival before the guns of Fort St. Louis, which guarded the southern approaches to Toulon's harbor. Dressed in a white uniform with gold trim, the bespectacled port captain introduced himself as Capitaine Antoine-Pierre Mercier.

Mercier sat down on the chair next to the bed and removed several sheets of paper from his satchel. "It is easier," he observed wryly, "to get past the Swiss guards at the Vatican or at Versailles than past your ship's surgeon." They were conversing in French, the post captain having been informed that Richard was fluent in that language.

"I can imagine," Richard replied. He took a sip from the mug of the hot Ceylon tea that Captain Mercier had kindly brought in for him.

"I realize you are not entirely healed, Captain Cutler," he mused as he searched through his papers, "so I will limit my time here today." He put down one sheet of paper, picked up another. "I have but a few questions to ask . . . ah, here we are." He scanned his notes before glancing up. "You sailed here to Toulon from Algiers, correct?"

"That is correct."

"At your government's request?"

"At *your* government's agreement to my government's request to let us use these facilities."

Mercier smiled. "Yes, of course. My apologies. Now, then, if you don't mind, let us go back to the beginning. What was your purpose in going to Algiers?"

"My purpose was to ransom American sailors taken by Barbary pirates aboard one of my family's merchant vessels. My brother is among those sailors."

"Yes, I was sorry to learn that. When did this attack on your family's vessel occur?"

"Two years ago."

"Your government supported you in this mission?"

"Yes, it did. I was granted diplomatic status for the mission."

"Ah. Then as a diplomat, surely you must have met our esteemed consul in Algiers, Monsieur de Kercy?" Mercier's face remained impassive, though Richard thought he detected a twinkle of mirth in the Frenchman's eyes.

"I met him," Richard replied noncommittally.

Mercier leaned forward, spoke in confidence. "As I have, Captain. Let me just say that in my opinion, and in the opinion of others, Monsieur de Kercy is not the flower of the French diplomatic corps. He is, in fact, more like a weed. Why he was appointed to such a critical post I cannot explain to you." Mercier leaned back, cleared his throat, and resumed an official tone of voice. "Now please tell me, Captain, as best you can, exactly what happened in Algiers."

Richard told him, as best he could.

"I see. And you sailed from there . . . one moment, please . . . " Mercier checked his notes. "You sailed from there the evening of September the second?"

"That is correct."

"Captain, please tell me what happened on the morning of September the third."

Richard knew that Mercier had been through all this with Micah Lamont and several other members of his crew who had emerged unscathed from the sea battle. He said as much to the port captain.

"That is true," Mercier acknowledged. "And I must add that they have been most cooperative. Their testimony is the basis for my notes." He held up the sheets of paper. "But Mr. Cutler, you must understand that when it comes to the morning of September the third, what they told me was . . . well, shall I say that what they told me is an account I would appreciate hearing again from the mouth of the schooner's captain."

As Richard conveyed the details of the battle in a matter-of-fact tone, Mercier chewed lightly on his lower lip. At the conclusion of the account he stared at Richard, mouth slightly agape. "You are telling me, Captain, that your schooner, a merchant vessel armed with six guns, was attacked by two Algerian xebecs, each armed with twenty guns, and that in the ensuing battle you succeeded in destroying *both* of them before sailing on to Toulon. Is that what you are telling me?"

"That is what I'm telling you, sir."

"Monsieur . . . Forgive me for asking . . . I do not mean to doubt you . . . Your mate and surgeon have collaborated every detail . . . but my dear man . . . *how*?"

Richard shrugged, and instantly regretted it as pain knifed through his arm. "I sail with good men, Captain."

Mercier shook his head repeatedly as he busied himself rearranging the papers on his lap. "You will appreciate, Captain Cutler, that my report on this subject will be met with some skepticism by my superiors. At the very least, they will think my brain has become addled with too much wine. And who could blame them, after hearing such an account?" He gave Richard a weak smile.

Richard smiled back.

"Well, Captain Cutler, I suppose that must do. Now, what is next for you? Once you have fully recovered."

"I must see to repairs of my schooner."

"Yes, of course. Those repairs will take time—and money."

"I have funds to pay for repairs. Can you recommend a good shipwright in Toulon?" When Mercier nodded, Richard continued, "I will remain here until my ship is almost ready to sail, then I will travel to Paris while my men remain with the ship. "My crew *will* be allowed to remain here, Captain, until the repairs are made?" Again Mercier nodded. "Thank you. Once I reach Paris, I will visit Captain John Paul Jones. You know of him, I trust?"

Mercier held up the palms of his hands in French fashion, as if to say, "Who in France has not?"

"Captain Jones will be leading a delegation to Barbary," Richard said. He saw no point in being secretive about Jones' mission. It seemed to be common knowledge in several parts of the world. "I have information that may prove useful to him."

"Yes. It is what I read in a dispatch from your consul, Mr. Jefferson, when he requested permission for you to use our medical facilities here. I had wondered if you still planned to travel to Paris."

"I do. After what happened in Algiers, nothing is more important to me."

"I understand, Captain. But I feel I must warn you . . ." Mercier paused.

"Warn me about what, monsieur?"

Mercier removed his eyeglasses and began wiping them with a handkerchief drawn from an inner pocket of his uniform dress coat. Richard waited in silence for the man to collect, assess, and finally articulate his thoughts.

"You are aware of . . . the difficulties we are having in France?"

Richard understood generally what Mercier meant, though he had little specific knowledge. Even before leaving home he had read in the Boston newspapers about the unrest in France and the disastrous state of the French economy. It was caused in no small part by excessive spending on the French military, specifically the French Royal Navy, by the government of King Louis XVI, who hoped to avenge the loss of French prestige and overseas possessions following the Seven Years' War against England. France's hatred for England had been the basis of the military alliance between France and America during the Revolutionary War.

Hunger and unemployment in France had been exacerbated by severe droughts in the south and bizarre summer hailstorms in the north that had all but destroyed the harvest for 1788. The price of bread had soared, and the government's efforts to stimulate the economy and get things back on an even keel had been badly bungled. Famine had gripped the nation with such severity that food riots had broken out in many cities. Peasants who could no longer afford to buy bread demanded relief from well-to-do landlords who continued to demand rents and other vestiges of feudal privilege. Those dressed in rags and barely able to scrounge together a few sous resented paying high rents to a landlord who spent the money on snuff to clear his nostrils and perfume to scent his powdered wig.

When the gathering storm finally broke and angry mobs began sacking Bordeaux and other French cities, shock waves of disbelief reverberated all the way across Spain to Gibraltar. Jeremy Hardcastle had informed Richard during his visit there that French citizens fueled by hate and desperation were breaking into bakeries and seizing shopkeepers accused of price-fixing or hoarding bread, lynching them on the spot or bludgeoning them to death in a fury of lawless retribution that enlarged to include local officials and tax collectors guilty only of doing their jobs. King Louis had pleaded for calm, promising reforms in a bankrupt system that had failed nearly everyone. He vowed to convene the États Généraux, a government body encompassing the three estates of the French societal pyramid that had not sat since 1614, during the reign of the Sun King, Louis XIV. The king's promises and the respect he still commanded among his subjects succeeded in restoring a semblance of order. But it was a tenuous truce at best, with dark whispers of insurrection continuing to threaten France like a fire-arrow of destruction aimed from the vast underbelly of the third estate, up through the heart and soul of French culture—the chevaliers of the second estate and the clergy of the first—all the way to the very tip of the pyramid: the court of Versailles where King Louis resided with his despised Austrian-born queen, Marie Antoinette.

"I regret that your country is suffering, Captain," Richard said, with a sincerity he truly felt. "France was a loyal ally of my country during the war. We could not have won our independence without your help."

Mercier bowed. "France was pleased and proud to help, monsieur." He gazed beyond Richard, his eyes misting with pride as if he were recalling an earlier age when the power and prestige of La Belle France had stirred the hearts of all Frenchmen, from the lowliest of the low to the grandest of nobles fêting one another in their magnificent *châteaux*.

He snapped to when Richard asked, "Is it safe to travel to Paris these days, Captain?"

"What? Oh. You are asking me if it is safe to travel to Paris?"

"Yes."

"The journey itself is safe, I should think. The danger is what may await you once you arrive there. Whatever is coming, it will begin and it will end in Paris. You are an American. Your country is much admired by my people, rich and poor alike. Ironic, is it not, that France fought for America's independence and now finds herself threatened by what America achieved. Those who would limit the powers of the monarchy, or abolish it altogether, call themselves 'patriots,' as you Americans did during your revolution. The marquis de Lafayette, a nobleman of ancient blood, is leading the call for reform in France, seeming to care nothing for his own class and privileged status." He smiled without humor, a man who had far more than privileged status to lose if *l'ancien régime* collapsed.

Under the circumstances, Richard thought it best not to mention that he was well acquainted with the marquis de Lafayette. He had served under him at the Battle of Yorktown, and his parents had met the Frenchman at a reception held at the Anchor Inn in Hingham when Lafayette traveled there during the war to confer with Brigadier General Benjamin Lincoln, Washington's second in command.

"Excuse me, Captain Cutler," Mercier said, rising from his chair. "I have kept you longer than I promised. I must take my leave. But first I must add that you needn't worry about the safety of your schooner or her cargo. The quays are patrolled night and day, and I have ordered a detail of marines to stand watch over her. Before I go, is there anything I might do for you? Or have sent to you?"

"Just the repairs to my schooner," Richard reminded him. "And I would be obliged, Captain, if you could have pen and paper sent to me. I have many letters to write."

"Of course. I will see to your requests immediately. Adieu, Captain Cutler. I have enjoyed our conversation and I wish you good luck." He offered a salute.

"*Bonne chance à vous aussi,*" Richard said, saluting in turn. "*Et, capitaine?*" he added as Mercier was about to make his exit. Mercier glanced back. "*Vive la France!*"

Mercier held Richard's gaze. "*Vive le roi!*" he said softly, passionately, before turning and disappearing through the folds of the curtains.

THE WEEKS ROLLED ONWARD. Though the calendar indicated that spring was approaching, the weather claimed otherwise. The winter of 1789 was the coldest in memory, the chill of Christmas descending to outright frigid conditions in January that heaped misery upon misery on the hapless French peasantry. Unable to procure food and firewood to keep themselves alive, many families died in their sleep, huddled together in scraps of clothing and blankets. Nor did winter's wrath spare the southern provinces. Throughout Provence, delicate grapevines and more sturdy olive trees remained encased in tombs of ice until the warming rays of April finally released them from the death grip—too late; the produce on which so many people relied had been destroyed.

In Toulon, windows of buildings designed to welcome in, not shut out, the soothing breezes of the Mediterranean remained shuttered for weeks on end. If one looked down toward the harbor and the massive La Bagne prison at the base of the mountains on the eastern shore, one could only imagine the suffering of the French radicals and other accused enemies of the state shivering inside in the cold while awaiting transport to some distant penal colony from which they would never return.

Richard saw a different view as he walked slowly alongside the quays of Toulon early one morning in May: a cloudless sky and glints of sunshine reflecting off *Falcon*'s newly rigged shrouds. She was tied to a dock nearby, a tiny vessel compared with the mammoth ships anchored out in the harbor: an array of battle cruisers the likes of which Richard had not witnessed since the summer of '74, when he and his brother Will had sailed past the British naval base at Spithead. *Falcon* had only recently come out of dry dock, her repairs delayed by the weather and the turmoil sweeping France—and thus extending by several months the time granted her crew to remain in Toulon. But her repairs were nearing completion; Richard had been informed just yesterday that she should be ready for sea trials within a fortnight. As he slowed his step still more to keep pace with Agreen limping along beside him, the thought again occurred to him that whatever else might be said about the French, they knew how to build and repair ships. *Falcon* had never looked better. He said as much to Agreen.

"Careful, matey," Agreen groused. "Ben Hallowell would have you flogged for speakin' such heresy," referring to the shipwright in Boston who had designed and built *Falcon*. "He'd set up a grate on the Common and invite all your rich friends up from Hingham t' come watch you get yours."

A glint shone in Richard's eye when he asked, "Do you think Lizzy would be there?"

"Damn right she'd be there. She'd be first in line, given what-all you've made me put up with ever since I signed on with your outfit. And I haven't even told her the bad things. I don't want her angrier at you than she already is." He shook his head. "Mark my words, matey, mark them well: if by some miracle we ever do get back t' Boston, I have half a mind t' quit your employ."

Richard squeezed Agreen's shoulder, gently. "That's okay, Agee. I'd miss you, but I'd understand. If you'd just do me the courtesy of leaving me the half of your mind that still works, I'd settle for that."

"What the hell kind of sense does *that* make? Jesus, Richard." Agreen lifted his face to the sun and ran his fingers through his unkempt reddish blond hair, pulling it back to expose as much of his face and neck as possible to the remedial heat. "Damn, that feels good," he sighed. "For a while there I thought I'd never feel this warm again."

"You and the rest of France," Richard commiserated.

They watched together as a team of workmen on *Falcon*'s deck heaved on ropes, using the leverage provided by her capstan to crank up a refurbished foretopsail yard to a second team of four perched high in the shrouds, ready to receive the spar and secure it into place. Elsewhere along the quays that stretched for a good quarter-mile in front of the medieval city that King Louis XIV had decreed would serve as his primary naval base, a host of shipwrights and carpenters and pursers and other petty officers toiled under the critical eye of white-uniformed officers.

Richard noticed Agreen leaning heavily against his cane for support. "Let's sit over there," he suggested, indicating a stone bench set well back from the quays, almost against the city walls. The tide was coming in, bringing with it the noisome flotsam and sewage from the great ships anchored out in the harbor. Away from the quays the stench was less offensive.

Agreen sat down with a sigh and stretched his injured leg out before him.

"How's it coming?" Richard asked. He glanced again at the newspaper he had been carrying before putting it aside. It reported, on page three, that in February the American Electoral College had elected George Washington as its first president. John Adams had received the second largest number of votes—a mere handful compared with Washington's count—and thus would serve as vice president. The oath of office was scheduled to be taken some time in late April in New York—which meant that today, as he was reading the old newspaper, a new president and a new Constitution had taken the helm in America.

"Right smartly," Agreen replied as he massaged the kneecap. "It does me good t' walk on it. Give me another week or two and I'll be dancing a jig. Have you given more thought t' my goin' with you t' Paris?"

Richard nodded heavily. They had covered this ground before, both in the hospital and more recently in the modestly priced *auberge* where they had found lodging in the heart of the medieval quarter of the city, near the grain market on the Place Puget. "My decision stands, Agee. Lamont needs your help sailing *Falcon* to Lorient. We have only sixteen men left as crew, and four of them can't do much. That leaves twelve able-bodied seamen. Besides, you've been to Lorient. You know the harbor and the town." When silence greeted his words, he added, from the heart, "You know my preferences here, Agee. And you know how much Captain Jones was looking forward to seeing you. I hated to tell him that you would not be coming with me. But *Falcon* and the men need you more than I."

Agreen folded his arms across his chest: "How long you reckon you'll be gone?"

"Not long. A week or so to get to Paris, two or three days there, and the time it takes to get to Lorient. So let's say three weeks. If it looks to be more than that, I'll send word to Lorient." After another silence he added: "I want to get home just as much as you do, Agee."

Agreen nodded, as though finally accepting the logic. "I know that, Richard. Just be sure t' bring along the letters you pick up in Paris. There should be a number for the men. And who knows, maybe one or two for me."

The subject of letters pained Richard, for it forced him to recall those he had written during the dreary weeks of winter. As hard as it had been to write to his own parents, it was infinitely harder to write the families of those who had died or been injured in battle, and of those of *Eagle*'s crew still held captive in Algiers or, in the case of Ashley Bowen, Nathan Reeves, and Joshua Winter, who had died there. He had limited himself to two letters a day, his frayed emotions more a barrier to further correspondence than his injuries. The last letter he wrote, to the parents of Phineas Pratt, was perhaps the hardest of all, for he had to inform them that while Pratt would be coming home aboard *Falcon*, it would be without his left leg, a victim of gangrene and amputation above the knee, and his left eye.

Two French naval officers strolled casually by the bench. One of them, apparently recognizing Richard, lifted his bicorne hat above his head and bowed respectfully. Richard acknowledged the courtesy with an American salute.

The officers having passed on, Agreen poked him in the ribs. "Introduce a few Arabs t' Davy Jones," he commented blithely, "and the French Navy bows an' scrapes at your feet."

When Richard did not reply, Agreen changed the subject. "So what have you told Lizzy in your letters home?" he asked, trying to stoke a jovial mood.

"I haven't told her anything. That's your job."

"Alright then, what have you told Katherine? You know she'll tell Lizzy everything you tell her. Surely you've written her."

"Surely I have."

"Well, what have you told her?"

Richard tapped the side of his head with his finger, as if trying to jog his memory. "I told her we're beached in Toulon, but the scenery around here is fabulous."

"Seriously, Richard. You know what I'm gettin' at. What have you told her about me?"

"About you? Not much. Just that you've been cavorting naked on the beach all day and that your sorry white ass is finally showing some color."

"Ha ha. Very funny. I'm dyin', I'm laughin' so hard. What else?"

Richard snapped his fingers. "Oh, yes. I told her that I stand in awe, every night, at the number of *jeunes filles* who leave our room at the *auberge* with a smile on their lips and a dreamy look in their eyes."

"Christ on the cross, Richard," Agreen snorted. "What the hell kind of friend are you? Makes me wonder why I'm so fired-up anxious t' have you stand up for me at my wedding."

Richard's eyebrows shot up. "Your wedding? You're getting married, Agee? To one of those *jeunes filles* you knocked up in the *auberge*?"

"Always the card, aren't you." Agreen stared ahead beyond the quays out to the great line of battle ships riding serenely at anchor, sails neatly furled on their yards and the white Bourbon flag of France fluttering high up on their mizzen backstays. "What I mean, my friend," he went on with a gravity and quality of purpose that Richard had rarely heard from him, "is that the first thing I do when I get home is ask Lizzy for her hand. I was hopin' you might agree t' stand up with me as my best man."

Richard did not respond until Agreen asked, in a tone that was more plea than query, "Why don't you answer? Don't ya think she'll have me?"

Richard laughed out loud, at the sincerity of the question and for his joy in answering it. "Yes, matey, I think she will. I'd wager serious money on it. And I'd be proud as hell to stand up with you. What a day *that's* going to be!"

Twelve

France, June–July 1789

THE RUGGED TOPOGRAPHY THAT protected Toulon's harbor and defenses also served to isolate the city. If not sent by military dispatch, word from Paris often arrived days after a significant event had occurred there, such as the violence that erupted in the Réveillon factory on April 23. As reported in the Toulon newspaper in early May, three hundred workers went on a rampage following unsubstantiated reports that the owner of the factory, Jean-Baptiste Réveillon, intended to cut the wages of his employees in order to lower the price he charged his élite clientele for the luxury wallpaper his factory produced. Fears of layoffs and destitution in an already crippled economy fanned the smoldering embers of rebellion into a raging inferno. Order was restored only after government troops were called in, but not before both the factory and the residence of Jean-Baptiste Réveillon had been burned to the ground and twenty-five people lay dead.

It seemed unfathomable to Richard and Agreen, after reading the account of the riot, that danger of this sort could lurk in Toulon. The hot sun glittering off the blue Mediterranean was too sensuous, too soporific, and the white sand on *la plage du Mourillon* too warm and inviting, to brood for long over anarchy and chaos in the French capital. The local population, military and civilian alike, appeared perfectly content with their lot. The arrival of summer had restored the natural order of things. And while local crops had been devastated by the brutal winter weather, harvests from the sea were, as always, plentiful.

In the course of Richard's five-hundred-mile journey to Paris in late June, however, his perception of things began to change. On June 22 he boarded a stagecoach in Marseilles, the southern terminus of a well-maintained road snaking northward through the Rhône Valley, to travel the main corridor linking northern and southern France. Early on, as the coach entered the province of Provence, he saw little of note beyond the natural beauty of a place studded with rocky plateaus, fields of neatly pruned olive trees, and terraced hillsides dotted with picturesque farmhouses. But as they left behind the old papal city of Avignon and approached Lyons, the second-largest city in France, the physical and psychological consequences of social upheaval became depressingly visible. Buildings that once had served as *patisseries*, government offices, or silk factories lay in ruins, their charred walls and roofs collapsed in blackened heaps. Farms bereft of crops stood abandoned, their fields gone to weeds, their great barn doors ajar, the animals gone—slaughtered, perhaps, for lack of feed. Citizens in the towns and villages the coach passed through went about their business furtively, studiously avoiding eye contact with the passengers inside the coach and with each other, save for the legions of beggars and waifs piteously pleading for coin and succor and the whores aggressively hawking their wares. It was as though such a fire of hate and despair burned within these townspeople that but one smoldering look, one fiery word, would ignite yet another deadly conflagration.

Richard tried talking with his fellow passengers, most of whom were of sufficient social standing to afford silk neck stocks and gold watch chains gleaming on their waistcoats, not to mention the luxury of travel in a coach-and-six featuring thickly padded cushions and armrests on its seats. He got no response. The door of ordinary civility remained closed to him, and Richard understood why. Although he might be fluent in their language, he was not one of them. Any conversation, however banal or benign its intent, would likely lead to places these men of privilege preferred not to go.

They had started out on their journey at a lively pace, making good time along the well-maintained road. Whenever the coach thundered into a *relais*, local personnel quickly exchanged the frothing horses with a fresh team of six. But as the coach jounced and shuddered into the heart of France, their pace began to slow. Here the road was pock-marked with deep ruts and sinkholes, and each day the number of hours they traveled on the road diminished. Despite the abundant hours of daylight afforded by midsummer, when the coach pulled into a *relais* during the late afternoon or early evening, it would likely as not remain there for the night, its passengers charged with finding their own food and lodging in some local *auberge*. Often it was midmorning the next day before they were on their way again.

A journey that should have taken a week was taking considerably longer. By the time the three passengers remaining aboard were within a day's ride of Paris, the coach's pace was reduced to a walk. Other coaches were slowed as well, trying to make headway against the streams of people afoot with various baggage and belongings and animals in tow, many of them dressed in decent clothing, their eyes blank with despair and hunger, coming the other way like refugees from a war zone. When the coach arrived within sight of the city, a squad of heavily armed soldiers ordered it to halt. Minutes stretched into a quarter-hour, a half-hour, an hour, and still the coach sat there, crowded in among the other coaches, with only wisps of hot, sticky air circulating inside and no explanation forthcoming.

"*Qu'est-ce qui se passe?*" the man next to Richard asked of his companion sitting across from him. He wiped his brow with a handkerchief already damp with perspiration.

The two men had come aboard the previous day in Troyes and had ignored Richard ever since, even after the other passengers had disembarked at various towns along the way and it was clear that the three of them were the only ones going on to Paris. The two men had chatted back and forth on various subjects of a mostly trivial nature, although their conversation did offer occasional interesting tidbits. Richard heard of a lawyer named Robespierre, whom the fatter of the two passengers described as a godless rabble-rouser. They also mentioned a writer named Mirabeau, described as a traitorous pig for forsaking his noble heritage and speaking out in support of the National Assembly—the self-proclaimed parliamentary body comprising the peasants and bourgeoisie in the third estate and those few nobles and clerics in the first and second estates who chose to join them. Their voices grew ever more agitated when the subject of the dauphin came up, not because the young heir to the throne had recently died, but because the death of his oldest son had caused the grieving King Louis to further withdraw from his duties as the leader of the upper classes.

The conversation then turned to something that sounded very odd: an oath that had been sworn a week or so ago on a tennis court in Versailles by what Richard understood to be outcast delegates of the third estate. Exactly why the delegates had been cast out, what the oath was, or what its ramifications might be—or why it was taken, of all places, on a tennis court—Richard could not determine since apparently the two men did not know themselves. When he asked, the man sitting across from Richard glanced out the window and shrugged, "*Qui sait?*"

Boredom and stifling heat coupled with curiosity about what seemed to be a continuing chorus of church bells clanging in the far distance brought Richard out of the coach. The heat was more tolerable outside, although the sun was bright and high, and a slight breeze stirred the tall grass on the gentle rise on which Richard found himself standing alongside clusters of other disgruntled passengers. They were stopped southeast of Paris. To the north, beneath a powder blue sky dotted with cotton puffs of clouds, Richard could make out tiny spires sprouting above the capital city and the deeper blue of the great river running through it. Directly below, the main artery leading into the heart of Paris was swallowed up by dense thickets of trees, though Richard could see where the road eventually led, for it broke into the open perhaps a mile farther on.

On the hill and in haphazard lines down each side were soldiers, hundreds of them, many wearing the familiar white of the regular French army, others in uniforms reminiscent of the American Continental Army: white trousers and white cross-belts, and a blue coat lined with bright scarlet on the collar and cuffs. Still others wore uniforms Richard could not identify, though he assumed the various black, yellow, and white colors represented one or more of the German states: Bavaria or Prussia, perhaps, or Saxony. Whatever their uniforms, these soldiers stood ill at ease as they stared out toward Paris, listening, as Richard was, to the bells and waiting for word. Whatever was happening down there in Paris clearly had implications for every person up there on the hillside, soldiers and civilians alike.

As Richard walked around the area, keeping a close eye on the trunk at the back of the coach in which he had stowed his baggage, he approached several officers to learn what he could. Finding himself ignored, he tried a different tack, remembering something he had read in a Toulon newspaper that was subsequently corroborated by Captain Mercier. He walked up to a young officer wearing the tricolor uniform who was studying Paris through a long glass.

"*Excusez-moi, monsieur. Votre uniforme: est-il l'uniforme de la Guarde Nationale?*"

"*Oui,*" the officer acknowledged. The way he expressed that one word and continued to peer through the glass suggested that he was not inclined to continue the conversation.

"*Ensuite, monsieur,*" Richard persisted, "*le général, le marquis de Lafayette, est-il ici?*"

The officer skewered him with a harsh glare. "You are not French," he stated in English.

The brusqueness of the observation took Richard aback. He tried an ingratiating smile. "The fact that I'm not is all too obvious around here."

The officer was not amused. "You are English?"

"No. American."

"*Américain? C'est ça?*" The man's hard Gallic features softened. "What are you, an American, doing here? And what business do you have with the marquis? Have you made his acquaintance?"

"Yes, sir, I have."

"How, may I ask?"

"I served with him in our revolution against England. He was my commanding officer."

"I see. That is most interesting, monsieur." For several moments the officer studied Richard's face, as if to confirm what his instincts were telling him. "What is your name please, monsieur?"

"Richard Cutler."

"*Très bien,* Mr. Cutler. If you will wait by your coach, I will pass word to the general. I cannot say when he will see you, or if he will see you at all."

"I understand, monsieur. *Merci.*"

The sun well along its downward arc found Richard waiting patiently by the coach. Impatience would serve no purpose, he realized. He had nowhere to go and no one to talk to, including his two traveling companions, who had finally disembarked and were pacing back and forth nearby, cursing the heat and whatever it was that was interrupting their journey.

As he waited, Richard's thoughts drifted to *Falcon*. Agreen, in command, had planned to weigh anchor three or four days after Richard departed Toulon, once final provisions had been stowed aboard and *Falcon* and her remaining crew had been cleared by local authorities. Richard dead-reckoned the schooner's progress, as he had done many times each day. Barring strong headwinds, *Falcon* should now be through the Strait of Gibraltar and approaching the Portuguese coast.

Pirate corsairs cruising those waters posed a threat, but Richard was not overly concerned. Before leaving Toulon he had posted a letter by military dispatch to Gibraltar, to apprize Jeremy of events and to request that the Mediterranean Squadron keep *Falcon* under its wing until she was safely within the Bay of Biscay. Richard had no doubt that his brother-in-law would make every effort to comply with that request.

His thoughts were drifting inevitably away from Europe toward home—to Katherine and their sons and daughter—then back again to Africa and Caleb and *Eagle*'s crew, when suddenly he heard a commotion behind him and a man shouting: "*Vous avez raison!* Richard Cutler, *ici en France!*"

Richard whirled toward the voice. Fast approaching up the gentle incline, his long stride leaving behind two soldiers struggling to keep pace with him, came Marie-Joseph-Paul-Yves-Roch-Gilbert du Motier, the marquis de Lafayette. He was dressed impeccably in a red, white, and blue uniform, his rank indicated by a tricolor cockade pinned to his bicorne hat. He came close to Richard before he removed his hat and bowed low in courtly fashion, just as Richard had watched him do when they had first met aboard *Bonhomme Richard* in Lorient a decade earlier. He took Richard's extended hand in both of his and pressed it warmly.

"*Bonjour, mon général,*" Richard greeted him, adding, with a smile, "It is good to see you again."

"The joy is mine, sir," Lafayette replied gallantly in practiced English. His leaf-green eyes took in Richard at equal height, though it came at once to Richard that height was one of the few traits they still had in common. They were of similar age, both approaching thirty, but the years since the war had been less kind to the French general. His hairline was receding, as had become evident the moment he removed his hat, and what hair remained was streaked with white. But it was his eyes that told a more distressing story. They were bloodshot and red-rimmed, and beneath them were dark shadows of fatigue. His grayish skin was etched by worry. Even when he smiled, as he was doing now, it seemed forced good cheer, strained optimism, the antithesis of the dashing young *chevalier* Richard had so admired in America who had radiated *la gloire de la guerre* as he led his men into battle. "Though I wish to God we were meeting under better circumstances," the marquis added glumly. He indicated a grove of stately oaks where they could speak in private.

"What is happening here, General?" Richard asked after they had walked away from the astonished gape of his two fellow coach passengers. "Why are we being detained? Why are there German regiments in France? And why are you wearing the uniform of the National Guard?"

Lafayette smiled. "So many questions, my friend," he said. "Alas, I have little time to answer them. I must return to my post. Still, I had to come here, for the joy of seeing you. I also came to warn you. You have chosen a bad time to travel to Paris."

"The timing was not of my choosing," Richard replied. He asked again what was happening in Paris.

"The Germans are mercenaries," Lafayette replied disgustedly to one of Richard's questions, sidestepping the more important ones. "They fight for profit. We saw them in America fighting for the British. Now we see them in France preparing to fight for our king—or rather his queen, if you believe the rumors that say it was she who invited them. Whoever is responsible, it was a very foolish thing to do. It has made the people very angry and it has made the crisis much worse. I fear the consequences will be terrible." Lafayette's gaze shifted northward. "Those bells in the distance? It is the signal that many of us in France have prayed we would never hear."

"The signal for what?"

"For the people to take to the streets. They have already sacked Les Invalides and the Abbé de Saint-Lazare. Do you understand what I am telling you, *mon ami*? The good citizens of Paris have plundered a hospital and they have looted a monastery. A monastery! A house of God!"

"Why?" Richard struggled to make sense of what Lafayette was telling him. "Why would they do such things?"

"Les Invalides? To seize weapons. Muskets, pistols, cannon, every weapon you can imagine is stored in there. I should say *was* stored in there, since the citizens have taken the forty thousand muskets to the streets. It is a hospital, yes, but also a royal arsenal. The monastery? Inside, the people believe, is grain that the priests have been hoarding for months, enough to feed many mouths. But the hospital and the monastery, these were not enough. Not for these citizens. Now they have their sights set on a bigger prize. We are informed that the Bastille is under siege."

"The Bastille? Isn't that a royal fortress?"

"It once was a fortress. Today it serves as a prison. Inside there are only six prisoners. Two have been judged insane and a third is the son of a marquis who had him put there for disobedience. But that is of minor consequence. It is not freedom for the prisoners that the citizens desire."

"What, then?" Richard was almost afraid to ask.

"Powder. For the muskets and cannon they took from Les Invalides. No arsenal in France holds more powder than the Bastille. That is why it is guarded by a hundred soldiers of the Royal Army."

"Can a hundred soldiers defend it against such a mob? *Will* they?"

Lafayette gave a typically Gallic shrug, then said, "I fear we shall soon find out."

Powder? Muskets? Cannon? Richard's brain was unwilling to grasp the ramifications. "This is not just another bread riot, is it, General." The instant he said it, he felt foolish.

Lafayette sadly shook his head. "No, my friend, this is not just another bread riot. This, God save us, is the revolution."

THE REALITY OF WHAT was happening in France became clearer to Richard the next day, July 15. His coach remained where it was—military units had cordoned off Paris, denying access or egress to anyone not on official business—but Lafayette arranged accommodations for him in his base camp after he understood Richard's purpose in going to Paris. He strongly advised him, however, to finish his business quickly and leave. He feared the worst, he told Richard, and if his fears were justified, no one in France was safe.

It was a warning Richard took seriously, given its source. Lafayette, he soon came to learn, was in a most precarious position, notwithstanding his military rank and appointment as vice president of the National Assembly. In these deeply troubled times, with the nerves of the nation shredded to ribbons, Lafayette was, at least for the moment, a leader acceptable both to the king and to those demanding that the king's power either be checked by a parliamentary body or checkmated and done away with altogether. As a marquis, scion of an old line of titled blood, he had the trust even of Marie Antoinette, a queen who publicly professed concern and sympathy for her subjects but who, the rumors accused, privately urged her husband to send troops into the National Assembly and arrest the ringleaders of the revolution. Too, she had urged him to seek military intervention from her mother, the Hapsburg Empress Maria Theresa, she who had arranged a marriage for her daughter at the tender age of fifteen to strengthen ties with France.

At the same time, honored for his service in an American army that had overthrown royal authority, Lafayette remained the third estate's champion for his widely publicized view that France should follow the American example, but with a constitutional monarchy. With the consent of the National Assembly, King Louis had recently

appointed Lafayette commander of the newly formed National
Guard, a quasi-military, quasi-police force that had the unenviable
task of preventing the French Royal Army from crushing the will
of the people, on the one hand, while on the other preventing the
will of the people from spilling over into senseless violence aimed at
France's élite.

His friend's duty was as difficult for Richard to fathom as it was for
Lafayette to execute. Here, on the outskirts of Paris, all was quiet. The
National Guard and French army units mingled, at ease with each other,
mindful of, but no longer stricken by, the sporadic gunfire and puffs of
smoke rising into the sky just a few miles away. The Bastille had fallen;
reports were filtering in that the commander of the royal garrison had
opened fire on the mob, and that in retaliation the mob had perpetrated
unspeakable acts of barbarism on the soldiers and on the commander
himself once he had yielded to the inevitable and ordered his men to
stand down. An untold number of corpses littered the streets near the
Bastille. Why, Richard wondered, was the French military doing nothing to restore order?

During a rare moment with Lafayette on the second day, the six-
teenth, Richard asked that question as the two of them sat together
outside the French general's tent.

Lafayette gave him a rueful smile. "You have never witnessed a mob
in the heat of passion, have you?" he asked.

Richard confessed that he had not.

"I thought as much. I can assure you, my friend, it is not something
you would wish to see. There is no sense to anything; violence becomes
irrational, insane. Everyone realizes it, even the rioters, but no one can
stop it; it takes on a life and purpose of its own. It is like a fire raging out
of control, and like such a fire, it must burn itself out. Marshal Broglie
of the Royal Army agrees that our intervention would make matters
worse, especially since many of my soldiers, and even some of his own,
would break ranks and join the rioters. When the riots end—which they
must do soon because people cannot sustain such rage for long—we
will go in and do what we can."

"When will that be?"

"Perhaps tomorrow. We shall see. King Louis is at Versailles, and he
has ordered his soldiers to disperse and the Germans to go home. It is
a wise decision, though he had no choice and it comes too late. When
we go in, you may go in with us. I will provide an escort to take you to

your consul, Mr. Jefferson. He is my friend and a friend of the National Assembly. He is helping the Assembly prepare a new constitution, one I have seen and one I approve. You will be safe in his company, although again I urge you to leave France as soon you can."

"Thank you, General. You have been most helpful to me, and I am glad for this opportunity to renew our friendship, whatever the circumstances. I will take your advice. My schooner should already be in Lorient. I will leave Paris after I report to Captain Jones. I must meet with him, General. I owe it to my brother, and to many others as well."

"I understand, my friend." Lafayette offered his hand. "*Bon chance, mon ami.* We have been through much together, you and I. When you return to America, I ask you to send my regards to General Washington. I love him as a father—I have named my own son George Washington Lafayette—and I was delighted to learn that he is America's first president. I would give much to see him again, but alas, that day will never come." He made to take his leave, turned back as if with an afterthought. "If I may be of further service to you during your stay in Paris, you may approach any National Guard soldier and ask for me. He will know where to find me."

ELEVEN YEARS HAD PASSED since Richard had last entered Paris. When the war with England was in its most critical stages, Richard had served as aide-de-camp to Captain John Paul Jones and had stayed in Passy in what had then served as the first American consulate in Europe. Richard had found both excitement and romance in France's capital—a city grander and more gratifying than anything his imagination had dreamed. Paris had seemed to him the cradle of civilization, a magnificent city preserving the best of its past while opening its future to the contemporary thinking of Rousseau, Voltaire, Locke, and other intellectuals busily sowing the seeds of the Enlightenment in the fertile soil of Parisian cafés and salons.

What Richard witnessed today, through the flaps of the enclosed military wagon in which he rode with two National Guardsmen, was a sight he had rarely seen during those earlier days: the actual citizens of Paris—people of humble birth dressed not in fine silks and linens and gold thread but in homespun cloth or rags, people who for centuries had remained invisible to *la haute société* as they huddled in the shadows of the great buildings rising above the broad boulevards. The

Florentine architecture, a stately reminder of the Italian influence on Parisian architecture during the glorious age of construction following the marriage of Catherine de Médicis to King Henri II three centuries earlier, remained, but Paris was today a very different place. The once invisible poor were visible everywhere now, and those in hiding were the people who for so long had disdained and tormented them. Nor did citizens avoid eye contact with Richard as they had in Lyons and other stops along the way to Paris. They stared back at him with defiance, as they did at anyone who might dare blame them for the rape and pillage of their once beautiful city.

As the covered wagon lumbered past the Louvre on its way to La Place Louis XV, Richard caught a glimpse of the Tuilleries Palace and its majestic gardens, where colorful hot-air balloons had once enticed the well-to-do to pay for lofty rides over Paris on warm summer afternoons. As he looked out, a wave of fond remembrance washed over him. It was here, at the Théâtre de la Nation, that he and Anne-Marie had attended a performance of *The Barber of Seville,* a play by Beaumarchais performed by the Comédie Française. It had been her gift to him on his eighteenth birthday, and he smiled at the recollection. They had stayed only through the first act in the private alcove Anne-Marie had reserved for them before rising in a mutual desire to return to the privacy of her château in Passy. In the intervening years he had not forgotten her or that night, or the nights that followed until duty and his captain commanded him back to his ship. He had not seen her since, but the memory of her remained forever tucked away in that secret refuge of the mind where life's most cherished memories are kept.

The military wagon had approached Paris from the south to avoid the area around the Bastille on the Right Bank, where remnants of rioting lingered, as well as the Hôtel de Ville, where thousands of Parisians had gathered to cheer King Louis for ordering the German regiments out of France. They thus avoided the sight of angry citizens dismantling the Bastille brick by brick and the spectacle of dead bodies heaped one on top of another in horse-drawn carts. The rank smell of the dead fouled the air nonetheless, and the stench turned Richard's stomach. Or perhaps it was just the thought of those putrefying corpses, their rotting flesh food for rabid, half-starved dogs.

Suddenly there came a sharp *bang!* against the wooden base of the wagon, followed by another and another and another. The two horses reared up as the driver pulled hard on the reins, causing the wagon to shudder and lift, throwing Richard and the two soldiers off the plank on which they had been sitting and into crates of what had been neatly stacked supplies. Cursing, Richard got to his knees and crawled to the back of the wagon. He pulled aside the canvas flap to see a knot of young boys, several not yet in their teens, running away—needlessly, for there was no one in pursuit. Hurling rocks at a military wagon, an offense that a week ago would have been dealt with severely, was today *une petite délinquance.*

When the wagon arrived at 19, avenue des Champs-Élysées, the wagon creaked to a halt in front of a three-story gray building of modest yet attractive design. The three rectangular windows facing the avenue on each of the upper two floors were embraced by blue wooden shutters on each side and intricate black ironwork beneath. Above the red mansard roof fluttered the stars and stripes of the American flag.

The driver glanced back at Richard. "*Nous sommes arrivés,*" he said, adding, as if in apology for the broadside of rocks, "*Je regrette le dérangement, monsieur.*"

"*Pas de quoi,*" Richard said, stepping down. A National Guard soldier handed him his sea bag and satchel, and the driver flicked the reins. As the wagon rumbled on, Richard walked up the shrub-lined pathway to the front of the building and knocked on the door.

His knock was answered by a liveried servant wearing a glossy red coat and a white peruke, its long strands tied back at the nape of his neck with a black silk bow. The man did not step aside and offer entrance, but instead remained standing in the doorway, his eyes asking who this visitor was and what he wanted.

"*Bonjour,*" Richard said. "*Je m'appelle Richard Cutler. Je suis américain et je viens pour voir Monsieur Jefferson.*"

"*Très bien, Monsieur Cutler,*" the footman replied deferentially. "*Attendez ici pour un moment, s'il vous plaît.*"

His footsteps clicked across the black-and-white-tiled floor until he reached a door at the far end of the hallway, on which he knocked and announced the visitor. The door opened and a man emerged. Even at that distance Richard could see that he was tall—taller than himself— and appeared gangly, gawky even. He was dressed in a suit of brown cloth that at first blush did not seem to fit him properly. But that impression vanished as the man began walking toward him. It was his smile that first captivated Richard, so open and sincere, but he quickly noted the man's handsome patrician features—long face, thin lips, and aquiline nose—and the easy, fluid way he walked. He was, Richard knew, in his middle fifties, married with two daughters, and came from Charlottesville, Virginia. That was almost all he knew about the man, except that he had served as American minister to France since taking the reins from Benjamin Franklin.

"Good day, Mr. Jefferson," Richard said. He removed his tricorne hat and bowed from the waist. "I am Richard Cutler. I trust you have received my letters?"

"I have indeed, Mr. Cutler," Jefferson replied in the aristocratic accent of Tidewater Virginia, "and I am relieved to see that you have arrived safely. That, in and of itself, is no small feat. I have received three letters from you, and I am holding a number of others on your behalf. No doubt you wish to review them. But first, if you are agreeable, I was just having a cup of chocolate with an acquaintance. You are most welcome to join us. I'll have the letters and your baggage sent upstairs to your room while we chat. I am eager to hear what you have to report."

Richard was struck by what Jefferson had just said. "You are offering me lodging, sir? Here, in your home?"

"By all means, Mr. Cutler. My home, as you refer to it, serves as the American consulate in Paris. You are an American, are you not? On a mission for our country? Then of course you are most welcome to stay here. Had you alternative lodgings in mind?"

Richard hesitated. It was an obvious question, but he lacked an obvious answer because the person he had hoped to stay with had not replied to his messages. "I had thought perhaps with Captain Jones," he said.

"Yes, I see. That would be a possibility were Captain Jones in sufficient health to receive you in that capacity. I am sorry to report that he is not. Do not be overly concerned; he is most anxious to see you. But the poor man has not been well recently. I believe it is nothing serious, but since he refuses to see a doctor, one cannot be certain." Jefferson sent the footman upstairs with Richard's bag and satchel and motioned to Richard to follow him down the hall. "Perhaps you will understand better after you see him. Tomorrow morning, perhaps?"

"I had hoped to visit him today," Richard said frankly.

"That I cannot permit, Mr. Cutler," Jefferson said with equal frankness. "It is a long walk across the river to his lodging, and it would be dark before you could return. Surely you have seen for yourself that the streets of Paris are not safe during the daytime, let alone at night. Allow me to send a messenger to him announcing your visit in the morning. Shall we say ten o'clock?"

Richard nodded his assent and allowed himself to be led into a room that apparently served as Jefferson's study. Three of the four walls were lined with books, many with gold-blocked spines, and most appearing in mint condition, either recently published or, if not, long in the care of a bibliophile. Brightly colored oil paintings of wildflowers and rural landscapes graced the walls above the shelves. On the right was a desk holding an inkwell, quills, and neatly stacked papers. In the center of the room was a round table with four chairs drawn up to it. On one of them sat a man with many of Jefferson's physical attributes, except that he wore a peg leg attached by leather straps to his thigh and knee. Despite this infirmity, he rose with surprising agility when Richard entered the room.

"Mr. Morris," Jefferson said, "allow me to introduce Richard Cutler, from Boston. You may recall my mentioning his recent voyage to Algiers. He has come from there to share information with Captain Jones, who, as you know, is our president's choice to lead a delegation to the Barbary States. Mr. Cutler, this gentleman is Mr. Gouverneur Morris. He is our commercial attaché here in Paris, an office I held when I first came to France in '84. He will continue in that position after I have returned to Philadelphia to serve as President Washington's secretary of state."

"Congratulations, Mr. Jefferson," Richard said. "I had heard rumors to that effect, and I am pleased to learn they are true. And I am honored to meet you, Mr. Morris," he added, bowing courteously to the richly attired man. "Your reputation precedes you. As you may know, my family is engaged in the carrying trade. We appreciate what you have done to promote American commerce overseas."

"That is generous of you, Mr. Cutler," Morris said, retaking his seat, "most generous indeed. And you are most welcome. You clearly understand that I best serve my country by serving your family's interests. I have long maintained that commerce holds the key to our prosperity as a young nation."

"I could not agree more, sir," Richard countered, "especially if our young nation is prepared to invest in a navy to protect our commerce."

"Here, here," Jefferson said, clapping his hands. "It seems we three are of equal mind on that score. You may be assured, Mr. Cutler, that I will be advancing that position once I hold office. Now then, please be seated. May I offer you a cup of chocolate?"

"I'd prefer tea if it's no trouble."

"No trouble whatsoever."

Jefferson made a small gesture to the liveried servant, who bowed and departed. He returned a few minutes later with a silver tray on which was set an elegant silver pot with three tiny legs at its base and a straight wooden handle opposite its spout. The servant poured tea into a porcelain cup and placed little bowls of cream and sugar nearby. He then bowed and took his leave, gently closing the door behind him.

"I must say, Mr. Jefferson," Richard commented after he had sampled the tea, "the atmosphere in here is very different from what it is outside. Did you happen to witness the recent riots?"

"No, I did not. Mr. Morris was with me that day, and we thought it wise not to venture out. This uprising is a nasty business, Mr. Cutler. God alone knows how, where, and when it will end. I have lived in Paris for five years now, and during those years I have grown to love this city. I cannot tell you how deeply it saddens me to watch it disintegrate at the hands of a mob."

"I met General Lafayette on my way into Paris," Richard informed him. "He told me that many people in the third estate are hoping to establish a new form of government much like our own."

"Yes, I have often heard that said. The general may also have told you that I have been invited on several occasions to express my opinions on a new manifesto. It's called the Declaration of the Rights of Man and of the Citizen, and it was introduced to the National Constituent Assembly by Lafayette. This manifesto is fashioned after our own Bill of Rights, so I suppose we should be flattered. But there is one thing that people tend to overlook in contemplating an American basis for a new government in France. We Americans fought the British. The French are fighting themselves. It's a critical distinction."

Richard understood that distinction, but to him it did not seem so critical. Before the revolution that carved America out of the British Empire, the vast majority of Americans were, after all, British. To his mind, the American Revolution was just as much a civil war as the looming French Revolution would be, and just as much a war fought for principles and ideas rather than for territory and commercial advantage.

"Personally, I agree with Mr. Jefferson," Morris cut in, warming to the subject, "though perhaps I would take what he said a step further. To be frank, I do not believe that the French can duplicate our republican form of government. And they have no business overthrowing their king. I favor what Lafayette favors, a constitutional monarchy based on the British model."

Richard nodded, then shifted the topic of conversation toward the subject uppermost on his mind. "Mr. Jefferson, Mr. Morris," he said, "please do not think me rude. You have been most kind in receiving me today. But since I have little time in Paris, I must be blunt. In Algiers, I was unable to ransom my brother and other Americans held there. There were a number of reasons for that, most of them, perhaps, outside anyone's control. But I was informed there, by the dey himself when I was brought before him in the royal palace, that you, Mr. Jefferson, have let it be known that the United States henceforth will not pay ransoms to Algiers or any of the Barbary States, or treat with them under any circumstances. Is that truly your position, sir? And will that be your position as secretary of state? If so, there can be no dialogue with these people. Captain Jones will have failed in his mission before he leaves Paris. I mean no disrespect in asking such questions. But it is imperative to me, as I am sure it is to Captain Jones, that our government's position be clarified. My brother's life is at stake, as are the lives of many American sailors."

Jefferson frowned. He placed his cup of chocolate delicately back on its matching saucer as Morris said: "It appears, Mr. Cutler, that you have no difficulty coming straight to the point."

"Forgive me, sir, but I have no choice. I am meeting with Captain Jones tomorrow and I will be leaving Paris the following day. I have no time for diplomacy or genteel discourse."

Jefferson uttered a sharp laugh. "*Time* for diplomacy, Mr. Cutler? I believe what you mean to say is, there is no *opportunity* for diplomacy in this topsy-turvy world, here or anywhere else. But no matter. I can see that you are disappointed with me and I understand why." Richard drew a breath to temper the word "disappointed," but was waved off. "I admit I may have made an error in diplomacy," Jefferson continued, "but I stand by my position. I had hoped, in saying what I did, that the Barbary States would do exactly what you want them to do: stop seizing our ships and imprisoning our sailors. If they were convinced that our government would not parlay with theirs and would pay no ransoms under any circumstances, then what would be the advantage of taking hostages, especially if other nations were to follow our lead? Representatives of several other nations have assured me they will, if we have the courage to use this weapon. France and England have declined, which should come as no surprise. France is distracted by internal issues at the moment, and England is quite content to let the Arabs continue to wash their dirty linen for them."

"By 'dirty linen' I assume you mean attacking our commerce to destroy competition," Richard said, echoing the words of Captain Dickerson in Algiers.

"Exactly. I admit I may have been naïve in my choice of words," Jefferson went on, his voice rising, his inborn southern gentility giving way to steely resolve, "but I stand by my conviction that negotiating with pirates and paying them tribute is not only foolish, it is counterproductive. I realize that not everyone agrees with me. Mr. Jay does not. Nor do Mr. Adams and Mr. Hamilton. They maintain it is cheaper to pay tribute than to build a strong navy. God's mercy, Mr. Cutler, how naïve is *that*? You ask for my position as secretary of state? Here it is: I may uphold the rights of the individual states, but America, as a nation of states, must build a navy that can and will confront any nation that seeks to meddle in our affairs. A single broadside of cannon will do more to protect our interests than millions of dollars in tribute. I apologize if your brother has suffered as a result of what I said. But I submit to you that your brother and your commerce and your country will prosper far more, in the long haul, if governments will stop mollycoddling these pirates and start fighting them!"

Richard was astonished to hear Jefferson espouse a view that could just as well have been advanced by his father-in-law, as crusty and ornery a hard-liner as the Royal Navy ever loosed upon the sea. During the war with England, when prices charged to England for ship's stores began to skyrocket, Captain Hardcastle's solution was to dispatch a fleet of battle cruisers to Stockholm and blast the Swedish capital to kingdom come. Such action, he thundered, would bring down prices, by God, and quickly.

"No apologies required, sir," Richard said, realizing that he had been put roundly in his place; realizing also that President Washington had selected the right man to manage America's foreign affairs.

The conversation veered to more practical matters regarding Algiers. As it continued over a supper of chicken fricassee, greens, and two bottles of claret, the turmoil and despair of Paris just outside the door seemed a world apart. Jefferson and Morris were keen to learn about Richard's voyage to North Africa via Gibraltar, and thence to Toulon, especially the details of the sea battle with the two Arab xebecs, an account that sent a servant scurrying down to the wine cellar for a third bottle. Richard related as much as he could remember to his hosts that evening, as he had months ago to Captain Mercier in Toulon, and as he would tomorrow to Captain Jones.

LATER THAT EVENING, his mind besotted with fatigue and wine, Richard excused himself for the night and climbed the stairways winding up to his lodgings on the third floor of the consulate. It was a snug room with a high ceiling to mitigate the effects of summer heat and humidity. The twin windows had been pushed outward, allowing the moist breeze to ruffle the yellow lace curtains and circulate the muggy air within. Richard walked to a window and listened. His senses came alert at what he first took to be cannon fire but which turned out to be a distant roll of thunder. On this night, at least, Paris seemed at peace.

On the oaken dresser table next to his bed, three candles burned brightly, revealing the large leather satchel Thomas Jefferson had told him would be there, thick and heavy with letters from home. Richard opened the satchel, removed the letters, and placed them on the bed in appropriate piles according to recipient. Every member of his crew had at least two letters, even those, Richard noted with remorse, who were no longer alive to read them. The dates inscribed on them indicated that some of the letters had been written almost a year ago.

The largest pile belonged to Agreen. Each of the letters in his stack was written in the familiar cursive of Lizzy Cutler and carefully numbered, one to twenty-two, each number circled in red. Richard almost laughed as he counted them. "Think she'll have you, Agee?" he asked out loud. He waved the pile of letters back and forth in the air. "Here's your answer, my friend."

He flipped through his own pile of letters. Most were from Katherine, and he ached to read them. But he opened first a letter from his father dated 15 May, just two months ago.

"*Dear Richard,*" it began, "*your letter written from Toulon arrived yesterday. Your mother and I feel your remorse in every word. There are no words to send you that will ease your sorrow and frustration. I wish there were. I can only assure you that no one here blames you for what happened, least of all your parents. It was the will of God. You did everything you could.*" The letter went on to say that everyone was well at home except for Richard's mother, who had endured another round of physical suffering over the winter. She was better now, as she normally was come spring, though her health remained fragile. "*Lavinia and Anne ask me to send their love to you and will be writing letters of their own. Please send our family's respects to Mr. Jefferson and to Captain Jones, and sail home to us when you are able. God in His mercy will watch over us all."*

"Thank you, Father," Richard whispered, his words catching in his throat. He glanced at his letters strewn out atop the bed. True to his father's prediction, Lavinia and Anne had both written him—to add their support to their father's words, Richard was certain: he knew his sisters that well. But it was the fourteen letters from Katherine that he opened next. He read them in chronological order, starting with the letter dated the day after *Falcon* sailed from Boston.

Each of the long letters—five, six, seven pages—was written in the form of a diary, the events or impressions of one group of days added on to those that preceded it. Clearly it was her intent to keep her husband informed of what she was doing and, more important, what his sons and daughter were doing, on a daily basis, as though he were there with them in Hingham and she was simply recounting for his benefit those often mundane events of a child's life that have meaning only to a parent, and those character-defining decisions that only a parent can make.

Richard smiled longingly, grateful for the love of a woman who after nearly a decade of marriage took such care keeping him involved in the daily lives of his children, even with him half a world away. *"You are in Paris as you read this,"* she concluded in her last letter, dated May 18. *"You will meet with Captain Jones and then, God willing, you will be returning home to us. Will, Jamie, and Diana send their dearest love, as do I, my darling husband. You are forever in my thoughts, forever in my prayers, forever in my heart. Katherine"*

Thirteen

Paris, France, July 1789

RICHARD HAD TO WALK the nearly two miles from the American consulate to the building where John Paul Jones lived on the Left Bank. Public conveyance was not available. The hackney coaches that had once graced the Champs-Élysées and rue de Rivoli no longer conveyed better-off Parisians to the Tuilleries Gardens for a stroll or to the open-air food stalls at Les Halles. The élite these days did not rendezvous at the Palais-Royal, a festive hub of restaurants, gambling dens, and theaters opened to the public not long ago by its royal proprietor, the duc d'Orléans, in a desperate attempt to stave off financial ruin. Today its cafés and private clubs sat deserted, as forlorn and cheerless as the once-bustling boulevards where jugglers, drink peddlers, illusion-show aficionados, and animal-fight hawkers had regaled the crowds while hurdy-gurdy players cranked out their jangling tunes.

Adding to the gloom of the day was a heavy mist, the aftermath of a summer storm that had rumbled through Paris during the night, spreading in its wake a muggy shroud of gray over the buildings and bridges, the public bathhouses along the banks of the river, even the stained-glass magnificence of Notre Dame. By the time Richard had crossed over the Seine, the white cotton shirt he was wearing under his coat clung to his skin and sweat oozed from under his black felt tricorne hat. He dared not doff the hat. That morning, before allowing him to leave the consulate, Thomas Jefferson had pinned a rosette on the front of Richard's hat with a warning to keep it visible at all times.

That simple clump of blue, white, and red ribbons identified him as
un partisan of the National Assembly; without it, Gouverneur Morris
had added his own warning, the knife and small pistol Richard had
concealed on his person would hardly be sufficient to keep the human
wolves at bay.

Jones' residence was located east of the Luxembourg Palace, a grand
Florentine establishment that served as the Left Bank's equivalent of the
Right's Tuilleries Palace. On another day, in another era, Richard would
have enjoyed walking through these cramped city neighborhoods that,
he suspected, had changed little since the early Middle Ages. There was
no spring to his step this morning, however. Not with the eyes of Paris
upon him. Those eyes were everywhere—in bread lines, in windows, in
the dark shadows of doorways—scrutinizing everyone who appeared
different or well-to-do. People did not shout at him or taunt him; that
sort of innocuous human behavior he could have tolerated with equa-
nimity. What unnerved him was their ominous silence, their menacing
glares transmitting incomprehensible depths of hatred, resentment, and
anger. For the first time ever in Paris, Richard felt panic niggling at his
gut, and he had to force himself to slow down, to appear nonchalant,
to deny the wolves the smell of fear. When finally he rounded onto the
rue de Tournon, it was with considerable relief that he climbed the short
flight of steps leading up to number 52, and thence upstairs to the *pre-
mier étage* where he knocked on a door on the left side.

"Enter," a familiar voice commanded from within. Richard might
have been entering the after cabin of *Bonhomme Richard* to report to
his captain as officer of the watch, except that here there was no steward puttering in the pantry, no green-coated marine standing at ramrod
attention outside with a musket held at his side.

Richard clicked open the door, and there sat John Paul Jones on a
high-backed chair of pastel blue and yellow, turned partly toward the
entryway. Nearby was a second chair of similar pattern and design, and,
between the chairs, a rectangular library table. Richard's gaze quickly
took in Jones and a room reminiscent of the one where they had first
met back in '77 in the Hingham residence of Benjamin Lincoln. It had
the same crowded bookshelves, the same sort of rug and couch and
hearth and writing desk, the same snug feeling of home. So sharp was
the remembrance that Richard half-expected Lincoln's faithful servant,
Caleb, in whose honor Richard's brother had been named, to material-
ize behind him to take his coat and hat.

"Richard, my boy!" Jones boomed. Instantly he was assailed by a hacking cough. When the coughing subsided he said, in a voice much subdued and raspy, "It gives me great joy to see you this day."

As Jones struggled to rise, Richard noted with concern the swelling in his legs and the yellow hue of his skin. Such signs of affliction would have seemed foreign to the intrepid sea captain who had saluted him farewell from the quarterdeck of the captured British frigate *Serapis,* hove to in enemy waters off the cliffs of Dover until Richard had been delivered ashore. Yet evidence of the officer and gentleman remained: his reddish brown hair might be streaked with gray, but it was neatly combed back and tied at the nape with a perfectly formed black bow. And he was impeccably dressed, from the white silk of his neck stock to the dark green cotton of his waistcoat and knee-breeches to the finely polished silver buckles on his black leather shoes. He still appeared to Richard every bit the naval officer he had known those many years ago: a man born to command wherever duty and destiny required it of him.

"It brings me greater joy, Captain." Without hesitation he walked up to Jones and embraced him as a son would his father, an act of open affection that took Jones momentarily aback. "Or should I address you as 'Admiral'?"

He was referring to the rank of rear admiral bestowed upon Jones by Her Most Catholic Majesty Catherine the Second, Tsarina of Russia. Three years ago, fed up with the U.S. government's reluctance to invest in a navy, Jones had accepted the invitation from Empress Catherine to join her Black Sea fleet in an attack against the crumbling Ottoman Empire. That fleet, under the titular command of a Romanov prince, Admiral Potemkin, was vested with wresting Constantinople away from the Muslim Turks who had occupied the city for three centuries. Having liberated the Christians there, the empress expected to receive, as just compensation for doing God's work, a warm-water port for her navy and an outlet to the Mediterranean Sea.

Once aboard the Russian flagship, Jones had quickly concluded that Potemkin had no future as a naval commander. It took considerable effort and tact to convince Potemkin that Russia would be better served were he to hand over the reins of commander in chief to Jones, advice the reluctant prince finally accepted. At the Battle of Liman, having secretly reconnoitered the enemy fleet the night before from a rowboat, Jones destroyed fifteen enemy warships while killing three thousand Turks and taking sixteen hundred prisoners—all at the cost of one

Russian frigate and eighteen Russian sailors. When reports of the stunning victory reached the capital, all Russia rejoiced except for one man, Prince Potemkin, who, stung by what he deemed a usurpation of glory rightfully his, publicly accused Jones of molesting a ten-year-old girl in Saint Petersburg. Disgusted and disillusioned, Jones left Russia as soon as the charges were dropped and returned to Paris, where details of his heroic adventures were widely published.

Jones shot Richard a mock frown. "Then it would be Kontradmiral Pavel Ivanovich Jones, if you please, Lieutenant."

As Richard bowed low in mock deference to such grandeur, Jones slapped him on the shoulder and laughed out loud, an act that set off another round of harsh coughing. He groped for the arms of his wing-back chair and sat down, motioning to Richard to do the same. He removed a white handkerchief from a waistcoat pocket and held it against his mouth until the coughing had quieted.

"Forgive me, Richard," he said weakly. "I can't seem to shake this illness, try as I may. I am disciplining myself not to get overagitated or to talk too loudly. I do better if I keep calm—which as you know better than anyone is a type of behavior that does not come naturally to me." He cleared his throat and spat into the kerchief. "Now, then, to answer your question, 'Captain Jones' will do just fine, thank you. While I may admire the courage of Russian sailors, I am most proud of my service to our country. On that service may my life be judged." He glanced at what he had coughed up, which Richard could see was flecked with blood, then folded the handkerchief and replaced it in its pocket.

"Have you seen a doctor, Captain?" Richard asked, certain that he already knew the answer.

Jones shook his head. "I'd sooner face a mosque full of fanatic Muslim imams babbling to Allah than the ministrations of one French doctor."

"Even so," Richard persisted, "that doctor might be able to prescribe something to help you recover."

Jones waved that idea away, and with it the entire French medical profession. "Speaking of fanatical Arabs," he said, "we've something to discuss along those lines, do we not? But first, catch me up a little. What mischief have you been up to these past few years? Sailing the high seas, I presume, and making babies with that lovely wife of yours. Talk about piracy, sir," he chuckled, "snatching her away from Captain Horatio Nelson himself, one of the most esteemed officers in the Royal Navy, whilst he was on his way to the altar. What a feat!"

Richard grinned. "It wasn't quite like that, sir," he said. "As Fate would have it, I had occasion to visit Captain Nelson in Antigua not long ago. I hope that someday you two will have the opportunity to meet. You have a lot in common. As to my married life, Katherine and I now have three children: two sons, Will and Jamie, and a daughter, Diana."

"Congratulations. Will was the name of your older brother, as I recall."

"Yes, sir."

"And Jamie was Katherine's brother, the midshipman who saved your life on the deck of *Serapis.*"

"Yes, sir."

"Well, that explains why you didn't name one of your sons 'John Paul.' I was about to be offended. British newspapers gave that story quite a run. I read about it in Holland, after I saw you off at Dover. A very moving account, I must say. The British press made both you and Jamie out to be heroes. That account fueled considerable antiwar sentiment in England, in Parliament especially."

"So I understand."

Jones coughed lightly into his fist and was about to offer a further comment when there came a light rap on the door. Jones checked his waistcoat watch. "Enter," he called out.

The door opened and an elderly woman dressed in a simple ankle-length brown dress, olive-colored shoulder wrap, and white apron walked into the room. The white mobcap on her head covered all but fringes of her silver hair, and she stood before them slightly stooped as she gently wrung her long, gnarled fingers and flashed inquisitive eyes about the room, settling them on Richard for several awkward moments.

"*Bonjour,* Carlotta," Jones greeted her. "*Ponctuelle comme d'habitude, n'est-ce pas?* Richard, this is my housekeeper, Carlotta. She cleans and cooks and darns for me four mornings a week. I'd be hard-pressed without her, though she speaks little English and my French, I regret to say, is not much better today than it was yesterday."

"*Bonjour, madame,*" Richard greeted her cordially.

She inclined her head at him but offered no word in reply.

"*Merci,* Carlotta," Jones added, dismissing her to her duties when she seemed to hesitate.

Richard watched as she disappeared off to the left into the kitchen. "Did you see the way she looked at me?" he whispered. "I don't think she trusts me."

Jones shrugged and smiled. "Take no offense, Richard. She means nothing by it. No one trusts anyone in Paris these days. Not since the fall of the Bastille." He gave Richard a contemplative look and let it linger there, as though he were weighing the pros and cons of something. "No doubt you have heard what happened at the Bastille?"

"A little, yes. I arrived outside Paris on the fourteenth, and I was fortunate to come across General Lafayette. He offered me transport to the American consulate two days later."

"I'm not surprised. General Lafayette was always very fond of you."

"The feeling is mutual." Richard glanced toward the kitchen. "What is going to happen in Paris, Captain?" he asked sotto voce, still feeling the eyes of the city upon him.

Jones cleared his throat, coughing after he did so. "I can't predict the future any better than you can," he responded. "But of this I am certain: the monarchy cannot survive as it is currently constituted. King Louis may defend the divine right of kings, but I assure you there is nothing divine about the man or his rule, or even much that is admirable. About the only thing he does these days with any sort of proficiency is stuff his gullet. Did you happen to see him at the Hôtel de Ville? No? I didn't either, but from what I hear he's become so fat it's a wonder his pants don't split. But as bad as he might be, his queen is far worse. Versailles is a *grand bateau* of pomp and ceremony, Richard, floating upon a sea of misery and despair. This country is bankrupt in every sense of the word, and Marie Antoinette is first in line to claim responsibility. The people still seem to abide their king. But they despise their queen. They call her 'Madame Deficit' in addition to other, less flattering epithets."

"Will the monarchy fall?"

"In my opinion, yes, it will. And I say good riddance to it. One would think that the nobles would be doing everything they can to save it, did they find it worth saving. Apparently they don't. They are on the run, like rats from a sinking ship. Except that these rats once ruled from the quarterdeck. Even the comte d'Artois, the king's brother, has fled to Holland. That should tell you something."

"What happens to a nobleman caught trying to flee?"

Jones shrugged. "There are rumors that certain aristocrats have been arrested and never seen again. Other rumors insist that aristocrats have a new method of execution awaiting them, a machine of death designed by a member of the National Assembly, a doctor named Guillotin. True or not, these rumors offer a rather gruesome picture of just how much the French people have come to hate their nobles and clergy."

"What about the army? Are its soldiers still loyal to the king?"

"Some are; some aren't. The fact is, French soldiers will do whatever Lafayette commands them to do. They'll follow him against any general in France, and that includes Marshal Broglie, the king's commander in chief. Since you met with Lafayette, you are no doubt aware that he favors a constitutional monarchy. That's a giant step down from royal absolutism, and less of a step up from republicanism. In any event, you may be assured that Lafayette would never wage war against his own people. He loves his country too much. And he certainly would not fight to save the dainty white derrière of an Austrian-born queen."

Richard asked, going to what for him was a critical issue, "If that's true, Captain, are you not in danger yourself? I understand from Mr. Jefferson that you have been awarded the status of *chevalier.*"

"I have. And I have the sword King Louis presented to me to prove it." He pointed toward the wall where a finely polished, gold-hilted ceremonial sword hung horizontally above the writing desk. "She's a beauty, eh? Have a closer look if you'd like. You can test your Latin on the phrase engraved on the blade. I had to have it translated for me."

Richard gave the sword an appreciative glance. "But that makes you a nobleman, does it not?"

Jones smiled condescendingly as he held out his arms. "Look around you, Richard. Does this look like the grand salon of a château? Am I a lord overseeing his estates?" He chuckled at the very thought of it. "No, to the French people I am simply Captain Jones of the Continental Navy, defender of the faith and slayer of the British lion. The French people may hate their nobles, but they hate the British more. Nothing will change that, no matter what form of government may emerge from the mists. May it ever be so. It's my best protection.

"Now, then," he said, "I want to hear about Algiers. Later, we'll return to the Bastille. I suspect something is missing from the accounts you've heard thus far, and I feel it my duty to tell you what it is. But for now, may I suggest a mug of ale? You may be surprised to learn that I've developed quite a taste for it. It helps soothe my throat."

He called out to Carlotta, who appeared shortly from the kitchen carrying a salver with two tall pewter mugs of ale. She placed the tray on the rectangular table and returned to whatever it was she had been doing. Jones took a healthy swig of the frothy liquid and settled back in his chair. "That's better," he sighed. "Right, Richard, go to it. I've done all the talking thus far. Now it's your turn. Tell me about Algiers."

Two hours later Richard had told Jones everything he could recall; most of it was also detailed in the written report he had brought with him: his conversations with Jeremy Hardcastle in Gibraltar, his audience with the dey of Algiers, his impressions of the city of Algiers and its defenses, the disturbing allegations related to him by Caleb and Captain Dickerson, his cruise northward across the Mediterranean, and what information he had gleaned from Captain Mercier and others in Toulon. Coughing only sporadically, Jones listened with rapt attention, especially to the details of the battle with the two xebecs and the destruction wreaked by the three fire-arrows. He sipped his ale, offering no comment until Richard had withdrawn some folded papers from his satchel. After transferring the tray from the table to the floor, he spread those sheets out between them. Each was an intricate depiction of Algiers drawn by the hand of Peter Chatfield.

"These are well done," Jones said as he perused the drawings a second time. "Extremely well done. I should like to meet the artist."

"I'm afraid that's not possible, Captain. He died in the naval hospital in Toulon of wounds he received in the battle."

"I see." Apparently Jones had caught the anguish in Richard's voice, for his tone turned sympathetic. "I am sorry for your loss, Richard. And I'm sorry for mine. I had hoped I might persuade you to join me on my mission to Barbary. Now that is not possible. I doubt the dey of Algiers would want to negotiate peace terms with an American schooner captain who had the temerity to run out his guns and destroy two of Islam's finest warships." He said that not as a reprimand, but with the pride of a father who has witnessed his son's mastery of a special skill he had taught him.

Richard nodded his understanding. "When do you expect to depart, sir?" he asked when Jones fell silent, seemingly preoccupied with the ramifications of Richard's report.

Jones glanced up. "As soon as Jefferson is installed as secretary of state, which I think will be soon. A ship is sailing from America to Brest in mid-October to take my delegation to Morocco. From there we will sail to Algiers, where the real negotiations will take place. I have been informed that representatives from Tunis and Tripoli will be attending."

"Can we send word of this to the prisoners in Algiers? It would boost their morale."

"I think so, and so, apparently, does Mr. Jefferson. He has discussed this very issue with the Spanish ambassador, who has agreed to intervene with bin Osman on our behalf."

"I am glad to hear it, Captain." Richard was surprised by Jefferson's cooperation in the matter, given his stand on peace negotiations. "Is there anything else I can tell you? Anything I might have omitted?"

"No, I don't believe so," Jones said. "You have done a commendable job, and I thank you for your report. My only regret, aside from not having the pleasure of your company and your rather odd sense of humor on my cruise to Barbary, is not knowing what effect your little escapade at sea will have on our negotiations. Or on the prisoners, should bin Osman decide to exact his revenge on them. You have given that matter some thought, I presume?"

"I have indeed, Captain. Many times."

"And what have you concluded?"

"Forgive me if I sound naïve, but I don't believe the prisoners are in greater danger as a result of that battle. I believe the opposite is true, that they are in less danger. Bin Osman realizes that negotiations are imminent. Why would he jeopardize what he regards as an advantageous negotiating position by harming his captives? Are they not worth more to him in good physical condition? His interests are served by making it appear as though his prisoners have been well treated. The greater concern, as I see it, is that you will not be granted the funds you need to pay whatever ransoms you are able to negotiate. Mr. Jefferson is dead set against paying any sort of tribute to anyone, or even negotiating with the Arabs under these circumstances."

"He has told me that himself," Jones conceded. "And I must say that under normal circumstances I would agree with him. But these are not normal circumstances. In any case, he seems to be relenting a bit in private, whatever he might say in public. Political pressure from home," Jones explained to Richard's quizzical look. "Freedom for our sailors has become quite the issue in the American press. Citizens put pressure on Congress, Congress puts pressure on the president, Washington puts pressure on Jefferson, and around it goes. My prediction? These atrocities in the Mediterranean will finally persuade our government to invest in a navy. I've been pounding that drum for years, and people are beginning to listen—people who matter, people who can get things done."

"God grant you are right, Captain," Richard said.

"And it could be," Jones said, "that your victory at sea might actually help keep whatever ransoms we have to pay at a reasonable level.

The last thing bin Osman wants is other nations following your example. I'm betting he'll want to conclude the negotiations as quickly as possible and get on with business."

When neither of them seemed to have anything further to add to the subject, Richard steered the conversation back to Paris. "You said there was something you wanted to tell me about the Bastille, Captain?"

"Yes, I did." Jones did not look at Richard as he answered. He stared instead at the wall directly across from him, as though deep in thought. At length he placed his hands resolutely on the armrests of his chair. "Help me up, would you? I get cramps when I sit for too long and I need to stretch my legs. Let's walk over to that window and see what's outside, shall we?"

Richard rose from his chair and put a hand under his former commander's elbow. Jones rose slowly to his feet. After taking several tentative steps, he began walking with more assurance toward an open window at the far end of the room. On the way there, Richard happened to glance into the kitchen. Carlotta was standing at the opposite end of a table littered with white flour and other ingredients, a bread board, and some bread pans. When he looked in at her, she quickly dropped her gaze and went back to kneading a lump of dough.

Outside, the mist and fog had cleared, and the breeze wafting in through the open window was fresher, less humid. Across the street they could see a four-story building capped with a blue slate roof. At its base, huddled in a heap against the dirty brick wall, was a woman dressed in coarse gray cloth. She was nursing a baby while an older child, a boy, judging by the narrow-brimmed hat he was wearing, rested his head on her knee. Approaching them was a young woman clearly of the upper class riding piggy-back on a man bent over by her weight.

Jones followed Richard's gaze. "He's a gutter-leaper," he explained, and they watched as the man paused in the middle of the street, balancing himself before jumping over a two-foot-wide channel running freely with human and animal waste mixed with rainwater. "Charming profession, isn't it? I wouldn't mind having a go at it myself, were all my passengers as buxom as that one."

Richard grinned at the mental image.

When the young woman was deposited on the other side of the street, near where the woman was feeding her baby, she deposited a coin in the gutter-leaper's hand. "Chivalry lives on," Jones commented wryly, "at a price." His tone then turned deadly serious, as did the look he gave Richard.

"What exactly do you know about what happened at the Bastille?"

Richard shrugged. "Not a lot. A thousand people marched there and demanded that the royal garrison surrender. They were armed with muskets and cannon taken from an army arsenal. Les Invalides, as I recall. Their goal, they claimed, was to free the prisoners. But according to General Lafayette, what they really wanted was to destroy this symbol of feudal authority and seize the powder stored inside."

"Lafayette is correct. Go on."

"At first, the governor of the Bastille refused to surrender. He ordered his troops to fire on the crowd. Some people were killed. He sent word to the mob that he would personally blow up the Bastille if they didn't disperse. Since something close to twenty thousand pounds of gunpowder was stored inside, that was no small threat."

"That's not exactly how it happened. Yes, the governor did order his men to fire, but into the air, over the heads of the mob. He wanted to scare them, to bring them to their senses. And yes, the governor did threaten to blow up the Bastille, but only if the leaders of the mob refused to accept his terms of surrender—which basically were to allow his garrison to leave the prison unharmed. He was simply trying to defuse the situation, to avoid further bloodshed on both sides and guarantee the safety of his soldiers. He realized he couldn't defend the Bastille with a hundred aging veterans and a few Swiss guards dispatched from Versailles. He lost all hope when three hundred Gardes Françaises defected from the regular army and marched into Paris to join the ranks of the mob. But the governor had his honor to consider."

"What happened next?" Richard asked, caught up in the telling and seeing no point in recounting events that Jones obviously knew far better than he.

"When a leader of the mob—a man named Aubriot—refused the governor's terms, the mob stormed into the outer courtyard, which was undefended, and cut the chains on the drawbridge leading into the inner yard. When they did that, the garrison opened fire. Many people were killed, which only served to inflame the mob further. They stormed inside in ever greater numbers until the governor finally was forced to surrender. When he did, he and his officers were seized and dragged off to the place de Grève, a spot where traitors and criminals have traditionally been executed. He was defiant to the end. He was even able to free himself long enough to kick one of his captors in the balls and spit in Aubriot's face. The mob pounced on him like a pack of dogs after that. They tore at his body and cut into his neck with a dull knife. As the lifeblood flowed out of him, he managed to gurgle out '*Vive le roi!*' before he died. They cut off his head, impaled it on a pike, and paraded it through the city streets followed by rioters shouting, 'Death to all aristocrats!'"

Jefferson had briefly mentioned this horrific incident to Richard, but not in such detail. Richard understood why. Such savagery and butchery might have been part of the ancient world—perhaps even of the modern world in places like Algeria or Damascus or Bombay—but never would one expect to witness such acts of brutality in a city as civilized and enlightened and universally beloved as Paris. Perplexed nonetheless as to why Jones was telling him all this, Richard waited for him to continue.

"The governor died a brave and honorable man, wouldn't you agree?"

"I would," Richard said.

"Has anyone told you his name?"

"I recall General Lafayette mentioning his name, but I don't remember it."

"His name was Bernard-René de Launay. He was a marquis from one of the oldest and most respected families in France."

Richard sensed they had arrived at the crux of the matter. "Yes? And so?"

"You've never met him. But you know his wife."

"His wife? How can that possibly be, Captain?"

"You met her when we were together in Passy, during the war. You two grew quite fond of one another. Her name at the time was Anne-Marie Helvétian."

Richard's jaw dropped. "Anne-Marie? De Launay's *wife*? Dear God no! It can't be true, Captain!" Even as he spoke he realized that it was true.

Jones made a hand gesture: keep your voice down.

"I thought you said we could trust her," Richard whispered bitterly.

"That is not what I said. What I said was, no one trusts anyone in Paris these days."

Richard's hand went to where the old wound throbbed high on his forehead. He shook his head, trying to clear it. He felt an overpowering urge to sit down. And so he did. "Where is Anne-Marie now?"

"She lives at 22, rue Saint-Antoine. It's not far from the Bastille."

"Does she live alone?"

"She lives with her two young daughters. And with Gertrud."

"Gertrud is still with her?" Richard inquired, asking the obvious. Gertrud was a sturdy Swiss-born woman of German descent whom the Helvétian family had hired as a nursemaid shortly before Anne-Marie was born. She had remained with the family after Anne-Marie had reached maturity because she was devoted to her mistress. When he was in Passy with Captain Jones, Richard had been frequently in her presence, though she lived at that time in a small cottage separate from the château. He had never known her last name. She was, and presumably always would be, simply "Gertrud," a woman of substance, no nonsense, and severe loyalties who had regarded Richard's intentions toward her charge with extreme skepticism until near the end of his stay in Passy, when she finally warmed to him a little.

"Yes. She is all that is left of the family's many servants and attendants. She stays because of her love for Anne-Marie. She has become a surrogate mother now that Anne-Marie's real mother is dead."

"Why did Anne-Marie's other servants leave?"

"They were frightened, scared of being associated with her. Anne-Marie understood. She did not try to stop them. She gave each of them a substantial amount of money before they left. Many wept as they went out the door."

"I see." Richard willed himself to stay calm, to think, to reason this out. It proved to be no easy task. The questions were hard to put in logical order, the solutions even harder to determine. "Does Anne-Marie know I'm here?"

"Here today in my quarters? No. But here today in Paris, yes."

"Who told her?"

"I did. She visited me several times this past year, the last time only a fortnight ago. She told me she feared her family was in danger. Bear in mind that was *before* the Bastille. She wanted to leave Paris—if not with her husband, at least with her two daughters—and she came to ask me for help. At the time, I was in no shape to help anybody." As if on cue, a round of harsh coughing assailed him. Jones held his hand-kerchief to his mouth until the coughing stopped. "But it didn't matter. She and I both understood that at the end of the day, she could not leave her husband. Her sense of duty and loyalty would not permit that."

Richard used the coughing interlude to try to think things through. His business in Paris was concluded. *Falcon* and home beckoned. But he could not just abandon Anne-Marie to her fate. It didn't matter whether or not she knew he was in Paris. The fact that many years had passed since he had last seen her or heard from her was also of no consequence. What did matter was what they had shared together back then. Those few unforgettable weeks had established a bond between them for life, a bond that not even love for another, and marriage and children and the passage of time, could change. He had to try to help her. He had no idea what he could do, but he had to try something. Of this he was certain: were their roles reversed and it was his life that was on the line, she would wade into the fires of hell to try to save him.

"I apologize if I spoke out of turn," Jones said slowly. "I debated whether or not to tell you this, but I thought you ought to know. And I must confess, I have always felt rather . . . avuncular toward Anne-Marie. I love her too, in my own way."

That brought Richard back. "You did the right thing, telling me. Please, Captain, I have kept you long enough. You should rest now. I have but one last question to ask you. How much danger is Anne-Marie in?"

Jones twisted his mouth. "As the widow of one of the most reviled nobles in France, and the mother of his two daughters, I would think that she is in grave danger."

"Is she guarded?"

"She is closely watched, which amounts to the same thing. She can't go anywhere without being followed. Whatever she needs, Gertrud gets. The guards leave Gertrud alone, probably because they're afraid to confront her. I would be were I not in her good graces. Most days, Anne-Marie stays at home with her daughters. They mean everything to her. She would do anything to protect them."

Richard gathered up his belongings. He left the written report for Jones, but as Jones had suggested, he slipped the drawings of Algiers back into his satchel to give to Jefferson to take back with him to Philadelphia.

"Where are you going?" Jones asked when Richard made ready to leave. "And what will you do?"

"I don't know," Richard replied. He walked over to Jones and embraced him. Jones replied in kind this time, embracing Richard in return as a father would his son. "God's blessings on you, Captain," Richard whispered. "I'll come by or send word, one way or another."

Jones looked up from his chair with pleading eyes. "Be careful, my boy. Please God, be careful."

"That I will, sir." Richard saluted Jones in naval fashion, then turned toward the door leading out.

IT WAS NOT UNTIL Richard had retraced his steps back across the Petit Pont and the Pont de Notre Dame that he decided on his immediate course of action. He could know nothing for certain until he had met with Anne-Marie and assessed the situation. She was a woman of considerable influence and means, he reasoned, and she was not French by birth, but Swiss. That heritage might somehow protect her. Perhaps she had already managed to escape from France. Or perhaps she and her children were not in as much danger as Captain Jones presumed.

His pace quickened as he followed the rue de Rivoli past the grand Renaissance façade of the Louvre, heading east toward the rue Saint-Antoine. Clusters of soldiers milled about, both of the regular army and of the National Guard. Increasingly as he approached the more affluent districts near the Bastille, he saw elements of what appeared to be a citizen's militia, men and women clad in everyday dress and wearing a red stocking cap with a small tricolor rosette attached. Many carried a musket over one shoulder and a powder bag at the waist. Intermingling easily with the more traditional armed units, they formed yet another quasi-military force of uncertain loyalties and purpose in this city of confused allegiances.

As Richard approached 22, rue Saint-Antoine, a four-story affair of graceful white brick construction, his way was blocked by two of these musket-wielding militiamen.

"State your business here, citizen," the taller of the two demanded in French. He was foul-breathed, scruffy, and unshaven, yet the coal black eyes that bored into Richard's remained steady and uncompromising.

Richard met his gaze without faltering. "I am here to see Madame de Launay," he replied, also in French.

"On what business?" the other militiaman demanded. Richard found the man's officious self-importance obnoxious.

Above, on the second floor of the building he caught a glimpse of a curtain being drawn back and a form appearing briefly at a mullioned window. It was a shadow, gone in an instant.

"I am here on a personal matter, monsieur," he replied, forcing himself to sound respectful. "I am an American. I travel frequently to Paris on business. I made Madame de Launay's acquaintance some years ago when I was here with Captain John Paul Jones and Dr. Benjamin Franklin during the war with England. I am staying as an official guest of the

American consul and I have papers with me to prove it. Captain Jones told me where I might find Madame de Launay, and I have come to pay my respects."

Richard gambled that the calm of his voice, reinforced by the names of Jones, Franklin, and Jefferson, would have the desired effect. He did not want to invoke, yet, the name of General Lafayette. That was a card he might have to play later. "I can assure you, citizens," he said in brasher tones when the two militiamen stood their ground, "that you have nothing to fear from me unless you insist on detaining me further. Now, if you will please excuse me."

As Richard stepped forward, the two Frenchmen grudgingly stepped aside.

"As you wish, monsieur," the taller one allowed, but with a warning: "You have one hour. One hour only. We will be waiting here to make certain you do not overstay your welcome. If you do not leave by then, there will be consequences for you and for Madame." It was as if he were granting Richard leave to visit a condemned man in a prison rather than a marchioness living in one of the more stylish residences of Paris. The other guard added with a sneer, "An hour should give you plenty of time to pay your respects, eh, monsieur? In more ways than one? Before *die Fräulein* returns?" He poked his companion in the ribs, and the two started laughing.

"*Merci, monsieur,*" Richard spat out. Hot fury welled up within him. His right hand coiled into a fist, and he had to summon all of his willpower not to swing it against the militiaman's jaw. He used it instead to knock on the door.

His bile yielded to more tender emotions when, a moment later, the door opened, he was whisked inside, the door was bolted behind him, and Anne-Marie was in his arms. Her embrace was not that of a lover but of a woman greeting her savior, one who had risked all to honor what the two of them had once meant to each other.

"Richard, *mon plus cher,*" she wept. "I knew you would come. I *knew* it." She clutched him tighter, her body trembling with sobs.

"How could I not?" Richard whispered, feeling the emotion as much as she. Nevertheless, he gripped her by the shoulders and urged her gently away from him, on the pretext of wanting to look at her but in truth because the feel of her lithe body pressed against his had unsettled him.

As if in tacit understanding, she took one step backward. He put a handkerchief in her hand, and as she wiped her eyes and straightened herself he gazed upon a woman who had lost little of her allure over the years. Her hair remained thick and long, and it curled down to frame a face that even at the age of twenty-nine could still fetch an amorous glance from any man of normal persuasions, notwithstanding the marks of fear and worry etched on her brow and at the corners of her eyes. She wore an ankle-length dress of eggshell blue, finely embroidered in white at the wrists and neck, and a white shawl of light cotton across her shoulders, both garments attractively accentuating the ebony gloss of her hair and the sky blue of her eyes. Composed now, she stood before him both as the dignified aristocrat she was and as the beautiful young woman who, years ago, had so eagerly initiated him into the blissful rites of manhood.

"You look well, Richard," she said with feeling. "You've changed hardly at all."

"And you, Anne-Marie. You're as lovely as the first day we met. And as gracious," he added with a smile.

She gave him a weak smile in return. "You must forgive me," she said. She dabbed a final time at her eyes with the kerchief and handed it back to Richard. "I am not in the habit of erupting in such fashion. I know perfectly well what came over me, but that is no excuse."

"Apologies are not necessary, Anne-Marie. Not between us." Then, somewhat lamely, "I'm sorry about what happened to your husband."

She acknowledged that with a brief nod. "He did his duty," she said, four words that Richard suspected encapsulated quite well her husband's adult life.

"You have children, Captain Jones tells me."

Her countenance brightened considerably. "Yes, Richard, I do. Come, I shall introduce them to you." She walked the few steps to the foot of a grand stairway and called upstairs, clapping her hands. "*Adélaide! Françoise! Venez en bas, s'il vous plaît!*"

There was a patter of feet followed by a moment of silence before two little girls dressed similarly in purple damask dresses and black slippers descended the stairs, one behind the other, in a decorous manner that no doubt had required many lessons. When they reached the bottom, they stood side by side and swept him graceful curtseys, their heads demurely bowed.

"*Bonjour, monsieur,*" they said together. "You were welcome to her house," added the older one, whom Richard guessed was close in age to Will, in English.

Anne-Marie smiled at her daughter's word usage. "We're working on Adélaide's English," she said.

Richard smiled at the pretty young girl who, like her sister, was blessed with her mother's physical attributes, in miniature. Adélaide de Launay was a pleasing image of what Anne-Marie must have looked like at that age. In reply, he extended his left leg and bowed in courtly fashion, his right hand over his heart.

"*Bonjour, mes enfants. Cela me fait plaisir de faire votre connaissance.*" He straightened and pointed to himself. "*J'ai une fille aussi. Elle s'appelle Diana et elle est très belle, comme vous. Et j'ai deux fils: Will et Jamie.*"

Françoise giggled, and her older sister shot her a searing look of disapproval. The giggling ceased abruptly.

"That will be all, children, thank you," their mother said in French.

They bobbed another curtsey before marching back upstairs to what Adélaide had announced was a game of skittles. When they heard a distant door close shut, Richard said: "They're lovely, Anne-Marie. They would make any parent proud."

"Yes, Richard, they would." She led him away from the stairway toward the parlor. Once they were inside, she closed the twin doors. "I am very proud of them, which is why I am so fearful for them. Children like Adélaide and Françoise are no longer admired in Paris. Their breeding is slandered and denounced as something shameful and wicked. Because of that, I won't let them out of my sight. I fear what might happen if I did."

"Surely the revolutionaries wouldn't harm children?"

Anne-Marie faced him. "Not today, perhaps, but tomorrow, yes. The worst is still to come. We have seen nothing yet. These so-called revolutionaries mean to destroy everyone and everything of noble heritage. A child's innocence means nothing. Age and gender mean nothing. If you are of noble blood, you are guilty as charged and condemned to prison or death. It is only a matter of time before the slaughter begins. My husband warned me of this, and he was right. It is why so many nobles have left France."

"Why haven't *you* left?"

She gave him a rueful smile. "If you had known my husband, Richard, you would not ask such a question. He was twenty years my senior and very stubborn. I cannot imagine him running from anything, least of all his birthright. And of course I could not leave France without him."

"But now . . . now you are free to go. You have nothing to hold you here."

"Ah, but I do. I have my two children to hold me here. And I have Gertrud. How could I possibly slip past the guards outside with the three of them in tow? And where would I go?"

"To America, with me," Richard said.

Her eyebrows shot up. "Richard, you cannot be serious!"

"I have never been more serious, Anne Marie. My schooner is anchored in Lorient. There's plenty of room on board. You and Gertrud and your daughters can have my cabin. It's hardly the accommodations you're used to, but I promise you there will be no militiamen lurking outside your door."

She shook her head. "Richard, that is impossible. It is simply not possible! My dear love, for years I have prayed that I would see you again. Today, God has answered my prayers. *You* have answered them. It means everything to me that you wanted to come here. But I cannot ask you to put your family's welfare at risk for the sake of mine. That is too much to ask of anyone."

"I don't recall you asking." Richard glanced around the parlor, with its rich tapestries and elegantly appointed furniture. "Is there a way out of this building other than by the front door?"

"Richard . . ."

He clutched her shoulders, stared deep into her eyes. "Answer me, Anne-Marie. For the sake of your daughters, answer me."

Her lower lip quivered. She shook her head. "No. Not from this one. Even the servants' entrance is guarded. But from the building next to us, yes. It has a back door."

"Who lives there?"

"No one does, now. The owner has left. Some say he is in prison."

"Can you get over to it? And inside? Through a window, perhaps?"

She considered that. "I think so. There is a small iron crosswalk that connects the rooftops. I don't know why it was put there. Bernard-René imagined that young lovers once used it to sneak across to each other. That, I believe, was the most romantic thing he ever said to me."

"Then you *can* get into that building."

"I can find a way, yes."

"Can you leave by the back door? Without being seen?"

"Yes, I believe we can. They will not be guarding an empty house. The back door leads into a cul-de-sac. It's very dirty in there, full of refuse and rats and . . . Richard, what are you thinking?"

Richard grimaced. A plan of sorts had formed in his mind. He had no way of knowing how realistic it was or whether it had a hair of a chance of succeeding, but he had no choice: he had to trust his instincts. He glanced down at his waistcoat watch: 3:18. He must leave at once and never return to the rue Saint-Antoine. His coming here a second time might arouse suspicion.

"Anne-Marie, do you remember the night we walked together down by the quays near the Île Saint-Louis?"

She smiled. "How could I forget that night?"

"Be there tomorrow night at 11:00. Dress your daughters in plain clothes. You and Gertrud do the same. Don't carry much with you. And plan a circuitous route. Do not go directly there from here. Above all, do everything you can to make sure you are not followed. Do you understand?"

"Richard, I told you, you must not—"

He again gripped her shoulders, harder this time. "Do you *understand*, Anne-Marie?"

She nodded. Tears trickled from her eyes and ran down her cheeks. She brought her hand to the side of his face and caressed him, her touch as soft and gentle as a peacock's feather.

"Richard . . . my dear . . . We will meet tomorrow at the quays at 11:00 . . . What then?"

"Let me worry about that. Just be there, Anne-Marie."

Fourteen

Paris and Lorient, France, July 1789

THE TWO MILITIAMEN WERE waiting for him when Richard emerged from the de Launay residence. They had been joined by three others, and the group talked quietly among themselves as Richard walked by, satchel in hand, his gaze set rigidly ahead. One of them offered a remark to the others that triggered a spark of laughter, but it was a cruel laugh, void of any humor. Richard could feel their hostility toward him as he made his way up the rue Saint-Antoine.

His objective was the quays at the base of the rue Saint-Paul, in an area along the Right Bank known locally as the port des Célestins. It was a ten- or fifteen-minute walk, had he gone there directly. He decided instead to take his own advice and follow a more circuitous route, starting out along the rue de Fourcy before circling back down the rue de Figuier, across the rue Saint-Paul, and on another hundred feet or so until he came upon a cozy, two-story café busing with customers. The loud and boisterous chatter one would expect to find in such a place filled the air, and waiters wove around crowded tables, balancing trays overhead on one hand. Slipping inside, Richard felt immediate relief, and not just from the summer heat. This high-ceilinged, pleasantly cool establishment was one of the few places he had been in Paris that appeared halfway normal.

Finding no place to sit, he ordered a lemon water from a waiter, then sidestepped through clusters of customers to a mullioned window where he could observe passers-by on the street. He froze when he spotted someone he thought he recognized. He could not be certain; the man wore his tricorne hat low on his forehead, and the barrel of the musket that hung off his left shoulder partially obstructed Richard's view. But he looked, in profile, very much like the tall, lanky militiaman who had first challenged him outside Anne-Marie's residence. And he appeared to be searching for someone. When he paused in front of the coffeehouse to peer through a window, Richard stepped back into the crowd and waited. If the man came in, and if he turned out to be the militiaman from the rue Saint-Antoine, Richard decided to walk straight up to him and demand in a loud voice to know why he was being followed. Such an unexpected and bold approach in a public place, he had learned over the years, tended to fluster an adversary, and perhaps, in doing so, expose a weakness. But the man walked on.

Richard waited a quarter-hour before paying the waiter and leaving the café. Once outside, he retraced his steps to the rue Saint-Paul, where he turned a sharp left and made his way down to the river.

The port des Célestins was a major docking area along the banks of the Seine, across from the Île Saint-Louis in mid-river and upstream from the neighboring Île de la Cité. It had changed little during the last decade, Richard mused as he scanned the sturdy wooden quays and the equally sturdy thick-planked river barges nestled up to them. Everywhere were watermen, as hardy and ageless as the barges from which they were offloading the wheat, vegetables, fruits, and other commodities on which Paris and countless other riverside communities depended. Threats of social upheaval and insurrection did not seem to concern these men. They had serious work to do. Without the goods they transported, meager as these might be in this year of withered crops, Paris would starve.

Richard walked slowly along the hundred-foot quay, studying the barge captains as he went. It was almost 5:30, and a long and hot workday was, for most of them, drawing to a close. Nevertheless, Richard's attention and admiration were drawn by the degree to which these men joined in with their small crews to put everything shipshape on board and ashore, including faking out in Flemish coils the excess ropes by the bollards. Their chores might be tedious and dirty compared with those performed aboard a merchant brig, and their vessels might not have the graceful lines of a frigate or a sloop-of-war, but these watermen went about their business with a pride and purpose as keen and briny as any sailor on the open sea.

Richard had already decided on the sort of individual he would approach: a barge captain seasoned enough in the ways of the world not to be easily swayed by new political ideology yet enterprising enough to be enticed by the prospect of easy money. That captain also needed to command a barge large enough to accommodate four passengers yet small enough for two men to handle going downstream.

Finally he made his choice, having taken the measure of a grizzled, powerful man of perhaps fifty years whose craggy face reflected much about the quality of his life, yet who chatted amicably with his three-man crew and with other barge captains. He was of medium height with a chest-length russet beard and bulging forearms, and his eyes had a perpetual squint, as though he had spent the better part of a lifetime peering into a sun-sparkling sea. And he walked with a sailor's roll, further suggesting he had spent time on a heaving deck.

Richard trailed after him, keeping his distance. When they were out of earshot of anyone else, he approached cautiously from behind. "*Pardonnez-moi, capitaine,*" he said respectfully. "*Un moment, s'il vous plaît.*"

The man turned around. "*Oui? Qu'est-ce que vous voulez, monsieur?*" His tone was neutral, inquisitive, giving Richard hope.

"I am an American, sir," he declared in French, "a sea captain, like yourself. My schooner lies at anchor in Lorient. I am hoping I might hire your barge for several hours tomorrow night."

"Hire my barge? For tomorrow night? That is a most unusual request, monsieur."

"Yes, Captain, it is," Richard had to confess.

"Where do you wish to go?"

"To Le Bois, across from Auteuil." It was a place near Passy and the Bois de Boulogne where he and Anne-Marie had often strolled together arm-in-arm, along with countless other lovers similarly enchanted by those magnificent acres of woods, greens, ponds, and intimate pathways.

"Auteuil?" The man laughed. "Monsieur, you could walk there from here had you a mind to. Or you could hire a private carriage."

"I could, sir, but I would prefer to go by water."

"Why?" Suspicion had entered his voice. "And why at night?"

"I prefer not to answer that now, Captain. Tomorrow night I will reveal everything to you, I promise." Richard held firm, hoping for the Frenchman's complicity if not his trust. When the captain offered no immediate reply, Richard drew a Spanish piece of eight from a trouser pocket and squeezed it into the man's leathery hand. "That's for listening to me. I'll give you ten more of these if you are here tomorrow night. Twenty more when we reach the quay across from Auteuil."

The amount he was offering, Richard suspected, was about what a river-barge captain could expect to earn in three or four months, per- haps considerably more now that the French economy was on the brink of collapse. Still the Frenchman did not respond. He scratched the back of his neck with his left hand as he stared down at the thick silver coin in his right.

"Please, Captain," Richard pressed. "This matter is of great personal importance to me. That is why I am prepared to pay so much."

The captain slowly raised his eyes. "At what time tomorrow night, monsieur?"

"Eleven o'clock," Richard told him. "And, Captain, bring no one with you. I will help steer the barge downriver."

The Frenchman pocketed the coin. "*À demain, monsieur,*" he said, and moved off down the quai des Célestins.

WHEN RICHARD RETURNED to the American consulate, he was informed by *le maître* that His Excellency the consul was in conference with the Neapolitan ambassador and could not be disturbed. Richard asked that Mr. Jefferson be advised that Richard wished to see him immediately after the ambassador departed, and the servant bowed his assent.

In his room on the third floor Richard paced back and forth, working through a possible sequence of events that depended on out- comes linked together by little more than a hope and a prayer. Step one: would Anne-Marie do as he had urged? Would she be able to? He realized that he was putting her at grave risk; any attempt to flee France would have dire consequences should the attempt fail. But, he rationalized, by her own admission, she and her daughters were doomed did she decide to stay put and do nothing. Step two: would the barge captain be at the quay? If not, what then? He could not bring Anne-Marie and her daughters here to the consulate. Such an act would violate American neutrality in French internal affairs. Jefferson would not, could not, offer them sanctuary. Then . . . what? He had no answer. And there were other links involved, each of which had to work independently yet cohesively with the others if the overall plan had any chance of succeeding.

That plan, at this moment, seemed hopeless, outlandish, utterly without merit. Worst of all, it provided no safety net, nothing to fall back on save for Richard's deep-seated conviction that if all else failed, he could somehow tap into the prestige and influence of his friend the marquis de Lafayette. Yet that, he had to concede when he judged things squarely, was the weakest link of all. Even if Lafayette should want to intervene on his behalf, more than likely he could not, else he too might suffer the consequences. Could Richard ask his friend and former commanding officer to compromise the vital authority on which so many people, noble and commoner alike, depended? A sickening dread began to take hold of him, a gut-wrenching fear that in going to Anne-Marie he had opened up a Pandora's box that could wind up putting not only her and her daughters in jeopardy, but everyone else he held dear in Paris.

Still, there was no turning back. The wheels were in motion. Nor, he realized, would he turn back under any conditions, and he forced himself to ask why. Was it simply to save the life of a woman he had once cherished and the lives of two children as innocent of wrong-doing as was his brother Caleb? Or was something else involved, something darker and more primeval, a dormant beast perhaps, stirred to life when she had pressed her body against his, a body he had once held— so young, warm, and eager—lovingly in his arms? An image sprang to mind of Katherine standing on the Hingham docks, her graceful form gradually receding in the distance as she held up Diana for him to see one last time before waving her final good-bye to him. He shook his head, casting out the demons of deceit and betrayal.

The somber fingers of dusk were probing their way through the dank streets of Paris when Richard was informed by a liveried servant that the consul would receive him in his study. He found Jefferson seated at his desk, pouring out a glass of *vin ordinaire*. A second glass was already filled, its rich crimson essence accentuated by the glow of two candles set nearby in gold sconces.

"Good evening, Mr. Cutler," Jefferson greeted him. "Please, have a seat. That glass is for you. How fared your day?"

"Well, thank you, sir." Richard sat down and gratefully accepted the glass.

"I am pleased to hear it. How did you find Captain Jones?"

"Better than I expected," Richard replied. "He had some interesting insights to offer, and he was most pleased to receive my report on Algiers. At his suggestion, I brought back the maps I showed him so that you can take them back to America."

"Excellent. President Washington will want to review them, as will Henry Knox," referring to the recently appointed secretary of war.

Jefferson crossed his right leg over his left and settled back in his chair, his fatigue evident as he ran his fingers through his long reddish hair; it was hanging loose, the bow at the nape discarded now that his official duties were dispensed with. He held his glass pensively in hand, reflecting, perhaps, on what the ambassador from the Kingdom of Naples had said or someone else within the legions of foreign dignitaries demanding the consul's attention and trying his patience. Suddenly he glanced over at Richard.

"Excuse my wandering mind, Mr. Cutler. Was there something you wanted to ask me? Or tell me? I was informed by my butler that you attached some urgency to our meeting."

"Yes, sir. May I ask, does Monsieur de Chaumont still reside in Passy?" He was referring to Jacques-Donatien Leary de Chaumont, a man of considerable wealth formerly attached to the French Ministry of Marine. It was in his château—more accurately, in a guest house built in the shadow of his château—that Benjamin Franklin and two other commissioners had maintained the first foreign consulate of the United States during the war with England. Chaumont had proven himself a true friend of America, smuggling food and munitions to the starving Continentals during a period when all of Europe, France included, professed a strict *laissez-faire* policy toward an infant republic that few dared believe could prevail over the world's strongest military. He had also proven himself a true friend of Richard Cutler in his *affaire de coeur* with Anne-Marie Helvétian.

"He does," Jefferson informed him. "He remains one of the king's few close confidants in Versailles. Rumors point to Chaumont as the one who finally persuaded Louis to dismiss the German regiments from France. I put stock in those rumors. During my stint here in Paris I have come to know Monsieur de Chaumont quite well, and I have grown fond of him. If the monarchy is to survive in any form, it will be because of men like him and Lafayette. Why do you ask?"

"I made his acquaintance when I was here with Captain Jones and Dr. Franklin during the war," Richard explained, quickly adding, "If I were to write a message to Monsieur de Chaumont tonight, could you have it delivered to him by post rider early in the morning?"

Jefferson sat upright, folded his hands before him on the desk. "I could, yes. But I must ask, why an official dispatch? Why not deliver your message to Monsieur de Chaumont yourself in the morning?"

Jefferson waited for Richard's response, which, in coming, was not what he expected.

"I have one other request, sir. I need to have a post rider sent to my schooner in Lorient. Can you arrange for that as well?"

Jefferson furrowed his brow, narrowed his eyes. "An American consul can work wonders," he said in a voice peppered with sarcasm, "*if* the consul understands the request being made of him and *if* he approves of that request. What is this all about, Mr. Cutler? And why this sense of urgency?"

"The reason for the dispatch to Lorient is to advise my sailing master to have *Falcon* made ready for immediate departure."

"Yes? And the message to Monsieur de Chaumont? I don't seek to meddle, Mr. Cutler, but intuition tells me that this matter is not strictly a private one. Are you concerned, perhaps, that you might arouse a suspicion if you were seen entering the home of a highly placed noble?"

The brief period of silence that greeted that last question confirmed his intuition.

"By your leave, sir," Richard said quietly, "I have no wish to involve you or this consulate in my affairs. I ask only that you trust me, and that you believe me when I say my intentions are honorable."

Jefferson heaved a sigh of exasperation. He thrummed his fingers lightly on the table, never taking his eyes off the youthful-looking American, who returned his gaze without flinching. "Is Captain Jones in any way involved in this scheme of yours?"

"No, sir. I made no mention of Monsieur le Chaumont to Captain Jones."

"I see." Jefferson took a healthy swig of wine. He set the glass down, twirling the stem with his fingers, considering. "Very well, Mr. Cutler," he said at length. "I grant your requests. Your message to Monsieur de Chaumont will be delivered tomorrow morning, and I will dispatch a post rider to your schooner in Lorient. I have other correspondence I need sent to Brest, so I can tie your needs to my own. Neither of your requests, by itself, is out of the ordinary or cause for my immediate concern. Now, if there is nothing else . . . ?"

"There is nothing else, sir."

"Excellent. I shall speak no more on this matter, except to warn you, Mr. Cutler, that should you come to grips with the French authorities as a result of whatever it is you are about, this consulate must and will disavow any knowledge of your activities. We may not be able to come to your aid."

"I understand, sir."

AT 8:00 THE NEXT MORNING, two post riders appeared at the front door of the U.S. consulate. They had been chosen from among a group of men, all Americans, who provided security and performed other official functions for the embassy staff. Many had been appointed to their positions by the former ambassador, Benjamin Franklin, and several had served as officers in the Continental Army. One of the two present this morning, a barrel-chested man sporting a gold earring and plaited queue, had served as boatswain aboard a Continental frigate. Jefferson had tapped him to carry the dispatches for Lorient and Brest, and the man assured the consul that he would have them delivered to their respective destinations the very next day.

When he heard that, Richard realized that by this time the following day his plan would either have succeeded or failed. Should it succeed, he would be somewhere between Paris and Lorient, bound for his ship and the open sea. Should it fail, he would be bound, literally, and soon to face a revolutionary tribunal not likely disposed to grant mercy to anyone of any nationality abetting the escape of a despised aristocrat.

Shortly after the two riders had galloped off and the consulate was settling into its daily routine, from *le centre ville* came the distinct and ominous peal of church bells. Within the hour, a ragtag mob of people, most of them women, came marching up the Champs-Élysées from the direction of the now-defunct Palais-Royal. They were heading westward, their ranks swelling by hundreds, soon by thousands, of others similarly clad in homespun garb streaming in from all directions. They were chanting slogans hard to distinguish at first because of the distance, but which became chillingly clear as the mob stormed past the American consulate, its mood growing uglier by the minute. Many citizens waved fists in the air. Others waved hatchets, kitchen knives, pitchforks, spears, muskets.

"Dear Mother of God," Jefferson said, awestruck, as he and Richard watched the procession through partially open French windows giving out onto a small wrought-iron balcony and a clear view of the street below. "They're marching on Versailles! They mean to attack the queen! Can this really be happening?"

Yes, it was really happening, William Short confirmed later that morning. A well-dressed and handsome man with graceful manners, Short had been Jefferson's private secretary since 1784 and would serve, it had been announced, as America's chargé d'affaires in Paris from the time Jefferson departed France for America until a new ambassador had been installed. Though youthful in appearance and slight of frame, he had held Jefferson's absolute trust and confidence since Jefferson had served as one of his examiners for the Virginia bar following Short's graduation in 1779 from Jefferson's own alma mater, the College of William and Mary.

"What set this off?" Jefferson asked him after Short had summarized what he had gleaned from other embassies and from his acquaintance within the corridors of power at the Hôtel de Ville.

"I can't determine that," Short reported. "No one has offered a satisfactory explanation. I can only conclude, Mr. Jefferson, that this affair has been planned in secret by revolutionary leaders, perhaps for some time. You heard the bells. It was the same call to arms that summoned the people on the fourteenth."

"How do you keep something like this a secret?" Richard wondered aloud. He, too, was watching in awe as the rearguard of the mob disappeared up the broad avenue and their shouts grew ever more distant.

Short gave him a condescending look. "It is not difficult, Mr. Cutler. It takes only a few people to arrange it. Citizens here are prepared to march at a moment's notice whenever the call comes, much like your Massachusetts Minutemen during our own revolution. That is the state of Paris these days."

"What steps are being taken to protect the royal family?" Jefferson inquired of Short. "Surely *something* is being done."

Short nodded. "I am informed that General Lafayette is leading National Guard units to intercept the mob before it reaches Versailles. Under whose authorization, I cannot determine. Surely not the king's— presumably he knows nothing about this, as yet. And not the National Assembly: this uprising plays directly into their hands. I must conclude that Lafayette is acting on his own accord. What will happen when he actually confronts the mob . . . " He left that speculation hanging.

"I see. Thank you, Mr. Short. Please keep me informed."

While Jefferson and Short were pondering the implications of today's events for France and the future of the monarchy, Richard pondered its implications for the future of his plan to flee Paris. One fact was indisputable: however horrific this insurrection, or assault, or whatever one chose to call it, it provided a much-needed diversion for Richard and Anne-Marie. National Guard and militia units remaining in the city would be focused on Versailles, not on the River Seine or Passy. Something else was indisputable: Lafayette was no longer a factor in Richard's plans. Were Richard to be detained, his plight would seem absurdly trivial compared with Lafayette's in facing down a rabble horde and an overt threat to the monarchy, a trifle unworthy of Lafayette's passing thought let alone his active intervention. Oddly, that realization gave Richard more comfort than regret.

There was another advantage: the events occurring at Versailles and concern about the status of the royal family kept Jefferson and his staff occupied during the remainder of the day, as embassy observers rode back and forth to Versailles bringing word of the latest developments from the front lines just a few miles away. Initial reports were somewhat encouraging. The mob had not attempted to force its way through the cordon of National Guardsmen blocking the road to Versailles and had agreed to hear Lafayette's plea to disperse. As yet, however, few citizens had heeded that appeal. The mob remained in a virtual standoff with the Guard. Many citizens were screaming for the head of Marie-Antoinette—and, for what witnesses reported was the first time in public, also for the heads of King Louis and his two surviving children, Louis-Charles, the dauphin, and Marie-Thérèse-Charlotte, a princess of the blood.

"Please God that Lafayette chooses his words carefully," Jefferson ruminated over his daily cup of chocolate in the late afternoon, "else many of his soldiers could defect. If that happens, Versailles will fall. There are too few Swiss Guards at the palace or Royal Army units in Paris to protect the royal family." He was seated in his study speaking to no one in particular, having just been informed by a staff member that although the standoff continued, the worst seemed to be over: more and more citizens were now straggling back to Paris. Those in his presence, including Richard, understood the reality. It was not the French Royal Army, which was stationed mostly along the Austrian border; nor the National Guard, stationed mostly in and around Paris; nor the National Assembly that preserved the last vestiges of law and order in the French capital. It was Lafayette alone.

At 9:00 that evening, after spending much of the day in his room pacing back and forth and fretting over the perverse links of his escape plan, Richard took leave of Jefferson and the consulate, taking with him only his seabag containing a few personal belongings and the letters addressed to his crew. Concealed in an inner pocket of his coat was the small St. Etienne pistol he had carried with him from Toulon. In another inner pocket he carried a small bag of powder and extra rounds of shot.

His only other weapon was a foot-long sheath knife attached to his belt on his right hip.

There were no formal farewells. Jefferson was aware that Richard was leaving Paris, presumably for good, but decorum dictated that he act as though Richard were simply going out side for a brief reconnaissance. Richard left with him a letter addressed to Captain Jones, to be hand-delivered by an embassy courier to the le Tournon in two days' time. In it he outlined his plan. He concluded t e letter with a prayer for Jones' blessing and his hope that God would g ant Jones a full recovery from his illness and every success in Algiers.

Daylight lingered tenaciously, as though re uctant to allow a Stygian cloak to settle over a city so in need of illumin tion. To westward, from his vantage point outside the American consu ate, Richard could make out the giant blue needle towering above No e Dame. Like many foreigners in Paris, he used that spire in the sar e way that foreigners in Algiers used the Qasbah to get their bearing before setting out for a destination.

Everything was quiet at the port des C estins when he arrived. There was only a quarter-moon—another ad ntage—and in its feeble light Richard could discern the darker outlin of the two isles in midriver. The barges tied up to the docks bumped hythmically against each other. He checked his waistcoat watch: 9:45. ime to kill, he thought, then smiled at the unintended irony. Spotting stone bench out of the way but within sight of the quays, he went o r to it and sat down. As a precaution he removed his pistol from the nner folds of his jacket, where it was hard to get at, and carefully slid t e barrel between the belt and waist of his black cotton trousers, then b ttoned his coat over it.

And settled in to wait.

By 10:15 he found himself searching abo t for the barge captain, though he realized it was too early for that. By o:30 he could sit still no longer. Anxiety nibbled at his lower gut; he ha to get up, do something. He began strolling back and forth along the s eet bordering the quays, forcing himself to appear relaxed, studiously oiding any indication of interest in the few citizens who happened by.

At 10:55, with no sign of anyone familiar, e was debating what to do next when a low male voice intruded from behind: "*Bonsoir, monsieur. Vous êtes prêt à partir?*"

Startled, Richard whirled around to find le barge captain regarding him with a solemn expression. "*Ah, bo oir, capitaine,*" Richard greeted him. He tried his best to sound relaxed, nonchalant. "*Je suis heureux de vous voir. Un moment, s'il vous plaît. J'attends quartre autres personnes.*"

"What four other people?" the captain inquired in French. "You made no mention of other passengers."

"I mentioned nothing at all to you," Richard reminded him. "As I promised, I will tell you everything when the others arrive."

"When will that be, monsieur? I am an honest man and I do not like being here so late at night. It arouses suspicion."

"I understand, monsieur," Richard replied. "It should not be long now. I—" He paused, his senses alert to the sudden sound of footsteps coming toward him at a good clip from the direction of the rue Saint-Paul. Emerging from the darkness, dressed in plain clothes with a muslin shawl drawn over her head, came Anne-Marie at a fast walk, holding Françoise's hand. Behind her trudged Gertrud, holding Adélaide's hand and breathing hard. Arrayed as she was in a light cotton knee-length cloak, and with her hair pulled back severely under a wide-brimmed hat, Gertrud could have passed for either man or woman. She gave Richard a brief nod, her sole acknowledgment of a man she had not seen for many years, before looking furtively behind and around her.

"Are you being followed?" Richard asked Anne-Marie. He had never seen Gertrud so on edge. In his experience, she was the one who inspired unease in others.

Anne-Marie shook her head. "I don't think so. We did what you told us to do and took a roundabout route here."

"Who are these people?" the captain demanded gruffly.

Richard faced him. "Captain," he said respectfully, "it is best for you not to know who these people are. I have hired you to take us to Auteuil. That is all the information you need. Please, sir, for your own safety, ask nothing more of me. Trust me."

The Frenchman spat at Richard's feet. "*Trust* you?" he snarled. "Why should I trust you, monsieur? You lied to me. You have deceived me." He gave Anne-Marie a cursory glance. "I must assume that these are enemies of the people and you are asking me to help them escape. I am not a traitor, monsieur. I will not do it. I will not take you to Auteuil." He turned to go.

The sharp click of a hammer being thumbed back brought him to a standstill. He turned and stared at the barrel of the pistol trained at his chest.

"I am sorry, monsieur," Richard said. "I'm afraid I must insist."

"What is this?" the Frenchman scoffed, his eyes glued to the barrel. "You will shoot me if I refuse?"

Richard thumbed the hammer back another click to full cock. "Have no doubt, monsieur." He waved the barrel toward the quays. "Shall we?"

The captain glowered at Richard but did as he was told. He stepped down onto the quay, and as he cast off the docking lines of his barge from their bollards, Richard whisked Anne-Marie, Gertrud, and the two little girls on board. He pointed forward toward an empty wooden-planked storage area. "Hide in there. Keep low and out of sight. Gertrud, pull that tarp over them. Captain," he said to the Frenchman as the barge, free of her moorings, began swinging out toward mid-river and the sluggish flow swirling in great loops between the quays and the Île Saint-Louis, "if you please, take station to larboard amidships. I have the tiller. And as you are well aware, monsieur, I speak French and I am armed. I warn you not to call out to anyone."

Working a river barge was a laborious process but generally not a difficult one. The barge's course was controlled by the tiller; all the crew had to do, going downstream, was fend off other craft, the shore, and river debris. Additional speed was available from sets of poles walked down simultaneously on each side from bow to stern. The Seine was shallow here, less than a fathom in most places, and pole propulsion could increase headway by several knots depending on the weight of the craft, the number of poles employed, the direction of the wind, and the craft's heading. Tonight, they would rely strictly on the current to get them to Auteuil. The distance was only five miles, but the journey would take perhaps two hours.

Richard held course as the great Gothic arches of Notre Dame towered up in the darkness to larboard. To starboard, the Hôtel de Ville loomed into view, its immense stone façade dark at this hour save for tiny flickers of candlelight visible in an upper-story window—a bureaucrat working late, perhaps, or a cadre of revolutionaries plotting their next move. On and on slogged the barge, its pace agonizingly slow but going unchallenged until they approached Le Pont Neuf at the western tip of the Île de la Cité.

"*Attention, citoyen*," a voice called down from the bridge. "*Où allez-vous à cette heure?*"

"*Prenez garde, capitaine!*" Richard hissed under his breath. He could not determine if the man on the bridge was armed or in what capacity he had asked the question. The amber light cast by the lantern he held up in his right hand revealed little about him or his uniform, if in fact he was wearing one. More clearly discernible was Anne-Marie watching him, wide-eyed, from beneath the tarp.

"*Où allez-vous?*" the man repeated.

Richard held his breath. He gripped the pistol in his coat's side pocket as the captain cupped his hands to his mouth.

"I am Captain Édouard Baudouin," he called up in French as the barge approached the stone-block bridge. "I am moving my barge downriver to the Quai de Tuilleries for on-loading early tomorrow morning. If you are militia, please send my respects to Captain Michel de Lisle. He will remember me. Understood?"

The resonating gurgle and suck of swirling water close by was the only sound as the barge passed under an arch of the bridge and emerged on the other side. Richard kept his gaze firmly ahead on the barge captain, who looked back at the bridge and waved. Although Richard wondered why the man had mentioned the name of a militia officer, he decided not to ask. He would not likely be told the truth if he did.

"Understood, Captain Baudouin," they heard the man on the bridge shout out from behind.

Free at last of the bridges and narrow channels fashioned by the two islets, Richard steered the barge to mid-river. Out here, with more than three hundred feet of water on either side of them, they would not likely be challenged from the shore. The farther they went downstream, the less activity appeared along the river's sandy banks. He signaled to Anne-Marie that it was safe to come out. She crawled from her hiding space and walked aft.

"*Capitaine,*" she said in a low voice to the barge captain standing amidships, "*merci beaucoup pour votre service ce soir.*"

The Frenchman regarded her warily, said nothing.

She came to Richard and stood quietly beside him at the tiller. Time drifted as she gazed out upon buildings and parks and byways she knew by heart but could barely identify on this quiet, moon-silvered night, save for the massive frontage of the Louvre to starboard, an enormous rectangle of jet black passing slowly by aft. A northerly breeze kicked up, stirring the muddy river water and loosening strands of ebony hair at her forehead. Richard jogged the tiller slightly to larboard to counteract the effects of the breeze as the Seine rounded to westward.

"How are the children?" he asked at length.

She started, as though awakened from a dream. "They are excited, if you can believe it, Richard. This is a grand adventure to them, something they might take from a storybook. Such is the advantage of youth: they are too young to understand."

"And Gertrud?"

She smiled. "Gertrud is old enough to understand."

"Have you told her we are going to America?"

"Yes."

"And?"

She shrugged. "She knows little about America. But she is relieved to be leaving Paris. She has been faithful to me over the years, Richard, more than I had any right to expect. You remember my dear mother. Gertrud is very much like her, only stronger. When the . . . when the troubles began, I gave everyone in my employ the option to leave. Everyone chose to go except Gertrud. She wouldn't hear of it. Not only did she stay, she worked harder than ever, doing her chores and the work of those who had left. God is my witness, I would not want any harm to come to her for the devotion she has shown me and my daughters."

"No harm will come to her. People in America will welcome Gertrud. She will become one of us."

"Then America is a place I too wish to go . . . Richard?" she asked.

"Yes?"

She leaned in close to him. "Would you *really* have shot the captain had he refused to take us?"

His face remained expressionless. "What do you think?"

Some time later, as the Seine flowed in a more southwesterly direction and their speed increased a knot or two with the freshening breeze, Anne-Marie asked, staring straight ahead: "When we arrive in America, Richard, what will become of us? Where will my family live? And *how* will we live? I brought very little with me. I am no longer a woman of means."

These were questions in which Richard had invested considerable thought. As yet, he had no definite answers. "There are many possibilities," he hedged. "I suggest we hold off discussing them until we're at sea." He was grateful when she let it go at that.

A half-hour later the barge captain pointed ahead to larboard. They were approaching the quays across from Auteuil. Richard checked his watch: 12:40. They had made decent time. His first inclination was to send Anne-Marie back into hiding, but he decided against it. Although the post rider sent to Passy had confirmed that Monsieur de Chaumont had received his message, Richard had no way of knowing what, if anything, Chaumont might do in response. If he had done nothing, they could walk to Passy and seek refuge in the château of another of Anne-Marie's acquaintances in the area. But given the marked status of those aristocrats remaining in Passy and the number of militia patrolling the area, it would be a decision, and a route, fraught with peril.

As the barge bumped against the quay on the left bank, he heard the high whinny of a horse coming from behind what appeared to be a long, low storage facility built perhaps twenty feet back from the riverbank.

"Wait here," Richard whispered to Anne-Marie. He stepped onto the dock, secured the stern of the barge to a bollard with a clove hitch, and, in a hush broken only by the whispered rustle of leaves and the chirping of a few crickets, cautiously approached the building.

Suddenly two men appeared from around the corner. They were similarly dressed in sugar white trousers, coats, and cross-belts. One carried a lantern, the other a musket held out horizontally at his waist. At its tip a silver bayonet gleamed menacingly in the yellow light of the lantern.

"*Qui est là?*" the man wielding the musket demanded.

"*Je m'appelle Richard Cutler,*" Richard answered candidly. It was a gamble, because he did not know who these men were or whether he had just walked into a trap. But he had no other card to play. "*Et vous, messieurs? Avez-vous connaissance de moi?*"

"*Oui,*" the same man confirmed, relaxing his grip on his weapon and standing down. "*Bonsoir, Capitaine Cutler. Votre voiture est prête. Nous sortirons tout de suite à Lorient.*"

The relief Richard felt at that moment was immeasurable, and what he saw on the other side of the warehouse went far beyond what he had dared hope for. Not only was there a stagecoach ready to depart—a comfortable coach with cushioned seats yet not too conspicuous in its luxury—it was drawn by six powerful horses that were even now snorting impatiently and pawing the dirt. As if that were not enough, he learned that the two men who had challenged him were Royal Army soldiers assigned to escort his party to the coast. Clearly, Monsieur de Chaumont still wielded considerable influence in French affairs, notwithstanding the upheavals of revolution. "God bless you, monsieur," Richard muttered under his breath.

He hurried back to the barge and urged everyone out of hiding and ashore to the carriage. Gathering up his seabag, he withdrew a leather pouch heavy with coins and handed it to the barge captain. "For your services tonight, Captain," he said, before jumping ashore.

"*Merci, monsieur,*" Anne-Marie called out softly to him from the quay. "*Vive la France!*" She took her daugh ers' hands in hers and started running toward the soldier holding u a lantern as if it were a beacon of salvation. Richard and Gertrud foll wed close behind.

The barge captain stood mutely, staring fi t down at the pouch he held in his hands, then up at those now fleein his country.

Inside the coach Richard took position fa ing aft, beside Gertrud, while Anne-Marie sat facing forward betweer her two daughters. With a light crack of the driver's whip the coach lu ched forward and maintained a slow but steady pace. The two heavil armed escorts followed behind on horseback, their army uniforms si naling to any highwayman or other miscreant lurking along the ro d that he would be well advised to keep his distance.

With the coach under way, Adèlaide and F nçoise leapt excitedly to the windows to see what they could through tl e darkness. Their mother levered up the low, scrolled armrests to allov room for her daughters to stretch out to sleep when their interest war d. The tense glances the three adults exchanged amongst themselves cc firmed that sleep would not come easily for any of them this night.

The road westward from Paris to Lorien was as well maintained with tight-fitting stones as the road winding n rth from Marseilles, and for the same reason. Each road led to a Frenc naval base: one in Toulon, the other in Brest. And in Lorient, not f   down the Breton coast from Brest, was the headquarters of the quasi- nilitary and now defunct French East India Company, once the proud and mighty conveyor of spices, silks, exotic woods, and other Asian g ods coveted by those in French *haute société* who could afford such it ms.

As dawn crept into the eastern sky and tl e driver could see better the road ahead, he picked up the pace. It wa not unusual, along this military road, for a coach to be traveling at hi gh speed and escorted by Royal Army soldiers. At *relais* stations along ie route, and at a coaching inn near Mayenne where they put in the ollowing night, *les propriétaires* and other citizens they encountere paid them scant notice. With the first streak of dawn the next mornir g they were on their way again, in the company now of but one soldi , who, at the first *relais* station of the day some distance west of R nnes, whipped his horse around and galloped back toward the old pro incial capital of Brittany.

"Where is Stéphane going?" Richard ask d Aubert, the driver, as the horses, hot and sweaty with foam, were eing replaced by a fresh team of six. "And where is Paul-Henri?" refe ring to the other escort, whose company he had come to enjoy and who had treated him and his entourage with every courtesy. Gertrud had gone into town in search of food and drink while Anne-Marie's daughters, giggling like the little girls they were, chased each other around the coach under the watchful eye of their mother. It was a sultry and cloudless day, though a brisk westerly breeze mitigated what otherwise would have been oppressive conditions.

"Paul-Henri took ill, monsieur," Aubert replied wearily. Unlike the horses, their driver was not replaced when fatigue set in. "He stayed behind in Mayenne. Stéphane? He is going back to Rennes to check on something. He didn't tell me what. He will return soon. Do not worry, monsieur," Aubert encouraged when he noted Richard's concern. "These men are your friends, as am I. They will not betray you. Besides, we are now very close to our destination. We will arrive in Lorient this afternoon."

Richard nodded, although he did not fully share the driver's optimism. Something about this turn of events unsettled him: exactly what, he could not identify. He waited impatiently until the coach was ready for its final surge toward the Breton coast.

THE SUN WAS WELL UP when Richard awoke with a start. He had been sleeping fitfully, dreaming of something he could not quite pull up from the depths of his subconscious, and had come awake with a sharp jounce of the coach as it sped past open pastureland interspersed with ancient hedgerows, rocky outcrops, and clumps of trees. Beside him Gertrud breathed deeply, her head resting on his jacket, propped up as a pillow and put near a half-open window. Across from him Adélaide and Françoise slept, each with her head on her mother's lap. Anne-Marie was gazing down at them, stroking the hair of one, then the other, while humming a tune Richard did not recognize but assumed was a favorite nursery rhyme of the girls. She lifted her gaze to his when she sensed him watching her.

She smiled at him, and he at her. A comfortable silence ensued as they sat, the eyes of one upon the other, each silently recalling sweet moments of yesteryear.

"So, Mr. Cutler," she murmured at length. "What will Mrs. Cutler think when her sailor returns home from the high seas and deposits me and my two daughters at her feet?"

His smile faded but did not altogether leave his lips. "Katherine and I keep no secrets, Anne-Marie. I told her about you long ago. It's a good thing I did, since she already knew about you . . and about us."

"How?"

"My cousin Lizzy Cutler told her. She has been Katherine's best friend since they were children in England. Her father, my uncle, was a close friend of Lord Stormont. Remember him? He was the British ambassador to France during the war and an acquaintance of Dr. Franklin. He was the one who helped gain my release from Old Mill Prison and who told my uncle about our . . . relationship. When my uncle told Lizzy, the words were hardly out of his mouth before she was galloping off to tell Katherine." He said that humorously, with affection.

"Did Katherine not object to our . . . relationship?"

"She was hardly in a position to object. At the time, she was engaged to marry a British sea officer."

"Ah, I see. My, my, Richard Cutler. What a fascinating life you have led."

He shrugged. "No more fascinating than yours, Madame."

Their eyes locked a second time and stayed that way until Françoise stirred in her slumber, muttering something incomprehensible. She turned, facing forward now, and curled up like a baby. Her mother spoke softly to her, stroked her arm, coaxed her back to sleep. When she had succeeded, she looked up.

"Richard, forgive me, but I must ask you something."

"Ask me anything."

She drew a deep breath, hesitated. "You love her very much, don't you." It was a statement more than a question, and she said it with a note of resignation, as though steeling herself for the answer she knew he would deliver.

"Yes, Anne-Marie, I do. Very much."

She nodded her understanding. With a gentle sigh she said: "Then God has blessed your union, Richard. What bliss it must be, to be married to someone you truly love. Katherine is a most fortunate woman."

"And I, a most fortunate man."

She held his look for another moment before dropping her gaze to her daughters. She resumed her singsong lullaby as Richard closed his eyes, feeling sleep overcoming him anew.

He sprang suddenly awake at the distant *bang!* of a pistol and a shout from someone approaching from behind. Aubert yanked in the reins, and the coach shivered to a stop on the western edge of a Breton village of timber-framed white stucco homes and shops crowded close together.

Fumbling for his pistol from the seabag placed under the seat, Richard shot a glance out the right side of the coach, to see the soldier Stéphane closing in on them. When he was abreast of the coach, Stéphane drew hard on the reins, causing his horse to rear up on its hind legs. He spoke directly to Richard, who had opened the window to its full extent.

"Monsieur Cutler," he cried, "I must warn you, we are being followed. I heard rumors of this in Rennes and went back to see for myself. It is true. The semaphore confirms it," referring to a recently constructed system of communication that transmitted messages from one relay station to another by manipulating two long white arms according to a prescribed code.

"Who is following us?"

"Militia."

"How many?"

"Four, five, I cannot say for certain. I have not seen them."

"How far away are they?"

"Ten miles, monsieur, maybe less."

Richard cursed under his breath and heard Gertrud gasp beside him. He reached over to pick up his coat, which had fallen to the floor when she jerked awake. From an inside pocket he withdrew the pouch of extra shot and powder.

"Monsieur," the soldier hesitated.

"Yes," Richard replied irritably, his mind awhirl. "What is it, Stéphane?"

"Monsieur, I am sorry. I cannot stay with you. I cannot protect you."

Richard instantly grasped what the soldier was saying. It was what he had suspected from the start of their journey. The army escort was for the sake of appearance only, to ward off any isolated troublemaker who might think to waylay the coach and rob its passengers. It was unlikely that a king's soldier would defy a citizens' militia, certainly not a militia force chasing a fleeing aristocrat. To do so could have dire consequences, not only for the soldier but for France.

"I understand," he said, his tone much subdued. "Stéphane, may I beg you to ride ahead to Lorient, to warn my vessel at anchor there? Her name is *Falcon*. She is schooner-rigged and has a yellow hull. Ask for Monsieur Crabtree. Tell him what has happened here."

"I will do as you ask, monsieur."

"Thank you, Stéphane. God be with you."

"And with you, monsieur. And with the kind lady and her children." He saluted and galloped off westward.

Richard knew precisely how many rounds of shot he had in the pouch, but he counted them out anyway, to buy a few seconds in which to think. Giving up was out of the question. That would spell disaster for everyone inside the coach. They could make a stand here, but he had only one small weapon which he could not reload fast enough to have much effect against a force of men coming at him on horseback. Or they could make a run for it. The militia was five to ten miles behind them and catching up fast. The coach was still fifteen miles from Lorient. Quickly he estimated the different rates of speed of coach versus horse, the relative distances involved, and the time required to reach the coast, assuming both pursued and pursuer were traveling at full tilt. It would be close. Very close.

He glanced out the window. Scores of local Bretons had emerged from their homes and shops and were cautiously approaching the coach, drawn as much by their natural curiosity as by the pistol shot. He looked across at Anne-Marie. She held a hand of each of her daughters, both girls wide awake now, and wide-eyed with fear.

"Put the pistol away, Richard," she commanded in a half-whisper. "I will not tolerate gunfire. I will not put my children at such risk; nor these innocent people outside. Put the pistol away."

"I'll put it away," he said, "in a moment. Keep the children close to you and brace yourself. You too, Gertrud."

He clicked open the coach door and stepped outside, closing the door with a loud bang.

"Driver!" he barked up in French. "Step down from there this instant!"

Aubert gaped down at him. "Monsieur?"

"You heard me, damn your eyes! Get down from there!" He raised his pistol, aimed it. "I mean *now*, monsieur!"

Aubert climbed down. When he was on the ground next to Richard, he said in a voice laced with spleen, "There is no need for such words, Monsieur Cutler. And no need for the pistol."

Richard grabbed a fistful of Aubert's shirt and pulled him in close. His mouth twisted in a sneer as he bent to address the man. He kept his voice low, conspiratorial, as he held the pistol against the French-man's head. "Forgive me, my friend, but there *is* a need. I want these Bretons to bear witness that I am forcing you at gunpoint to surrender your coach. It may save your life, Aubert. If you have any wish to save mine, delay the militia as long as you can when they get here." With that, Richard shoved Aubert in the chest so hard the driver staggered backward and fell down. "Now back off!" he shouted out loud. "I warn you, monsieur: make no further attempt to stop us!"

Richard tucked the barrel of the pistol under his belt and clambered up the footholds leading to the driver's seat. Releasing the reins from their hold, he raised them high and flicked them with all his might.

"*Vite! Vite!*" he commanded the horses. The coach surged forward. "*Allez! Vite!*"

TWO HOURS LATER, aboard *Falcon*, Agreen Crabtree trained the lens of a long glass on the semaphore soaring above the fort guarding the southern approaches to Lorient's harbor, clearly visible a quarter-mile away down an ever-widening estuary from the town's center. For greater stability in these relatively calm inner-harbor waters, he had the glass set up on a tripod erected on the after deck. Through the lens he could clearly see the semaphore's outstretched bony arms moving in spasmodic gestures up and down, sideways this way, sideways that way. But since he had no knowledge of the code, he could not determine what message was being relayed to the authorities in Lorient from the next-closest semaphore.

He swung the glass to his left, focused the lens until the steep-sided rocks and sandy beaches of the Île de Groix leapt into view. Yes, she was still out there. The French frigate he had noticed earlier continued to stand off and on at the entrance to Lorient Harbor, between the fort and the strip of island a mile or so offshore. Her sails were full and white, making it difficult to discern the white Bourbon flag fluttering high on the wind abaft her ensign halyard. Was she on maneuvers, Agreen wondered, or was there another reason for her presence there? He glanced up from the glass to the American ensign snapping above him. The breeze had strengthened, he noted, and was blowing at perhaps fifteen or twenty knots. Of greater significance, it continued to hold steady from the west-northwest.

"Coach-and-six approaching from across the river, Mr. Crabtree."

Agreen wheeled about. He saw the coach before his name was out of Micah Lamont's mouth.

"And unless my eyes deceive me," Lamont's voice rose in excitement, "that's the captain driving it."

"Your eyes do not deceive you, Mr. Lamont." Agreen snatched a speaking trumpet from its becket on the binnacle and held it to his mouth. "Stations t' set sail! Stand by t' weigh anchor!"

As quickly as naval protocol allowed, Agreen walked forward to the bow of the schooner and directed the trumpet to starboard, to the long stone jetty ashore and the schooner's gig bobbing alongside, its four oarsmen sitting on the thwarts. He had originally assigned six oarsmen to the task, to transport Richard as quickly as possible over to the schooner, but the French soldier Stéphane had informed him a short time ago of the other passengers in the coach who would be coming aboard as well. The gig would be considerably slower than he had hoped, but nothing could be done about that.

"Whiton!" he shouted to the coxswain. "Stand by, the captain!" He gestured to where the coach was approaching the jetty. It was moving at a much slower pace now, weaving in and around the shore traffic afoot and in carriages, winding its way down the wide cobblestone street set between the harbor and the low-lying wooden structures with large, faded block lettering that announced in peeling paint the name of the bankrupt owner: La Compagnie Française des Indes Orientales.

Abel Whiton waved back in reply. He removed the gig's forward line from a bollard and held it in one hand, waving with the other at the coach. Aboard the gig, the two starboard oarsmen slid their oars between their thole pins and held the blades in the water.

Agreen swapped the trumpet for a short spyglass and held it to his eye. The carriage had stopped a hundred feet or so shy of the jetty, stalled by the waterfront congestion. Good, Richard had seen the gig. He was waving back at Whiton. As Agreen watched, Richard climbed down from the driver's seat and opened the carriage door. A woman stepped down, followed by another woman. Two little girls followed, helped down by the first woman—the younger one—their mother, presumably. Together, hand-in-hand, the small party ran up the street toward the gig.

"Look there, Mr. Crabtree!"

Agreen slid his gaze to where Isaac Howland was pointing. Seven men a-horse, five with muskets strapped across their backs, had bypassed the town of Lorient and were riding at a hard pace along the dirt road leading to the fort at the southern entrance to the harbor. Compared with the other dangers *Falcon* now faced, their firepower was negligible. To get free of land *Falcon* would have to pass within point-blank range of the fort's great guns, three tiers of them on the east-facing wall, perhaps thirty cannon total, most of them 32s or 54s, the dreadnoughts of shore batteries. One well-placed cannonade from that east-facing battery could reduce an admiral's flagship to kindling wood.

"Heave the anchor short, Howland," Agreen said. "We'll be under way in a few minutes."

"Aye, Mr. Crabtree."

As the party ashore scrambled into the gig and her starboard oarsmen backed oars to point her bow toward *Falcon,* Agreen scanned the deck and top-hamper. All was primed for departure. The two square sails remained furled—the ship would be on a starboard tack leaving the harbor—but the two giant fore-and-aft sails had been released from their stops, and the foresails lay loose on the foredeck and bowsprit. Amidships, the small capstan creaked and groaned under the pressure of the anchor rope being heaved aboard; only the anchor itself now rested on the harbor bottom.

The gig bumped against the schooner's larboard side, and sailors leaning through the open entry port helped Anne-Marie, Gertrud, and the children aboard. Richard was up next, with his gear, his eyes sweeping the deck before alighting upon Agreen. They shook hands as the four tired oarsmen and Abel Whiton clambered aboard.

"Whiton," Richard said, "show these women to my cabin. And have my gear stowed below in Mr. Crabtree's cabin. Dr. Brooke, good to see you, sir. I'd advise you to go below as well. Cates," he ordered the sharp-eyed topman, "lay aloft and keep me informed about everything you see. We'll tow the gig behind," he said to Jacobs, one of the oarsmen, "and sway her aboard later. Now, lads, let's get her to sea!"

The anchor was up and was being catted to the starboard side of the schooner as sailors in the bow backed the jib to windward, forcing the bow to swing to leeward until the ship was headed southward toward the harbor entrance. *Falcon*'s two great sails, hoisted up their masts moments before and thundering in protest as the schooner made her turn, had caught the wind and had fallen silent, their clamor replaced by the more pleasant gurgles and splashes of a vessel moving smoothly, rapidly through water.

"What do you make of our situation, Agee?" Richard asked. They were standing together in the bow by the jib sheets, peering ahead at the fort through a glass. It was clear sailing only in the sense that, at the moment, no other vessels were sailing in or out of Lorient. They noted only the French frigate on patrol outside the entrance. "By the way, in case I forgot to mention it, it's goddamn wonderful to see you again."

"Likewise, Richard," Agreen replied. "And I'm glad t' see you haven't lost your taste for beautiful women. Can t wait t' hear *this* story. Now, then, t' answer your question, those Frog know what we're about. Before you arrived, the arms of that semaphore were movin' around like an old hag givin' her husband what-for. Whatever the message was, it hardly matters now. Whoever was chasin' you has arrived. I saw them ridin' south toward the fort."

"I saw them too. There's nothing for it but to wait and see what happens. Unless you have a better suggestion."

"We could run out our guns," Agreen offered, "an' scare the livin' shit out of 'em."

"We could," Richard acknowledged, "though I doubt that's the choice I'll make." His expression turned sober when he thought he detected movement on the fort's parapets and below at openings cut out of the stone façade near sea level. Cannon positioned on that lowest tier could prevent even the smallest vessel from stealing in or out of the harbor beneath the arc of those placed higher up.

Richard cupped his hands to his mouth and looked up. "Anything to report, Cates?"

"They're running out their guns, sir," Cates shouted down.

"Damn," Agreen cursed under his breath.

"What else would you expect, Agee?" Richard pointed to the flag fluttering above the fort. "See that? That's the Bourbon flag. King Louis' flag. They may run out their guns, but would the French Royal Army fire on an American vessel?"

"You bet your life," Agreen remarked as a puff of smoke issued from one of the cannon ports, "because that's exactly what they're doin'."

The roar of a cannon resounded throughout the estuary, sending scores of gulls and terns screeching into the air in protest. Orange flame belched from the massive black muzzle of a cannon protruding through merlons on the battlements. Twenty yards ahead, off to the left near the opposite shore, a menacing plume of water spewed up.

"A warning shot, Agee? Perhaps, but I'm not so sure," Richard said, answering his own question. He walked aft along the starboard rail until he had Micah Lamont in sight.

"Steady as she goes, Mr. Lamont," he shouted the order.

"Steady as she goes, aye, Captain," Lamont shouted back.

They were close up to the fort now, no need for a spyglass to scrutinize details or movement ashore. As Richard's gaze swept the embankment, he saw the seven militia soldiers who had pursued the coach, standing on foot now, outside the north-facing wall of the fort. They were watching *Falcon*'s progress, though the massive fortress wall was about to obstruct their view. Why, he wondered, had they not been allowed inside the fort? He had a hunch, and he was playing that hunch for all it was worth.

His speculations ended with the deafening blast of a cannonade. Instinctively he grabbed for the railing, bracing himself against an impact that could reduce his ship to driftwood within seconds. But . . . no. The waters ahead were roiled into white spume, but not one ball had landed near *Falcon*. A glimpse ashore confirmed from vanishing clouds of acrid smoke that the shots had been fired from cannon placed on the three tiers farthest away from them, at the southern edge of the wall. The cannon closest to them, and now bearing on them, had remained silent.

"Richard," Agreen barely managed to ask, "are you thinkin' what I'm thinkin'?"

"I dare not think," Richard said.

Just then, another series of ear-splitting explosions rocked their senses. Cannon shot whined and shrieked overhead like demonic prehistoric birds swooping in on a defenseless prey. Again Richard seized the railing, but this time he glanced ashore as he did so. To his extreme satisfaction, he noted that the shots fired came from the highest tier of cannon, too high to have an impact on so small a vessel as a schooner sailing so close to shore. The shot lobbed over them fell harmlessly far off to larboard.

"We're through," Agreen breathed moments later. And they were. With her sails full in the stiff breeze, *Falcon* lunged out of the estuary into the mildly choppy waters of the Bay of Biscay. White froth spewed from her yellow stem.

"Mr. Lamont," Richard shouted aft. "Fall off two points and round the island to southward."

That decision, he realized, would bring them close to the French frigate, which was now standing some distance away to southward of the entrance to the Lorient estuary. But to round the Île de Groix to northward would bring *Falcon* into range of the fort's south-facing cannon. Despite what had just happened, dealing with a frigate seemed preferable to again challenging the proclivities of the soldiers stationed within the fort. At least with a frigate, seamanship might play a hand. *Falcon* was a fast vessel, though slowed a knot or two by the gig trolling in her wake.

"Remember the charts of this area?" Agreen cautioned. "Off the south end of that island there's a mess of reefs and shoals."

"I remember, Agee. It's why we're falling off. We could use the tops'ls on this tack had we time to set them, but we don't. We have to round the island ahead of that frigate. Ship to ship, in a race, we'll show her our heels. And I'd wager that frigate captain has orders to remain inshore, on station. She won't pursue us for long into the Atlantic."

Richard walked aft to the helm, never taking his eyes off the French warship bearing down on them to larboard. As Cates had reported, she had hauled her wind and was giving chase.

Richard squinted through a long glass. He could clearly see the press of sails but could not make out, at this distance, much about her hull or deck.

"Deck, there!" Cates yelled from above. "Shoals ahead, to starboard!"

Richard cursed under his breath. The damned shoals extended farther out from the island than he had calculated. He had no choice. He had to fall off further, toward the frigate. Whatever the French navy had in mind for them, what the reefs and shoals had in store was not in question.

"Bring her off another point, Mr. Lamont.

"Another point, aye, Captain. New course: southwest by south, a half south."

Agreen joined them by the helm. "Damn, Richard," he said, his gaze following the frigate closing in fast off to larboard. "For a rube from Maine, this here's a little too much excitement for one day."

"I have to agree, Agee," Richard replied, squinting through the glass. "But stay with me. The excitement will be over, one way or another, in a few minutes."

"I'll stay. Where else would I go?"

Just then, a hundred yards away across a white-capped span of seawater, the frigate veered off the wind to present her starboard battery.

"Captain!" came the cry from above.

"I see it, Cates," Richard shouted up. He held the glass on the frigate as he held his breath. When he focused the lens, his head jerked back at what he saw. He brought the glass down to chest level, stared out at the frigate with his naked eye, then brought the glass up again. "I'll be goddamned," he exulted. He handed Agreen the glass. "Her ports are closed, Agee. Have a look."

Agreen looked. A gun roared. And another. And then a third, in perfect sequence. Three discharges, yet nary a trace of smoke swept across her deck, as should have been the case with the wind on her starboard beam. What smoke there was flew off quickly from the larboard side.

"Sweet Jesus," Agreen breathed when he realized the implication. "That frigate just *saluted* us!"

Richard bowed his head and gripped the larboard railing with such intensity that the sunburned skin on his hands turned pale. For long moments he could not speak. A full minute passed before the naval commander in him finally took control.

"Dip our ensign in reply, Agee. It's the least we can do. Mr. Lamont, bring her up full and by once we've cleared the shoals."

"Where are you going, Richard?" Agreen asked after Lamont had repeated the order.

"Below. To see our passengers. I'm bunking with you on this cruise, you lucky devil. Though I doubt I'll see much of you. You'll be too busy reading."

"Reading what? A letter?" Agreen inquired eagerly. "Lizzy sent me a letter?"

"Not *a* letter. A sack full of letters. Enough to sink us if we're not careful." He disappeared down the after hatchway. At the doorway to his cabin, he knocked softly.

"*Entrez,*" a tentative voice called out.

Richard opened the door. Ducking his head, he stepped inside and removed his tricorne hat. Anne-Marie was sitting on the edge of his bunk with her arms gathered protectively around her children. They had been crying but, disciplined aristocrats that they were, had composed themselves to an admirable degree by the time he entered. Gertrud sat nearby on a chair by the writing desk, white-knuckled hands clutching its armrests.

"Richard . . . ?"

"It's alright, Anne-Marie. The danger has passed. Our next port of call is Boston, three weeks from now. Sooner, if this wind holds."

"God be praised," Gertrud murmured. She crossed herself repeatedly.

"I'll have some extra bunks brought in for Gertrud and your daughters. It'll be cramped in here, and the food served by the ship's cook is hardly royal fare. But it's what we have and it will see us home."

Anne-Marie released her daughters and walked toward Richard, steadying herself against the rhythmic sway of the schooner. Her lips were trembling; her eyes were bloodshot from fatigue and worry; her hair had come undone in places, and long ebony strands hung in disorderly fashion upon her shoulders. Still, to Richard's mind, she remained a figure of astounding grace and composure.

She stopped short of him, took his hands in hers. "Richard . . . my dear . . . I fear you have burdened me with a debt I can never repay. How can I ever thank you for what you have done for me and my family?"

He squeezed her hands.

"You can thank me by loving my family in return, Anne-Marie. And by loving my country. You'll see. A new and wonderful life awaits you in America."

Glossary

aback A sail is aback when it is pressed agains the mast by a headwind.

abaft Toward the stern of a ship. Used relative y, as in "abaft the beam" of a vessel.

able seaman A general term for a sailor with c nsiderable experience in performing the basic tasks of sailing a ship.

after cabin The cabin in the after part of the hip used by the captain, commodore, or admiral.

aide-de-camp An officer acting as a confider ial assistant to a senior officer.

alee or *leeward* On or toward the sheltered s de of a ship; away from the wind.

amidships In or toward the middle of a vessel.

athwart ship Across from side to side, transve ely.

back To turn a sail or a yard so that the wind ows directly on the front of a sail, thus slowing the ship's forward mc ion.

back and fill To go backward and forward.

backstay A long rope that supports a mast anc counters forward pull.

ballast Any heavy material placed in a ship's h ld to improve her stability, such as pig iron, gravel, stones, or lead.

Barbary States Morocco, Algiers, Tunis, and T poli. All except Morocco were under the nominal rule of the Ottoman sultan in Constantinople.

bark or *barque* A three-masted vessel with th foremast and mainmast square-rigged, and the mizzenmast fore-and ift rigged.

bar-shot Shot consisting of two half cannonb lls joined by an iron bar, used to damage the masts and rigging of enc ny vessels.

before the mast Term describing common sail rs, who were berthed in the forecastle, forward of the foremast.

before the wind Said of a ship sailing with the vind directly astern.

belay To secure a running rope used to work the sails. Also, to disregard, as in "Belay that last order."

belaying pin A fixed pin used onboard ship to secure a rope fastened around it.

bend To make fast. To bend on a sail means to make it fast to a yard or stay.

binnacle A box that houses the compass, found on the deck of a ship near the helm.

boatswain or *bosun* A petty officer in charge of a ship's equipment and crew.

bollard A short post on a ship or quay for securing a rope.

bowsprit A spar running out from the bow of a ship to which the forestays are fastened.

brace A rope attached to the end of a yard, used to swing or trim the sail. To "brace up" means to bring the yards closer to fore-and-aft by hauling on the lee braces.

brig A two-masted, square-rigged vessel having an additional fore-and-aft sail on the gaff and a boom on her mainmast.

Bristol fashion Shipshape.

buntline A line for restraining the loose center of a furled sail.

burgoo A thick porridge.

burnoose or *burnous* A long, loose hooded cloak worn by Arabs.

by the wind As close as possible to the direction from which the wind is blowing.

cable A strong, thick rope to which the ship's anchor is fastened. Also a unit of measure equaling approximately one-tenth of a sea mile, or two hundred yards.

cable-tier A place in a hold where cables are stored.

canister-shot or *case-shot* Many small iron balls packed in a cylindrical tin case and fired from a cannon.

capstan A broad revolving cylinder with a vertical axis used for winding a rope or cable.

caravel-built Describing a vessel whose outer planks are flush and smooth, as opposed to a clinker-built vessel, whose outer planks overlap.

cartridge A case made of paper, flannel, or metal that contains the charge of powder for a firearm.

casbah or *qasbah* A general term for the walled citadel of many North

African cities, the Qasbah of Algiers being the most famous.

cathead or *cat* A horizontal beam at each side of a ship's bow used for raising and carrying an anchor.

catharpings Small ropes that brace the shrouds of the lower masts.

chains or *chain-wale* or *channel* A structure projecting horizontally from a ship's sides abreast of the masts, used to widen the basis for the shrouds.

clap on To add on, as in more sail or more hands on a line.

close-hauled Sailing with sails hauled in as tight as possible, allowing the vessel to lie as close to the wind as possible.

commodore A captain appointed as commander in chief of a squadron or station.

companion An opening in a ship's deck leading below to a cabin via a companion way.

cordage Cords or ropes, especially those in the rigging of a ship.

corvette or *corsair* A warship with a flush deck and a single tier of guns.

course The sail that hangs on the lowest yard of a square-rigged vessel.

crosstrees A pair of horizontal struts attached to a ship's mast to spread the rigging, especially at the head of a topmast.

cutwater The forward edge of the stem or prow that divides the water before it reaches the bow.

deadlight A protective cover fitted over a porthole or window on a ship.

dead reckoning The process of calculating position at sea by estimating the direction and distance traveled.

dogwatch Either of two short watches on a ship (1600–1800 hours and 1800–2000 hours).

East Indiaman A large and heavily armed merchant ship built by the various East India companies. Considered the ultimate sea vessels of their day in comfort and ornamentation.

ensign The flag carried by a ship to indicate her nationality.

fathom Six feet in depth or length.

felucca A small Mediterranean vessel with lateen sails on two masts, used chiefly for coastal trading.

fiferail A rail around the mainmast of a ship that holds belaying pins.

figgy-dowdy A pudding with raisins popular in the West Country of England.

flag lieutenant An officer acting as an aide-de-camp to an admiral.

fo'c'sle or *forecastle* The forward part of a ship below the deck where the crew was traditionally quartered.

foot-rope A rope beneath a yard for sailors to stand on while reefing or furling.

furl To roll up and bind a sail neatly to its yard or boom.

gangway On deep-waisted ships, a narrow platform from the quarter-deck to the forecastle. Also, a movable bridge linking a ship to the shore.

gig A light, narrow ship's boat normally used by the commander.

grape or *grapeshot* Small cast-iron balls, bound together by a canvas bag, that scatter like shotgun pellets when fired.

grapnel or *grappling hook* A device with iron claws attached to a rope and used for dragging or grasping, such as holding two ships together.

grating The open woodwork cover for the hatchway.

haik A large outer wrap worn by people from North Africa.

half-seas over Drunk.

halyard A rope or tackle used to raise or lower a sail.

hawser A large rope used in warping and mooring.

heave to To halt a ship by setting the sails to counteract each other, a tactic often employed to ride out a storm.

hull-down Another ship so far away that only her masts and sails are visible above the horizon.

impress To force to serve in the navy.

jack The small flag flown from the jack-staff on the bowsprit of a vessel, such as the British Union Jack and Dutch Jack.

jolly-boat A clinker-built ship's boat, smaller than a cutter, used for small work.

keelhaul To punish by dragging someone through the water from one side of the boat to the other, under the keel.

langrage Case-shot with jagged pieces of iron, useful in damaging rigging and sails and killing men on deck.

lateen sail A triangular sail set on a long yard at a forty-five-degree angle to the mast.

laudanum An alcoholic solution of opium.

lee The side of a ship, land mass, or rock that is sheltered from the wind.

leech The free edges of a sail, such as the vertical edges of a square sail and the aft edge of a fore-and-aft sail.

Levant Name for the eastern shores of the Mediterranean Sea between Greece and Egypt.

lighter A boat or barge used to ferry cargo to and from ships at anchor.

Maghrib Arabic term referring to the coastal regions of the Barbary States, literally "the west."

manger A small triangular area in the bow of a warship in which animals are kept.

muster-book The official log of a ship's company.

ordnance Mounted guns, mortars, munitions, and the like.

orlop The lowest deck on a sailing ship having at least three decks.

parole Word of honor, especially the pledge made by a prisoner-of-war, agreeing not to try to escape or, if released, to abide by certain conditions.

petty officer A naval officer with rank corresponding to that of a non-commissioned officer in the army.

pig An oblong mass of metal, usually iron, often used as ballast in a ship.

polacca A two- or three-masted merchant vessel of the Levant and the Mediterranean having a lateen sail on the foremast and sometimes on the mizzen.

poop A short, raised aftermost deck found only on very large sailing ships.

privateer A privately owned armed ship with a government commission authorizing it to act as a warship.

prize An enemy vessel and its cargo captured at sea by a warship or a privateer.

purser An officer responsible for keeping the ship's accounts and issuing food and clothing.

quadrant An instrument that measures the angle of heavenly bodies for use in navigation.

quarterdeck That part of a ship's upper deck near the stern, traditionally reserved for the ship's officers.

quay A dock or landing place usually built of stone.

queue A plait of hair; a pigtail.

quoin A wooden wedge with a handle at the thick end used to adjust the elevation of a gun.

ratlines Small lines fastened horizontally to the shrouds of a vessel for climbing up and down the rigging.

reef A horizontal portion of a sail that can be rolled or folded up to reduce the amount of canvas exposed to the wind.

rig The arrangement of a vessel's masts and sails. The two main categories are square-rigged and fore-and-aft rigged.

rode A rope securing an anchor.

round-shot Balls of cast iron fired from smooth-bore cannon.

royal A small sail hoisted above the topgallant sail used in light and favorable winds.

scupper An opening in a ship's side that allows water to run from the deck into the sea.

sheet A rope used to extend the sail or to alter its direction. To "sheet home" is to haul in a sheet until the foot of the sail is as straight and as taut as possible.

ship-rigged Carrying square sails on all three masts.

shipwright One employed in the construction of ships.

shrouds A set of ropes forming part of the standing rigging and supporting the mast and topmast.

slops Ready-made clothing from the ship's stores.

slow-match A very slow burning fuse used to ignite the charge in a large gun.

stay Part of the standing rigging, a rope that supports a mast.

staysail A triangular fore-and-aft sail hoisted upon a stay.

stem The curved upright bow timber of a vessel.

sternsheets The rear of an open boat and the seats there.

studdingsail or *stunsail* or *stuns'l* An extra sail set outside the square sails during a fair wind.

swivel-gun A small cannon mounted on a swivel so that it can be fired in any direction.

tack A sailing vessel's course relative to the direction of the wind and the position of her sails; in a "starboard tack," the wind is coming across the starboard side. Also the corner to which a rope is fastened to secure the sail.

taffrail The rail at the upper end of a ship's stern.

tampion A wooden stopper for the muzzle of a gun.

thole pin or *thole* One of a pair of pegs set in a gunwale of a boat to hold an oar in place.

three sheets to the wind Very drunk.

top A platform constructed at the head of each of the lower masts of a ship to extend the topmast shrouds. Also used as a lookout and fighting platform.

topgallant The third mast, sail, or yard above the deck.

top-hamper A ship's masts, sails, and rigging.

topsail The second sail above the deck, set above the course or mainsail.

touchhole A vent in the breech of a firearm through which the charge is ignited.

tumble-home The inward inclination of a ship's upper sides that causes the upper deck to be narrower than the lower decks.

waist The middle part of a ship's upper deck between the quarterdeck and the forecastle.

wardroom The mess room onboard ship for the commissioned officers and senior warrant officers.

watch A fixed period of duty on a ship. Watches are four hours in length except for the two two-hour dogwatches.

wherry A rowboat used to carry passengers.

windward Facing the wind or on the side facing the wind. Contrast *leeward*.

xebec A three-masted Arab corsair equipped with lateen sails. Larger xebecs had a square sail on the foremast.

yard A cylindrical spar slung across a ship's mast from which a sail hangs.

yardarm The outer extremity of a yard.

About the Author

WILLIAM C. HAMMOND was born in 1947 in Boston, Massachusetts, and grew up in Manchester-by-the-Sea, Massachusetts. An amateur historian and sailing enthusiast, he is the author of the Cutler Family Chronicles, which take place amid the rise of the American Navy. Hammond lives in New Zealand with his wife, Sheree.